Praise for Rosamunde Pilcher

'Rosamunde Pilcher weaves her magic delightfully'
Publishers Weekly

'I don't know where Rosamunde Pilcher has been
all my life – but now that I've found her, I'm not
going to let her go' *New York Times*

ROSAMUNDE PILCHER OMNIBUS

The Carousel
Voices in Summer

ROSAMUNDE PILCHER

sphere

SPHERE

This omnibus edition first published in Great Britain by Warmer Books in 2001
Reprinted by Sphere in 2007
Rosamunde Pilcher Omnibus Copyright © Rosamunde Pilcher 2001

Previously published separately:
The Carousel first published in Great Britain by Severn House Publishers Ltd 1983
Published by Sphere Books Ltd 1987
Reprinted 1989 (twice), 1990, 1991 (twice)
Reprinted by Warner Books 1992
Reprinted 1993, 1994 (twice), 1995, 1996, 1997 (four times),
1998 (five times), 1999 (twice), 2000, 2001 (three times)
Reprinted by Time Warner Books in 2005 (twice)
Reissued by Sphere in 2007
Copyright © 1982 by Rosamunde Pilcher

Voices in Summer first published in Great Britain by Severn House Publishers Ltd
1985 by arrangement with Sphere Books Ltd
Published by Sphere Books Ltd 1986
Reprinted 1989 (three times), 1990 (three times), 1991
Reprinted by Warner Books 1992
Reprinted 1993, 1994 (twice), 1995, 1996 (three times), 1997,
1998 (four times), 1999, 2000, 2001
Reprinted by Time Warner Paperbacks in 2002
Reprinted 2002, 2003, 2004
Reprinted by Time Warner Books in 2006
Reissued by Sphere in 2007
Copyright © 1984 by Rosamunde Pilcher

The moral right of the author has been asserted.

A CIP catalogue record for this book is available from the British Library.

ISBN 978-0-7515-3168-8

Papers used by Sphere are natural, recyclable products made from
wood grown in sustainable forests and certified in accordance with
the rules of the Forest Stewardship Council.

Printed and bound in Great Britain by Clays Ltd, St Ives plc
Paper supplied by Hellefoss AS, Norway

Sphere
An imprint of
Little, Brown Book Group
Brettenham House
Lancaster Place
London WC2E 7EN

A Member of the Hachette Livre Group of Companies

www.littlebrown.co.uk

The Carousel

Chapter One

My mother stood in the middle of her pretty sitting room, filled with September sunshine, and said, "Prue, you must be going out of your mind."

She looked as though she were about to burst into tears of disappointment, but I knew that she would not, because tears would destroy her faultless maquillage, would make her face swell, turn down her mouth, and accentuate unbecoming lines. However exasperated, she would never cry. Her appearance mattered to her almost more than anything else, and now she stood across the hearth rug from me, immaculately turned out in a raspberry pink woollen suit and a white silk shirt, with her gold earrings and her charm bracelet, and pretty silvery hair crisp and curly.

She struggled, however, to contain a conflict of destructive emotions: anger, motherly concern, but mostly disappointment. I felt very sorry for her.

I said, "Oh, come on, Ma, it's not the end of the world." Even as I said it, it sounded pretty feeble, which it probably was.

"For the first time in your life, you seem to have got involved with a really suitable man . . ."

"Darling, 'suitable's a terribly old-fashioned word . . ."

"He's charming, he's steady, he's got a good job, and he comes from the right sort of family. You're twenty-three and it's time you settled down, got married and had children and a home of your own."

"Ma, he hasn't even *asked* me to marry him."

"Of course he hasn't. He wants to do it properly—take you home, introduce you to his mother. There's nothing wrong with that. And it's obvious the way his mind is running. You only have to see the two of you together to known that he's wildly in love with you."

"Nigel is incapable of being wildly anything."

"Honestly, Prue, I don't know what you're looking for."

"I'm not looking for anything."

We had had this conversation so often that I knew my part word for word, as though I had sat down and learned it by heart. "I've got everything I want. A job I like, a little flat of my own—"

"You can hardly call that one-room basement a flat—"

"And I don't feel like settling down."

"You're twenty-three. I was nineteen when I was married."

[2]

I nearly said, *and divorced six years later,* but I didn't. However maddened by her, you couldn't say things like that to my mother. I knew that she had a will of iron and an inner core of steel, which nearly always ensured that she got her own way, but there was something vulnerable about her—her delicate build, her enormous blue eyes, her rampant femininity—that precluded harsh words.

So I opened my mouth and then shut it again, and looked at her hopelessly. She gazed back at me, reproachful but not reproaching, and I understood for perhaps the thousandth time why my father, from the moment they set eyes on each other, had been lost. They had married because she was totally irresistible, and he was exactly what she had been searching for ever since she first realised that there was such a thing as an opposite sex.

My father is called Hugh Shackleton. In those days he worked in London, in a merchant bank in the City, with a life-style that was solid and a future that was bright. But he was basically a fish out of water. The Shackletons were a Northumberland family, and my father had been brought up there on a farm called Windyedge, where the pasture fields ran down to the cold North Sea and the winter gales blew straight in from the Ural Mountains. My father never lost his love of the country, or ceased to yearn for it. When he married my mother, the farm was being managed by his older brother, but about the time that I was five years old, this brother tragically was killed in a hunting accident. My father travelled to Northumberland for the funeral. He stayed away for five days, and by the time he returned to us, his mind was made up. He told my mother that he intended resigning from his job, selling the house in London, and returning to Windyedge.

He was going to be a farmer.

The rows and arguments, the tears and recriminations that followed this announcement are amongst the earliest of my truly unhappy memories. My mother tried everything to make him change his mind, but my father remained adamant. In the end she fired her final gun. If he returned to Northumberland, he would return alone. Rather to her surprise, he did this. Perhaps he thought that she would follow, but she could be just as stubborn. Within the year they were duly divorced. The house in Paulton Square was sold and my mother moved to another, smaller one, near Parson's Green. I, naturally, stayed with her, but I always went to Northumberland for a couple of weeks every year, just to keep in touch with my father. After a bit he married again; a shy, horsy girl whose tweed skirts were always slightly seated and whose clear and freckled face had never known so much as the touch of a powder puff. They were very happy. They are still very happy. And I am glad.

But for my mother it was not so easy. She had married my father because he seemed to conform to a pattern of masculinity that she could understand and admire. She never delved beneath the veneer of the pinstripe suit and the briefcase. She had no wish to uncover any hidden depths. But the Shackletons were full of surprises, and to my mother's horror, I inherited most of them. My dead uncle had not only been a farmer but an amateur musician of some achievement. My father in his spare time stitched the most beautiful tapestries. But it was their sister Phoebe who was the true rebel. An artist and an accomplished painter, she was a character of such originality, with such careless regard of day-to-day conventions, that my mother had a hard time coming to terms with her sister-in-law.

As a young woman Phoebe had based herself in London, but in her middle years she wiped the dust of the city from her shoes and went to live in Cornwall, where she cohabited happily with a charming man, a sculptor, called Chips Armitage. They never married—I think because his wife would not divorce him—and when he died he left his little Victorian Gothic house in Penmarron to Phoebe, and she had lived there ever since.

Despite this small social hiccup my mother could not completely write Phoebe off, because Phoebe was my godmother. Every now and then my mother and I would be invited to stay with her. The letters always made it perfectly clear that Phoebe would be happy to have me on my own. But my mother feared her bohemian influence, and on the principle that if she couldn't lick the Shackletons, she would join them, she always—at least when I was a child—accompanied me on these visits.

The first time we travelled to Cornwall, I was filled with anxiety. I was only a child, but I knew well that my mother and Phoebe had nothing in common, and I dreaded two weeks of disagreements and prickly silences. But I underestimated Phoebe's perception. She took care of the situation by introducing my mother to Mrs. Tolliver. Mrs. Tolliver lived in the White Lodge at

Penmarron and had a perfectly conventional little circle of friends, who were charmed to include my pretty mother in their bridge afternoons and small dinner parties.

With them, she would contentedly play cards on the bright days while Phoebe and I walked on the beach, or set up our easels by the old seawall, or drove inland in the battered old Volkswagen that Phoebe used as a mobile studio, to climb the moor and lose ourselves in landscapes that lay drowned in a white and shimmering light that seemed reflected from the very sea itself.

Despite my mother's antagonism, Phoebe exerted enormous influences on my life. Unconscious influences, in the shape of my inherited talent for drawing. And other, more practical influences—pressures, maybe— which bolstered my determination to study in Florence, to go to art school, and which finally culminated in getting me my present job with the Marcus Bernstein Gallery in Cork Street.

And now it was because of Phoebe that we quarrelled. Nigel Gordon had come into my life some months ago. He was the first totally conventional person I had ever even mildly liked, and when I brought him home to meet my mother, she could not hide her delight. He was charming with her, flirting a little and bringing her flowers, and when she learned that he had invited me to Scotland to stay with his family and meet his mother, her excitement knew no bounds. She had already bought me a pair of tweed knickerbockers to wear "on the moor," and beyond this I knew that her imagination was in full flight to the final climax of engagement notices in the *Times*, engraved invitations, and a London wedding with me in a white creation designed to look well from the back.

But at the last moment, Phoebe had put an end to all these pretty fancies. She had, of all things, broken her arm, and the day she returned from hospital to Holly Cottage, her little house, with the arm rigid in a plaster cast, she telephoned to beg me to come and keep her company. It wasn't that she couldn't perfectly well look after herself, but she was not able to drive the car, and to remain immobilised until the cast came off was more than she could bear.

As I listened to her voice over the phone, I was filled with an extraordinary sense of relief, and it was only then that I admitted to myself that I didn't want to go north to stay with the Gordons. I was not ready to become so deeply involved with Nigel. Subconsciously I had been longing for some sound excuse to wriggle out of the arrangement. And here it was, presented to me on a plate. Without even hesitating, I told Phoebe that I would go. Then I told Nigel that I couldn't go to Scotland. And now I was telling my mother.

She was, predictably, devastated.

"Cornwall. With Phoebe." She made it sound like the worst sort of dead end.

"I must go, Ma." I tried to make her smile. "You know she's hopeless at driving that old car of hers, even with two arms."

But she was beyond amusement. "It's so rude, crying

off at the last moment. You'll never be invited again: And what will Nigel's mother think?''

"I'll write to her. I'm sure she'll understand.''

"And with Phoebe . . . you'll meet nobody with Phoebe except a lot of unwashed students and extraordinary women in hand-woven ponchos.''

"Perhaps Mrs. Tolliver will come up with some suitable man for me.''

"It's nothing to joke about.''

I said, gently, "It is *my* life.''

"You've always said that. You said it when you took yourself off to live in that gruesome basement in Islington. Islington, of all places.''

"It's very trendy.''

"And when you enrolled at that horrible art school . . .''

"At least I've got a perfectly respectable job. You must admit that.''

"You ought to be married. And then you wouldn't have to have a job.''

"Even if I were married, I wouldn't want to give it up.''

"But, Prue, it's not a future. I want you to have a proper life.''

"I think it is a proper life.''

We eyed each other for a long moment. Then my mother sighed deeply, resigned and apparently mortally wounded. And I knew that for the time being, the argument was over.

She said, sounding pathetic, "I'll never understand you.''

I went to give her a hug. "Don't try,'' I told her. "Just

cheer up and go on liking me. I'll send you a postcard from Cornwall."

I had decided not to drive a car to Penmarron but to travel by train. The next morning I took a taxi to Paddington, found the right platform and the right coach. I had reserved a seat, but the train was not full; by the middle of September the flood of holidaymakers had ceased. I had just stowed my luggage and settled myself in a seat when there was a tap on the window, and I looked up and saw a man standing outside, carrying a briefcase in one hand and a bunch of flowers in the other.

It was, astonishingly, Nigel.

I got up and went back to the door and stepped down onto the platform. He was walking towards me, smiling sheepishly.

"Prue. I thought I wouldn't find you."

"What on earth are you doing here?"

"I came to see you off. Wish you bon voyage." He held out the bunch of flowers, which were small and shaggy yellow chrysanthemums. "And to bring you these."

I was, despite myself, very touched. I recognised that his coming here to the station was a generous gesture of forgiveness, and to make it clear that he had understood why I was letting him down. This had the effect of making me feel more of a heel than ever. I took the flowers in their collar of crisp white paper and buried my nose in them. They smelt delicious. I looked up at him and smiled.

"It's ten o'clock. Oughtn't you to be at your desk by now?"

He shook his head. "No hurry."

"I didn't realise you were so high up in the banking world."

Nigel grinned. "I'm not, but I don't exactly have to clock in. Anyway, made a phone call. Said I'd been held up." He had a solid, mature sort of face, with fair hair beginning to thin on top, but when he grinned like that, he looked quite boyish. I began to wonder if I was mad, abandoning this personable man in order to go and nurse my unpredictable aunt Phoebe. Perhaps my mother had been right, after all.

I said, "I'm sorry about letting you down. I wrote to your mother last night."

"Perhaps, another time . . ." said Nigel generously. "Anyway, keep in touch. Let me know when you get back to London."

I knew that he would be waiting for me, if I asked him. Ready to meet my train, to drive me back to Islington, to pick up the threads of our relationship as though I had never been away.

"I'll do that."

"I hope your aunt recovers quickly."

"It's only a broken arm. She's not ill."

There came a short, uncomfortable pause. Then Nigel said, "Well. . . ." He moved forward to kiss my cheek. It was more of a peck than a kiss. "Good-bye, and have a good journey."

"Thank you for coming. Thank you for the flowers."

He stepped back, made an indeterminate gesture of farewell, turned and walked away. I watched him go, making his way through the shifting confusion of porters, barrows, families with suitcases. At the barrier he turned back for a final time. We waved. Then he was gone. I got back into the train, stowed the flowers in the luggage rack and sat down once more. I wished that he had not come.

I was very much a Shackleton, but every now and then stray emotions would float to the surface of my mind, which I recognised as stemming straight from my mother. This was just such a time. I must be mad not to want to be with Nigel, to become involved with him, even to spend the rest of my life with him. Normally, I bucked like a horse at the very idea of settling down, but at this moment, sitting in the train, gazing out the window at Paddington Station, it suddenly seemed enormously attractive. Security; that's what this dependable man would give me. I imagined living in his solid London house, going to Scotland for my holidays; only working if I wanted to, and not because I needed the money. I thought about having children . . .

A voice said, "I'm sorry, is this seat taken?"

"What . . . ?" I looked up and saw the man standing there in the aisle between the seats. He carried a small suitcase, and there was a child beside him, a small thin girl about ten years old, dark haired and wearing round, owllike spectacles.

"No, it's not taken."

He said, "Good," and lifted the suitcase up into the rack. He did not look in the mood for any sort of pleasantry, and a certain impatience of manner made me not ask him to watch out for my bunch of chrysanthemums. He was dressed, as Nigel had been, for some City office, in a navy chalk-striped suit. But the suit sat ill upon him, as though he had lately put on a good deal of weight (I imagined enormous expense-account luncheons), and as he reached up with the suitcase, I had a direct view of his expensive, bulging shirt and straining buttons. He was dark, and once, perhaps, had been good-looking, but now his jowls were heavy, his complexion florid, and his greying hair worn long on the back of his collar, possibly to atone for the lack of it on top.

"There you are," he said to the little girl. "Go on, sit down."

She did so, cautiously, perched on the very edge of the seat. She carried a single comic paper and wore a red leather purse slung by a strap across one shoulder. She was a pale child, with hair cut very short, exposing a long and slender neck. This, and her spectacles, and her expression of stoic misery gave her the appearance of a small boy, and I was reminded of other small boys I had observed on station platforms, dwarfed by stiff new uniforms, fighting tears, and being told by beefy fathers how much they were going to enjoy being at boarding school.

"Got your ticket all right?"

She nodded.

"Granny'll meet you at the junction."

She nodded again.

"Well . . ." He ran a hand back over his head. He was obviously longing to be off. "That's it, then. You'll be all right."

Once more she nodded. They looked, unsmiling, at each other. He began to move away and then remembered something else.

"Here . . ." He felt in his breast pocket, produced a crocodile wallet, a ten-pound note. "You'll need something to eat. When it's time, take yourself along to the restaurant car and get some lunch."

She took the ten-pound note and sat looking at it.

"Good-bye, then."

"Good-bye."

He went. At the window he paused to wave and give a cursory smile. Then he disappeared, hurrying in the direction of some sleek, showy car that would restore him to the safe, masculine world of his business.

As I had already told myself that Nigel was nice, I now told myself that this man was horrible and wondered why such an unengaging person had been given the job of seeing the little girl off. She sat beside me, still as a mouse. After a little she reached for her handbag, undid the zipper, put the ten-pound note inside, and shut the zipper again. I thought about saying something friendly to her, but there was a shine of tears in her eyes behind the spectacles, so I decided, for the moment, to leave well alone. A moment later the train started to move, and we were off.

I opened my *Times,* read the headlines and all the gloomy news, and then turned with a pleasant sensation of relief to the Arts page. I found what I was looking for, which was the review of an exhibition that had opened a couple of days before in the Peter Chastal Gallery, which was only a couple of doors away from where I worked for Marcus Bernstein.

The artist was a young man called Daniel Cassens, and I had always been interested in his career because, when he was about twenty, he had spent a year in Cornwall living with Phoebe and studying sculpture with Chips. I had never met him, but Phoebe and Chips had become very fond of him, and when he left them to continue his career in America, Phoebe had followed his progress avidly and enthusiastically as if he had been her own son.

He had travelled and spent some years in America and then had taken himself on to Japan, where he had engrossed himself in the intricate simplicities of Oriental art.

This latest exhibition was a direct outcome of his years in Japan, and the critic was enthusiastic, revelling in the tranquillity and formality of Daniel Cassens's work, praising the controlled brushwork of the watercolours, the subtlety of detail.

". . . This is a unique collection," he finished his piece. "The paintings are complementary, each one a single facet of a total and rare experience. Take an hour or so off from your daily round and visit the Chastal Gallery. You will certainly not be disappointed."

Phoebe would be delighted, and I was glad for her. I closed the paper and looked out the window and saw that we had left the suburbs behind and were now out into the country. It was a damp day, with large grey clouds rolling across the sky, revealing every now and then a patch of limpid blue. Trees were beginning to turn, the first leaves to fall. There were tractors ploughing out in the fields, and cottage gardens, as we rocketed past, were purple with Michaelmas daisies.

I remembered my small companion and turned to see how she was getting on. She had not yet opened her comic or unbuttoned her coat, but the tears had receded and she seemed a little more composed.

"Where are you going to?" I asked her.

She said, "Cornwall."

"I'm going to Cornwall, too. Whereabouts are you going?"

"I'm going to stay with my grandmother."

"That'll be nice." I thought about this. "But isn't it term time? Shouldn't you be at school?"

"Yes, I should. I'm at a boarding school. We all went back, and then the boiler blew up, so they closed the school for a week till it's mended and sent us all home again."

"How terrible. I hope nobody was hurt."

"No. But Miss Brownrigg, our headmistress, had to go to bed for a day. Matron said it was shock."

"I'm not surprised."

"So I went home, but there's nobody there but my father. My mother's on holiday in Majorca. She went at the end of the holidays. So I've got to go to Granny."

She didn't make it sound a very attractive prospect. I was trying to think of something comforting to say to jolly her along when she picked up her comic and settled down, rather pointedly, to read it. I was amused but took the hint, found my book, and began to read. The journey progressed in silence until the waiter from the restaurant car made his way down the train to tell us that luncheon was being served.

I laid down my book. "Are you going to go and have some lunch?" I asked her, knowing about the ten-pound note in her bag.

She looked agonised. "I . . . I don't know which way to go."

"I'm going. Would you like to come with me? We could have lunch together."

Her expression changed to one of grateful relief. "Oh, could I? I've got the money, but I've never been on a train by myself before, and I don't know what I'm meant to do."

"I know, it's muddling, isn't it? Come along, let's go before all the tables get booked up."

Together we made our way down the lurching corridors, found the restaurant car, and were shown to a table for two. There was a fresh white cloth, and flowers in a glass carafe.

She said, "I'm a bit hot. Do you think I could take off my coat?"

"I think that would be a good idea."

She did this, and the waiter came to help her, and fold the coat, and lay it over the back of her seat. We opened the menus.

"Are you feeling hungry?" I asked her.

"Yes I am. We had breakfast *ages* ago."

"Where do you live?"

"In Sunningdale. I came up to London with my father in his car. He drives up every morning."

"Your . . . ? Was that your father who saw you off?"

"Yes." He hadn't even kissed her good-bye. "He works in an office in the City." Our eyes met, and then she looked hastily away. "He doesn't like being late."

I said, soothingly, "Few men do. Is it his mother you're going to stay with?"

"No. Granny's my mother's mother."

I said, sounding chatty, "I'm going to stay with an aunt. She's broken her arm, and she can't drive her car, so I'm going to look after her. She lives at the very end of Cornwall in a village called Penmarron."

"Penmarron? But I'm going to Penmarron too."

This was a coincidence. "How extraordinary."

"I'm Charlotte Collis. I'm Mrs. Tolliver's granddaughter. She's my granny. Do you know Mrs. Tolliver?"

"Yes, I do. Not very well, but I do know her. My mother used to play bridge with her. And my aunt is called Phoebe Shackleton."

And now her face lit up. For the first time since I had set eyes on her, she looked a natural and excited child. Her eyes were wide behind the spectacles, and her mouth opened in a delighted gasp of surprise, revealing teeth too big for her narrow face.

"*Phoebe!* Phoebe's my best friend. I go and have tea with her and things, every time I go and stay with Granny. I didn't know she'd broken her arm." She gazed into my face. "You . . . you're not Prue, are you?"

I smiled. "Yes, I am. How did you know?"

"I *thought* I knew your face. I've seen your photograph in Phoebe's sitting room. I always thought you looked *lovely.*"

"Thank you."

"And Phoebe used to tell me about you when I went to see her. It's lovely going to tea with her, because it's not like being with a grown-up person and I'm allowed to go on my own. And we always play with the carousel that used to be a gramophone."

"That was mine. Chips made it for me."

"I never knew Chips. He was dead before I can remember."

"And I," I told her, "never knew your mother."

"But we go and stay with Granny most summers."

"And I am usually there at Easter, or sometimes for Christmas, so our paths have never crossed. I don't think I even know her name."

"It's Annabelle. She was Annabelle Tolliver. But she's called Mrs. Collis now."

"And do you have brothers and sisters?"

"One brother. Michael. He's fifteen. He's at Wellington."

"And the boiler at Wellington hasn't blown up?"

It was an attempt to add a little levity to the conversation, but Charlotte did not smile. She said, "No."

I studied the menu and thought about Mrs. Tolliver. My memories of her were of a tall, elegant, and rather chilling lady, always immaculately turned out, her grey hair neatly groomed, her skirts pleated and pressed, her long, narrow shoes polished like chestnuts. I thought of White Lodge, where Charlotte was going to stay, and wondered what a child would find to do in those neatly manicured gardens, that quiet and orderly house.

I looked across the table at the child and saw that she, too, with furrowed brow, was trying to decide what she would have for lunch. She seemed a sad little person. It couldn't have been much fun, being sent home from school simply because the boiler there had blown up.

Unexpected and probably unwanted, with your mother abroad and no person to take care of you. It couldn't have been much fun, being put by yourself on a train and shunted off to the end of the country to visit your grandmother. I wished, all at once, for Mrs. Tolliver to be dumpy and cosy, with a round, warm bosom and a passion for knitting dolls' clothes and playing Clock Patience.

Charlotte looked up and saw me watching her. She sighed hopelessly. "I don't know what I want."

I said, "A moment ago you told me you were feeling very hungry. Why don't you have everything?"

"All right." She decided on vegetable soup, roast beef, and ice cream. "And do you think," she added wistfully, "there might be enough money over for a Coca-Cola?"

What is there so magical about travelling by train to Cornwall? I know I am not the first person to have known the enchantment as the line crosses the Tamar by the old Brunel railway bridge, as though one were entering the gates of some marvellous foreign country. Each time I go I tell myself that it cannot be the same, but it always is. And it is impossible to pinpoint the exact reasons for this euphoria. The shapes of the houses, perhaps, pink-washed in the evening sun. The smallness of the fields; the lofty viaducts soaring over deep, wooded valleys; the first distant glimpses of the sea? Or perhaps the saintly names of small stations that we rocket through and leave behind, or the voices of the porters on the platform at Truro?

We reached St. Abbatt's Junction at a quarter to five. As the train drew alongside the platform, Charlotte and I were ready by the door, with our suitcases and my bunch of chrysanthemums, by now distinctly worse for wear. When we stepped down from the train, we were assailed by a blustering west wind, and I could smell the sea, salty and strong. There were palm trees on the platform, rattling their leaves like old, broken umbrellas, and a porter opened the door of the guards' van and manhandled out of it a crate of indignant hens.

I knew that Mr. Thomas was going to come and meet me. Mr. Thomas owned the only taxi in Penmarron, and Phoebe had told me over the telephone that she had engaged his services. As we walked up towards the bridge, I saw Mr. Thomas waiting, bundled up in an overcoat as though it were winter and wearing on his head the hat that he had bought at a jumble sale and that had once belonged to some noble chauffeur. When he was not driving a taxi, he was a pig farmer, and for this occupation he had another hat, felt, and of great antiquity. Phoebe, who had a Rabelaisian wit, once wondered what sort of hat he wore when he was getting into bed with Mrs. Thomas, but my mother had pursed her lips and lowered her eyes and refused to be amused, so Phoebe had not wondered it again.

There was no sign of Mrs. Tolliver. I could feel Charlotte's anxiety.

"Perhaps your grandmother's waiting on the other side of the bridge."

The train, which never stopped long anywhere, drew

out. We scanned the opposite platform, but the only person who waited was a fat lady with a shopping bag. Not Mrs. Tolliver.

"Maybe she's sitting in the car in the station yard. It's a cold evening to be standing about."

"I hope she hasn't forgotten," said Charlotte.

But Mr. Thomas was to reassure us. "Hello, my dear," he said to me, coming to meet us and to relieve me of my case. "How are you? Nice to see you again. Have a good journey, did you?" He looked down at Charlotte. "You're Mrs. Tolliver's little girl, aren't you. That's right. My orders are to pick up the pair of you. Take the little girl to White Lodge, and then you on to Miss Shackleton's. Travel together, did you?"

"Yes, we did; we met on the train."

"Your aunt would have come, but she can't drive her car with that dratted arm of hers. Come on now," he turned to Charlotte, "give me your case, too, easier to carry two than one . . ."

And thus burdened, he trudged up the wooden steps and over the bridge, and Charlotte and I followed him. Settled in his taxi, which had moulting leather seats and always smelt faintly of pig, I said, "I hope Mrs. Tolliver hasn't broken her arm, too."

"Oh, no, she's lovely." In Cornwall, lovely means well. "Nothing wrong with her. But didn't seem much point two cars coming . . ." And with that he started up his engine, and the taxi, after backfiring twice, ground into gear and shot forward up the hill that led to the main road.

I sat back and felt annoyed. Perhaps it was the most sensible thing to do, arranging for Charlotte and me to share the taxi, but it would have been more welcoming if Mrs. Tolliver had come to the station to meet Charlotte herself. It was, after all, a drive of only two miles. Charlotte was looking away from me, out the window, and I suspected that once more she was fighting tears. I didn't blame her.

"That was a good idea, wasn't it, for us to share the taxi?" I tried to sound enthusiastic, as though I approved.

She did not turn round. She said, "I suppose so."

However, we had arrived. We were here. Along the main road on that windy afternoon, and down the hill beneath the oak trees. Past the gates of what used to be the Squire's house, and then into the village. Nothing ever seemed to change. Up the hill again, past the cottages and the shops, an old man walking his dog, the petrol station, the pub. We turned down the road that led to the church and the sea, the copse of ancient oaks, the farm with its slated steadings, and so to the open white gates of White Lodge.

Mr. Thomas changed down with a hideous clash of gears and turned into these gates. We came up the short drive, between overhanging trees, and I saw the swept verges and the fading banks of hydrangea. We rounded a clump of these and drew up on the gravel sweep in front of the house. It was a stone house, whitewashed and solid. A wisteria clambered up the wall to the upstairs windows, and a flight of stone steps rose to the

closed front door. We all got out of the taxi, and Mr.
Thomas went up the steps to ring the bell. The wind
suddenly blew up a gust and swept a scatter of dead
leaves into a whirlpool at our feet. After a short wait, the
door was opened and Mrs. Tolliver appeared. She
looked just the same as I had remembered her and came
down the steps towards us with her smoothly coiffed grey
hair and her slender, elegant figure. Her face was neatly
arranged in a smile of welcome.

"Charlotte. Well, here you are." She stooped to kiss
the child briskly. She straightened up. I am tall, but she
was taller. "Prue. How very nice to see you. I hope you
didn't mind sharing the taxi."

"We didn't mind in the least. We met on the train in
London, so we've travelled all the way together."

"How very nice. Now, Charlotte, is this your suitcase?
In you come. There's just time to wash your hands, and
then we'll have tea. Mrs. Curnow's made a sponge cake.
I expect you like sponge cake."

Charlotte said, "Yes." It did not sound convincing.
She probably hated sponge cake. She would much have
preferred fish fingers and chips.

". . . And Prue, I hope you find Phoebe well. Perhaps
you'll come for lunch one day. How is your mother?"

"She's well."

"I'll get all the news some other time. Come along
now, Charlotte."

"Good-bye," Charlotte said to me.

"Good-bye, Charlotte. Come and see us."

"Yes, I will."

I waited by the taxi until they had gone up the steps and through the door. Mrs. Tolliver carried the suitcase, and Charlotte, still clutching her comic, trod cautiously at her heels. She did not turn to wave. The door closed behind them.

Chapter Two

It seemed all wrong that Charlotte should have been given a reception of such little warmth, while I, twenty-three years old and perfectly able to stand on my own two feet, had Holly Cottage waiting for me, and Phoebe. At Holly Cottage there was no driveway; just a patch of gravel between the gate and the house. At Holly Cottage the garden was a mass of dahlias and chrysanthemums, the front door stood open to the evening breeze, and from an upstairs window a pink cotton curtain blew in the wind, like a person waving a cheerful greeting. No sooner was the taxi turning in at her gate than Phoebe herself appeared. Her left arm was strapped up in a bulky white plaster cast, but her right arm signalled its own exuberant welcome, and she came running forward so unexpectedly that Mr. Thomas very nearly ran her over.

Before the car had stopped, I was out of it and into Phoebe's one-armed embrace. The one I gave back to her did double duty for both of us.

"Oh, my darling," she crowed, "what an angel. Never thought you'd be able to come. Couldn't believe it. I'm going nearly insane trying to get myself about. Can't even ride a bicycle. . . ."

Laughing, I let her go, and we stood back and looked at each other with the greatest of satisfaction. Looking at Phoebe is always a pleasure. Unpredictable, but always a pleasure. She was at that time well into her sixties, but it has always been impossible to equate Phoebe to the passing years.

I saw the thick stockings, the stout boots, the worn and faded blue-jean skirt. Over these she wore a man's shirt and cardigan (probably inherited from Chips); there were gold chains about her neck, and a tartan scarf, and on her head, inevitably, a hat.

She always wore hats, broad-brimmed, deep-crowned, rather dashing. She had taken to wearing them to protect her eyes, while painting out of doors, from the cold, white glare of the Cornish light, and they had become so much part of her that she very often forgot to take them off. This one was a rich brown, decorated with grey gull feathers stuck into the ribbon band. Beneath its kindly shade, Phoebe's face, the skin netted with lines, twinkled and smiled at me. The smile revealed teeth that were even and white as a child's, and her eyes were the deepest speedwell blue, their brightness challenged only by the turquoise-and-silver earrings that dangled on either side of her face.

I said, "You're a fraud. You may have broken your arm, but you're as beautiful as ever."

"What rubbish! Do you hear that, Mr. Thomas, she says I'm beautiful. She must be either mad or blind. Now, what's this? Your suitcase. And what are the dead flowers for? I don't want any dead flowers . . ." Holding the poor things, she began to laugh again. "Now, Mr. Thomas, you'll have to send me a bill. I can't pay you just now—I've mislaid my handbag."

"I'll pay, Phoebe."

"Of course you won't. Mr. Thomas doesn't mind, do you, Mr. Thomas?"

Mr. Thomas assured her that he didn't. He got back into his taxi, but Phoebe pursued him in order to put her head through the window and ask after Mrs. Thomas's bad leg. Mr. Thomas began to tell her, at some length. Halfway through his dissertation, Phoebe decided she'd had enough. "So glad she's better," she said firmly, and withdrew her head from the window. Mr. Thomas, halted in full spate, was not in the least disconcerted. It was just Miss Shackleton, and heaven only knew, she had some funny ways. The old taxi was set into motion once more and the next moment had sped away, scattering gravel through the gate and up the road.

"Now." Phoebe took my arm. "Let's get indoors. I want to hear all the news."

Together we went through the open door and into the house. I stood in the hall, looked about, and loved everything for being the same. I saw the polished floors scattered with rugs; the uncarpeted wooden staircase that led to the upper floor; the whitewashed walls hung, haphazard, with Phoebe's tiny, jewel-bright oil paintings.

The house smelt of turpentine and wood smoke and linseed oil and garlic and roses, but its greatest charm was the effect of airy lightness engendered by pale colours, lacy curtains, straw rugs, and polished wood. Even in the middle of winter, it always felt summery.

I took a deep breath, savouring it all. "Heaven," I said. "Heaven to be back."

"You're in the same old room," said Phoebe and then left me, heading for the kitchen. I knew she would spend some time trying to resuscitate Nigel's poor flowers, even though she had more than enough of her own. I picked up my case and went upstairs to the room that had been mine since I was a very small girl. I opened the door and was assailed by a gust of cold air pouring in from the wide open window. I shut the door, and everything stopped billowing. Putting down my case, I went to the window and leaned out to gaze at the familiar view.

The tide was out, and the evening smelt of seaweed. You were never far from the sea smells at Holly Cottage, because the house had been built on a grassy bluff overlooking a tidal estuary, which penetrated inland like a huge lake and was filled and emptied each day by the tides.

Below the house was a wide seawall, where once a single-line railway siding had led to a busy shipyard. The shipyard was closed now and the railway sleepers removed, but the wall still stood, solid as a cliff. At high tide the water reached nearly to the rim of this wall, and in summer it made a good place to swim, but at low tide there was nothing but acres of empty sand, with a few weedy rocks and shallow pools scattered here and there and a dozen or so derelict fishing boats that had been pulled up on the shingle winters ago and for some reason never floated again.

On this, the south side of the house, the garden was unexpectedly large. An irregularly shaped lawn, edged here and there with random flower beds, sloped down to a boundary hedge of escallonia. In the middle of this was a gate, and over the gate the clipped escallonia had been trimmed into an arch, which gave the garden a charmingly formal and old-fashioned aspect. To the right, beyond a high brick wall, where Chips Armitage used to grow peach trees, was a sizeable vegetable garden, and at the bottom of this, scarcely visible from the house, he had built his studio. All I could see was the pitch of the slate roof and, sitting on it, a single herring gull. As I watched, it spread its wings, screaming defiance at nothing in particular, and then took flight, soaring and gliding away, out over the wet, empty sands.

I smiled, closed the window against the cold, and went down to Phoebe.

We sat facing each other across the hearth rug, with a blazing log fire to warm us, and the light outside gradually dying into evening. There was a big brown teapot on the trolley, hand-painted earthenware cups and saucers, a plate of fresh scones, yellow farm butter, and homemade cherry jam.

"You didn't make these scones, Phoebe. You couldn't, with only one hand."

"No, Lily Tonkins made them this morning. Darling

woman, she comes in every day, and she's simply taken over the kitchen. I never realised what a marvellous cook she is."

"But how did you break your arm?"

"Oh, my dear, too stupid. I was down in the studio looking for some old folios of Chips's . . . I knew they were on the top shelf of his bookcase, and I stood on a chair, and of course some worm, unknown to me, had burrowed into the wood, and the leg gave way, and down I came!" She roared with laughter as though it were the best joke in the world. She was still wearing her feathered hat. "Very lucky not to break my leg. I came back to the house, and by great good fortune there was the postman, delivering the afternoon mail. So I hopped in beside him and he drove me to the cottage hospital and they tied me up in this tiresome cast."

"You poor thing."

"Oh, never mind, it doesn't hurt much; it's just a nuisance, and maddening not being able to drive. I've got to go back to the hospital tomorrow to let the doctor see it . . . I suppose he thinks I'm going to get gangrene or something . . ."

"I'll drive you . . ."

"You won't have to, because they're sending an ambulance. I've never been in an ambulance before. I'm rather looking forward to it. Now, how's Delia?"

Delia was my mother. I said she was well.

"And what sort of a train journey did you have?" Before I could tell her, she remembered the arrangement she had made with Mrs. Tolliver. "Heavens, I forgot to ask about Charlotte Collis. Did Mr. Thomas remember to collect her at the station as well?"

"Yes."

"How fortunate. I hope you didn't mind sharing the ride with her. Personally, I thought Mrs. Tolliver might have gone to fetch the poor child herself, but she seemed to think it was pointless if Mr. Thomas was going anyway."

"I thought she might have come to meet her, too."

"How is she, poor little mite?"

"She seemed a bit anxious. Not at all excited at the thought of staying with her grandmother. The only person she showed any enthusiasm for was you. She adores you."

"It's funny, isn't it. You'd think she'd rather be with children of her own age. Except that there aren't many children in this village, and even if there were, she's always been something of a loner. The first time we met, I found her wandering on the beach by herself. She said she was out for a walk, so I asked her back for tea and rang Mrs. Tolliver to say she was with me. After that she came quite often. She's fascinated by my pictures and paints and sketchbooks. I gave her a sketch pad and some felt pens for herself, and she has a remarkable talent and a marvellous imagination. Then she loves being told stories; hearing about Chips and all the stupid things he and I used to do together. Extraordinary, really, in such a young child."

I said, "You know, I don't think I ever knew that Mrs. Tolliver had a grandchild. I don't think I ever realised that she had a daughter. Or a husband, for that matter. What happened to Mr. Tolliver?"

"He died, some years ago. When Chips and I first came here, he was still alive, and they lived in great style. You know the sort of thing—a Bentley in the garage and two gardeners and a cook and a housemaid. Annabelle was impossibly spoiled and indulged—a real only child. But then Mr. Tolliver had a heart attack—keeled over on the seventh green of the golf course—and never recovered. After that nothing was quite the same again. Of course, Mrs. Tolliver never said anything—she's the most reserved woman I know—but the big car was sold and a general cutting back rather obviously took place. Annabelle had been sent to some ridiculously expensive school in Switzerland, and she had to leave and come home and attend the local Comprehensive. She simply hated it. I think she felt that life had deliberately humiliated her. Silly girl."

"What was she like?"

"Very beautiful, but without the vestige of a brain. After she was married and had her little boy, she used to come down for the summers and stay with her mother, and every time there were three or four lovelorn fellows dancing attendance. At a party you couldn't see her for men. Just like bees round a honey pot."

"She's in Majorca just now. Charlotte told me that much."

"I know. I've heard all about that. I think Mrs. Tolliver rather felt that she should come back and look after Charlotte herself. She was annoyed about the school boiler blowing up. She felt it was inefficient. I was horrified. It might have killed all the children. But Mrs.

Tolliver was far more concerned at the prospect of having Charlotte to stay."

"But doesn't she like Charlotte?"

"Oh, I think she quite likes her," Phoebe told me in her airy way. "But she's never been interested in children, and I think she finds Charlotte very dull. And, as well, she's never had the child on her own before. I think she's wondering what on earth she's going to do with her."

Outside, the wind was getting up, rattling the window sashes and whistling around the corners of the house. It was nearly dark, but the room in which we sat was warm with dancing firelight. I reached for the kettle that simmered on a brass hob near the flames and refilled the teapot.

"What about Annabelle's husband?"

"Leslie Collis? I could never stand him, gruesome man."

"I thought he was gruesome, too. He didn't even kiss Charlotte good-bye. How did Annabelle meet him?"

"He was staying at the Castle Hotel in Porthkerris with three other stockbrokers, or whatever it is he does in the City. I don't know how they met, but the moment he set eyes on her, that was it."

"He couldn't have been attractive."

"In a funny way, he was. He had a certain sort of dark, flashy charm. Spent money like water, drove around in a Ferrari."

"Do you think Annabelle was in love with him?"

"Not for a moment. Annabelle was in love only with

herself. But he could give her everything that she'd ever wanted, and she didn't like being poor. And of course Mrs. Tolliver encouraged it madly. I don't think she ever forgave her poor husband for leaving her in straitened circumstances, and she was determined that Annabelle should marry well."

I thought about this. Then I poured myself another cup of tea and lay back against the cushions of the deep and friendly old chair. I said, "I suppose all mothers are the same."

"Don't tell me Delia's been at you again."

"Oh, no, she's not been at me. But there's this man . . . he brought me those chrysanthemums . . ." And I told her about Nigel Gordon and the invitation to Scotland.

Phoebe listened sympathetically, and when I had finished, she said, "I think he sounds very nice."

"He is. That's the trouble. He's terribly nice. But my mother's already got wedding bells banging to and fro and keeps reminding me that I'm twenty-three and ought to be settling down. Perhaps if she didn't go on about it so, I might marry him."

"You mustn't marry him unless you can't imagine life without him."

"That's just it. I can. Quite easily."

"We all need different things from life. Your mother needs security. That's why she married your father, and a fat lot of good it did her, because she never took the time to get to know him before she made that spectacular entrance up the aisle. But you're a special person. You need more than a man to bring you flowers and pay the bills. You're intelligent and you're talented. And when you do settle down with a man, it is absolutely vital that he makes you laugh. Chips and I laughed all the time, even when we were poor and unsuccessful and didn't know how we were going to pay the grocer's bill. We were always laughing."

I smiled, remembering them together. I said, "Talking of Chips, did you know that Daniel Cassens has an exhibition on at the Chastal Gallery? I read a rave review in the *Times* this morning."

"I read it too. So exciting. Dear, clever boy. I intended going up to London for the opening day, but then I went and broke this stupid arm and the doctor said I wasn't to travel."

"Is he in London? Daniel, I mean."

"Heaven knows where he is. Probably still in Japan. Or Mexico, or somewhere mad. But I'd love to see that exhibition. Perhaps, if I'm able, I'll come back to London with you and we'll go together. What fun that would be! Something to look forward to."

That night I had a dream. I was on some island—a tropical island, palm-fringed and white-sanded. It was very hot. I was on a beach, walking down towards the silent, glass-clear sea. I meant to swim, but the water, when I reached it, was only inches deep, scarcely covering my ankles. I walked for a long time, and then, all at once, the sand fell steeply away, and I was out of my depth, swimming, and the water was dark as ink and the current like a rushing river. I felt myself borne along on its flow, towards the horizon. I knew that I should turn back, swim for the beach, but the current was too strong, and there was no resisting it. So I stopped fighting and let myself be carried along, knowing that I could never return, but so marvellous was the sensation of going with the tide that I did not care.

I woke with the dream still sharp and clear in my mind. I could remember every detail of it. I lay in bed, thinking about the clear water and the sensation of peace as I was borne along in the wash of that warm and tranquil sea. All dreams have meaning, and I wondered how some professional would analyse this one. It occurred to me, in an unworried sort of way, that it might be about dying.

Chapter Three

The early morning turned into a beautiful day. Breezy and bright, the blue sky was patched with large, sailing white clouds blown in from the Atlantic. The sun blinked in and out of these clouds, and during the morning the flood tide slowly filled the estuary, creeping up the sands, filling the tide pools, and finally, by about eleven o'clock, reaching the seawall below the house.

Phoebe had gone to keep her appointment at the Cottage Hospital, borne there in some style by the local ambulance. For the trip she had donned yet another hat, black velours, bound by a tussore scarf, and she had waved enthusiastically through the open window as though she were setting off on a jaunt. She would be back for lunch. I had offered to prepare this, but Lily Tonkins, already busy with the vacuum cleaner, said that she already had a bit of lamb in the oven, so I found a sketch pad and a stick of charcoal, stole an apple from the fruit bowl, and took myself out of doors.

And now, at eleven o'clock, I sat on the grassy slope above the seawall, with the sun a dazzle on the wind-ruffled waters of the estuary and the morning freshness filled with the scream of gulls. I had done a rough sketch of the derelict fishing boats with their ramshackle chains and anchors, their empty masts piercing the sky. As I filled in some detail of a weather-scarred hatchway, I heard the morning train from Porthkerris come through the cutting behind Holly Cottage and draw up at the little halt by the edge of the shore. It was a very small and infrequent train, and a moment or two later it gave a hoot and moved on again, around the curve of the line and out of sight.

So engrossed was I in maddening perspectives that I was scarcely aware of this happening, but when I next looked up to study the keel of an upended dinghy, a movement caught the corner of my eye. I looked and saw a solitary figure walking towards me. He approached from the direction of the station, and I presumed that he had alighted from that train, crossed the line, and so followed the track of the disused siding. There was nothing unusual about this. People often took the train from Porthkerris to Penmarron and then walked back to Porthkerris, following the footpath that led for three miles or more along the edge of the cliff.

I lost interest in my drawing. I laid down the sketch pad, picked up my apple, and began to eat it. I watched the stranger's progress. He was a tall man, long-legged, with an easy, loping stride. His clothes at first were simply a blur of blue and white, but as he came closer I saw that he wore denim jeans and a faded shirt, and over this a white knitted jacket, the sort that people bring home from holidays in Ireland. The jacket was unbuttoned, flying open in the wind, and a red and white handkerchief, like a gipsy's, was knotted around his throat. His head was bare, his hair very dark, and though he did not appear to be in any sort of hurry, he was covering the ground at considerable pace.

He looked, I decided, a man who knew where he was going.

Now he had come to the far end of the seawall. Here he paused and looked out over the dazzling water, shielding his eyes from the glare. A moment later he moved on once more, and it was then that he spied me, sitting there in the long grass, eating my apple, watching him.

I thought that he would probably walk past me, perhaps with a casual "good morning," but as he drew level with me, he stopped and stood there, with his back to the water, his hands in the pockets of that voluminous jacket, his head tilted back. A gust of wind ruffled his dark hair. He said, "Hello."

His voice was boyish, his demeanour youthful, but his thin, brown face was not a boy's face, and there were strong lines etched around his mouth and his deeply set eyes.

"Hello."

"What a lovely morning."

"Isn't it?" I finished my apple and tossed the core away. A gull instantly pounced on it and bore it off to consume in private.

"I just got off the train."

"I thought you must have. Are you going to walk back to Porthkerris?"

"No, as a matter of fact, I'm not." And with that he began to climb the grassy slope, picking his way between the bramble patches and the clumps of bracken. When he reached my side, he collapsed, a sprawl of long boney limbs. I saw his old canvas shoes had holes in the toes, and the warmth of the sun made his jacket smell sheepy, as though it had been knitted straight off some oily fleece.

I said, "You can walk by the cliffs if you want to."

"Ah, but then you see, I don't want to." He spied my sketch pad and before I could stop him had picked it up. "That's very nice."

I hate people looking at my work, especially when it's not even finished. "It's just a scribble."

"Not at all." He surveyed it for a moment longer and then laid it down without further comment. He said, "There is a deadly fascination about watching a flood tide. Is that what you've been doing?"

"For the past hour."

He felt in his capacious pocket and brought out a thin packet of cigars, a book of matches, and a dog-eared paperback, obviously much read and consulted. Interest stirred when I saw that it was *Vanishing Cornwall* by

Daphne du Maurier. The book of matches had "The Castle Hotel Porthkerris" printed upon it. I felt like a detective and as though, already, I knew quite a lot about him.

He selected a cigar and lit it. His hands were beautiful; long and narrow, with spade-tipped fingers. On one wrist he wore a cheap and unremarkable watch, on the other a chain of gold links, very old-looking and heavy.

As he put the matches and the cigars back into his pocket, I said, "Are you staying at the Castle?"

He looked up in surprise and then smiled. "How did you guess that?"

"Deduction. Matches. Sharp eyes."

"Of course. How stupid of me. Well, I spent last night there, if you can call that staying. I came down from London yesterday."

"So did I. I came by train."

"I wish I had. I got a lift. I hate driving. Hate cars. I'd much rather sit and look out of the window or read a book. Infinitely more civilised." He settled himself into a more comfortable position, leaning on an elbow. "Are you on holiday, or staying here, or is this where you live?"

"Just staying."

"In the village?"

"Yes. Right here, actually."

"What do you mean by right here?"

"In the house up there."

"Holly Cottage." He began to laugh. "Are you staying with Phoebe?"

"Do you know Phoebe?"

"Of course I know Phoebe. That's why I'm here. To see her."

"Well you won't find her just now, because she's gone to the Cottage Hospital in an ambulance." He looked horrified. "It's all right, she hasn't had a stroke or anything, just broken her arm. It's been put in a cast, and the doctor wants to have a look at it.".

"Well, that's a relief. Is she all right?"

"Of course. She'll be back for lunch."

"And who are you? A nurse, or one of her perpetual students?"

"No, I'm a perpetual niece."

"You wouldn't by any chance be Prue?"

"Yes, I would." I frowned. "But who are you?"

"Daniel Cassens."

I said, ridiculously, "But you're in Mexico."

"Mexico? Never been to Mexico in my life."

"Phoebe said you were probably in Mexico or somewhere mad."

"That was charitable of her. In fact, I've been in the Virgin Islands, on a boat with some American friends, but then somebody said there was going to be a hurricane, so I decided the time was ripe to get out. But back in New York, I was instantly bombarded with cables from Peter Chastal to say I had to be in London for the opening day of this exhibition he's mounted for me."

"I know about that. You see, I work for Marcus Bernstein. We're practically next door to Peter Chastal. And I read the reviews of your exhibition. I think you've got a success on your hands. Phoebe read it, too. She was enormously thrilled."

"She would be."

"Were you at the opening?"

"Yes, I was. I finally made it. At the last moment I gave in and caught a flight over."

"Why were you so reluctant? Most people wouldn't miss it for anything. All the champagne and the adulation."

"I hate my own exhibitions. It's the most ghastly form of exposure, like putting one's children on display. All those eyes, staring. Makes me feel quite ill."

I understood. "But you did go?"

"Yes, for a little. But I wore a disguise—dark glasses and a concealing hat. I looked like an insane sort of spy. I only stayed for half an hour, and then when Peter wasn't looking, I slunk away and went and sat in a pub and tried to decide what to do next. And then I got talking to this man, and I bought him a beer, and he said that he was driving to Cornwall, so I hitched a lift with him and arrived last night."

"Why didn't you come and stay with Phoebe?"

Without thinking I asked the question and immediately wished that I hadn't. He looked away from me, pulled at a tuft of grass with his hand, and let the wind blow it from his fingers.

"I don't know," he said at last. "So many reasons. Some high-minded, some not so."

"You know she would have welcomed you."

"Yes, I know. But it's been a long time. It's eleven

years since I was here. And Chips was alive then."

"You worked with him, didn't you."

"Yes, for a year. I was in America when he died. Up in the Sonoma Valley in northern California. I was staying with some people I knew who had a vineyard. Phoebe's letter took a long time to find me, and I remember thinking then that if nobody ever told you that people you love have died, then they would live forever. And I thought then that I could never come back to Cornwall. But dying is part of life. I've learned that since. But I hadn't learned it then."

I thought of the carousel that Chips had made for me out of an old gramophone; he and Phoebe laughing together; the smell of his pipe.

"I loved him, too."

"Everybody did. He was such a benevolent man. I studied sculpture with him, but I learned from Chips a lot about living that, when you're twenty, is infinitely more important. I never knew my own father, and it always made me feel different towards other people. Chips filled that gap. He gave me a great sense of identity." I knew what he meant, because that was just the way I felt about Phoebe. "Coming down from London yesterday, I kept having second thoughts; wondering if I was doing the right thing. It isn't always wise to return to the place where you've been young and dreamed dreams. And had ambitions."

"Not if your dreams and ambitions came true. And surely that's happened for you. The Chastal exhibition must have proved that. There can't be a painting left unsold . . ."

"Perhaps I need to be unsure of myself."

"You can't have it all."

We fell silent. It was noon now, and the sun was very warm. I heard the soft buffet of the breeze, the lap of water against the seawall. Across the flooded estuary, from the distant causeway, came the hum of passing cars. A flock of gulls fought over a piece of rotting fish.

He said, "You know, once, centuries before Christ, in the Bronze Age, this estuary was a river. Traders sailed all the way from the eastern Mediterranean, around the Lizard and Lands End, laden to the gunwales with all the treasures of the Levant."

I smiled. I said, "I've read *Vanishing Cornwall*, too."

"It's magic." He opened the book and it fell open at a much-studied page, and he read aloud:

For the watcher to-day, crouching amidst the sand dunes and the tufted grass, looking seaward to where the shallows run, imagination can take a riotous course, picturing line upon line of high-prowed, flat-bottomed craft, brightly coloured, their sails abeam, entering the river with the flood tide.

He closed the book. "I wish I had that sort of perception, but I haven't. I can only see the here and the now, and try to paint it the way it happens to me."

"Do you take that book everywhere with you?"

"No. But I found it in a shop in New York, and when I first read it I knew that someday, sometime, I had to come back to Cornwall. It never leaves you. It's like a magnet. You have to return."

"But why to the Castle Hotel, of all places?"

Daniel looked up at me, amused. "Why? Don't you think I fit in there?"

I thought of the rich Americans, the golfers, the twin-setted ladies playing bridge, the genteel teatime orchestra.

"Not exactly."

He laughed. "I know. It was a fairly incongruous choice, but it was the only hotel I could remember and I was tired. Jet-lag tired, London tired, everything tired. I wanted to get into an enormous bed and sleep for a week. And then when I woke up this morning, I wasn't tired any longer. And I thought about Chips and knew that all I wanted to do was come and see Phoebe again. So I walked down to the station and caught the train. And then got off the train and met you."

"And now," I told him, "you're coming back to the house with me, and you're going to stay for lunch. There's a bottle of wine in the fridge and Lily Tonkins has got a bit of lamb in the oven."

"Lily Tonkins? Is she still going?"

"She runs the house. She's doing all the cooking as well just now."

"I'd forgotten Lily." He picked up my sketch pad once more, and this time I didn't mind. He said, "You know, you're not only exceptionally pretty, but you are talented as well."

I decided to ignore the bit about being pretty. "I'm not talented. That's why I work for Marcus Bernstein. I found out the hard way that there was no hope of me earning a living by being an artist."

"How wise of you to realise," said Daniel Cassens. "So few people do."

Together, with the sun on our backs, we climbed the slope of the hill. I opened the wooden gate in the escallonia hedge, and he went ahead of me, cautiously, as a dog will go, nosing his way into once-familiar territory. I shut the gate. He stood looking up at the face of the house, and I looked, too, and tried to see it with his eyes, after eleven years away. To me, it looked as I had always know it. I saw the pointed Gothic windows, the garden door open to the brick terrace and the morning's warmth. There were still geraniums blooming in their earthenware tubs, and Phoebe's ramshackle garden chairs had not yet been put away for the winter.

We walked up the gentle slope of the lawn, and I led the way indoors.

"Phoebe?" I opened the kitchen door, from whence came delicious smells of cooking lamb. Lily Tonkins was at the kitchen table, chopping mint, but she stopped when I appeared.

"She got home about five minutes ago. Went upstairs to change her shoes."

"I've brought a visitor for lunch. Is that all right?"

"Always plenty to eat. Friend of yours, is it?"

Daniel, behind me, moved into view. "It's me, Lily, Daniel Cassens."

Lily's mouth fell open. "Aw, my dear life." She laid down the chopping knife and put a hand to her meagre chest, conveying heart-stopping shock. "The sight of you! Like a body out of the past. Daniel Cassens. It must be nearly twelve years. What are you doing here?"

"Come to see you," he told her. He walked around the table and stooped to kiss her cheek. Lily gave a crow of laughter and went pink. "You villain. Turning up like a bad penny. Just you wait till Miss Shackleton sets eyes on you. Us thought you'd forgotten all about we."

The Cornish frequently mix their pronouns, but Lily did this only under great stress, her voice shrill with excitement. "Did you know she'd broken her arm, poor soul? Been at the hospital all morning she has, but the doctor says she's doing nicely. Wait now, till I give her a shout." And she disappeared into the hall, and we heard her calling upstairs to Miss Shackleton to come down immediate, because there was some lovely surprise waiting for her.

Daniel followed her, but I stayed in the kitchen because for some reason I felt that if I witnessed their reunion I should probably burst into tears. As it was, it was Phoebe who cried. I'd never seen her cry before, but they were tears of joy and over in a moment. But still, she cried. And then we all found ourselves back in the kitchen, and I took the wine out of the refrigerator and Lily forgot about chopping mint and went to find some glasses, and the occasion then and there suddenly turned into a tremendous celebration.

He stayed for the rest of the afternoon. The day, which had started so brightly, became overcast, with low clouds blowing in from the sea on a rising wind. There were showers, and it became chilly, but none of this mattered, for we were indoors by the fire, and the hours flew by in talk and reminiscence and a general catching up on everything that had been happening to both of them.

I had little to add to the conversation, but that did not matter. Listening was a joy, because not only did I feel that I was involved with both of them as people but because my interests and my work were relevant to everything that they discussed. I knew about this painter; I had heard of that exhibition; I had actually seen that particular portrait. Phoebe spoke of one Lewis Falcon, who was now living in a house out at Lanyon, and I remembered him because we had held an exhibition of his work at Marcus Bernstein's not two years before.

And we talked about Chips, and it was not like talking about a person who had died six years ago but as though at any moment he would walk into the firelit room to join us, sink into his own sagging armchair, join in the discussion.

Finally, they got onto the subject of Phoebe's own work. What was she doing now? Daniel wanted to know, and Phoebe laughed in her usual self-deprecating way and said that she had nothing to show him, but under pressure she admitted that there were a few canvases that she had completed last year, whilst on holiday in the Dordogne, but she had never got around to sorting them out and they were down in Chips's studio, still stacked haphazardly beneath dust sheets. Daniel at once sprang to his feet and insisted on seeing them, so Phoebe found the studio key and pulled on a raincoat and they set off together, down the brick path, to go and search them out.

I did not accompany them on this expedition. It was half past four and Lily Tonkins had gone home, so when I had collected our coffee mugs and washed them up, I laid a tea tray, found a fruitcake in a tin, and took the empty kettle off the Aga to fill it at the sink.

The sink in Phoebe's kitchen was beneath the window, which was pleasant, because it meant that while you were washing up, you could enjoy the view. But the view now was lost, drowned in a mistlike rain. The clouds were low, the wet, emptying sands of the estuary reflecting their leaden darkness. Flood tide, ebb tide. They made a pattern of time, like the minute hands of a clock, ticking life away.

I felt philosophic, peaceful. And then, suddenly, very happy. This happiness caught me unawares, as I used to be caught unawares by the random ecstasies of childhood. I looked around me, as though the source of this reasonless euphoria could be seen, pinned down, remembered. I saw everything in that familiar kitchen with a rare and heightened perception, so that each humble and ordinary object appeared both pleasing and beautiful. The grain of the scrubbed table, the bright colours of the crockery on the dresser, a basket of vegetables, the symmetry of cups and saucepans.

I thought about Daniel and Phoebe, rooting around together in Chips's dusty old studio. I was glad that I had not gone with them. I liked him. I liked his beautiful hands and his light, quick voice and dark eyes. But there was also something disturbing about him. I was not sure if I wanted to be disturbed.

He had said, "You are not only exceptionally pretty, but you are talented as well."

I was not used to being told I was pretty. My long straight hair was too pale, my mouth too big, my nose snub. Even Nigel Gordon, who—according to my mother—was in love with me, had never actually got around to saying that I was pretty. Smashing, maybe, or sensational, but never pretty. I wondered if Daniel was married and then laughed at myself, because my thought processes were so painfully obvious, and because it was exactly the question that my mother would have asked. My own self-ridicule broke the spell of that extraordinary moment of perception, and Phoebe's kitchen dissolved into its usual mundane self, left neat by Lily Tonkins before she had donned her head scarf and bicycled home to get her husband's tea.

When tea was over, Daniel pushed back his cuff, looked at his watch, and said that he must go.

"I wish you were staying here," said Phoebe. "Why can't you come back here? Fetch your things and then come back to us."

But he said that he wouldn't. "Lily Tonkins has got quite enough on her plate looking after the pair of you."

"But we'll see you again? You're down for a little?"

He stood up. "A day or two, anyway." It sounded vague. "I'll be back to see you."

"How are you going to get back to Porthkerris?"

"There's probably a bus . . ."

I said, "I'll drive you in Phoebe's car. It's a mile to the

bus stop and it's still raining and you'll get soaked."

"Don't you mind?"

"Of course I don't mind."

So he said good-bye to Phoebe and we went out and got into her battered old car, and I backed it cautiously out of the garage and we drove off, leaving Phoebe silhouetted in the lighted doorway of Holly Cottage, waving her good arm and wishing us a safe journey, as though we were setting off on some marathon rally.

We bowled up the hill through the rain, past the golf club, onto the main road. "You're so clever to drive," he said admiringly.

"But you can surely drive a car. Everybody can drive a car."

"Yes, I can drive, but I simply hate it. I'm a total fool about anything mechanical."

"Have you never had a car?"

"I had to have one in America. Everybody has a car in America. But I never really felt at home with it. I bought it secondhand, and it was enormous, long as a bus, with a radiator like a mouth organ and huge, phallic headlights and exhaust pipes. It had automatic gears, too, and electrically operated windows, and some sort of supercharged carburetor. I was terrified of it. When I'd had it three years, I finally sold it, but by that time I'd only just worked out how to operate the heater."

I began to laugh. I suddenly thought of Phoebe saying, when you settle down with a man, it is absolutely vital that he makes you laugh. Nigel, it was true, had never made me laugh much. On the other hand, he was a wizard with cars, and spent a good deal of his spare time either with his head under the hood of his M.G., or else prone beneath it, with only his feet sticking out, and conversation reduced to requests for a larger monkey wrench.

I said, comfortingly, "You can't be good at everything. If you're a successful artist, it would be too much to ask to be a mechanic as well."

"That's what's so fantastic about Phoebe. She paints like a dream. She could have made a really great name for herself if she hadn't happily subjugated her talent in creating a home for Chips . . . and for all the stray students like myself who lived with them and worked with them and learned so much from them. Holly Cottage was a sort of refuge for so many young and struggling artists. There were always immense, delicious meals, and order and cleanliness and warmth. You never forget that sort of security and comfort. It instills in you a standard of good living—and I mean 'good' in the true sense of the word—for the rest of your life."

It was marvellously satisfying to hear another person state aloud what I had always felt myself about Phoebe, and yet, somehow, had never been able to express.

I said, "We're the same, you and I. When I was a child, it was just about the only time I ever cried, when I had to say good-bye to Phoebe, and get on the train and go back to London. And yet once I was home again, back with my mother, and with my own room, and all my own things around me, it was all right. And by the next day, I was always quite happy again, and involved, and glued to the telephone, ringing up all my friends."

"The tears would have been the direct result of the

insecurity of two different worlds touching. Nothing makes one more miserable."

I thought about this. It made sense. I said, "I suppose so."

"Actually, I can't imagine you being anything but a happy little girl."

"Yes, I was happy. My parents were divorced, but they were both wise and intelligent people. And it all happened when I was very little, so that it didn't leave what you might call a lasting scar."

"You were lucky."

"Yes, I was. I was always loved and I was always wanted. You can't ask more than that out of any childhood."

Now the road sloped and curved towards Porthkerris. Through the murk, the lights of the harbour sparkled far below us. We came to the gates of the Castle Hotel, and turned in, and made our way up the winding drive, the avenue of oak trees. There was an open space, with tennis courts and putting greens, and then a wide gravel sweep in front of the hotel. Lights shone from windows and the glassed revolving door. I drew up between a Porsche and a Jaguar, pulled on the brake and turned off the engine.

"I can't help feeling very slightly out of place. Do you know, I've never been here before. Nobody's ever been rich enough to bring me."

"Come in and I'll buy you a drink."

"I'm not suitably dressed."

"Neither am I." He opened the door. "Come on."

We left the car, looking dusty and forlorn between its aristocratic neighbours, and Daniel led the way through the revolving doors, and inside it was tremendously warm and thickly carpeted and expensive-smelling. It was that slack period between tea and cocktail time, and there were not many people about; only a man in golf clothes, reading the *Financial Times,* and an elderly couple watching television.

The hall porter gave us a cold glance, then recognised Daniel and hastily rearranged his expression.

"Good evening, sir."

"Good evening," said Daniel and headed straight in the direction of the bar. But it was my first visit to the Castle, and I wanted to linger and inspect. Here was a writing room, and here, visible through open double doors, an overheated, overupholstered apartment arranged as a card room. In this, by a blazing fire, sat four ladies around a bridge table. I paused for a moment, my attention caught; the scene was so reminiscent of some play from the thirties. I felt that somewhere I had seen it all before: the long brocade curtains, the chintz-covered chairs, the set piece of the elaborate flower arrangement.

Even the ladies wore the correct clothes: the cashmere cardigans, the strings of good pearls. One smoked a cigarette with a long ivory holder.

"Two no trumps."

"Prue." Daniel, impatient, had retraced his steps to urge me on. "Come *on.*"

I was about to follow him when the lady who faced me

across the card table looked up. Our eyes met. I had not instantly recognised her, but now I was face to face with Mrs. Tolliver.

"Prue." She looked politely pleased to see me, though I found it hard to believe that this was so. "What a surprise."

"Hello, Mrs. Tolliver."

"What are you doing here?"

I did not want to go and talk to them, but confronted by the situation, I couldn't think of anything else to do. "I . . . I was just looking around. I've never been here before." I moved forward into the room, and the other ladies looked up at me from their hands of cards with smiling mouths and eyes that did not miss a detail of my windblown hair, my old pullover, my faded jeans.

Mrs. Tolliver laid down her cards and introduced me to her friends. ". . . Prue Shackleton. You must know Phoebe Shackleton, who lives at Penmarron. Well, Prue is her niece . . ."

"Oh, yes. How nice," said the ladies in their various ways, obviously longing to get on with their game.

"Prue was so kind to Charlotte yesterday. She travelled down with her from London on the train."

The ladies smiled again, approving of this. I realised with some dismay that I had not thought of Charlotte all day. For some reason this made me feel guilty, and the guilt was not assuaged by the sight of Mrs. Tolliver sitting here in her element and playing bridge.

I said, "Where is Charlotte?"

"At home. With Mrs. Curnow."

"Is she all right?"

Mrs. Tolliver fixed me with a cold eye. "Is there any reason she shouldn't be?"

I was taken aback. "No reason . . ." I met her eye. "It's just that, on the train, she seemed very quiet."

"She's always quiet. She never has much to say. And how did you find Phoebe? Not bothered by her broken arm? I'm so glad. Is she with you now?"

"No. I just drove someone back . . . he's staying here . . ."

I remembered Daniel then, standing behind me, and in some confusion turned to include him in this little encounter and introduce him to Mrs. Tolliver.

"Daniel, this is Mrs. . . ."

But he wasn't behind me. I saw only the open doors and the empty foyer beyond.

"Your friend took one look at us and left," one of the other ladies remarked, and I turned back and saw them laughing as though it were a joke. I smiled too.

"How silly of me. I thought he was still there."

Mrs. Tolliver picked up her cards once more and arranged them in a neat fan. "So nice to have seen you," she said. I found myself, for no reason, blushing. I made my excuses, said good-bye to them, and left.

Back in the foyer, I searched for Daniel. There was no trace of him, but I saw the lighted sign of the Cocktail Bar and headed for it, and found him, a solitary figure, sitting on a high stool with his back to me.

I was indignant. "What did you go off like that for?"

"Bridge-playing ladies aren't really my scene."

"They aren't my scene either, but sometimes you have to talk to people. I felt such a fool. I was going to introduce you and you'd evaporated into thin air. It was Mrs. Tolliver, from Penmarron."

"I know. Have a drink."

"If you knew it was Mrs. Tolliver, that was even ruder."

"You sound like an etiquette writer. Why should I be bothered with Mrs. Tolliver? No, don't tell me, because I don't want to know. Now I'm having a Scotch. What do you want to drink?"

"I don't know if I want a drink." I was still feeling put out.

"I thought that having a drink was what we'd come to do."

"Oh, all right." I climbed up onto the stool beside him. "I'll have a lager."

He ordered it for me. We then proceeded to sit in silence. At the back of the bar the shelves of bottles were backed by mirrored glass, and our two reflections gazed back at us from behind them. Daniel took out a cigar and lit it, and the barman brought me my lager and made a few remarks about the weather. He gave us a dish of peanuts. When he had gone back to the other end of the long bar, Daniel said, "All right, I'm sorry."

"What for?"

"For insulting Mrs. Tolliver, and for being bloody to you. I am in fact quite often bloody. It's as well to know before we embark on some deathless friendship." He looked at me and smiled.

"You didn't insult her." I added ruefully, "To be perfectly truthful, I don't much like her either."

"How do you come to be on such intimate terms with her?"

"Talking to someone at a bridge table isn't exactly being intimate."

"But you do know her quite well?"

"No, I don't. But my mother used to play bridge with her when we came down to stay with Phoebe. And then yesterday I travelled down on the train from London with her little granddaughter, Charlotte Collis. Her mother is Annabelle Tolliver. She was sitting next to me and she looked rather miserable, so we went and had lunch together. There was . . ." I decided not to go into the details of Charlotte's predicament, ". . . some complication, and she can't be at her boarding school, so she's spending a week with Mrs. Tolliver. Phoebe says she's a lonely child; she's always at Holly Cottage, just to have someone to talk to."

Daniel, quietly smoking his cigar, said nothing. I wondered if I was boring him stiff and looked to see if he was politely stifling yawns. But he wasn't. He was simply sitting, his elbow propped on the bar, his profile showing no expression, his eyes downcast. The smoke of his cigar made a fragrant, curling plume.

I took a mouthful of delicious icy lager. "Mrs. Tolliver didn't really want her to stay, according to Phoebe. She didn't even come to the junction to meet Charlotte off the train, and Charlotte and I had to share Mr. Thomas's taxi. And now, today, Mrs. Tolliver's playing bridge, and she's left the child with her housekeeper. It can't be much fun for Charlotte. She's only about ten. She should be with other children."

After a little, Daniel said, "Yes." He put out his half-smoked cigar, grinding the stub into the ashtray as though he had a grudge against it. He finished his drink and set down the empty glass, then turned and smiled at me and said, surprisingly, "Tomorrow. Will you come and have lunch with me?"

Taken unawares, I did not immediately reply. He went on, swiftly, "That is, if Phoebe can spare you. And lend you her car again."

"I think she could. I don't think she'd mind."

"Ask her, then, when you get back."

"All right. Shall I come here? To the hotel?"

"No. I'll meet you in the Ship Inn on the harbour in Porthkerris. We'll get a ploughman's lunch and a glass of beer, and if it's fine we'll go and sit on the harbour wall and pretend we're tourists."

I smiled. "What time?"

He shrugged. "About half past twelve."

"All right." I was very pleased that he had asked me. "Half past twelve."

He said, "Good. Now finish your lager and I'll take you back to the car."

We emerged from the revolving doors, ejected into wet darkness. We found Phoebe's car, and Daniel opened the door for me, but before I could get into it, he had put his hand around the back of my neck and drawn my face towards his and kissed my mouth. His face was damp with the rain, and for an instant we stood there, and I felt the cool pressure of his cheek against my own.

We said good night. I drove giddily back to Penmarron, feeling drunk, as though I had consumed a great deal more than a single half-pint of lager.

I was bursting to tell Phoebe about everything and to indulge in more long and illuminating discussions about Daniel and Mrs. Tolliver and Charlotte, but when I got back to Holly Cottage, I disturbed her dozing by the fire, and when she woke up, she admitted that she was very tired. Her arm ached, the cast was heavy, the day had been long and exciting. She looked tired, too, her face, beneath the obliterating brim of her hat, thin and shadowed. So I told her only that Daniel had asked me to have lunch with him the next day and asked if this would be all right and if I could borrow her car. She was, as I had known she would be, perfectly agreeable, so I went off to the kitchen and poured her a glass of restoring wine, and then I made scrambled eggs and we ate them in front of the fire.

After that, although it was only half past eight, she decided that she would go to bed, so I helped her upstairs and switched on the electric blanket and drew the curtains against the chilly darkness. When I left her, cosy in her huge bed, she was reading a book by the light of the bedside lamp, but as I shut the door and took myself downstairs, I knew that very soon she would be asleep.

Chapter Four

Next morning I was out of bed before she could be, and downstairs. It was too early for Lily Tonkins, so I laid a tray for Phoebe's breakfast, made coffee and toast, and carried the lot upstairs. She was already awake, watching through her open window the sun climb the sky. When I appeared through the door, she turned her head on the pillow and saw the tray and said, with all her usual energy, "You are an idiot, Prue; you know I never have breakfast in bed."

"You are this morning." She pulled herself up on her pillows, and I laid the tray across her knees and went to close the window.

"Red sky at morning, shepherd's warning. I suppose it's going to rain today."

"Don't be so gloomy. You haven't brought a coffee cup for yourself."

"I thought you'd like to be left in peace."

"I hate being left in peace. I like chatting over break-fast. Go and get a mug." She took the lid off the coffee pot and peered inside. "You've made enough for ten people; you'll have to help me drink it."

In bed, which was about the only place she did not wear one of her dashing hats, she looked different: femi-nine; older, perhaps; vulnerable. Her thick, wiry hair hung in a plait over one shoulder, and she was wrapped in a fleecy shawl. She looked so comfortable that I said, "Why don't you stay there for the morning? Lily Tonkins can cope with everything, and there's not much that you can do to help with only one arm."

"I might," said Phoebe, not committing herself. "I just might do that. Now go and get a mug before the coffee gets cold."

I fetched not only a cup but a bowl of cereal as well, and ate it sitting on the edge of the great, carved pine bed that Phoebe and Chips had shared for all those happy, sinful years. She had once told me that everything she really enjoyed in life was either illegal, immoral, or fattening, and then had roared with laughter.

But somehow they had got away with it, she and Chips. Even in this small, parochial village, they had ridden out the inevitable storm of prejudice by sheer strength of character coupled with their disarming charm. I remem-bered Chips playing the organ in church when the regu-lar organist had flu, and Phoebe busily baking enormous, lopsided cakes for the Women's Institute tea.

She cared for everybody, and yet for no person's opin-ion. I looked at her eating toast and marmalade and loved her. She caught my eye. She said, "How nice that you're having lunch with Daniel. What time are you meeting him?"

"Half past twelve at the Ship Inn in Porthkerris. But I won't go unless you promise me that you'll be all right."

"For heaven's sake, I'm not in a wheelchair. Off you go. But I shall want to hear all about it when you get back. Blow-by-blow descriptions." Her eyes twinkled, her cheeks bunched up in wicked laughter, and she was so obviously back to her normal good spirits that I started to tell her about the previous evening and our encounter with Mrs. Tolliver.

". . . And it was very embarrassing, because I thought Daniel was just behind me, and I said something stupid like, 'I want you to meet my friend,' and when I turned round, he wasn't there. Disappeared. Bolted to the bar."

"Did Mrs. Tolliver see him?"

"I've no idea." I thought about this. "Does it make any difference?"

"No-o-o . . ." said Phoebe.

I frowned at her. "Phoebe, you're holding something back."

She laid down her coffee cup and gazed abstractedly out the window. After a bit she shrugged and said, "Oh, well, I don't suppose it matters talking about it now. It all happened so long ago, anyway. Water under the bridge. And it wasn't anything very desperate even then."

"What wasn't desperate?"

"Well . . . when Daniel was living with us, when he was

a very young man, Annabelle Tolliver came down from London to spend the summer with her mother, and . . . well . . . I suppose you could say that they had a little fling. A flingette," she added hopefully, trying to make it sound trivial.

Daniel and Annabelle Tolliver. I stared at Phoebe. "You mean, he fancied Annabelle."

" 'Fancied.' " She chuckled. "Such a lovely old-fashioned word. Like 'frock.' Nobody wears frocks anymore." She gave a sigh and got back to the point. "No. Not exactly. If truth be told, I think it was Annabelle who fancied Daniel."

"But she must have been much older than he was."

"Oh, certainly. At least eight years."

"And married."

"Yes, married, too. But I told you, that never made much difference to Annabelle. She had a child by that time. Michael. He must have been about four years old. Poor child, even then I remember, he looked exactly like his father!"

"But. . ." Phoebe's endless digressions did nothing to clarify the situation. "What *happened?*"

"Oh, heavens, nothing happened. They used to go to parties together, picnics on the beach, swimming. She had a very flashy car that summer. It had a hood you could put down, and they used to drive all over the place together; very dashing they looked, too. Very eye-catching. Oh, you can imagine it, Prue."

I could. Only too clearly. "But I wouldn't have thought that Daniel. . ." I stopped, because I wasn't sure what I did think.

"You wouldn't have thought that Daniel was the social type. Perhaps he wasn't, but he was a very attractive young man. Still is, for that matter. And it must have flattered his ego to have her so eager to spend her time with him. I told you, she was beautiful. There were always queues of men swooning around her like lovesick cows. Or do I mean lovesick bulls? But Daniel was always a very quiet person. I think it was his quietness that intrigued Annabelle."

"How long did this go on?"

"The whole summer, on and off. It was just a little flirtation. Perfectly harmless."

"What did Mrs. Tolliver have to say about it?"

"Mrs. Tolliver never says anything about anything. She's the sort of woman who truly believes that if you don't look, it will go away. Besides, she must have realised that if it wasn't Daniel, it would have been some other man. Perhaps she reckoned that he was the lesser of a lot of other evils."

"But the little boy . . . Michael?"

"There was a starchy nanny taking care of him. He never got in the way at all."

"And her husband . . ." I could hardly bear to say his horrid name. "Leslie Collis?"

"He was left in London, running his office. I suppose living in some service flat or other. I've no idea. It's not important, anyway."

I thought carefully through this extraordinary revelation. I finally said, "Then last night . . . you think that's why Daniel didn't want to talk to Mrs. Tolliver."

"Maybe. Maybe he just didn't want to get involved with four bridge-playing ladies."

"I wonder why he didn't tell me himself."

"There was no reason he should. It has nothing to do with you, and it was a total nonevent, anyway." She poured herself more coffee and said, quite briskly, "You're not to make anything of it."

"I'm not. I just wish it had been anybody but Annabelle Tolliver."

Red sky at morning, shepherd's warning. But it was the sort of day when you couldn't be sure what would happen to the weather. A warm, west-wind sort of day, with gusts that tore leaves from trees and sent them flying and flecked the indigo sea with white horses. The sky was a brazen blue swept by high clouds, and the very air seemed to glitter. From the top of the hill above Porthkerris, I could see for miles, long beyond the lighthouse to the distant spur of Trevose Head. From the harbour far below me, a solitary fishing boat butted out into the choppy sea, making for the deep water beneath the cliffs of Lanyon.

The way led steeply downhill, through the narrow streets of the little town. Most of the summer visitors had now departed. Only a handful, looking chilly in shorts, stood about outside the news agent's or made their way down the hill to where a bakery was redolent with the smell of fresh, hot pasties.

At Porthkerris the Ship Inn stands, where it has stood

for three hundred years or more, on the harbour road by the old quay where the fishermen used to land their pilchards. I drove by it, but there was no sign of Daniel, so I found a place to park the Volkswagen and then walked back along the cobbles and went in, dipping my head beneath the low, smoke-blackened lintel. Inside, after the brightness of the day, it was very dark. A small coal fire burned in the grate, and an old man sat by this, looking as though he had sat there all his life or had, perhaps, grown up out of the floorboards.

"Prue."

I turned. Daniel was sitting in the deep window seat with an empty pint tankard on a wobbly table that had been made out of a barrel. He stood up, easing himself from behind this table, and said, "It's too good a day to have lunch indoors. What do you think?"

"So what shall we do?"

"Buy something. Eat it on the beach."

So we went out again and down the road until we reached one of those convenient shops that seem to sell everything. We bought fresh pasties, so hot that the man had to wrap them in newspaper. We bought a bag of apples, and some chocolate biscuits, and a packet of paper cups, and a bottle of dubious red wine. When the kindly man realised we were going to drink it right away, he threw in a corkscrew as well.

We went back out into the sunshine and crossed the cobbled street, and climbed down the stone steps that were dry at the top and coated with green weed at the bottom. The tide was on its way out and had left behind it a sickle of clean yellow sand. There was a cluster of rocks pounded smooth by the seas of centuries, and we settled ourselves on these, sheltered from the wind and with the sun on our faces. Screaming gulls wheeled in the windy air, and from where some men worked peacefully on a boat came the pleasant sounds of hammer blows and muted voices.

Daniel opened the bottle of wine, and we unwrapped the pasties. I was suddenly very hungry. I bit greedily into mine, and it was so hot that I nearly scalded my mouth and bits of steaming potato fell out of the pasty onto the sand, to be spied and scooped up in an instant by a great, greedy gull.

I said, "This was a brilliant idea."

"I have them, every now and again."

And I thought that if it had been Nigel, we would in all probability have been lunching at the Castle Hotel, with white tablecloths and waiters hovering, hampering conversation. Daniel had taken the cork out of the bottle; now he took a mouthful of wine, considered its taste, and swallowed it.

"An amusing and unpretentious little wine," he said, "if you don't mind it being stone cold. I don't suppose it improves its bouquet, drinking it out of a paper cup, but beggars can't be choosers. The only alternative seems to be the neck of the bottle." He took a bite out of his pasty. "How's Phoebe this morning?"

"She was tired last night. She went to bed early, and this morning I took her up her breakfast in bed, and she promised she'd stay there till lunchtime."

"What would she have done if you hadn't been able to come to Penmarron and take care of her?"

"She'd have managed. Lily would have looked after her, but Lily can't drive, and Phoebe hates being without her car."

"Were you able to get away from work just like that? What does Marcus Bernstein do without you?"

"I was on holiday anyway for two weeks, so that was no problem. He'd already engaged a temp to take over while I was away."

"You mean you had two weeks' holiday and you weren't going to do anything with it? What were you going to do, stay in London?"

"No. As a matter of fact, I was meant to be going to Scotland."

"Scotland? For heaven's sake, what were you going to do there?"

"Stay with people."

"Have you ever been to Scotland?"

"No. Have you?"

"Once. Everybody kept telling me how beautiful it was, but it rained so hard that I never found out if they were telling the truth or not." He took another mouthful of pasty. "Who were you going to stay with?"

"Friends."

"You're being cagey, aren't you? You might as well tell me all, because I'll just go on asking questions until you give me some answers. It's a boyfriend, isn't it?"

I would not look at him. "Why should it be?"

"Because you're far too attractive not to have some man languishing with love for you. And you've got the most extraordinary expression on your face. Confused nonchalance."

"I'm sure that's a contradiction of terms."

"What's he called?"

"Who?"

"Oh, stop being coy. The boyfriend, of course."

"Nigel Gordon."

"Nigel. Nigel's one of my most unfavourite names."

"It's no worse than Daniel."

"It's a wet name. Timothy's a wet name, too. So is Jeremy. And Christopher. And Nicholas."

"Nigel is not wet."

"What is he, then?"

"Nice."

"What does he do?"

"He's an insurance broker."

"And he comes from Scotland?"

"Yes. His family lives there. In Inverness-shire."

"What a frightfully good thing you didn't go. You'd have hated it. A great unheated house, with bedrooms cold as refrigerators and baths encased in mahogany, like coffins."

I said, "Daniel, you make more ridiculous sweeping statements than any man I've ever met."

"You won't marry him, will you, this Highland insurance broker? Please don't. I can't bear the thought of you in kilts and living in Inverness-shire."

I very nearly laughed but managed to keep a prim face. "I wouldn't be living in Inverness-shire. I'd be living in Nigel's desirable residence in South Kensington." I threw what remained of my pasty to the gulls and helped myself to an apple, rubbing it to a shine on the sleeve of my sweater. "And I wouldn't have to work, either. I wouldn't have to go trudging off to Marcus Bernstein's every morning. I could be a lady of leisure, with time to do all I want to do, which is paint. And it wouldn't matter if nobody bought my pictures, because my husband would be there, ready and willing to pay all the bills."

He said, "I thought you thought like Phoebe. I'm disillusioned."

"Perhaps sometimes I think like my mother. She likes life to be neat and squared off and conventional and safe. She adores Nigel. She's longing for me to marry him. She can't wait to start planning a wedding. St. Paul's, Knightsbridge, and a reception in Pavilion Road . . ."

"And a honeymoon at Budleigh Salterton, with the golf clubs in the boot of the car. Prue, you can't be serious."

I took a great bite of the shiny apple. "I might be."

"Not about a man called Nigel."

I was beginning to feel irritated. "You know nothing about him. And anyway, what's so bad about getting married? You think the world of Phoebe, you thought the world of Chips. But, you know, they would have been married, years ago, if only Chips could have gotten a divorce. But he couldn't. So they compromised, and made the very best of their life together."

"I don't think there's anything wrong in getting married. I just think it's insane to get married to the wrong person."

"I suppose you've never made that mistake."

"No, as a matter of fact, I haven't. I've done just about everything else. Made every other sort of mistake, but getting married wasn't one of them." He appeared to be considering this state of affairs. "Never even thought about it, as a matter of fact."

He smiled at me, and I smiled back, because for no particular reason I was filled with gladness, simply because he had never married. And yet I was not surprised. There was something nomadic, free, about Daniel, and I found I was envious of this.

I said, "I wish there was time in life to do everything."

"You've got time."

"I know, but already I seem to be in a sort of rut. I like the rut. I like my job and I'm doing exactly what I want to do, and I love Marcus Bernstein, and I wouldn't change my job for anything in the world. But sometimes, on a certain sort of morning, I drive to work, and I think, I'm twenty-three and what am I doing with my life? And I think of all the places I long to see. Kashmir and the Bahamas and Greece, and Palmyra. And San Francisco, and Peking and Japan. I would like to have been to some of the places you've been to."

"Then go. Go now."

"You make it sound so simple."

"It can be. Life is as simple as you make it."

"Perhaps I haven't got that sort of courage. But still, I would like to have done some of the things you've done."

He laughed. "Don't wish that. Some of it was hell."

"It can't still be hell. Everything's going so well for you now."

"Uncertainty is always hell."

"What are you uncertain about?"

"About what I'm going to do next."

"That shouldn't be too frightening."

"I'm thirty-one. Within the next twelve months I've got to make some sort of a decision; I'm frightened of drifting. I don't want to drift for the rest of my life."

"What do you want to do?"

"I want . . ."

He leaned back against the knobby granite of the harbour wall and turned his face to the sun and closed his eyes. He looked like a man who longed for the oblivion of sleep. "When this exhibition at Peter Chastal's is over and finished with, I want to go to Greece. There's an island called Spetsai, and on Spetsai there is a house, square and white as a sugar cube. And there's a terrace with terra cotta tiles on the floor, and geraniums in pots along the tops of the wall. And below the terrace there's a mooring and a boat with a white sail like the wing of a gull. Not a big boat. Just large enough for two." I waited. He opened his eyes. He said, "I think I shall go there."

"Do that thing."

"Would you come?" He held out his hand to me. "Would you like to come and visit me? You just told me you wanted to go to Greece. Would you come and let me show you some of its glories?"

I was very touched. I laid my hand in his and felt his fingers close about my wrist. How different this was, how frighteningly different, from the invitation Nigel had painfully offered me, to visit his mother in Invernessshire. Two different worlds. *The insecurity of two different worlds touching.* I wondered if I was about to burst into tears.

"One day," I told him, in the voice of a mother placating an insistent child. "One day, maybe, I'll be able to come."

The sky clouded and it grew cold. It was time to stir ourselves. We gathered up the picnic rubbish and found a little bin by a lamp post, and threw all the trash into that. We walked back to where I had left Phoebe's car, and there was the smell of rain in the air and the sea had turned angry and leaden.

Red sky at morning, shepherd's warning. We got into the car and slowly drove back to Penmarron. Phoebe's heater did not work, and I felt cold. I knew that there would be a fire ablaze at Holly Cottage, and possibly crumpets for tea, but I wasn't thinking about these things. My mind was filled with images of Greece, of the house above the water and the boat with a sail like the wing of a gull. I thought of swimming in that dark Aegean sea, the water warm and clear as glass . . .

Memory stirred.

"Daniel."

"What is it?"

"That night I got off the train from London, I had a dream. It was about swimming. I was on a desert island, and I had to walk a long long way through shallow water. And then all at once it was deep, but so clear I could see right to the bottom. And once I had started to swim, there was a current. Very fast and strong. It was like being swept down a river."

I remembered again the sensation of peace, of blissful acceptance.

"What happened then?"

"Nothing. But it was nice."

"Sounds a good dream. What brought it to mind?"

"I was thinking about Greece. Swimming in Homer's wine-dark seas."

"All dreams have meaning."

"I know."

"What do you think that one signified?"

I told him, "I thought perhaps it was about dying."

But that was before Daniel had come into my life. Now I was wiser, and I knew that the dream was not about dying at all but loving.

When we got back to Holly Cottage, there was no sign of Phoebe. The firelit sitting room was empty, and when I called up the stair, thinking that perhaps she had spent the whole day in her bed, there was no reply.

But sounds of clashing crockery and opening drawers came from the kitchen. I went down the hall with Daniel behind me to open the door and investigate, only to discover Lily Tonkins engaged in whisking up a bowl of batter.

"You're back then," she said. She did not look too pleased to see us, and I wondered if she was in one of her cross moods. Lily could get very cross. Not with us in particular but just with the world in general, which included her morose husband, the cheeky girl who worked in the grocer's, and the man in the town hall who dealt with Lily's pension.

"Where's Phoebe?" I asked.

Lily did not look up from her task. "Gone down to the water."

"I hoped she'd stay in bed today."

"Stay in bed?" Lily set down the bowl with a thump and faced me with her arms akimbo. "Some chance she's had of staying in bed. We've had that little Charlotte Collis here all day, ever since ten o'clock this morning. I'd just taken Miss Shackleton a nice cup of tea and was polishing up the brasses when I heard a ring at the bell. Dratted nuisance, I said to myself, and went to the door, and there she was. And been here ever since."

"Where's Mrs. Tolliver?"

"Gone over to Falmouth for some meeting—Save the Children or Save the Church or something. Seems funny to me. I mean, I can understand some people don't like looking after children. There are some that do and some that don't. But she's that little girl's granny. No business to be up and about all the time, playing cards and saving things. Somebody's got to look after the little girl."

"Where's Mrs. Curnow?"

"Betty Curnow, she's there all right, up at White Lodge, but she's got her own work to do. Mrs. Tolliver can't be bothered to look after the child, then she should pay some other person to do the job."

"So what happened?"

"Well, I let her in, poor little soul, and I said Miss Shackleton was still in bed and you were out, gone for lunch. So she went up the stairs to see Miss Shackleton, and I heard them talking together. Talk, talk, you'd think that child had never had a soul to talk to the way she carries on when she's here. Then she came down, the little girl, and said Miss Shackleton was getting up and getting dressed. And that vexed me because I knew she needed a good rest. So I went up and gave her a hand with her clothes, and then down she came and phoned Betty Curnow and said that we were keeping Charlotte here and giving her lunch. Luckily there was a bit of cold lamb, and I peeled a few potatoes and made a custard, but it's not right Miss Shackleton being landed with the child to take care of, and her with that bad arm and everything."

I had never seen Lily so loquacious or upset. She was concerned, and naturally so, for Phoebe. But, as well, she had a kind heart. The Cornish love children, and Lily was no exception. She had decided that Charlotte was being neglected, and all her hackles were well and truly up.

I said, "I'm sorry. I should have been here to help you."

Daniel had listened to all this in silence. Now he said, "Where are they?"

"Went down to the shore to do their drawing. That's what they like to do when they're together, like a pair of old women." She turned from the table and went to the sink to peer out the window. Daniel and I followed her. We saw the empty estuary, the deserted sands. But at the far end of the seawall we could discern the two distant figures: Phoebe, unmistakable in her hat, and the child beside her, wearing a scarlet anorak. They had taken camp stools with them and sat side by side, very close. There was something touching about the pair of them. Oblivious to the rest of the world, they looked as though they had been washed up by some unimaginable storm and forgotten.

As we stood there, there came the first sharp rattle of

raindrops against the glass of the window, and Lily said, "There now!" as if she had forecast this very thing happening. "That's the dratted rain come on. And Miss Shackleton won't even notice. Once she starts her sketching, that's the end of it. Might as well shout your heart out, and she'd never take notice. And her with that cast on her arm, poor soul . . ."

The time had obviously come to intervene. "I'll go and get them," I said.

"No." Daniel laid a restraining hand on my arm. "It's pouring. I'll go."

"You'll need a mackintosh, Daniel," Lily warned him, but he found an umbrella in the hall and set off armed with that. I watched his progress, the umbrella held high over his head, as he walked down across the lawn and disappeared through the gate in the escallonia hedge. Moments later he came into view once more, making his way along the edge of the seawall towards the two unsuspecting artists.

Lily and I turned away from the window. "What can I do to help you?" I asked.

"You could lay the table for tea."

"Let's all have it in here. It's so nice and warm."

"I'm making a batch of pancakes." She picked up her bowl and started whisking again. She looked more cheerful, having aired her grievances, and I was grateful for this.

I said, "Tomorrow I'll do something with Charlotte. Take her somewhere in the car, perhaps. She's been on my conscience ever since I arrived, only there doesn't seem to have been much time to arrange anything."

"Mind, she's a nice enough little girl."

"I know. But somehow that only makes it worse."

The table was laid, the drop scones made, and the kettle boiling, and still they had not returned.

"That Daniel," observed Lily. "He's as bad as the rest of them. Probably forgot what he went for, and he's sat down with them to paint a picture for himself . . ."

"I'd better go." I found an old raincoat of Phoebe's and a man-eating sou'wester that had once belonged to Chips and let myself out the garden door. It was now raining hard and very wet, but as I crossed the grass Daniel and Phoebe appeared at the gate, Daniel holding the camp stools under one arm and the umbrella high over Phoebe's head with the other. Phoebe, except for her hat, was dressed as though for a sunny outing, and her cardigan, buttoned bulkily over her plaster cast, was sodden, her shoes and stout stockings mud-splashed. She carried in her good hand her painting bag, a sturdy and familiar piece of equipment made of canvas, and as Daniel opened the gate for her, she looked up and saw me.

"Hello! Here we are, a lot of drowned rats!"

"Lily and I wondered what had happened to you all."

"Charlotte hadn't quite finished, and she wanted to."

"Where is she?"

"Oh, coming. Somewhere," said Phoebe, airily.

I looked past her, down the hill, and saw Charlotte at the foot of it. She stood with her back to me, peering into the depths of a dripping bramble bush.

I said, resigned, "I'd better get her," and set off down the wet and slippery slope. "Charlotte! Come along."

She turned and looked up and saw me. Her hair clung to her head, and her glasses were misted with rain.

"What *are* you doing?"

"I'm looking for blackberries. I thought there might be some."

"You're not meant to be looking for blackberries, you're meant to be coming up to the house for tea. Lily's made pancakes."

She moved reluctantly. "All right." Even the lure of hot pancakes did not kindle much enthusiasm. I thought that it would be easy to be maddened by her, and yet I understood her reluctance to end an afternoon spent in Phoebe's delightful company. I remembered myself at Charlotte's age, trailing home after a day with Phoebe, spent perhaps on the beach or picking primroses or riding in the little train to Porthkerris. It had always been an effort to drag oneself back to routine, and meals, and everyday, mundane life.

I held out my hand to her. "Do you want a pull up the hill?"

She took her hand out of her anorak pocket and gave it to me. It felt thin and small and wet and cold. I said, "What you need is a good rubdown with a towel and a hot drink." We set off up the slope. "Did you have a good afternoon with Phoebe?"

"Yes. We've been drawing."

"I don't suppose you even noticed the rain."

"No, not really. My paper was beginning to get a bit wet, but then that man came and held the umbrella over it and I could finish."

"His name is Daniel."

"I know. Phoebe's told me about him. He used to live with her and Chips."

"He's a famous artist now."

"I know that, too. He said my drawing was very good."

"What did you draw?"

"I tried to draw some gulls, but they kept flying away, so I did a made-up picture."

"That was enterprising."

"He said it was very good."

"I hope you haven't left it behind?"

"No. Phoebe put it in her bag."

Breathless by now, we toiled on in silence. We reached the gate. I opened it, and as Charlotte went through, I said, "I've been wondering how you've been getting along. I would have rung you up or asked you to tea, only I've been so . . ." I hesitated, searching for the right word. "Busy" seemed scarcely truthful.

"It's not much fun," said Charlotte with a child's uncompromising honesty.

I made a cheerful face. "Well, perhaps tomorrow we could do something together." I shut the gate behind us. "Go somewhere in the car if Phoebe doesn't need it."

Charlotte considered this. Then, "Do you think," she said, "that Daniel would like to come too?"

As soon as we were inside the kitchen, Lily, half-irritated and half-laughing, pounced on Charlotte, unzipping her drenched jacket, kneeling to struggle with the buckles of her sandals.

"I don't know, some people can be that silly. Miss Shackleton, well, I've never seen a soul so wet. I told her to go upstairs and change down to the skin, and all she would do was laugh and say it didn't matter. It'll matter all right when she gets pneumonia. Didn't you notice the rain?"

"Not really," said Charlotte.

Lily produced a dry towel, removed Charlotte's spectacles, carefully dried the lenses, and then gently put them on again, setting them straight across the bridge of Charlotte's small nose. Using the same towel, she began to dry the child's hair, rubbing as though she were drying a wet puppy, scolding on. I left them to it and went to take off the mackintosh and the sou'wester and drape them over the radiator in the hall to dry.

The door to Phoebe's sitting room stood open. On the far side the fire blazed, the flames reflected in the brass fender and on all the little polished knickknacks that stood about—a copper jug, a silver photograph frame, a luster bowl. In front of the fire, with an elbow on the mantelpiece and a foot on the fender, stood Daniel. The profile of his downcast face was reflected in the mirror that hung above the mantelpiece, and in his hand he held a sheet of paper, which he appeared to be studying.

I came through the door, and he looked up.

"I've got Charlotte. She's with Lily, getting dried. She was looking for blackberries." I went to stand beside him, spreading my cold hands to the warmth of the fire. "What are you looking at?"

"This little picture she's done. She's very good."

He handed it to me and moved away from the fireplace to sink, recumbent, in the roomy depths of Chips's old armchair. He looked tired, his chin sunk on his chest, his long legs stretched out in front of him. I looked at Charlotte's drawing and saw at once what he meant. It was a child's effort, but imaginative and cleanly drawn. She had used felt pens, and the bright primary colours reminded me of Phoebe's own brilliant little oils. I saw the red boat bowling across a cobalt sea, the sail curved and set full in the wind. There was a small figure at the helm wearing a cap with a seagoing peak, and on the foredeck a large, whiskery cat.

I smiled. "I like the cat."

"I like the whole thing."

"It's a very cheerful picture. And that's odd, because I don't think she's a particularly cheerful child."

"I know," said Daniel. "It's reassuring."

I put the drawing on the mantelpiece, propped against Phoebe's clock. "Tomorrow I said I'd take her somewhere. She isn't having much of a time with her grandmother. I thought we could go somewhere in the car."

"That would be kind."

"She seemed to think it would be more fun if you came, too."

"Did she," said Daniel. He did not seem overexcited at the prospect. I wondered if he was already tiring of feminine company, or perhaps the idea of a day spent with Charlotte and myself had no allure for him. I wished now that I had said nothing about it. "You've probably got better things to do."

He said, "Yes," and then, "We'll see."

We'll see. He sounded like the adults who used to infuriate me as a child by using those very words when they

were unable, or possibly unwilling, to commit themselves.

Chips had made the carousel for me. It was mine. He
had said when he gave it to me that if I wanted, I could
take it back to London, but I chose not to. The carousel
was part of Holly Cottage, and I was such a traditionalist
that I chose to leave it here.

It lived where it always had, in the bottom half of the
huge French bombe cabinet that stood at one end of
Phoebe's sitting room. That evening, after tea had been
cleared away and washed up, Charlotte went to take it
out. She carried it carefully and set it on the table in front
of the fire.

Chips had made it from an old-fashioned gramophone. He had removed the lid and the needle arm and
cut a circle of plywood the same size as a regular record,
with a hole in the middle to fit over the gramophone's
central spindle. This disc was painted a bright scarlet,
and the animals were fixed around its perimeter. These,
too, had been cut from plywood with Chips's little jig-
saw. There was a tiger, an elephant, a zebra, a pony, a
lion, and a dog, each coloured with its own stripes or
spots and each sporting a brightly painted saddle with
tiny bridles and reins made of golden cord.

Various games could be played with it. Sometimes,
along with building blocks, farmyard people, and a few
wooden animals left over from a defunct Noah's Ark, it
became part of a fairground or a circus. But mostly I
played with it just as it was, winding the handle to power

the mechanism and switching the lever that made the turntable revolve. There was, as well, another lever to regulate the speed. You could start it up very slowly (to give people time to get on, Chips used to say) and then speed it up until the animals whirled so fast you could scarcely see them.

Charlotte did this now. It was like watching a spinning top. Finally the mechanism ran down, and the carousel came slowly to a halt.

She crouched down on her heels and moved the turntable with her hand, gazing at the face of each animal in turn.

"I simply don't know *which* is my favourite."

"The tiger was always mine," I told her. "He has such a fierce face."

"I know. He's a bit like the tigers in *Little Black Sambo*, isn't he. And you know, when the animals go round really fast they look a bit like the *Little Black Sambo* tigers going round the tree and turning into butter."

"Perhaps," said Phoebe, "Lily made our pancakes out of tiger butter, just the way Little Black Sambo's mother did."

"Why did you have to make old-fashioned gramophones go fast and slow? I mean, there's everything on my father's stereo at home, in Sunningdale, but I don't think there's a switch to make it go fast or slow."

"It was great fun," Phoebe told her. "You could put an ordinary record on very slowly and it sounded like an enormous Russian singing basso profundo. And then you'd make it go quickly and it was all squeaky and high. Like a mouse singing."

"But *why?* Why did that happen?"

Phoebe said, "I haven't the faintest idea," which was always her very sensible reply to a question to which she had no answer.

Charlotte turned to me. "Do you know?"

"No, I don't."

"Do you?" She turned to Daniel.

He had been silent all this time. He had, for that matter, been silent through most of tea. Now he was back in Chips's armchair, apparently watching the carousel with the rest of us and yet in some way remote and withdrawn. Now we all looked at him expectantly, but he had not even realised that Charlotte had spoken to him, and she had to say it again. "Do you, Daniel?"

"Do I what?"

"Do you know why the music goes squeaky when it's fast and basso profundo when it's slow?"

He considered this question with some care and then suggested that perhaps it had something to do with centrifugal force.

Charlotte screwed up her nose. "What's *that?*"

"It's what makes your spin dryer work."

"I haven't got a spin dryer."

"Well, when you're a big girl, perhaps you'll have one, and you'll look at it working, and then you'll know what centrifugal force is."

Charlotte began to wind the gramophone handle again. Above us, on the mantelpiece, Phoebe's clock struck five.

Phoebe said gently, "Charlotte, perhaps it's time you went home."

"Oh, do I *have* to?"

"No, you don't have to, but I said you'd be back about five."

Charlotte looked up, her expression all set to whine. "I don't want to go. And I can't walk back, because it's raining."

"Prue will take you in my car."

"Aw . . ."

Terrified of tears, I said quickly, "And don't forget, we've got a date for tomorrow. We're going out together in the car. Do you want me to come and fetch you?"

"No. I hate being fetched because I hate waiting. I'm always afraid people won't come. I'll come here. I'll walk down like I did this morning. What time shall I be here?"

"Oh, about half past ten?"

"All right."

Daniel had heaved himself to his feet. "Where are you off to?" Phoebe asked him.

"I must go, too," he told her.

"But I thought you were going to stay for dinner with Prue and me. Lily's made a chicken casserole . . ."

"No, really . . . I should get back. I've got a phone call to make. I promised Peter Chastal I'd get in touch with Lewis Falcon, and I've done nothing about it . . ."

"Oh, all right," said Phoebe, who always instantly accepted other people's decisions and never tried to argue. "Then you'd better go with Prue, and she'll drive you back to Porthkerris after she's dropped Charlotte."

He looked at me. "Do you mind?"

"Of course not."

But I did mind, because I wanted him to want to have dinner with Phoebe and me.

"Good-bye, Phoebe." He went to give her a kiss, and she gave him an affectionate little pat on the arm; letting him go, asking no questions.

That's the way I've got to be, I told myself, as I went to fetch my coat. *If I don't want to lose his friendship that's the way I've got to be.*

In the car, he sat in front, while Charlotte perched on the backseat, leaning forward so that the pale blur of her face hung between us.

"Where shall we go tommorow?" she wanted to know.

"I don't know. I hadn't thought. Where's a good place?"

"We could go up to Skadden Hill. We'd maybe find blackberries. And there's lots of rocks on the top of the hill and one of them has got a giant's footprint on it. Really. A real, huge footprint."

Daniel said, "You could go to Penjizal."

"What happens at Penjizal?" I asked.

"There's a cliff walk, and at low tide a great deep rock pool, and the seals come into it and swim there."

Charlotte instantly forgot about Skadden Hill. Giant's footsteps were tame compared to seals.

"Oh, let's go there. I've never seen seals, at least not close to."

I said, "I don't even know where Penjizal is."

"Will you show us, Daniel?" Charlotte banged on his shoulder with her fist to get his whole attention. "Will you come with us? Oh, do come with us."

Daniel did not at once respond to this impassioned appeal. I knew that he was waiting for me to intervene, perhaps make some excuse for him, but I stayed selfishly silent. Through the windscreen wipers' fan of clear glass I saw the road ahead, awash with muddy water; the oak trees, black against the sky, lashed with rain.

"Please," Charlotte persisted.

He said, "I might."

But she stuck to her guns. "Does that mean yes or no?"

"Well, all right . . ." He turned his head to grin at her. "Yes."

"Oh, *good.*" She actually clapped her hands. "What shall I bring, Prue? Shall I bring my gum boots?"

"Perhaps you'd better. And a proper raincoat in case it's wet."

"But we'll have a picnic, won't we, even if it's raining?"

"Yes, we'll have a picnic. We'll find somewhere to eat it. What do you like? Ham sandwiches?"

"Yes. And Coke."

"I don't think we've got any Coke."

"I think Granny's got some. And if she hasn't I'll go and buy some. They sell it in the village shop."

We had reached the gates of White Lodge. I drove through them and up the short drive, and the house, as before, waited for us, curtained in the rain, its face closed and blank, giving nothing away. We drew up at the foot of the steps, and Daniel got out in order to let Charlotte emerge from the backseat. He stood looking down at her. She was holding the picture she had drawn. Phoebe had taken it down from the mantelpiece and given it to

Charlotte as we were on the point of leaving.

"Don't forget this," she had said, and added hopefully, "Perhaps you'd like to give it to your grandmother."

But now Charlotte held it out to Daniel. "Would you like to keep it?" she asked him shyly.

"I'd like to very much. But isn't it for your grandmother?"

"Not really. She won't want it."

"In that case, I'll take it." He did so. "Thank you. I shall treasure it."

"I'll see you tomorrow then. Good-bye. Good-bye, Prue, and thank you for bringing me home."

We watched her climb the steps to the front door. As Daniel got back into the car beside me, the door opened. A wedge of yellow light shone out into the murk, and we saw Mrs. Tolliver standing there. She waved—perhaps to say thank you, perhaps to say good-bye—and then drew Charlotte indoors.

Chapter Five

We set off for Porthkerris. It was only a short journey, but it was made that evening, by Daniel and me, in total silence. Sometimes silences between two people are comfortable things; sometimes they speak more loudly than words. On other occasions they become strained and tense, and this was one of them. I wanted to break the constraint, to start some trivial conversation, but in the face of such noncooperation I could think of no words for the tall, quiet stranger who sat beside me. His hand, still holding Charlotte's present, lay against his knee. His head was turned away from me. He stared out at the drenched, grey-green fields, the stony walls, the rain. There seemed to be nothing to say.

We reached the gates of the hotel at last, turned up the driveway, parked with all the expensive cars. On that gloomy evening even the opulent Castle Hotel had an abandoned appearance, like a sinking liner, with its few lighted windows reflected in a sea of puddles.

I turned off the engine and waited for Daniel to get out of the car. Now there was only the sound of the rain drumming on the roof and the sough of wind blown up from the sea far below us. Listening, I heard the distant breakers crashing on the shore. Daniel turned his head and looked at me. "Will you come in?"

I couldn't think why he had even bothered to ask me. "No. You have to get in touch with Lewis Falcon. And I should get back . . ."

He said urgently, "Please. I want to talk to you."

"What about?"

"We can have a drink."

"Daniel . . ."

"Please, Prue."

I switched off the headlights and we got out of the car. Once more the revolving doors injected us into that warm, scented, carpeted, overheated interior. Today, perhaps because of the inclement weather, there were more people about. They sat grouped around tea tables, read their newspapers, chatted over knitting. The air was thick with late-afternoon boredom. Daniel headed for the bar, but it was too early and it had not opened yet.

He stopped before the shuttered door and said, "Bloody hell," so loudly that one or two pairs of eyes were raised to observe us. I felt embarrassed. I knew how we looked, untidy and incongruous; Daniel in his worn jeans and the sweater of dark rough wool; myself in an old navy blue duffle coat that had seen better days, and with my hair windblown and uncombed.

I wanted to go away. "I don't want a drink, anyway."

"I do. Come on, we'll go up to my room."

And without waiting for my response to this suggestion, he set off up the wide staircase, his long legs taking the steps three at a time. Because there didn't seem to be anything else to do, I followed him, aware of the interest that our behaviour was arousing. I knew that we would be suspected of the very worst, but so concerned was I by Daniel's behaviour, so apprehensive for myself, that I didn't care anyway.

His room was on the first floor, at the end of a long, wide passage. He took the key from his pocket and went in, turning on the lights, and I followed him and saw that he had been given one of the best rooms in the hotel, facing out over the small nine-hole golf course. The greens and fairways of this golf course sloped to a little wood, and so high on the hill were we that the sea's horizon lay above the topmost branches of these trees. This evening the horizon was not visible, but the window of Daniel's room stood open, and the wind poured in upon us and sent the long curtains flapping like badly set sails.

He shut the door and went to close the window. The curtains ceased their frantic dance. I looked at the large, comfortably furnished room, with its unexpected features that made it feel more like a bedroom in some well-loved country house than an impersonal hotel. There was a fireplace, and over this a pretty mirror, framed in rose-colour glass. Chintz-covered armchairs were drawn up before the fireplace, and the same chintz skirted the dressing table. A television set stood on a low table, and beside this was a small refrigerator. There were even flowers on the mantelpiece and a round basket of fresh fruit by the wide double bed.

When he had shut the window, Daniel went to switch on the electric fire. Sham logs instantly flickered. He was still holding Charlotte's picture. Now he placed it carefully in the middle of the mantelpiece. In the mirror I could see his quiet reflected face.

I watched him and waited.

He said, "She's my child."

Beyond his reflection, I could see my own, my face a pale blur, my hands deep in the pockets of my coat; the whole image distorted by some flaw in the glass so that I appeared ghostly, like a person drowned.

It was suddenly very hard to speak. I said, "Charlotte," and the word came out as a whisper.

"Yes, Charlotte." He turned from the fireplace, and across the room our eyes met. "She's my child."

"But why are you saying this?"

He said again, "She's my child."

"Oh, Daniel."

"You see, all those years ago, I had a love affair with her mother. I wasn't in love with Annabelle, she was married to another man, she already had a child. Everything was against us. But still, contrary to any sort of reason, it happened. And Charlotte is the outcome of a long, hot summer of what must have been total madness."

I said, "I know about it. I mean, I know about you and Annabelle Tolliver."

"Phoebe told you."

"Yes."

"I thought she might tell you. In fact, I was pretty sure that she would."

We stared at each other. My mind, like a panicky rabbit, scuttled to and fro, getting nowhere. I tried to remember the words that Phoebe had used. *I think it was Annabelle who fancied Daniel. Daniel was a very quiet person. It was a total non-event anyway.*

I said. "But I thought . . . I mean . . . I didn't realise . . ."

He rescued me from my delicate floundering. "You thought we'd just had a little walk out. I always hoped that that was what Phoebe and Chips thought too. But you see, it wasn't nearly as innocent as that."

"You're . . . you're sure she's your child?"

"I knew the moment I saw her this afternoon, sitting there on her camp stool, at the end of the sea wall. In the cold and the rain, trying to finish her picture. Prue, you've gone as white as a sheet. I think we'd better both have a drink."

I watched him go to open the refrigerator. He took out glasses and ice and soda water and a bottle of whisky and set these on the top of the cabinet.

"Daniel, I don't drink whisky."

"I haven't anything else." He unscrewed the top of the bottle.

I said, "She doesn't even look like you."

"She doesn't look like Annabelle, either. But I have a photograph of my mother when she was just about that age. Nine or ten. Charlotte is my mother all over again."

"Did you know that Annabelle was having your baby?"

"She said she was."

"Wasn't that enough?"

"As things turned out, no."

"I don't understand."

He shut the refrigerator door and stood leaning against it, a tumbler in either hand. "Prue, take off your coat. It makes you look impermanent. Besides, it's probably damp. You mustn't catch a cold."

I thought this the most irrelevant observation, but I did as he said, unbuttoning the coat and taking it off and laying it over the back of a chair. He held out my drink and I went to take it from him. The glass was icily cold.

I said again, "I don't understand, Daniel."

"You can't understand unless you understand about Annabelle." He frowned. "Did you never meet her? When you were staying with Phoebe?"

"No, our paths never crossed. I suppose because she used to come down in the summer, and I was usually in Northumberland then, with my father."

"That would explain it."

"Were you in love with her?" I sounded cool, as if it were of no importance.

"No, I wasn't in love with her. Come to think of it, I didn't even like her very much. But there was something . . . amazing about Annabelle that rendered every other emotion meaningless. I was twenty and she was twenty-eight. Married and a mother. None of that mattered, either."

"But didn't people . . . talk? Surely Phoebe and Chips . . ."

"They knew, of course, but they imagined it was just a jolly flirtation. And Annabelle was clever. She played the field. There were always plenty of other men."

"She must have been very beautiful." It was hard to keep the wistful note from my voice, but I had never been described as "amazing" and knew that I never would be.

"No, she wasn't beautiful. But she was very tall and slender and she had a face like a Siamese cat, with a neat little nose and a long upper lip and a smile that was full of secrets. 'Enigmatic,' perhaps, the word is. Her eyes were astonishing. Enormous, slanted, a very dark grey."

"How did you meet her?"

"Phoebe and Chips carted me off to this party. I didn't want to go, but they said I had to, I'd been invited, and I'd get boring if I did nothing but work. And Annabelle was there. I saw her the moment I walked into the room. She was over on the far side, surrounded by other women's husbands. I saw that face and my fingers itched to draw her. I suppose I was staring, because she suddenly looked up, straight at me, as though she'd known all along that I was there. And I forgot about drawing her." He gave a rueful grin and shook his head. "It was like playing a game of rugger and then getting a great kick in the guts."

"That's never happened to me."

I hoped my timid attempt at levity would make him smile, but he didn't seem to hear it, for now he was pacing up and down the room with his glass in his hand as though it were physically impossible for him to talk and stand still at the same time.

"The next time we met, it was on the beach. I'd got a surfboard, a Malibu, from Australia. A friend had brought it for me from Sydney. There was a north wind that day, and the rollers were pouring in from miles out. I surfed until the tide changed, and when I came in, blue with cold because I couldn't afford a wet suit, I saw Annabelle sitting up on the dunes, watching me. I had no idea how long she'd been there. She wore a red skirt and her hair was loose and black and blowing in the wind. There wasn't anyone else on the beach that grey day, and I knew that she was waiting for me. So I climbed up to where she sat, and we talked and smoked her cigarettes, and the rushes all around us were flattened by the gale. I remember thinking that they looked like stroked fur. And later we walked home, and the golf links smelled of wild thyme. And a couple of men, golfers, passed us, and I saw them looking at Annabelle and then at me, and there was envy in their faces. It made me feel good. And that's the way it always was; going into a pub with her, or sitting beside her in the car, with the roof down and the sun on our faces. We'd stop at traffic lights, and people on the pavements would turn their heads, and stare, and smile."

"They were probably thinking what a good-looking couple you made."

"More likely asking themselves what a sensational creature like Annabelle was doing with a callow, gangling boy."

"How long did this go on for?"

"Two months. Three months. It was a very hot summer. She said it was too hot to take her little boy back to London. So she stayed at Penmarron. She was always there."

"Did she talk about her husband?"

"Leslie Collis? Not much. Rumour had it that she'd married him for his money, and she certainly didn't talk of him with much obvious affection. That didn't bother me. I didn't want to know about him. I didn't want to think about him. I didn't want to feel guilty. If you're really determined, it's quite possible to stuff an uneasy conscience out of sight. I'd never realised that I had that ability. It made things much easier."

"Perhaps, at twenty, that's the way you're meant to live life."

He smiled. "You sound old and wise. Like Phoebe."

"I wish I were."

He was still pacing, a caged tiger, up and down the charming, pretty room. He said, "It was about this time of the year, the middle of September. Only it wasn't raining like it is now. They went on and on, the sunshine and the warmth. So that I was taken unawares when Annabelle suddenly announced that she was going back to London. We were on the beach again. We'd been swimming. It was a flood tide, one late afternoon. The tide had come in over the warm sand, and the sea was the colour of jade and very warm. We were sitting having a cigarette, and she told me about going back to London, and I waited for utter desolation, and then realised that I wasn't desolate. In a funny way, I was relieved. I wanted it to stop now, while we were still having fun. I didn't want it to get stale. Besides, I knew that I had to get back to work. Painting has always been the most important thing in my life, and it had started tugging at me. I wanted to turn my back on everything else and concentrate on my painting, drown myself in it. My year with Chips was just about over. I wanted to travel, to learn. I planned to go to America.

"I started to say something trivial, but Annabelle interrupted me. It was then that she told me she was having a baby. She said, 'It's your child, Daniel.'

"You know, when I was young, growing up, I used to scare the pants off myself by imagining just such a situation. A girl, pregnant by me. A girl I didn't want to marry. Paternity suits, furious fathers, shotgun weddings. Nightmarish. And now it had happened, only it wasn't happening that way. She went on talking, and it gradually sank into my paralysed brain that she wanted nothing of me. She didn't want me to act as corespondent for a divorce; didn't want me to elope; didn't want me to marry her. She didn't want money.

"I felt there had to be a catch in it somewhere. Finally, when she stopped talking, I said, 'What about your husband?' and Annabelle laughed and said that he wouldn't ask any questions. I told her I couldn't believe this; no man would accept another man's child. But Annabelle said that Leslie Collis would, to save his own face and his pride; he hated more than anything else in the world to be made to look foolish. He minded what his colleagues thought of him, what people said about him. He'd built up for himself this hard-headed image, and he would let nothing destroy it. And then she looked at the expression on my face and she laughed again, and she said,

'Don't worry, Daniel, he won't come gunning for you.'

"I said, 'But it's my baby,' and she threw her cigarette away and pushed her hair out of her face and said, 'Oh, don't bother about the baby. It'll have a good home,' and she made it sound as though she were talking about a dog."

He was still now, the restless pacing stopped. He stood in the middle of the room, looking down into his glass. There was still some whisky left in the bottom, and with a quick movement of hand and head, he tipped the last of it down his throat. I hoped that he would not pour himself another. He seemed to me, in this frame of mind, a man happy to drink himself into oblivion. But he went and put the empty glass back on top of the refrigerator and then, noticing that it was now dark, moved to the window and drew the heavy curtains, shutting away the dismal night outside.

He turned to face me. "You're not saying anything."

"I can't think of anything intelligent to say."

"You're shocked."

"That's a ludicrous word to use. I'm in no position to be shocked. I'm in no position to take up any sort of attitude. But for your sake, I'm sorry it happened."

"I haven't told you everything yet. Do you want to hear the rest?"

"If you want me to hear."

"I think I do. I . . . I haven't talked like this for years. I'm not sure if I could stop now, even if I wanted to."

"Have you never told anyone before?"

"Yes. I told Chips. At first I thought I wouldn't. I couldn't. For one thing, I was too ashamed. Leslie Collis wasn't the only man who hated to look foolish. But I was never much good at hiding my feelings, and after a couple of days of idiocy, shambling around Chips's studio and dropping things, he lost patience with me and came out with it, and said what the hell was the matter with me, anyway. So I told him then. I told him everything, and he never interrupted; never said a word. Just sat there in his saggy old chair, smoking his pipe and listening. And when I'd finished, got it off my chest, the relief was so great that I couldn't think why I hadn't told him straight away."

"What did he say?"

"He didn't say anything for a bit. Just went on smoking and gazing into space. Mulling things over. I didn't know what he was thinking. I half-expected to be told to go and pack my bags and never darken the doors of Holly Cottage again.

"But finally he knocked the ash out of his pipe and put it in his pocket and said, 'Young man, you are being taken for a ride.' And then he told me about Annabelle. He said that she had always been amoral, openly promiscuous. That summer was no exception. As for the baby, there was another man, a farmer from over Falmouth way, married and with a family of his own. In Chips's opinion, there was every likelihood that he was the father of Annabelle's baby. And Annabelle must know this.

"When he came out with this, I was in more of a quandary than ever. Half of me was relieved. But, as well, I felt cheated. My pride was badly bruised. I knew I was deceiving Leslie Collis, but it gave my newly found manhood a kick in the teeth to be told that Annabelle had been two-timing me. That sounds despicable, doesn't it?"

"No. It's understandable. But if it was true, why did she say the baby was *yours?*"

"I asked Chips that very question. And he told me that that had always been Annabelle's way. It was no fun creating havoc if she couldn't leave behind her a trail of guilt and remorse. Unbelievable, isn't it?"

"It sounds unbelievable to me. But if Chips said that, then it has to be true."

"I knew that, too. He went and saw Annabelle that very evening. Had it out with her. He walked up to White Lodge and got Annabelle on his own. At first she tried to bluff it out, insisting that it could be nobody's child but mine. But then he faced her with what he had told me. About the other man. And when he came out with his name, Annabelle broke down and admitted that he was right. It wasn't necessarily my child. She just liked to think that it might be. I never saw her again. She went back to London a couple of days later, taking the little boy and his nanny with her. And Chips and I agreed that it was time that I went, too. I'd been marking time for far too long."

"Does Phoebe know about all this?"

"No. I didn't want her to know, and Chips agreed that it would be better if she didn't. Hopefully, there would be no repercussions, and there was no point in upsetting her or creating any sort of trouble with Mrs. Tolliver. Penmarron is a small village. They had to go on living there, both of them part of a fairly tight community."

"What a wise man Chips was."

"Wise. Understanding. I can't begin to describe to you his kindness to me at that time. Like the very best sort of father. He fixed everything for me, even lent me some money to see me through till I found my feet. He gave me letters of introduction to friends of his in New York, but most important, he sent me off with a letter of introduction to Peter Chastal in London. In those days the gallery had been going only for a couple of years, but he'd already earned something of a name for himself in the art world. I took a great folio of my work for him to look at, and by the time I left for America, he'd agreed to exhibit for me and act as my agent. And that's what he's done ever since."

I thought of the ecstatic review I had read on the train. "He's done well for you."

"Yes. I've been fortunate."

"Chips used to say it was no good having a talent if you didn't work at it."

"Chips used to say a lot of sound things."

"Was it working that kept you away for eleven years?"

"I like to think so. I don't like to think I was trying to escape from what had happened. But perhaps I was. Running. Further and further away. New York first, and then Arizona, and then San Francisco. It was while I was there that I first became interested in Japanese art. There's a big Japanese community in San Francisco, and I found myself involved with a group of young painters. The longer I worked with them, the more I realised how little I knew. The traditions and disciplines of Japanese painting go back for centuries. It fascinated me. So I went to Japan, and there I became a student again, sitting at the feet of a very old and famous man. Time ceased to have any meaning. I was there for four years. Sometimes it seemed like a few days. At others, eternity.

"This exhibition at Peter Chastal's is a direct result of those years. I told you I didn't want to come back for it. Opening days do genuinely terrify me. But as well, I was afraid of coming back to England. On the other side of the world it was possible not to think about Annabelle and the child that might be mine. But coming back . . . I had nightmares about being in London and seeing Annabelle and my child walking up the pavement towards me."

"Wasn't coming to Cornwall something of a risk?"

"It all seemed predestined. Meeting a stranger in a pub, being offered a lift. I very nearly didn't come, but I wanted so much to see Phoebe again."

I thought back to yesterday. I remembered how quietly he had sat at the bar downstairs while I chattered on about Mrs. Tolliver and Charlotte. "Daniel, when I told you Charlotte was here, at Penmarron, staying with her grandmother, you must have realised that she was the baby."

"Yes, I realised. And I knew, too, for sure, inevitably, that I was going to meet her. It was all part of some extraordinary pattern, out of my control. When we got to Phoebe's this afternoon and got out of the car and went into the house, I knew that Charlotte was around, somewhere. I knew even before Lily told us. And as I walked out of the house and down the hill and along the seawall to fetch them back for tea, I kept telling myself that after all these years of uncertainty, I was finally going to know.

"They didn't notice me coming. They were both far too engrossed in their work. And then Phoebe caught sight of me and said my name. And Charlotte looked up, too. And there was that little face. And I knew then that, without knowing it, Annabelle had told me the truth."

So that was it. I seemed to have been standing forever, listening to Daniel's voice. My back ached, and I felt drained and exhausted. I had no idea what hour it was. From downstairs, from the busy heart of the hotel, came sounds and smells. Voices, the distant clash of dishes, the thin strains of an orchestra playing something undemanding out of *The Sound Of Music*. Sometime I had to return to Holly Cottage, to Phoebe and the chicken casserole. But not yet.

I said, "If I don't sit down I shall die." And I went over to the fireplace and collapsed in one of the chintz-covered armchairs. All the time we had talked the little fake flames had licked cheerfully around the pretend logs. Now I sat back, with my chin buried in the collar of my sweater, and watched them flickering busily, getting nowhere.

I heard Daniel pour himself another drink. He brought it over and sat facing me in the other chair. I looked up, and our eyes met. We were both very solemn.

I smiled. "So now you've told me. And I don't know why you told me."

"I had to tell someone. And for some reason, you seem to be part of it all."

"No. I'm not part of it." It was about the only thing of which I was certain. Otherwise the situation in which Daniel now found himself seemed to have no solution. I thought about it for a bit and then went on. ". . . and I don't think that you're part of it, either. It's over, Daniel. Finished. Forgotten. Water under the bridge. You thought that Charlotte might be your child; now you know that she is. That's all that's changed. Charlotte is still Charlotte Collis, Leslie Collis's daughter, Mrs. Tolliver's grandaughter, and Phoebe's friend. Accept that and forget about everything else. Because there really is no alternative. The fact that you've discovered the truth is irrelevant. It alters nothing. Charlotte was never your responsibility and she isn't now. You have to think of her as a little girl you met on the seawall who happens to share your talent for drawing and whose face reminds you of your mother's."

He did not answer me at once. And then he said, "If that were all I had to come to terms with, it wouldn't be so bad."

"What do you mean, exactly?"

"I mean exactly what you observed in the train, and what Lily Tonkins, who is nobody's fool, instantly put her finger on. Charlotte not only has to wear spectacles, but she bites her fingernails, she is lonely, she is unhappy and apparently neglected."

I looked away from him, turning to the fire for diversion. If it had been a proper one, I could have filled in the difficult moment by some small business with a poker or a fresh log. As it was, I found myself at a loss. I knew, and Phoebe knew and Lily Tonkins knew, that every-thing Daniel had just said was in all probability true. But to agree with him now could do no good for Charlotte and would only make the situation even more difficult for Daniel to accept.

I sighed, searching for words. "You mustn't take ev-erything that Lily says quite literally. She's always been inclined to overdramatize things. And you know, little girls of Charlotte's age aren't always very easy to under-stand. They become secretive and withdrawn. As well, I think she's rather a shy child . . ."

I looked up and met his gaze again. I smiled, making my face cheerful and matter-of-fact. ". . . And let's face it, Mrs. Tolliver would never win a competition for the world's cosiest granny. That's why Charlotte's so fond of Phoebe. And anyway, I don't suppose she's having a bad time staying at White Lodge. I know there are no other children to play with, but that's because all the other children in the village are back at school. And despite what Lily said, I'm sure Betty Curnow spends a bit of time with her and is kind. You mustn't let things exagger-ate themselves in your mind. Besides, tomorrow we're taking her out for a picnic. You haven't forgotten that, have you? You said you'd take us to Penjizal and show us the seals . . . you can't back out now."

"No. I won't back out."

"I understand why you were reluctant to come with us. It won't be very easy for you."

He shook his head. "I don't see that a single day is going to make much difference, one way or another, taken in the context of two separate lifetimes."

I tried to work this out. "I don't know what that means, but I'm sure you're right."

He laughed. Downstairs the orchestra had switched from *The Sound Of Music* to *The Pirates of Penzance.* I could smell delicious food.

I said, "Come back with me. To Holly Cottage. Phoebe would love it so much. We'll eat Lily's casserole, the way we planned. She's cooked enough to feed an army."

But he said that he would not come.

I looked at the empty whisky glass on the floor between his feet.

"You promise me you won't sit here all evening and drink yourself into a coma?"

He shook his head. "How little you know me. How little we know each other. I don't drink that way. I never have."

"But you'll get something to eat? You'll have dinner?"

"Yes. Later. I'll go downstairs."

"Well, if you won't come, then I must go on my own. Phoebe will think I've forgotten about her or crashed the car or something ghastly."

I got out of my chair and so did Daniel. We stood, like people at a formal party when it is time to leave.

"Good night, Daniel."

He put his hands on my shoulders and stooped to kiss my cheek. When he had done this, I stood for a long moment, looking up into his face. I put my arms around his neck and drew his head down to mine and kissed his mouth. I felt his arms come around me, felt myself held so close that I could feel the beating of his heart through the thick, rough wool of his sweater.

"Oh, Prue."

I laid my cheek against his shoulder. Felt his lips caress the top of my head. It was the most gentle of embraces, without passion, without apparant significance. So why did I suddenly feel this way, aching with a need I had never known before, my legs weak, my eyes burning with ridiculous, unshed tears? Could loving a person happen so suddenly? Like a rocket, fired into a dark sky, exploding into infinity and carrying with it a trail of shimmering, many coloured stars.

We stood silent, holding each other, like children clinging for comfort. It didn't seem to matter about not talking. Then Daniel said, "That house in Greece. I don't want you to think I didn't mean it when I asked you to come and visit me."

"Are you asking me to come with you now?"

"No."

I drew away from him and looked up into his face. He told me, "I can't go on running away from the inside of my own head. Maybe someday, sometime." He kissed me again, briskly this time, becoming practical, glancing at his wristwatch. "You must go. The casserole will be burned to nothing and Phoebe will think I've ravished you." He fetched my coat from the chair and held it out for me, and I put my arms into the sleeves, and he turned me around and did up all the buttons down the front.

"I'll come downstairs with you." He went to open the door, and we walked together, side by side, down the long corridor towards the head of the stairs. We passed rows of closed bedroom doors behind which people we

had never known had loved and honeymooned and holi-
dayed and laughed, and quarrelled and made up the
quarrels with laughter.

The foyer, when we reached the foot of the stairs, now
presented its most festive face. Guests emerged from the
bar or made their way towards the restaurant or sat
around those same little tables with cocktails before
them and dishes of nuts. The hum of conversation,
raised in order to be audible above the sound of the
orchestra, was considerable. The men wore black ties
and velvet dinner jackets, and the ladies were in evening
skirts or sequinned caftans.

We walked through it all, causing a slight stir with our
unexpected appearance, like ghosts at a feast. Conversa-
tions faltered as we walked by; eyebrows once more were
raised. We reached the main door and were turned out
into the darkness and the night. It had stopped raining
at last, but there was still a wind keening through the
high branches of trees.

Daniel looked up at the sky. "How will it be tomorrow?"

"Fine, perhaps. The wind may blow all the bad
weather away."

We came to the car. He opened the door for me.
"When shall I meet you?"

"About eleven. I'll come for you, if you want."

"No. I'll get a lift over to Penmarron or catch a bus or
something. But I'll be there, so don't go without me."

"We have to have you there, to show us the way."

I got into the car, behind the wheel.

He said, "I'm sorry about this evening."

"I'm glad you told me."

"I'm glad, too. Thank you for listening."

"Good night, Daniel."

"Good night."

He slammed the door shut, and I started the engine and set off down the curving drive, following the beam of the headlights; away from him. I do not know how long he stood there after I had gone.

Chapter Six

We talked that evening, Phoebe and I, far into the night. We indulged in memories, recalling the days when Chips was alive. We went even further back, to Northumberland, to Windyedge, where Phoebe had spent her childhood, running wild and riding her shaggy pony along the margins of those cold and northern beaches. We spoke of my father, and the contentment he had found with his new wife, and she remembered expeditions when they were all children together, to Dunstanbrugh and Bambrugh, and midwinter meets, with the pink coats of the huntsmen bright as berries in the frosty air and the foxhounds streaming across the snow-streaked fields.

We talked about Paris, where she had been a student, and the little house in the Dordogne she and Chips had bought one affluent year and to which she still returned for annual painting trips.

We talked about Marcus Bernstein, my job, my little flat in Islington.

"Next time I come to London, I shall come and stay with you," she promised.

"I haven't got a spare room."

"Then I shall sleep on the floor."

She told me about the new Society of Arts that had just been formed in Porthkerris and of which she was a founding member. She described for me the house of an old and famous potter, who had returned to Porthkerris to spend his final years in the warren of narrow streets where he had been born eighty years before, the son of a fisherman.

We talked about Lewis Falcon.

But we did not speak of Daniel. As though we had made some secret agreement, neither Phoebe nor I mentioned his name.

Past midnight she went at last to bed. I followed her up the stairs to draw her curtains and turn down the quilt and help her off with her more awkward clothes. I took a hot-water bottle downstairs and filled it from the boiling kettle and finally left her, warm in her huge and downy bed, reading her book.

We said good night, but I did not go to bed. My mind was seething, as alert and restless as if I had pumped myself with some enormously stimulating drug. I could not face lying in the darkness, waiting for sleep that I knew would not come. So I returned to the kitchen and made a mug of coffee and took it back to the fireside. The flames had died to a bed of grey ash, so I threw on more logs and watched them kindle and flare, and then curled myself up into Chips's old armchair. Its battered depths were comforting, and I thought about him and longed for his presence. I did not want him dead; I wanted him alive, here, in this room with me. We had always been very close, and now I needed him. I needed his counsel.

Like the very best sort of father. I thought of Chips, his pipe in his mouth, listening as the young Daniel told him about Annabelle Tolliver and the baby. Annabelle, with her dark hair and her cat face and her grey eyes and her secret smile.

It's your child, Daniel.

There were other voices. Lily Tonkins. *Mrs. Tolliver can't be bothered to look after the child, then she should pay some other person to do the job.* Lily shrill with indignation, beating out her resentment on a bowl of batter.

And my mother, exasperated because I would not conform to the pattern that she had endeavoured all her life to cut for me.

Honestly, Prue, I don't know what you're looking for.

I had told her that I wasn't looking for anything. But there was a word—"serendipity." It was such an odd, strange-sounding word that I had once looked it up in a dictionary.

serendipity *n:* faculty of making happy discoveries by accident

I had discovered. Daniel. Watched him walking from the little railway station, along the old seawall, towards me, into my life. This evening, "How little we know each other," he had said, and up to a point, that was true. A day. Two days. Too short, one would have said, to achieve anything but the most superficial relationship.

But this was different. For me time and events had become miraculously encapsulated, so that I felt as though I had lived an entire lifetime with him in the course of the past twenty-four hours. It was hard to realise that I had not known him forever, that our two separate existences were not already spun together, like strands in a single skein of wool.

I wanted it to go on being this way. I was prepared to let him go his way, as Phoebe had let him go. I was wise enough for that. But I did not want to lose him. And I knew that the odds were against me. Partly because Daniel was the man that he was—an artist, restless, seeking, he would always need to be free. But infinitely more formidable was the memory of Annabelle, the existence of Charlotte.

Charlotte. Who knew what traumas Charlotte had suffered, foisted upon a man who was not her father and who must surely know that he was not her father. I had taken an instant dislike to him during those brief moments I had seen him on the train, watched his impatience with the little girl and recognised a total lack of affection as he thrust the ten-pound note into her hand, as though he were paying off some tiresome debt.

And Annabelle. So much unhappiness to answer for. *It was no fun creating havoc if she couldn't leave behind her a trail of guilt and remorse.* She had done that, all right, with her wayward passions, destructive as a hurricane. Now the hurricane seemed to have blown up again, and I was afraid because I could see it tearing Daniel and me apart forever.

I can't go on running away from the inside of my own head.

I thought of the house in Greece, the sugar-cube house above the sea, with the whitewashed terrace and the bright geraniums. A scrap of poetry, half-learned, half-forgotten, flew like a ghost through the back of my mind.

Oh, love, we two shall go no more to lands of summer beyond the seas.

From the mantelpiece, Phoebe's clock chimed a single, silvery note. One o'clock. I laid down the empty coffee mug and with an effort pulled myself from the deep comfort of Chips's armchair. Still not sleepy, I went over to Phoebe's radio and fiddled with knobs, searching for some early-hour music. I found a recorded programme of classic pop, recognised a tune that dated back to the years of my growing up.

God bless you,
You made me feel brand new
For God blessed me with you.

The toy carousel still stood on the table where Charlotte had played with it. It had never been put back in its cupboard, and now I went to do this, for fear that dust should seep into its ancient mechanism and cause it to grind to a final halt. I couldn't bear to think of it broken, forgotten, never played with again.

I simply don't know which is my favourite . . .

I wound the handle and gently released the lever. Slowly, sedately, the brightly painted animals revolved, their tinselly bridles sparkling in the light from the fire, like decorations on a Christmas tree.

> Without you,
> Life has no meaning or rhyme
> Like notes to a song out of time.

There was always tomorrow. I could not be sure whether I dreaded the day we had planned or looked forward to it. There seemed to be too much at stake. I only knew that we would go, the three of us, to Penjizal and look for the seals. Beyond tomorrow I could not imagine, simply hope that some good would come of our being together. For Daniel's sake. For Charlotte. And, selfishly, for myself.

The mechanism ran down; the turntable slowly came to a halt. I stooped and lifted the carousel off the table and put it away in its cupboard; closed the doors, turned the key. I put the guard in front of the fire, switched off the radio, turned off the light. In the darkness, I went upstairs.

I awoke early, at seven, to the sound of a big old herring gull screaming at the new day from the roof of Chips's studio. My drawn curtains framed a sky of the palest blue veiled in a haze reminiscent of the hottest days of summer. There was no wind, no sound but the cry of the gull and the whisper of an incoming tide, trickling to fill the gullies and sand pools of the estuary. When I got up and went to the window, it was very cold, almost as though there had been a frost. I smelt the seaweed, tarry rope, and the clean saltiness of fresh seawater surging in from the ocean. It was a day made to order for a picnic.

I dressed and went downstairs and made coffee for myself and breakfast for Phoebe. When I took this up to her, I found her already awake and sitting up against the pillows, not reading but simply gazing with pleasure as the warmth of the sun on that perfect autumn morning burned away the last of the mist.

I put the breakfast tray on her knees.

"These are the sort of mornings," she said without preamble, "that I'm certain one remembers when one is very, very old. Good morning, my darling." We kissed. "What a day for a picnic."

"Come with us, Phoebe."

She was tempted. "It depends where you're going."

"Daniel's going to show us the way to Penjizal. He said something about a tidal rock pool where the seals come and swim."

"Oh, it's so beautiful! You'll be enchanted. But no, I think I'd better not come. The path down the cliffs is a little too precipitous for a person with only one arm. It would be too tiresome for you if I lost my balance and went flying over the cliff into the sea." She went into gales of her usual laughter at the very idea. "But the walk down from the farmhouse at the top is magical. There are wild fuchsias everywhere, and in summertime the valley is humming with dragonflies. What are you going to take with you to eat? Ham sandwiches? Have we got any ham? What a pity you can't make cold casserole sandwiches, there's so much left over from last night. I wonder if Daniel got in touch with Lewis Falcon. I've heard that he's got the most beautiful wild garden out there at Lanyon . . ."

She chattered on, her conversation, as always with Phoebe, darting from one intriguing subject to the next. It was tempting to forget about the day ahead; to lose all sense of time and simply to settle down to spending the rest of the morning sitting there on the end of Phoebe's downy bed. But, with the coffee pot empty and the sun's rays shining obliquely through the open window, I heard from downstairs the slamming of the kitchen door and knew that Lily Tonkins had arrived on her bicycle.

I looked at Phoebe's clock. "Heavens, it's past nine o'clock. I must get moving." I climbed reluctantly off the bed and started to gather up cups and plates, stacking them on Phoebe's tray.

"So must I."

"Oh, don't get up. Stay there for another hour or so. Lily likes it when you do that. She can get on with her polishing without having to shunt you around all the time."

"I'll see," said Phoebe, but as I went out the door, I saw her reach for her book. She was reading C. P. Snow, and I envied her her warm bed and that wonderful sonorous prose and guessed that it would be midday at least before she put in an appearance downstairs.

In the kitchen I found Lily tying on her apron.

"Hello, Prue, how are you this morning? Lovely, isn't

it? Ernest said last night, this was what was going to
happen. He said that wind was going to blow the dirty
weather away. And coming down the road from the
church, you'd think it was warm as June. Had a good
mind not to come in to work today; just go down to the
beach and put my feet in the tide."

From the hall, the telephone began to ring.

"Now," said Lily, as she invariably did when this happened, "who can that be?"

"I'll go," I said.

I went back to the hall and sat on the old carved chest
where the telephone lived and picked up the receiver.
"Hello."

"Phoebe?" A woman's voice.

"No. This is Prue."

"Oh, Prue. This is Mrs. Tolliver. Is Phoebe there?"

"I'm afraid she's still in bed."

I expected her to apologise for the early call and to say
that she would ring back later. But instead she persisted.
"I must speak to her. Can she come to the telephone?"
And there was an urgency to her voice, an unsteadiness,
that filled me with nameless apprehension.

"Is anything wrong?"

"No. Yes. Prue—I have to talk to her."

"I'll get her." I laid down the receiver and went upstairs. As I put my head around Phoebe's door, she
looked up placidly from her book.

"That's Mrs. Tolliver on the telephone. She wants to
speak to you." I added, "She sounds very odd. Upset."

Phoebe frowned. "What's it about?" She laid down
her book.

"I don't know." But my imagination had already scurried ahead. "Perhaps it's something to do with Charlotte."

Not hesitating any longer, Phoebe pushed back her covers and got out of bed. I helped her into her dressing gown, putting her good arm into the sleeve and wrapping the rest of its voluminous folds around her like a cape. I found her slippers. Her thick hair still lay in a plait over one shoulder, and her reading spectacles had slipped down her nose. She led the way down to the hall, sat where I had sat, picked up the receiver.

"Yes?"

The call was obviously important, and, possibly, private. Perhaps, realising this, I should have taken myself off out of earshot to the kitchen. But Phoebe sent me a glance that beseeched me to stay at hand, as though she expected to need my moral support, so halfway down the stairs, I sat, too, watching her through the bannister rails.

"Phoebe?" Mrs. Tolliver's voice was clearly audible from where I perched. "I'm sorry I had to get you out of bed, but I have to speak to you."

"Yes."

"I have to see you."

Phoebe looked a little nonplussed. "What, right away?"

"Yes. Now. Please. I . . .. I think I need your advice."

"I hope Charlotte's all right?"

"Yes. Yes, she's all right. But please come. I . . . I really want to speak to you very urgently."

"I shall have to get dressed."

"Just come as soon as you can. I shall expect you."

And before Phoebe could raise any objections, she had rung off.

Phoebe was left sitting there, holding the humming receiver. We looked at each other blankly, and I could tell by her face that she felt just as apprehensive as I did.

"Did you hear all that?"

"Yes."

Phoebe thoughtfully replaced the receiver, and the humming sound ceased.

"What on earth can be wrong? She sounds quite demented."

From the kitchen we could hear Lily wielding the floor polished and singing hymns. This was a sure sign that she was feeling on top of the world.

"Guard us, oh, thou Gre-hate Je-he-hovah . . ."

Phoebe stood up. "I'll have to go."

"I'll drive you in the car."

"You'd better help me get dressed first."

Back in her bedroom, she took from cupboards and drawers a selection of garments even more haphazard than usual. When she was ready, she sat at her dressing table, and I did her hair, replaiting it and winding it up into a knob at the back of her head, and holding it while she skewered it into place with her old-fashioned tortoiseshell pins.

I knelt to lace up her shoes. This done, "You go and get the car out," she told me. "I'll be down in a moment."

I found my coat and pulled it on and let myself out of the house. The pearly, brilliant morning shimmered all about me. I opened the garage and persuaded the old car to start. I had backed it out of the garage and was waiting by the front door when Phoebe appeared. She had put on one of her largest and most dashing hats, and, for warmth, had draped across her shoulders a brilliant poncho of wool, doubtless woven by some Middle Eastern peasant. Her spectacles were sliding down her nose; her hair, fresh from my inexpert hands, already looked as though it was about to collapse. None of this mattered. What did matter was that for once in her life she did not have a smile on her face, and this alone was enough to make me angry with Mrs. Tolliver.

She bundled herself into the seat beside me and we set off.

"What I can't understand," said Phoebe, giving her hat a tug to settle it even further down on her head, "is why me? I'm no particular friend of Mrs. Tolliver's. She's far more intimate with those nice ladies she plays bridge with. Perhaps it is something to do with Charlotte. She knows how fond I am of the child. That's it. It must be —" She stopped, abruptly. "Prue, why are we going so slowly? You're still in second gear." I changed up to third, and we continued our journey at a slightly increased speed. "We're meant to be in a hurry."

"I know," I said. "But I want to tell you something and I don't want to get to Mrs. Tolliver's before I've finished."

"What are you going to tell me?"

"It may have nothing to do with what she's going to talk about. But, on the other hand, I have an uncomfortable feeling that it has. I don't know whether I ought to say anything. But whether I ought to or not, I'm going to."

Phoebe sighed deeply. "It's about Charlotte, isn't it?"

"Yes. Daniel's her father."

Phoebe's worn hands stayed where they were, quietly clasped in her lap. "Did he tell you so?"

"Yes. He told me yesterday."

"You could have said something last night."

"He didn't ask me to."

We were moving so slowly that I had to change down again as the car ground on up the slight slope towards the church.

"So they did have an affair, he and Annabelle."

"Yes. You see, it wasn't just a little flingette after all. At the end of that summer, Annabelle told Daniel she was having his baby. And Daniel confided in Chips. And Chips pointed out that it wasn't necessarily Daniel's baby; it could easily be some other man's. And Chips confronted Annabelle with this, and she finally admitted to him that she couldn't be sure whose child it was."

"I always wondered why Daniel went off so precipitately to America. I mean, he'd been talking about it all summer, and I knew he planned to go. But all at once he was going. And then he'd gone."

"And didn't come back for eleven years."

"When did he realise she was his child?"

"As soon as he set eyes on her, sitting there on the seawall trying to finish her picture in the rain."

"*How* did he know?"

"Apparently she looks just the way his mother looked as a little girl."

"So there's no doubt."

"No. Not in Daniel's mind. No doubt."

Phoebe fell silent. Presently she sighed again, a long, troubled sigh. She said inadequately, "Oh, dear."

"I'm sorry, Phoebe. It's not a very nice thing to have to tell anyone."

"Perhaps in a strange way I already knew. I always had such a close relationship with Charlotte, just as I used to have with you. Just as I used to have with Daniel. And there were little things about her . . . mannerisms . . . that were strangely familiar. The way she holds a pencil, with her fingers all bunched up around it. Daniel holds a pencil that way."

"Chips never said anything to you?"

"Not a word."

"Perhaps I shouldn't have, either. But if you're going to be faced by some appalling revelation from Mrs. Tolliver, it's as well to have a few facts at your fingertips."

"I've got those all right. What a proper turn-up for the books." She added, without much hope, "Perhaps it's just going to be about the Women's Institute tea. And then your bombshell will have been all for nothing."

"It's not my bombshell. And if I hadn't told you, Daniel would have. And you know as well as I do that this isn't going to be about the Women's Institute tea."

There was no time for more. Even driving at my deliberate snail's pace, we had already covered the short distance between Holly Cottage and White Lodge. Here were the gates, the neatly kept drive, the gravel sweep in front of the formal house. But today the front door stood open, and as we drew up at the foot of the steps, Mrs. Tolliver came through the door and down the steps towards us. I wondered if she had been waiting for us just inside the hall, sitting on one of those ugly, uncomfortable chairs that are not meant to be used for sitting on but other purposes, like dumping overcoats and leaving parcels.

There was nothing outwardly dishevelled about her. I saw the usual well-cut skirt, the simple shirt, a cardigan of deep coral, the good pearls around her throat and set in the lobes of her ears, the well-coiffed grey hair.

But the inner turmoil was all too evident. She appeared distraught, her face blotched as though recently she had actually been crying.

Phoebe opened the door of the car.

"Phoebe, how good of you . . . how very good of you to come." She stooped to help Phoebe out and caught sight of me sitting behind the driving wheel. I smiled weakly.

"Prue had to come," said Phoebe briskly. "To drive me. You don't mind if she comes in, too, do you?"

"Oh . . ." Mrs. Tolliver obviously did mind, but it was a good indication of her immediate distress that this single word was as far as her objection went. "No. No, of course not."

I didn't want to go in in the very least. In the course of the last two days I'd had enough of the Tollivers, but Phoebe obviously wanted me with her, so trying to appear both disinterested and colourless, I too got out of the car and followed the two women up the stone steps and into the house.

The hall was flagged in stone, scattered with Persian rugs of great antiquity. A graceful staircase with a wrought-iron bannister curved to the upper floors. I closed the front door behind me, and Mrs. Tolliver led us across the hall and into her drawing room. She waited as we passed through the door and then closed it firmly, as though wary of possible eavesdroppers.

It was a large and formally furnished room, with long sash windows facing out onto the garden. The morning sun had not yet penetrated these windows, and the atmosphere was chilly. Mrs. Tolliver gave a shiver.

"It's cold. I hope you're not cold . . . so early . . ." Her instincts as a hostess rose to the surface. "Perhaps . . . light a fire . . . ?"

"I'm not in the least cold," said Phoebe. She chose a chair and sat firmly down in it, still bundled in her garish poncho and with her solid legs crossed at the ankle, like royalty. "Now, my dear. What is this about?"

Mrs. Tolliver crossed to the empty fireplace and stood there, supporting herself with a hand laid along the edge of the mantelpiece.

"I . . . I really don't know where to begin . . ."

"Try the beginning."

"Well." She took a deep breath. "You know the reason Charlotte is with me?"

"Yes. The boiler at her school blew up."

"That, of course. But the real reason is that her mother—Annabelle—is in Majorca. That was why there was nobody to take care of her at home. Well . . . I had a telephone call last night, at about half past nine . . ."

She took her hand from the mantelpiece and felt up her cuff and produced a tiny, lace-edged handkerchief. As she went on talking, she played with this, looking to me as though she were trying to tear it to pieces.

"It was my son-in-law, Leslie Collis. Annabelle has left him. She's not coming back. She's with this man. He's a riding instructor. South African. She's going back to South Africa with him."

The enormity of her statement silenced the lot of us. I was thankful that I was expected to say nothing, but I looked at Phoebe. She sat unmoving, and I could not see the expression on her face, because it was obliterated by the brim of her hat.

At last, "I am so sorry," she said, and there was a whole world of sympathy in her voice.

"But you see, that isn't the end of it. I . . . I really don't know how I'm going to tell you."

"I imagine," said Phoebe, "that it's got something to do with Charlotte."

"He says that Charlotte is not his child. Apparently he always knew this, but he accepted her for Michael's sake, because he wanted to keep his home together. But he's never liked the child. I always knew that he never had any time for her, though of course I had no idea exactly why. It used to distress me when I stayed with them. He was so impatient with her, sometimes it seemed as though she could do nothing right."

"Did you say anything?"

"I didn't want to make trouble."

"She's always seemed to me to be rather a lonely little girl."

"Yes. Lonely. She never fit in. And she was never pretty and engaging, the way Annabelle used to be. I don't want you to think that Leslie was *unkind* to her. It was just that all his time and affection seemed to be centred on Michael . . . and there wasn't enough left over for Charlotte.''

"What about her mother?"

Mrs. Tolliver gave an indulgent little laugh. "I'm afraid that Annabelle was never very maternal. Like me. I was never very maternal, either. But when Annabelle was a child, things were easier. My husband was alive then, and we were able to afford a nanny for Annabelle. I had help in the house as well. Things were easier.''

"Did your son-in-law know that Annabelle was having an affair with this man . . . the riding instructor?"

Mrs. Tolliver looked embarrassed, as though Phoebe had deliberately offended her. She looked away, toying with a china shepherdess that stood upon the mantelpiece. "I . . . I didn't ask him that. But . . . you know Annabelle, Phoebe. She was always . . .''

She hesitated, and I waited with interest. How does a mother describe her only daughter who is, by all accounts, a nymphomaniac?

" . . . attractive. Full of life. Leslie was in London all the time. They didn't see a great deal of each other.''

"So he didn't know," said Phoebe bluntly. "Or perhaps he just suspected.''

"Yes. Perhaps he just suspected.''

"Well," said Phoebe, coming to the point. "So what is now going to happen to Charlotte?"

Mrs. Tolliver set the china figure down neatly, exactly, in its customary position. She looked back at Phoebe and her mouth was trembling, but whether with incipient tears or indignation, I could not tell.

"He doesn't want Charlotte back. He said that she's

not his child and she's never been his child, and now that Annabelle has left him, he intends washing his hands of Charlotte."

"But he can't do that," said Phoebe, her hackles rising at the very suggestion of such behaviour.

"I don't know whether he can or not. I don't know what to do."

"Then she must be with her mother. Annabelle must take her to South Africa."

"I . . . I don't think that Annabelle will want her."

The enormity of this silenced both Phoebe and myself. We stared, unbelieving, at Mrs. Tolliver, and a flush crept up her neck.

At last Phoebe said bluntly, "You mean that Charlotte would get in Annabelle's way."

"I don't know. Annabelle . . ." I waited for her to tell us next that Annabelle had no more fondness for Charlotte than Leslie Collis had. But Mrs. Tolliver could not bring herself to come out with this. "I don't know what I'm trying to say. I feel torn in all directions. I'm sorry for the child—but, Phoebe, I cannot have her here. I'm too old. This isn't a house for a child. I haven't got a nursery, I haven't even got any toys. Annabelle's dollhouse went years ago, and I gave all her children's books to the hospital."

I thought, *No wonder Charlotte loved the carousel.*

"And I have a life of my own. My own commitments, my friends. It isn't as though she seems particularly happy here. She mopes around most of the time, without saying or doing anything. I admit, I find her difficult. And Betty Curnow only comes in in the mornings. It isn't as

though I have good help. I . . . I don't know which way
to turn. I'm at my wit's end."

Tears had never been far away. Now, at the end of her
tether, she lost control. The tears of older women are
ugly. Perhaps ashamed of them or wishing to spare us
embarrassment, she turned from the fireplace and took
herself over to the long window, where she stood, her
back to us, as though admiring her own garden. There
came the sound of painful sobs.

I knew that I was very much in the way and longed for
escape. I looked beseechingly in Phoebe's direction and
caught her eye.

Phoebe said instantly, "You know, I think a nice hot
cup of coffee would do us all good."

Mrs. Tolliver did not turn, but presently in a choked
voice she said pathetically, "There's no one to get it. I
sent Betty Curnow and Charlotte up to the village. Charlotte wanted to buy some Coca-Cola. We've . . . we've
run out. And it seemed a good excuse to get her out
of the house. I didn't want her here while I spoke to
you . . ."

I said, "I can get coffee."

Mrs. Tolliver blew her nose. This seemed to help a bit.
Slightly recovered, she looked at me over her shoulder.
Her face was blurred and swollen. "You won't know
where to find anything."

"I can look. If you don't mind me going into your
kitchen."

"No. Not at all. How kind . . ."

I left them. Let myself quietly out of the drawing room
and shut the door and leaned against it, like people do

in films. I couldn't like Mrs. Tolliver, but it was impossible not to feel dreadfully sorry for her. Her well-organised existence seemed to be collapsing about her head. Annabelle was, after all, her only child. Now Annabelle's marriage had come to pieces and she was off with her new love to the other end of the world, abandoning both her children and all her responsibilities.

And yet I knew that the bitterest blow of all to the pride of a woman like Mrs. Tolliver was the shaming revelation that Charlotte was not Leslie Collis's child but the unfortunate result of one of Annabelle's many love affairs.

I wondered if she had any idea which love affair it was. For all our sakes, I hoped not.

And Charlotte. *That little face.* I couldn't think about Charlotte. I pulled myself away from the door and went in search of Mrs. Tolliver's kitchen.

By a process of trial and error, opening cupboard doors and pulling out random drawers, I finally assimilated a tray, cups and saucers, a sugar bowl, some spoons. I filled the electric kettle and found a jar of instant coffee. I decided that we could do without biscuits. When the kettle had boiled, I filled the three cups and carried the tray back to the drawing room.

They were still at it, but Mrs. Tolliver, in my absence, seemed to have stopped crying and pulled herself together. Now she sat in a wide-lapped Victorian chair, facing Phoebe.

". . . Perhaps," Phoebe was saying, "your son-in-law will have second thoughts about Charlotte. After all, she has a brother, and it's always been considered very wrong to split up families."

"But Michael is so much older than Charlotte. So much more mature. I don't believe they've ever had very much in common . . ."

She looked up as I appeared through the door, and at once a polite smile turned up the corners of her mouth. She was a lady to whom social graces came automatically, even in times of stress.

"How kind, Prue. So clever." I set down the tray on a low stool. "Oh," a small frown creased her brow. "You've used the best teacups."

"I'm sorry. They were the first I found."

"Oh. Well, never mind. It won't matter for once."

I handed Phoebe her coffee. She took it and stirred it thoughtfully. I sat down, too, and for a moment there was silence, broken only by the tinkling of stirring teaspoons, as though we were gathered together for an enjoyable occasion.

Phoebe broke this silence. "In my opinion," she said, "I think there can be no question of Charlotte returning home. At least until things have simmered down and your son-in-law has had time to sort himself out."

"But her school."

"Don't send her back to that school. I don't like the sound of it, with the boiler blowing that way. It must be very inefficiently administrated. She's far too young for boarding school, anyway, and there can be no point in her returning there if her home life is in pieces. Enough to give any child a nervous breakdown." She sat with her cup and saucer in her lap and looked long and hard at Mrs. Tolliver. "You have to be very careful. You don't want the responsibility of Charlotte, and I can understand that, but for the moment, as far as I can see, you've got it. A life in your hands. A young, sensitive life. She is going to be hurt enough when she knows about her mother. Let us all see that she is not hurt any more than she has to be."

Mrs. Tolliver started to say something, but Phoebe, with unusual bluntness, overrode her.

"I said, I understand your situation. Things are going to be very difficult. For that reason I think it would be much better if you were here on your own, without Charlotte around the place, listening to talk and possibly overhearing telephone calls which she should not. She's an intelligent child, and she'll know instinctively that something is wrong. So I suggest that you simply tell her she's coming to live with me for a little while."

Oh, darling Phoebe. Oh, blessed Phoebe.

"I know I'm a bit of a crock just now, but Prue's with me for another ten days and Lily Tonkins is always a tower of strength in times of emergency."

"But, Phoebe, that's too much."

"I'm very fond of Charlotte. We shall get along very well."

"I know that. And I know that she is devoted to you. But . . . oh, don't think I'm not grateful . . . it will seem so strange to everybody. Leaving me, her grandmother, and coming to stay with you. What will people think? What will they say? This is a small village, and you know both Lily Tonkins and Betty Curnow will talk."

"Yes, they will talk. People always talk. But all the talk in the world is better than having that child hurt any more. Besides," Phoebe said as she set down her empty coffee cup, "we've both got broad shoulders, and," she gave a little chuckle, "let's face it, surely we're getting a bit long in the tooth for a scrap of gossip to bother us. So what do you say?"

Mrs. Tolliver, with obvious relief, finally succumbed.

"I don't mind admitting it would make things very, very much easier for me."

"Will you be in touch with your son-in-law again?"

"Yes. I said I would ring him up tonight. Yesterday evening we were both of us getting a little too emotional. I think he'd probably had far too much to drink. Not that I blame him for that, but neither of us was making much sense."

"In that case you can tell him that Charlotte's coming to stay at Holly Cottage for a little. And you can tell him as well that she's not going back to that boarding school. Perhaps we could get her into the local school here. You could talk it over with him."

"Yes. Yes, I'll do that."

"That's settled, then." Phoebe stood up. "Now Charlotte has already arranged to come to Holly Cottage this morning. Prue is taking her on a picnic. Pack a bag and let her bring that with her. But don't say anything to the child about her mother."

"But she'll have to be told."

"You are family, far too close, too involved. I shall tell her."

For a moment I thought that Mrs. Tolliver was going to object to this. She took a breath to say something but then met Phoebe's eye and didn't say it after all.

"Very well, Phoebe."

"It will be easier if I tell her. For all of us."

At the same snail's pace we trundled homewards. Down the drive of White Lodge, through the gates, past the oak copse. We turned the corner by the church, and the road to home sloped down and away from us, and we could see the whole long blue lake that was the estuary, the floodwaters dazzling with sun pennies.

"Prue, stop the car for a moment."

I did as she said, drawing the car in to the side of the road and switching off the engine. For a little we sat like two aimless tourists, gazing at the familiar view as though we had never seen it before. On the far shore, the gentle hills, patchworked in small fields, drowsed in the morning's warmth. A red tractor, minimised by distance to toy size, was out ploughing, drawing in its wake a flock of screaming white gulls.

At the end of the road, in the lee of the shore, Holly Cottage waited for us, hidden beyond the crest of the hill, slumbering in the sheltered sunshine. But here on the brow of the slope, the sea breezes were never still. Now the thin wind flattened the pale grasses in the roadside ditches and blew the first of the leaves from the topmost branches of the trees that bordered the ancient churchyard.

"So peaceful," said Phoebe, sounding as though she were thinking aloud. "You'd think that here, the end of the world, you'd be safe. I thought so, when I first came to live here with Chips. I thought I'd escaped. But there is no way you can escape reality. Cruelty, indifference, selfishness."

"All those things are part of people, and people are everywhere."

"Destroying." Phoebe thought this over for a bit, and then said in a changed voice, "Poor woman."

"Mrs. Tolliver. Yes, I'm sorry for her, too. But still, I wonder why she chose to confide in *you.*"

"Oh, my dear, it's obvious. She knows I'm an old sinner. She'll never forget that Chips and I lived in happy sin for years. She could talk to me, where she could never have confided in her other friends. Colonel Danby's wife, or the bank manager's widow from Porthkerris—they'd have been appalled. And, of course, what's hurting most of all is her pride."

"I thought that, too. But you were marvellous. You always are marvellous, but this morning you were more marvellous than usual."

"I don't know about that."

"I just hope you haven't bitten off more than you can chew. Supposing Leslie Collis really does refuse to have anything more to do with Charlotte; you'll be landed with her indefinitely."

"I wouldn't mind."

"But Phoebe . . ." I stopped, because you can't say to a person you love, You're too old, even if you think that she is.

"You think I'm too old?"

"Other things, too. You've as much a life of your own

[139]

as Mrs. Tolliver. Why should you be the one who gives it all up? And let's face it, we're all getting older. Even I'm getting older . . ."

"I'm sixty-three. If I manage to stay alive and kicking for another ten years, I shall still be only seventy-three. That's a young woman when you think of Picasso or Arthur Rubenstein."

"What have they got to do with it?"

"And by then Charlotte will be twenty and well able to take care of herself. I really don't see that that's much of a problem."

The windscreen of the Volkswagen was dirty. I found in some pocket a grubby rag and began to try in a desultory sort of way to clean the glass.

I said, "When I was in the kitchen getting the coffee, did she make any reference to Daniel?"

"None."

"You didn't say anything?"

"Heaven forbid."

I was making the smears on the windscreen, if anything, worse. I stuffed the rag back into its hiding place.

"He's coming here, you know, this morning, for the picnic. I offered to fetch him in the car, but he said he'd make his own way."

"That's just as well."

I looked at her. "You're going to tell Daniel about all this?"

"Of course I shall tell him. I shall tell him everything. Three heads are better than two, and I'm sick and tired of all of us keeping secrets from each other. Perhaps if we hadn't kept secrets, none of this would have happened."

"Oh, Phoebe, I hardly think so."

"Maybe you're right. But let's start being completely frank and truthful; then we'll all know where we stand. Besides, Daniel has a right to know."

"What do you think he'll do?"

"*Do?*" Phoebe gazed at me blankly. "Why should he do anything?"

"He's Charlotte's father."

"Leslie Collis is Charlotte's father."

It was just what I had said to Daniel, sitting with him by the pretend fire; trying to be down-to-earth and sensible, jollying him along. But surely, now, things were taking a different course.

"He may not *be* responsible," I pointed out, "but that's not going to stop him feeling that way."

"And what do you imagine he's going to do about it?"

"I don't know."

"In that case, I can tell you. Nothing. Because there is nothing that he can do. And because even if there were, he wouldn't do it."

"How do you know?"

"Because I know Daniel."

"I know him, too."

"I only wish you did."

"What's that supposed to mean?"

Phoebe sighed. "Oh, nothing. It's just that I'm afraid you've fallen in love with him."

Her voice, as always, was inconsequential, as though

she were talking of something of no importance. As a result, I was taken unawares. I said, trying to sound as casual as she did, "I don't think I know what falling in love actually means. It's always been a sort of nonword with me. Like 'forgive.' I never understand the word 'forgive.' If you don't forgive, then you're mean and resentful and grudge-bearing; and if you do, then you're smug and sanctimonious."

But Phoebe would not be waylaid into this interesting discussion. She stuck to her point.

"Well, 'love,' then. Perhaps that's an easier word to define."

"If you want definitions, then I feel as though I've known him always. I feel as though already we've shared a past. And I don't want to lose him, because I think we need each other."

"Did you feel this way before he unfolded to you the great saga of Annabelle?"

"I think so. Yes. So you see I'm not just feeling sorry for him."

"Why should you be sorry for him? He has everything —youth, a terrifying talent, and now fame and money and all the material things that go with them."

"But how can you discount what happened between Daniel and Annabelle? He's felt guilty for eleven years because he didn't even know if the child was his or not. Wouldn't you feel sorry for any man who had that load of guilt on his back for eleven years?"

"The guilt was of his own making. And he didn't need to run away."

"Perhaps he didn't run away. Perhaps he did what

Chips told him to do, which was the only possible, reasonable thing."

"Did he speak about this to you?"

"Yes. And he asked me to go to Greece with him. To Spetsai. That was before he told me about Annabelle and Charlotte. But afterwards we talked about it again, and he said that it wouldn't be any good, because he couldn't go on running away from the inside of his own head."

"Would you have gone? To Greece?"

"Yes."

"And afterwards?"

"I don't know."

"That's not good enough for you, Prue."

"You sound like my mother."

"At the risk of sounding like your mother—who, incidentally, is nobody's fool—I have to say it. You don't know Daniel. He is a true artist: impermanent, restless, impractical."

"I know he's impractical." I smiled. "He told me once that he had a car, and at the end of three years he'd only just learned how to work the heater."

But Phoebe ignored my small attempt at humour and went on doggedly.

"He's unreliable, too, because he's always lost in his own form of creation. It makes him, in a way, negative. Maddening."

"Oh, come off it, Phoebe, you know you adore him."

"I do, Prue, I do. But face him with day-to-day decisions and responsibilities, and I could never truly predict how he would react."

"Are you talking about Daniel as a prospective husband?"

"I wouldn't intrude that far."

"You knew him when he was twenty. You can't judge him by the person he was eleven years ago. He's a man now."

"Yes, I know that. And people mature, of course. But do their personalities change so much? You're such a special person, Prue, I wouldn't want you ever to be hurt. And Daniel could hurt you. Not deliberately, but by the sins of omission. His work fills his life, and I don't know how much room there is left over for personal things like loving people and being with them, and taking care of them.

"Perhaps I could take care of him."

"Yes, perhaps you could, for a little while. But I think not indefinitely. I don't see how it could be possible to stay forever with a man who I knew was afraid of permanency, emotional involvements, becoming trapped."

It was no good arguing with her. I sat saying nothing, gazing ahead of me through the dusty windscreen and seeing nothing. The funny thing was that we both seemed to be on the same side. She put out her hand and laid it over mine. Her fingers were warm, but I could feel the cold, hard pressure of her bulky, old-fashioned rings.

"Don't create fantasies about Daniel. They will probably never come true. And if you expect nothing of him, you will at least never be disappointed."

I was thinking of Charlotte. "I don't believe he will run away from this."

"And I believe that he has no alternative. Perhaps you

should run away, too. Go back to London. Get your life in perspective. Ring up that nice young man who brought you the dead chrysanthemums."

"Oh, *Phoebe.*" It took a small effort even to remember his name. "They weren't dead when he gave them to me."

"When you see him again, you may feel quite differently about him."

"No. I shan't do that. Anyway, he doesn't make me laugh." Nigel Gordon. I knew that now I should probably never get to go to Scotland.

"Well, you must make up your own mind." She gave my hand a pat and then sat back in her seat with her hands in her lap. "I've said it. Interfered. Cleared my muddy conscience. Now perhaps we'd better go home and break the news about Charlotte coming to stay to Lily Tonkins. If anything's going to stop her singing "Guard Us Oh Thou Great Jehovah," then that is. On the other hand, she always enjoys a drama, so maybe she'll take it quite well. As well, Charlotte will be turning up at Holly Cottage at any moment, and we've got the picnic to organise, as if life wasn't already sufficiently complicated."

I had forgotten the picnic. Now, starting the engine and letting off the brake, I wished that Phoebe had not found it necessary to remind me.

"Well, I don't know," said Lily when we told her about Charlotte coming to stay. "Leaving her granny and coming here. Seems funny." She looked from Phoebe's innocent face to mine. I hastily smiled, brightly and blankly.

"I suppose, come to think of it, it's not all that surprising. The child's here most of the time whenever she's meant to be staying with Mrs. Tolliver. Just as easy to make up a bed and be done with it."

Phoebe looked relieved. "You are good, Lily. And I hope it won't be too much extra work. I know you've got enough to do as it is just now, but once my arm's out of this dratted cast . . ."

"Don't you worry, Miss Shackleton, we'll manage lovely. Any road, she's no trouble. Quiet little soul. Doesn't even eat much." She moved her eyes once more from Phoebe's face to mine. She frowned. "There's nothing *wrong,* is there?"

There was a small pause. Then Phoebe said, "No. Not really. But Mrs. Tolliver finds it . . . awkward having Charlotte living at White Lodge. I don't think they find it too easy to get on together, and we all decided it might be better if she came here for a bit."

"Well, certainly more fun for her," Lily pointed out. "Betty Curnow's a nice enough person, but she was never much of a one for fun. Miss La-di-dah we used to call her when we were all at school together, and marrying up with a sanitary inspector didn't make her any more free and easy."

"Yes. Well, maybe Joshua Curnow isn't the jolliest of men, but I'm sure he's made Betty a marvellous husband," said Phoebe soothingly before bringing Lily back to the matter at hand. "Where do you think Charlotte should sleep?"

"We'll put her in Mr. Armitage's old dressing room. The bed's made up; just needs a bit of an airing."

"And the picnic, don't forget. They're all going on a picnic."

"That's right. Ham sandwiches I've made, and a little salad in a plastic box. And there's chocolate cake with orange icing . . ."

"How delicious. I wish I were going . . . my favourite . . . what a lovely picnic . . ." And Phoebe took herself off upstairs to divest herself of her poncho and change her shoes. We heard her footsteps cross the floorboards above us.

I said, "You are a tower of strength, Lily. That's what Phoebe always says about you."

"Get away," said Lily, pleased.

"I can help you. Give me something to do to help you."

"You can string beans for dinner tonight. One thing I can't abide is stringing beans. Give me a carrot to peel or a turnip and I'm happy as a sandboy. But fiddley old beans I can't abide . . ."

So I was in the garden, in the sunshine, in one of Phoebe's rickety old garden chairs, stringing beans, when Charlotte finally arrived. I heard the sound of a car and laid down the knife and the basket and went through to the front of the house, only to find both Phoebe and Lily there before me. Betty Curnow had brought Charlotte, driving Mrs. Tolliver's car. Charlotte was already out of it, and Lily had opened the boot and was lifting out her suitcase. Charlotte wore her grey flannel coat, with her red handbag slung across one shoulder. Her travelling clothes. I wondered how she had felt, putting them on; dressing herself for another journey, another house; shunted from pillar to post because nobody wanted her, nobody could be bothered to take care of her.

"Hello, Charlotte."

She turned and saw me. "Hello." She was very pale, unsmiling. Her spectacles were crooked. Her hair looked greasy, as though in need of a good wash, and somebody —perhaps Charlotte herself—had parted it carelessly and pinned back the front lock with a blue plastic slide.

"This is fun. Do you want to come upstairs and look at your bedroom?"

"All right."

Lily and Phoebe were engaged in conversation with Betty Curnow, so I took the suitcase, and we started together towards the front door. But then Charlotte remembered her manners and stopped.

"Thank you very much, Mrs. Curnow, for bringing me."

"That's all right, love," said Betty Curnow. "See and be a good girl, now."

We went upstairs. The little room that had been Chips's dressing room was next to mine. Lily had been through it like a dose of salts, and it smelt strongly of polish and clean, starched linen. Phoebe had found time to pick flowers for the dressing table, and the open window framed the same view that I enjoyed, of the garden and the escallonia hedge and the flood tide of the estuary beyond.

The room was so small and delightful, so exactly the

right size and shape for a little girl, that I expected a spark of enthusiasm. But Charlotte seemed unseeing; her expression showed nothing.

I set down her suitcase. "Do you want to unpack now, or later?"

"If I could just get Teddy out."

Teddy, flattened, was on the top of the suitcase. She lifted him out and set him on her pillow.

"What about everything else?"

"It doesn't matter. I'll do it later."

"Well . . . if you'd like to take off your coat, you can come down to the garden and help me. I'm stringing beans for Lily Tonkins and I could do with a bit of help."

She took off her red shoulder bag and laid it on her dressing table, then unbuttoned her grey flannel coat. I found a hanger and put it away in the wardrobe. Under the coat she wore a blue T-shirt and a faded cotton skirt.

"Do you need a sweater?"

"No. I'm all right."

We made our way downstairs again. In the chest in the hall I found an old car rug, in the kitchen took a second knife from the drawer. We went back out into the garden. I spread the rug and we sat on it together, with the basket of beans and Lily's largest saucepan between us.

"The knives are very sharp. You'll be careful not to cut yourself?"

"I've strung beans heaps of times."

Pause.

"Isn't it a lovely day? You haven't forgotten about our picnic, have you?"

"No."

"Daniel's definitely coming. He'll be here any moment now. He said he'd try and get a lift over from Porthkerris."

Pause.

"I wanted Phoebe to come with us to Penjizal, but she said that she was frightened that the wind would blow her over the edge of the cliff. Did you remember to bring the Coca-Cola?"

"Yes. Mrs. Curnow said she'd give it to Lily."

"Lily's made us ham sandwiches, just the kind you wanted. And a chocolate cake . . ."

Charlotte looked at me. "You don't have to cheer me up, you know."

I felt, and with some reason, extremely foolish.

I said, "I'm sorry."

She went back clumsily to slicing her bean.

"Charlotte . . . didn't you want to come and stay with Phoebe?"

"I've never stayed before."

"I . . . I don't know what you're trying to say."

"Something's happened. And nobody wants to tell me."

I was apprehensive. "What makes you say that?"

She did not reply, but a movement behind me caught her eye and she looked up, over my shoulder. I turned and saw Phoebe emerging through the garden door. She still wore her hat but had abandoned the gaudy poncho, and now her knotted scarf fluttered in the breeze like a little flag, and the sunlight winked back at us from the gold chains slung about her neck. She lugged, in her good arm, a deck chair, and I got up and went to take it from her and set it up by the rug where we sat. She sank into it, her knees jutting beneath the folk weave of her skirt.

There seemed no point in prevaricating. I caught and held her eye. "Charlotte and I were just talking." Phoebe's gaze was calm and untroubled. I knew that she understood. I settled down on the rung once more and picked up my knife. "She's wondering why she's here."

"Mostly," Phoebe told her, "because we want you."

"Mummy's not coming back from Majorca, is she?"

"Why do you say that?"

"She isn't coming, is she?"

"No," said Phoebe.

I selected a bean and began, very neatly, to string and slice it.

"I knew," said Charlotte.

"Would you like to tell us how you knew?"

"Because she had this friend. He was called Desmond. He used to come and see her. He had a riding school quite near our house in Sunningdale. They used to go riding together, and then he'd come back and have a drink or something. He was called Desmond. She went to Majorca with him."

"How do you know that?"

"Because there was one night at the end of the holidays. Before I went back to school and the boiler blew up. Daddy was in Brussels on business. And I had to get up in the middle of the night to go to the bathroom, and then I was thirsty, and I thought I'd go downstairs and get some Coke out of the fridge. I'm not meant to, but I do sometimes. And then when I was halfway down the stairs I heard voices. I heard a man talking and I thought perhaps it was a burglar. I thought perhaps it was a burglar and he was going to shoot Mummy. But then he said something and I knew it was Desmond. So I sat on the stairs and listened. And they were talking about Majorca. She told Daddy she was going on holiday with an old school friend. I heard her telling him at breakfast one morning, but I knew she was going with Desmond."

"Did you say anything?"

"No. Daddy never listens to me anyway, and I was frightened."

"Frightened of your father?"

"No. Just frightened. Frightened of her going and never coming back."

"Did you know that your father rang your grandmother last night?"

"I wasn't asleep. I heard the phone ringing. Granny's drawing room is under my bedroom. You can hear people talking, but you can't hear what they say. But I did hear her say his name. He's called Leslie. And I knew it was him. And I thought perhaps he'd just rung up to see how I was. But this morning everything felt so horrible, I knew it hadn't just been that. And Granny was all funny and cross, and then she sent me and Betty Curnow up to the village to buy Coke. So I knew something was wrong, because I'm always allowed to go to the village by myself."

"I think your grandmother didn't want you to overhear. To be distressed."

"And then when we got back again, Mrs. Curnow and me, Granny said I was coming to stay with you."

"I hope you were pleased."

All the time that she had been speaking, Charlotte had sat with downcast eyes, fiddling with a runner bean that she had slowly and deliberately torn to shreds. Now she looked up at Phoebe, her eyes anxious behind the lenses of her unbecoming spectacles. She was being very brave. "She isn't ever coming back, is she?"

"No. She's going to go and live in South Africa."

"What will happen to us? To Michael and me? Daddy can't look after us. At least, he wouldn't mind looking after Michael. They're always doing things together, like going shooting and watching rugger matches and things like that. But he wouldn't want to look after me."

"Maybe not," said Phoebe. "But I would. That's why I asked your grandmother if I could have you to stay with me."

"But not *forever?*"

"Nothing is ever forever."

"Won't I ever see Daddy and Michael again?"

"Yes, of course you will. After all, Michael is your brother."

Charlotte screwed up her nose. "He's not always very kind. I don't like him that much."

"Even so, he is your brother. Perhaps, next holidays, he'd like to come and stay with me as well. But I expect your grandmother might like to have him."

"She didn't want me," Charlotte pointed out.

"You mustn't think that. She just doesn't find it very easy to have a person of your age around the place. It's called not being good with children. Lots of the nicest people are like that."

"You're good with children," Charlotte told her.

"That's because I like them." Phoebe smiled. "Particularly you. That's why, for the time being at any rate, I want you to stay here."

"What about my school?" Charlotte was still being very wary. "I have to go back to school at the end of the week."

"I had a word with your grandmother about that. Do you like your boarding school?"

"No, I hate it. I hate having to be away all the time. And I'm much the youngest; there's nobody younger than me, not boarding. There are day girls, but they're all friends and they do things together at the weekend, and they don't want me. I wanted to be a day girl, too, but Mummy said it was much better to be a boarder. I don't know why it should be better. I thought it was horribler."

"Then you wouldn't mind too much if you didn't go back?"

Cautiously, Charlotte considered this. For the first time a gleam of something hopeful crossed her face. "Why? Don't I have to?"

"No, I don't think you do. If you're going to live with me, then it would be much easier for all of us if you went to our local school. Nobody's a boarder there, and I think you'd enjoy it."

"I'm not very good at lessons."

"People can't be good at everything. You're good at drawing and making things. And if you like music, they have a very good music master, and they have a proper orchestra and give concerts. I know one boy, he's only your age, and he plays the clarinet."

"Could I go there?"

"If you wanted, I think it could be arranged."

"I do want it."

"Then you'll stay with me?"

"You mean . . . never go back to Daddy?"

"Yes," said Phoebe gently. "Perhaps that is what I mean."

"But . . . you just said . . . you said nothing is ever forever." Her eyes were filling with tears, and it was almost too painful to watch. "I can't stay with you . . ."

"Yes you can. For as long as you like. So you see, although the worst has happened, the world hasn't come to an end. You can talk about things, to Prue and to me. You haven't got to keep everything to yourself any longer. Don't go on trying to be brave. It doesn't matter about crying . . ."

It was a dam burst of tears, uncontrollable. Charlotte's mouth went square in the manner of all weeping children, but the sobs that racked her small frame sounded more like the suffering grief of an adult.

"Oh, Charlotte . . ."

Phoebe leaned forward in her chair, her arms—the good arm, and the stiff one in its plaster cast—outflung, an open invitation to comfort and love. At any other time the effect of this typically expansive gesture might have been comic, but it wasn't funny now. ". . . come away, my darling."

And Charlotte scrambled to her feet and flung herself

into the lopsided embrace, winding her arms tightly around Phoebe's neck, burying her face in Phoebe's shoulder, knocking Phoebe's hat askew.

I picked up the beans and the saucepan and went indoors. Because it was their own private moment. Because she was Daniel's child. And because I thought I might be going to cry as well.

The kitchen was empty. Through the open back door I could see Lily out on the drying green, pegging out a line of snowy tea towels. Now she was onto another hymn.

> Do no sinful action
> Speak no angry wer-erd.

I put the beans and the saucepan down on the end of the scrubbed pine table and went upstairs to my bedroom. I had made my bed this morning, but since then Lily had been what she called through the room, which meant a strong smell of floor polish and everything on my dressing table arranged in a straight line. I sat on the edge of the bed and after a little realized that I wasn't going to cry after all. But I felt drained, disoriented, as though I had spent the last three hours in a dark cinema, absorbed in some deeply emotional film, and was now back in the street again, dazzled by the light, blundering my way along an unfamiliar pavement; incapable.

Mummy's not coming back from Majorca, is she? Daddy never listens to me anyway. He wouldn't want to look after me. I wanted to be a day girl, but Mummy said it was much better to be a boarder. My grandmother doesn't want me.

Oh, dear Lord, the things we do to our children.

The window was open, the curtains stirring in the warm breeze. I got off the bed and went to the window and leaned out of it, my elbows on the sill. Below me on the grass, Phoebe and Charlotte still sat. The tears seemed to be over, and now all that could be heard was the companionable murmur of their conversation. Charlotte was back on the rug again, cross-legged, absorbed in making a daisy chain. I looked down at her bowed head, the vulnerable back of her neck. I remembered being her age. My parents were divorced and I lived with my mother, but never was I unloved, unwanted, shunted off to boarding schools. I remembered travelling to Northumberland to stay with my father, willing the train to travel faster and faster as we rocketed north. I remembered being met by him at Newcastle Station and racing up the platform to be swept into his sturdy, tweed-smelling embrace.

I remembered my mother's little house in London, the bedroom she decorated for me exactly the way I wanted it. The clothes she bought me, which were the clothes that I was allowed to choose for myself. The fun of dancing classes in the winter, and Christmas parties; being taken to the pantomime at the Palladium and the *Sleeping Beauty* at Covent Garden.

I remembered shopping in Harrod's, the tedium of buying school clothes rewarded by the treat of a chocolate milk shake at the soda fountain. And summer outings down the Thames, by boat, with a party of small friends and all the shivery anticipation of a visit to the Tower of London.

And always Cornwall, and Penmarron. And Phoebe. *Oh, my darling, how lovely to see you again.*

Phoebe. I was suddenly filled with nameless apprehensions for her. What had she taken on, so impulsively, so lovingly? She was sixty-three and had already fallen from a worm-ridden chair and broken her arm. Supposing she had not simply broken her arm, but her hip, or her neck? Supposing she had struck her head and lain there, on the studio floor, concussed, with nobody knowing or coming to look for her? My imagination turned and fled but immediately came up with alternative and even more horrendous fabrications.

I thought of Phoebe driving her old car. She had never done this with much concentration, since she was always being diverted by the goings-on in the roads and streets down which she trundled, quite often on the wrong side of the white line, believing that provided she continued to blow the horn, nothing too dreadful could happen.

Supposing she had a heart attack and died? It happened to other people; why should it not happen to Phoebe? Supposing one summer day she went swimming from the old seawall, as she liked to do. Supposing she dived, wearing her old-fashioned bathing suit and her plastic bath hat, and never came up again? There seemed no end to the possible fatalities, and if anything happened to Phoebe, then who would take care of Charlotte? Once more my mind scurried ahead, searching for a solution to this hypothetical problem.

Who would have her? Myself? In a basement flat in Islington? My mother? Or perhaps my father? He was the sort of man who would take in any lame dog. I tried to picture Charlotte at Windyedge, but somehow nothing quite fit. My young stepmother would welcome any child who would ride her horses, muck out stables, clean tack, and go hunting, but she would have little in common with a small girl who only wanted to play the clarinet and draw.

These gloomy thoughts might have gone on forever, but at that moment I was brought back to reality by the sound of the morning train from Porthkerris, rattling through the cutting behind the house. It appeared busily around the curve of the single line to draw up at the halt, looking like a toy train, the kind that is wound up with a key. For a moment it stood there, and then somebody blew a whistle and waved a green flag, and it moved on, pulling away from the station and leaving behind it on the empty platform a single, lonely figure.

Daniel. Come for the picnic.

As soon as it was clear, he jumped down onto the line, crossed it, climbed a fence, and started down the track, past the small anchorage where the sailing boats bobbed at high tide and so onto the old seawall. He wore blue jeans, a navy blue sweater, a white canvas smock.

I watched his approach, ambling long-legged, his hands in his pockets, and longed for him to be the sort of person to whom I could run with all my problems, just as I used to run into the arms of my father on Newcastle

Station. I wanted to be embraced, reassured, loved. I wanted to gabble out to him everything that had occurred on that endless morning, and to be told that nothing mattered, I was never to worry again, he would deal with everything . . .

But Phoebe, who loved Daniel, was wiser than I.

Face him with day-to-day decisions and responsibilities and I could never truly predict how he would react.

I didn't want him to be that sort of person. I wanted him to take charge. To have taken charge. I watched him coming and knew that if what was happening to us all were a story I was making up, then this moment would be the beginning of the end. He would have everything solved, decisions taken and plans formed. I devised a film, slow motion, soft focus: Daniel coming through the gate in the escallonia hedge to run in floating strides up the slope of the lawn. To embrace Phoebe, scoop his child up into his arms, call me down from my open window in order to plan our future together. Violins would soar. "The End" would appear upon the screen. Credits would roll and we would all live happily ever after.

Don't create fantasies about Daniel. They will probably never come true. Instead, reality. Phoebe would take him aside, relate to him bluntly what had happened. No more secrets, Daniel. Annabelle has taken off and nobody else wants Charlotte. Nobody else wants your daughter.

And he? What would he do? I did not want to think about it. I did not want to know what was going to happen next.

He had moved out of sight, hidden from my view by

the slope of the bank and the height of the hedge. I closed my window and turned back to my room. In the mirror over my dressing table I caught sight of my reflection, and my appearance was so appalling that I spent the next five minutes doing things to improve it. Washed my face with a scalding-hot flannel, scrubbed my nails with Phoebe's lavender-scented soap, brushed and combed my hair. I took a fresh cotton shirt from a drawer, changed my shoes, applied mascara, sprayed scent.

"Prue!" Charlotte's voice.

"I'm here. In my bedroom."

"Can I come in?" The door opened, and her face appeared around the edge of it. "Daniel's here."

"I saw him get off the train."

"But Phoebe's taken him down to the studio. She says she wants to show him something that belonged to Chips. She says they'll be about ten minutes. What a lovely smell!"

"It's Dior. I always use it. Want a squirt?"

"Don't you mind?"

"Don't take it all."

She sprayed on some scent, breathing in the perfume with an ecstatic expression on her face. I picked up my comb and tidied her hair for her, straightening the parting and refastening the plastic slide.

When this was done, I said, "Perhaps we should go down to the kitchen and start packing our picnic basket. And it might be a good idea if you found your Wellingtons and an anorak."

"But it won't rain today."

"This is Cornwall . . . you never know what it's going to do."

So we were in the kitchen when Phoebe eventually came to find us. I saw her through the window, walking slowly up the brick path that led from the walled garden and the studio. She came towards us like an old person. She was alone. She came through the garden door and saw us standing, waiting for her. She told us that Daniel had gone. He would not, after all, be able to come with us on the picnic. He was sorry.

"But he promised . . ." Charlotte kept saying, near to tears. "He *said* he'd come . . ."

Phoebe would not meet my eyes.

So we never got to go to Penjizal. Somehow, by then, none of us had the heart to go anywhere. We ate the picnic right there, in the garden of Holly Cottage. We never saw the seals.

It was evening before I got Phoebe to myself. Charlotte was engrossed in television, and I cornered my aunt by the sink.

"Why did he go?"

"I warned you," said Phoebe.

"Where did he go?"

"I've no idea. Back to Porthkerris, I suppose."

I said, "I'm going to take the car. I'm going to go and see him."

"Don't do that."

"Why not? You can't stop me."

"Ring him first, if you must. Talk to him. Make sure that he wants to see you."

I went straight to the telephone. Of course he would want to see me. I dialled the number of the Castle Hotel, and when the girl on the switchboard answered, I asked for Daniel Cassens. But she put me through to the Reception desk, and a girl's voice told me that Mr. Cassens had gone, checked out, and left no forwarding address.

Chapter Seven

I washed Charlotte's hair and trimmed the ragged ends with Phoebe's sewing scissors. Clean, it was the colour of chestnuts shot through with unexpected copper lights.

Phoebe telephoned the headmaster of the local school and took Charlotte for an interview. She returned home full of excitement. She would have a new uniform, navy-blue and white. They had a pottery wheel in the art room. She was going to learn how to play the clarinet.

We watched, on television, a pretty girl showing us how to make a dolls' house out of cardboard boxes. We took the car into Porthkerris, and went to visit the wine merchant and were given four sturdy crates that had once held bottles of Scotch whisky. We bought a Stanley knife, and little pots of paint and some brushes. We bought tubes of glue. We came home and began to measure and mark out the door, the windows. The kitchen was littered with sheets of newspaper, scraps of card, all the tools of our trade.

Now there was a new moon in the night sky. It hung in the east, a silvery eyelash, and its pale reflection hung in the black waters of the estuary, drowned in trembling slivers of light.

"Prue."

"What is it?"

"Where has Daniel gone?"

"I don't know."

"Why did he go?"

"I don't know that, either."

"Is he ever coming back?"

"I expect he will. One day."

"People always go away. People I like. When Michael first went to school, the house was funny without him. All quiet and empty. And I had a nanny once, when I was very little, about six. I really liked her. But she had to leave and go and look after her mother. And now Daniel's gone."

"You scarcely know Daniel."

"But I've always known about him. Phoebe used to tell me about him. She used to show me bits in the newspaper about him, when he was having exhibitions and things in America. And she used to tell me about him."

"But, still, you scarcely knew him. You only met him for a day or so."

"I didn't want him to go away. It wasn't just the picnic. It wasn't just not seeing the seals. We can do that any time."

"Then what was it?"

"I wanted to tell him things, show him things. I wanted to show him the dolls' house. I wanted to *ask* him things. Daddy never has time to answer properly if you ask him things. And Daniel doesn't talk to you as though you're little, he talks as though you are a grown up person. He'd never tell you that you were being a nuisance or that you were stupid."

"Well . . . perhaps you have a lot in common. You're interested in the same sort of things. Perhaps that's why you feel so close to him."

"I wish he would come back."

"He's a busy man. An important man. And now he's a famous man. He has so many things that he has to do. And an artist is . . . different from other men. He needs to be free. It's hard for someone like Daniel to put down roots, to stay in the same place all the time, and be with the same people."

"Phoebe's an artist, and she stays in the same place."

"Phoebe is different. Phoebe is special."

"I know. That's why I love her. But I love Daniel too."

"You mustn't love him too much, Charlotte."

"Why not?"

"Because it's no good loving a person too much, if you

may never see them again . . . oh, don't start to cry.
Please don't cry. It's just that it's true, and it's no good
either of us pretending that it isn't."

We painted the door red, the frames of the windows
black. Lily found an old dress box, and we cut the roof
from the lid of this and scored a central line and bent it
into a gable. We painted tiles.

One day it rained, and there was a great wind, and
Charlotte and I walked over the golf links and down to
the beach. There was sand blowing everywhere, and the
breakers poured into the shore from half a mile out or
more. The rushes on the dunes were flattened by this
wind, and the sea gulls abandoned the coast and flew
inland to float and scream over fields of newly turned
plough.

No letter came for Charlotte, no postcard from South
Africa. We learned, through Betty Curnow and Lily Tonkins, that Mrs. Tolliver had gone to spend a few days with
a friend at Helford. Which made three people who had
run away.

We constructed furniture for the doll's house out of
empty matchboxes; we painted wallpaper. We raided
Phoebe's rag bag and made carpets from scraps of tweed
with fringed ends. Just like real, said Charlotte when we

laid them, and she closed the door of the dolls' house and put her face to the window, loving the smallness of everything, the little, safe, miniature world.

One night, "I can't bear to see you looking so un-happy," Phoebe told me, but I pretended that I had not heard her, because I did not want to talk about Daniel.

He was gone. Back to his nomadic, searching, restless life. Back to his painting, his exhibition, Peter Chastal. Perhaps, by now, back to America. Much later, when he felt able, maybe he would send me a postcard. I saw it, dropping through the letter box of my front door in Islington. A brightly coloured picture of the Statue of Liberty, perhaps, or the Golden Gate bridge, or Fujiyama.

Having a wonderful time, wish you were here. Daniel.

There was a future. My future. My job, my flat, my own friends. I would go back to London and pick up the threads again. But on my own, as I had never been alone before.

I had the dream again, the swimming dream. It was the same as before. The water first shallow, and then deep and warm. The racing current. The sensation of being swept along by this flood, not struggling but acquiescent. Not dying, I reminded myself at the end of the dream. Not dying, but loving. So why did I wake with tears wet on my cheeks?

The passing days had lost their names, just as I had lost all sense of their passing. Then suddenly it was a

Tuesday and time to be practical. Phoebe had decided the previous evening that I should drive her and Charlotte into Penzance, where we would buy the new navy-and-white school uniform. Perhaps, as a treat, we would have lunch in a restaurant or go down to the harbour and see if the Scilly Islands steamer was in.

But these plans did not come off, because early that morning Lily Tonkins rang to say that Ernest, her husband, had been taken poorly. Phoebe answered the telephone call, and Charlotte and I stood around and listened to the quaking voice over the line.

"Up all night," Lily told Phoebe.

Phoebe said, "Oh, dear."

Lily enlarged on the details. Phoebe's face took on an expression of horror. "Oh, *dear*." After this she hastily agreed that on no account was Lily to abandon her ailing husband until the doctor had seen him. She rang off. Lily was not coming to work today.

We hastily changed our arrangements. I would stay at Holly Cottage to do a bit of sketchy housework and cook the lunch, and Mr. Thomas, in his trusty taxi, would be asked to make the trip into Penzance with Phoebe and Charlotte.

Charlotte was slightly indignant about this.

"I thought we were going to have lunch in a restaurant."

"It wouldn't be any fun without Prue," Phoebe told her briskly. "We'll do it another day, when I have to go and see the bank manager or have my hair done."

A telephone call was duly made, and Mr. Thomas turned up in ten minutes with his chauffeur's hat on his head and the wheels of his car encrusted in pig manure. Phoebe and Charlotte clambered in, and I waved them away and then returned indoors to deal with the morning chores.

They were not very arduous. Lily cleaned the house so thoroughly every day that once I had made the beds, scoured the bath, and cleared the ashes out of the sitting room grate, everything looked more or less as usual. I went into the kitchen, made a cup of coffee and started to peel potatoes. It was a grey, still day, with rain in the air. When I had finished the potatoes, I pulled on a pair of rubber boots and went down to the vegetable garden to cut a cauliflower. As I returned to the house, I heard the sound of a car coming down the road towards the house. I looked at my watch and saw that it was only an hour since Phoebe and Charlotte had set off. There was no way that the shopping expedition could be over so soon.

The car came over the railway bridge, and I knew then that it was heading for Holly Cottage, for we were the last house on the road, and at the end of it lay only the dead end, the padlocked iron gates of the old shipyard.

I hurried back inside. In the kitchen I laid my knife and the cauliflower on the draining board, and then, still wearing Lily's apron and my boots, went through the hall and out the front door.

There, on the gravel, was parked an unfamiliar car. An Alfa-Romeo, long and sleek, dark green and travel-stained. The driver's door was already open, and behind the wheel, his eyes on my face, sat Daniel.

On that still, misty morning, there was little sound.

Then, from far away, I heard the scream of some gulls flying low over the empty sands of the estuary. Slowly, he climbed out of the car and straightened himself cautiously, arching his back, and putting up a hand to massage the back of his neck. He was wearing his usual strange assembly of clothes, and there lay the dark shadow of stubble on his chin. He shut the car door behind him, and it closed with a solid expensive-sounding thud. He said my name.

That proved it was true. He wasn't in London. He wasn't in New York. He wasn't in San Francisco. He was here. Back. Home.

I said, "What are you doing?"

"What do you think I'm doing?"

"Who's car is that?"

"Mine." He began to walk stiffly towards me.

"But you hate cars."

"I know, but it's still mine. I bought it yesterday." He reached my side and put his hands on my shoulders and stooped and kissed my cheek, and his chin felt rough and scratchy against my skin. I looked up at him. His face was colourless, grey with tiredness, but his eyes were bright with secret laughter.

"You're wearing Lily's apron."

"Lily's not here. Ernest's ill. You haven't shaved."

"Didn't have time. I left London at three o'clock this morning. Where's Phoebe?"

"She and Charlotte have gone to do some shopping."

"Aren't you going to ask me in?"

"Yes . . . yes, of course. I'm sorry. It's just that you were the last person I expected to see. Come along. I'll make you some coffee, or bacon and eggs if you want something to eat."

"Coffee would be fine."

We went back indoors. The house felt warm after the chilly dampness outside. I led the way through the hall and heard him close the front door behind us. In the kitchen I saw the cauliflower and the knife by the sink where I had left them, and for a moment, so disoriented was I, found myself wondering what I had intended doing with them.

I filled the electric kettle and plugged it in and switched it on. When I turned around, I saw that Daniel had pulled out a chair and was sitting at the head of the long scrubbed pine table. He had an elbow on the table and was rubbing his eyes with his hand, as though it were possible to erase exhaustion.

He said, "I haven't driven so far or so fast in my life, I don't think." He took his hand away and looked up at me, and I had forgotten the darkness of his eyes, the pupils round and dark as black olives. He still looked exhausted, but there was something else about him, an exhilaration, perhaps, that I could not fathom, because I had not seen it in him before.

I said, "What made you buy a car?"

"I wanted to get back to you all, and it seemed the quickest way."

"Have you found out how the heater works?"

It wasn't much of a joke, but it helped break the tension.

He smiled. "Not yet. Like I told you, I've only had it for a day." He crossed his arms on the tabletop. He said,

"Phoebe told me, you know. About Annabelle and Leslie Collis and Mrs. Tolliver."

"Yes. I know."

"And Charlotte."

"Yes."

"Was Charlotte disappointed about the picnic?"

"Yes."

"I couldn't stay, Prue. I had to get away. By myself. Do you understand?"

"Where did you go?"

"I went back to Porthkerris. I walked back, over the dunes and along the cliffs. When I got back to the Castle Hotel, I packed my suitcase without any clear idea of what I was going to do next. But then, when it was packed, I picked up the telephone and rang Lewis Falcon. I'd been meaning to get in touch with him ever since I got down here, but somehow with one thing and another I'd never got around to it. He was great. I told him who I was and said that we'd never met. And he said that he knew who I was, because he'd heard about me through Peter Chastal, and why didn't I come out to Lanyon to see him? So I said I'd do that, but what I needed was a bed for a couple of nights, and he said that would be okay too. So I checked out and got a taxi to drive me to Lanyon.

"He's a marvellous man. Immensely likeable, totally uncurious. With him, I found I could switch off; as though I were pulling down a great fireproof safety curtain between myself and everything that Phoebe had told me. The psychoanalyst's seventh veil, perhaps. He showed me his studio, and we looked at his work, and we talked shop as though nothing else existed for either of us.

"That was all right for a couple of days, and then I knew that I had to get back to London. So he drove me to the station and I caught the morning train.

"When I got to London I went to the gallery to see Peter. I was still in this extraordinary state of mind . . . it was like being insulated from reality. The curtain was still down, and I knew that Annabelle and Charlotte were behind it, but for the time being they had simply ceased to exist, and all I could do was carry on with my ordinary life as though nothing had happened. I didn't say anything about them to Peter. The exhibition is still on, the gallery still full of visitors. We sat in his office and ate sandwiches and had a glass of beer, and watched them through the glass of the door as though they were goldfish in a tank. Those were my pictures they were looking at, but I couldn't relate myself either to the pictures or to them. Nothing seemed to have anything to do with me.

"Then I left Peter and I went out and started walking. It was a beautiful afternoon. I walked for miles along the embankment, and eventually I realized that I'd reached Millbank and I was standing outside the Tate Gallery. Do you know the Tate?"

"Yes."

"Do you go there?"

"Often."

"Do you know the Chantrey collection?"

"No."

"I went up the steps and into the gallery. I made for

the room where the Chantrey collection is hung. There's a picture in it by John Singer Sargent. It's an oil. Quite big. Two little girls in a garden at night, lighting Japanese lanterns. They're wearing white dresses with frilled collars. There are lilies growing and pink roses. It's called *Carnation Lily, Lily Rose.* One of the little girls has short, dark hair and a very thin, delicate white neck, like the stem of a flower. She could be Charlotte.

"I don't know how long I stood there. But after a bit, very slowly, I realized that that safety curtain was going up, and little by little I was being flooded with—extraordinary instincts I'd never known I possessed. Tenderness. Protectiveness. Pride. And then anger. I began to be angry. Angry with all of them. Annabelle, and her husband and her mother. But most of all angry with myself. What the bloody hell was I doing, I asked myself, when she was my child, and I was her father, goddamn it. What the bloody hell was I doing, unloading all my responsibilities onto Phoebe? The answer was painfully simple. I was standing there doing nothing, which was what I had been doing for the past three days. Running on the spot, we used to call it at school. Getting nowhere. Achieving absolutely bugger all.

"I left the picture, and I went downstairs and found a telephone. I rang Directory enquiries and got Mrs. Tolliver's telephone number. And then I rang White Lodge. Mrs. Tolliver wasn't there . . ."

"She's visiting a friend in Helford," I told Daniel. I might just as well not have spoken.

". . . but her housekeeper answered the telephone and I told her that I was a friend of Leslie Collis and I wanted to get in touch with him, and she was able to give me the name of the firm where he works in the City."

The kettle was boiling, but we both seemed to have forgotten about coffee. I switched it off and then went to pull out a chair and to sit at the other end of the table, so that Daniel and I faced each other down its long scrubbed length.

"So, another phone call. I rang Leslie Collis. I said I wanted to see him. He began by saying that it wasn't convenient, but I insisted it was urgent, so he finally said that he could give me fifteen minutes or so if I could come right away.

"I went out of the Tate and got a taxi and went to his office. The City was looking very beautiful. I'd forgotten how beautiful it is, with all those ponderous buildings and narrow streets, and everywhere sudden unexpected glimpses of St. Paul's. One day I must go back and do some drawings . . ."

The words died. He had lost the thread of what he was telling me.

"Leslie Collis," I reminded him gently.

"Yes, of course." He put up his hand and ran his fingers through his hair. He began to laugh. "It was the most ludicrous interview. In the first place, I was looking even more reprehensible than I usually do. Again, I don't think I'd shaved, and I was wearing the shirt I'd worn on the train, and a pair of sneakers with holes in the toes. He, on the other hand, was all resplendent in his City gear, starched collar, pinstripe suit. We made the most incongruous pair of antagonists. Anyway, I sat down and started to talk, and as soon as I mentioned

Mrs. Tolliver and Charlotte, he immediately decided I'd come to blackmail him, and he was on his feet, shouting me down, threatening to call the police. And then I started shouting, too, just to try and make myself heard, and for a moment or two there was total pandemonium with both of us accusing each other, claiming responsibility, disclaiming responsibility, blaming each other, blaming Annabelle.

"But finally, just as I'd decided he was going to keel over with a heart attack and leave me with a corpse on my hands as well as everything else, it got through to him that I wasn't a villain come to bleed him white. After that things got a bit better. We both sat down again, and he lit a cigarette, and we started all over."

"You didn't *like* him, did you?"

"Why? Didn't you?"

"When I saw him that morning on the train, I thought he was the most horrible man."

"He's not that bad."

"But saying he never wants Charlotte again . . ."

"I know. That's rotten. But, in a way, I see his point of view. He's an ambitious man. He's worked his butt off all his life to make a lot of money and achieve his ambitions. I think he probably genuinely adored Annabelle. But he must have known all along, from the very first, that she could never be faithful to him. Even so, he stuck to her, gave her everything she wanted, bought the house in Sunningdale so that the boy could be brought up in the country. She had a car of her own, a maid, a gardener, holidays in Spain, total freedom. He kept saying, 'I gave her everything. I gave that woman bloody everything.' "

"Did he know from the first that Charlotte wasn't his baby?"

"Yes, of course he knew. He hadn't seen Annabelle for three months, and then she came back from Cornwall and told him that she was pregnant. And that's a pretty good kick in the balls for any self-respecting man."

"Why didn't he end it then?"

"He wanted to keep the family together. He's devoted to his son. He didn't want to lose face with his friends."

"He never liked Charlotte, though."

"It's hard to blame him for that."

"Did he say he didn't like her?"

"More or less. He said she was sly. He said she told lies."

"If she did, it was his fault."

"That's what I told him."

"That must have gone down well."

"Oh, it was all right. By then we'd reached the stage when all the cards were on the table, and we could insult each other as much as we liked, with no offence given or taken. It was almost as though we'd made friends."

It was hard to imagine. "But what did you *talk* about?"

"We talked about everything. I told him that Charlotte was going to stay with Phoebe, and in the end he finally admitted that he was grateful. And he was also quite pleased to hear that she wasn't going back to that school. Annabelle had chosen it for the child, but in his opinion it had never been worth the massive fees he'd had to fork out each term. I asked about the boy Michael, but Collis seemed to think that he was no problem. He's fifteen and apparently mature, well able to look after himself, do his own thing. I think the general feeling was that he'd out-grown his mother and, considering the way she was car-rying on, would be better away from her influence. Leslie Collis is going to sell the house in the country and get a place in London. He and the boy will live there to-gether."

"I'm sorry for Michael."

"I'm sorry for him, too. I'm sorry for everybody in this unholy mess. But I believe he'll probably be all right. The father thinks the world of him, and they appear to be the best of friends."

"And what about Annabelle?"

"He's spoken to his lawyer, and divorce proceedings are already underway. Leslie Collis is not a man to let the grass grow under his feet."

I waited for him to go on, but he didn't, so I said, "Which leaves us back at square one. What's going to happen to Charlotte? Or didn't you talk about her?"

"Of course we talked about her. That was the whole object of the exercise."

"Leslie Collis knows you're her father?"

"Sure, that was the first thing I told him. And he does-n't want her back."

"What about Annabelle? How does she feel about Charlotte?"

"She doesn't want her either, and even if she did, I don't think Leslie Collis would let her have the child. Call it sour grapes if you will, but it's the best thing that could happen to Charlotte."

"Why?"

"Because, my darling Prue, if Leslie Collis doesn't

want Charlotte and neither does Annabelle, then the way is clear for me to adopt her as my own."

I sat still as stone, staring at him in incredulous disbelief.

"But they won't let you."

"Why not?"

"You're not married."

"The law has changed. Now a single person is allowed to adopt. It takes longer to get through the courts; there's obviously a bit more red tape to be cut, but it is eventually perfectly possible. Provided, of course, that Annabelle agrees to it, and I honestly don't see why she shouldn't."

"But you haven't got a house. You haven't got anywhere to live."

"Yes I have. Lewis Falcon is off to the south of France to work there for a couple of years, and he said he'd rent me his house at Lanyon and the studio if I wanted them. So I'll be around. I don't suppose I'd be able to have Charlotte to live with me until the adoption is through the courts, but I'm hoping that Phoebe might be able to continue as her official foster mother until then."

"It sounds . . . Oh, Daniel, it sounds too good to be true."

"I know. And as I said, the extraordinary thing was that by the end of all this, it was almost as though Leslie Collis and I had made friends. We seemed to understand each other. Finally we went out to lunch together, to a scruffy place where none of his colleagues would spy him with a down-and-out like me. And at the end of the meal, there was another ludicrous pantomime while we both tried to pick up the bill. Neither of us wanted to owe the other anything. So in the end we split it down the middle and each paid half. And then we went out of the restaurant, and we said good-bye, and I promised to be in touch. And he walked back to his office, and I got into a taxi and went back to the gallery to see Peter Chastal.

"I knew I had to get a good lawyer, and I've never even had a bad one, because Peter's always done everything for me. I've never even had an accountant, either, or a banker, or an agent. Peter's handled everything ever since that first day when I went to him, raw and inexperienced, sent by Chips. He was marvellous. He put me in touch with his own lawyer, and he went and found out how much money I had put away, which is about ten times more than I thought I had, and then he said it was about time I matched up to this new family-man image and got over my dread of anything mechanical and bought myself a car. So I went out and did. And then Peter and I had dinner together, and after that I knew I couldn't wait another moment to see you all, so I got into the car and drove back to Cornwall."

"And now Phoebe and Charlotte aren't even *here*." I couldn't bear it for him.

But he only said, "I'm glad they're not. Because the most important thing I've got to tell you concerns you. Actually, it's not so much telling you as asking you. I'm going to Greece. For a holiday. In about ten days' time. I've told you about the house on Spetsai, and I've already asked you to come with me, but now I'm asking you again. I've got two seats booked on a flight to Athens. If Lily and Phoebe can cope with Charlotte, will you come with me?" The sugar-cube house that I had told myself I would never see. The whitewashed terrace with the geraniums, and the boat with a sail like the wing of a gull. "Come with me, Prue."

My mind raced ahead. I would have to do things, arrange things, tell people. My mother. Marcus Bernstein. And, somehow I should have to write a letter to poor Nigel Gordon.

I said, "Yes."

Down the length of the table our eyes met and held. He suddenly smiled. He said, "How little we know each other. Was it you who said that, or I?"

"It was you."

"After two weeks in Greece we'll know each other so much better."

"Yes. I expect we will."

"And after that—after we get home—perhaps we could think about coming back to Lanyon together. We'd have to get married first, but we don't need to think about that just now. It's better that way. After all, we don't either of us want to commit ourselves, do we?"

I knew that there was nothing I wanted more. And from the way Daniel was looking at me, I had a pretty good idea that he felt the same way.

I smiled, too. "No," I told him. "We don't want to commit ourselves."

When Mr. Thomas's taxi returned bearing Phoebe and Charlotte and all their shopping, we were still in the kitchen, though no longer sitting at either end of the table. We heard the ancient vehicle come grinding down the road and turn in at the gate, and we went out together to greet them.

Mr. Thomas was flummoxed by Daniel's car, which, unexpectedly parked in front of the house, had left him no room to turn. Phoebe was already out of the taxi, dramatic in her best brown tweed cape, and trying to give him directions.

"Left hand down, Mr. Thomas. No, I don't mean left, I mean right . . ."

"Phoebe," said Daniel.

She turned and saw him.

"Daniel!"

Mr. Thomas and his problems were forgotten. Disgusted, he switched off his engine and sat there, brooding, trapped, the radiator of his car nose-to-nose with Daniel's, the back wheels hard against the red brick kerbstone that protected Phoebe's border.

Daniel moved to meet her halfway. They embraced enormously, and her hat was knocked sideways.

"You wicked villain." She thumped his shoulder lovingly with her good fist. "Where have you been?"

But she did not give him time to tell her, because just then, over his shoulder, she caught sight of me standing there in Lily's apron and with a smile on my face that I could do nothing about. She let go of Daniel and came to me, and although she had no idea of what had happened, what was happening, what was going to happen, I saw my own happiness reflected in her face, and we held each other very tightly and laughed together, because Daniel had come back, and everything was suddenly so completely all right.

And Charlotte. At the same instant we remembered Charlotte. We looked and saw her cautiously alighting from the back of the old car, her arms filled with a perilous pile of wrapped boxes and packages. I knew that she had watched us all, was holding back, probably telling herself that she, Charlotte, had no place in all these loving reunions. Carefully, with her foot, she closed the door of the taxi. When she turned, her chin clamped over the topmost parcel, she found herself confronted by Daniel. Slowly her face tilted up to stare into his, her eyes unblinking behind the owlish spectacles. For a moment there was silence as they looked at each other. And then Daniel smiled and said, "Hello, my love. I'm back again."

He held wide his arms. It was all she needed.

"Oh, Daniel . . ."

The parcels began to slip. She let them go and flung herself at him, and he caught her and swung her up in his arms, round and round, and the packages lay unheeded where they had tumbled, higgledy-piggledy onto the gravel.

Voices in Summer

For Mark
for reasons that will be obvious to him

CONTENTS

1 Hampstead   1
2 Deepbrook   16
3 Islington   53
4 Tremenheere   68
5 Landrock   99
6 Penjizal   117
7 Saint Thomas   144
8 Roskenwyn   191
9 Homes   210

1

HAMPSTEAD

The doctor's receptionist, a pretty girl in horn-rimmed spectacles, saw Laura to the door, opened it for her, and stood aside, smiling, as though the visit had been a social one that they had both enjoyed. Beyond the open door, scrubbed steps led down into Harley Street, sliced by the houses opposite into bright sunlight and dark shadow.

'It's a lovely afternoon,' the receptionist remarked, and indeed it was; the end of July now, and fine and bright. She wore a crisp skirt and blouse and nylon tights on her well-rounded legs, and businesslike black court shoes, but Laura wore a cotton dress and her legs were bare. There was, however, a freshness to the brisk breeze that swept the summer streets, and she had tied a pale cashmere cardigan, by its sleeves, around her shoulders.

Laura said yes, but couldn't think of anything else to say about the weather. She said thank you, although the receptionist hadn't done anything very much except announce her arrival for her appointment with Dr Hickley and then, fifteen minutes later, appear to take her away again.

'Not at all. Goodbye, Mrs Haverstock.'

'Goodbye.'

The shiny, black painted door closed behind her. Laura turned her back on the façade of the handsome, imposing house and walked a little way down the pavement of the terrace, where she had found, by some miracle, an empty parking meter and had been able to leave her car. She stooped to unlock the door, and there was a stir from the back seat, and as she got in behind the wheel, Lucy leaped lightly over the back of the seat into her lap, stood on her back legs with plumy tail waving full tilt, and gave Laura's face a quick and affectionate wash with her long pink tongue.

'Oh, poor little Lucy, you must be boiling.' She had left a bit of window open, but still the inside of the car was like an oven.

She reached up and opened the sun roof, and at once everything felt a bit better. Cool air circulated, and hot sunshine struck the top of her head.

Lucy panted obligingly for a moment or two, as proof of her own personal doggy discomfort, her forgiveness, and her love. Her love was all for Laura. Despite this, she was a polite little creature, with charming manners, and made a point of greeting Alec each evening when he came back from work. Alec always told people that when he married Laura he got a sort of job lot, like a man at an auction sale: a new wife, with a dog thrown in.

When she was desperate for a confidant, Laura told Lucy things, secrets that she could safely divulge to no other person. Not even Alec. Especially Alec, because the secret thoughts were usually about him. Sometimes she wondered about other married women. Did they have secret thoughts from their husbands? Marjorie Anstey, for instance, who had been married to George for sixteen years and organized his entire life, from clean socks to aeroplane tickets. And Daphne Boulderstone, who flirted outrageously with every man she met and was constantly being spied in discreet restaurants lunching intimately with some other woman's husband. Did Daphne take Tom into her confidence, laughing, perhaps, at her own foolishness? Or was Tom cool and detached – disinterested, even – as he usually appeared? Perhaps he simply didn't care. Perhaps next week when they were all in Scotland together, at Glenshandra, for the long-planned fishing holiday, Laura would have time to observe these marriages and come to some sort of a conclusion. . .

She took a deep breath, maddened by her own stupidity. What was the point of sitting here fabricating these random possibilities, when, now, she wasn't even going to Scotland. Dr Hickley had minced no words about this. 'Let's get it over as soon as possible, waste no time. A couple of days in hospital and then a good rest.'

What Laura had dreaded had happened. She put Daphne and Marjorie out of her head. Alec. She must concentrate on Alec. She must be dynamic and decisive, and work out a plan of action. Because whatever happened, Alec must go to Glenshandra with the others. Laura would have to be left behind. This, she knew, would take some persuasion. It was necessary to think up some convincing and foolproof plan, and nobody could do this but herself. Now.

Slumped in the seat behind the wheel of her car, Laura did not feel capable of being dynamic or decisive.

Her head ached, her back ached, her whole body ached. She thought about getting home, which was a tall, thin house in Islington, not very far, but far enough when you were tired and despondent on a hot afternoon in July. She thought about getting home and going upstairs and lying on her cool bed and sleeping away the remainder of the afternoon. Alec was a great believer in emptying one's mind and giving the subconscious a chance to solve apparently unsolvable problems. Perhaps Laura's subconscious would come up trumps and, beavering away while she slumbered, would present her, on waking, with some brilliant and obvious plan. She considered this and sighed again. She hadn't that much faith in her subconscious. To be truthful, she hadn't that much faith in herself.

'I've never seen you look so pale,' Dr Hickley had said, which was disturbing in itself, because Dr Hickley was a cool and professional lady and seldom moved to make such impulsive remarks. 'Better take a little blood test just to be sure.'

Did it really show so much?

Laura pulled down the sunshield and inspected herself in the mirror set in its back. After a bit, without much enthusiasm, she took a comb from her bag and tried to do something with her hair. And then a lipstick. The lipstick was too bright, the colour wrong for the pallor of her skin.

She looked into her own eyes, which were a very dark brown and fringed with long, bristly lashes. They gave the impression, she decided, of being too large for her face, like two holes cut in a sheet of paper. She met her gaze sternly. *Going home and going to sleep isn't going to solve anything. You know that, don't you?* There had to be somebody who could help, some person to talk to. At home there was nobody, because Mrs Abney, who lived in the basement, took firmly to her bed every afternoon between two and four. She objected strongly to disturbance, even if it was something important like the man come to read the meter.

Someone to talk to.

Phyllis.

Brilliant. *When I come out of hospital, I could stay with Phyllis. If I was with Phyllis, then Alec could go to Scotland.*

She could not think why this obvious scheme had not

occurred to her before. Delighted with herself, Laura began to smile, but at that moment a short toot on a car horn jerked her back to reality. A big blue Rover was drawn up alongside her car, the driver a red-faced man who made it clear that he wished to know whether she was about to vacate the parking space or if she intended sitting there, primping and preening in the mirror, for the rest of the day.

Embarrassed, Laura pushed the sunshield out of the way, started the engine, smiled more charmingly than was necessary, and, a little flustered, manoeuvred herself out into the street without actually hitting anything. She made her way out into the Euston Road, edged along as far as Eversholt Street, in the three-deep stream of traffic, and there turned north and headed up the hill, towards Hampstead.

At once she felt marginally better. She had had an idea and she was doing something about it. The traffic was thinner, the car picked up a little speed, air poured through the open roof. The road was friendly and familiar, because when she was young and living with Phyllis, she had travelled this way each day by bus – first to school, and then to college. Stopped at traffic lights, she remembered well the houses on either side, shabby and tree-shaded, some of them coming up in the world, with freshly painted faces and brightly coloured front doors. The sunny pavements were crowded with people in flimsy clothes: bare-armed girls and mothers with half-naked children. As well, small shops had put up awnings and spilled their wares out onto the pavement. She saw vegetables, piled artistically, a set of scrubbed pine chairs, and green buckets packed with roses and carnations. There were even a couple of tables set up outside a little restaurant with striped umbrellas and white iron chairs. *Like Paris,* thought Laura. *I wish we lived in Hampstead.* And then the car behind her blared its horn and she realized that the light had gone green.

It wasn't until she was actually driving up Hampstead High Street that the thought occurred to her that perhaps Phyllis wouldn't be in.

Laura should have stopped to telephone. She tried to imagine what Phyllis could be doing on a fine summer afternoon, but it wasn't difficult because the possibilities were endless. Shopping for clothes or antiques; prowling around her

4

favourite art galleries; sitting on a committee dedicated to bringing music to the masses; or raising money to preserve some crumbling Hampstead mansion.

It was too late now to do anything about it, however, because Laura was almost there. A moment later, she turned out of the main road and into a lane that narrowed, curving uphill, and then straightened, and she saw the terrace of Georgian houses that climbed with it, each just a step higher than its neighbour. Front doors stood flush with the cobbled pavement, and in front of Phyllis' house was parked her car, which was at least a hopeful sign, although it didn't necessarily mean that Phyllis was in, because she was an indefatigable walker and only took the car when she had to go 'down to London'.

Laura parked her own car behind it, closed the sun roof, gathered Lucy up, and got out. There were tubs of hydrangeas on either side of Phyllis' front door. Laura banged the knocker and crossed her fingers. *If she's not in, I shall simply go back down the hill, go home, and telephone her.* But almost at once came the sound of Phyllis' busy tapping footsteps (she always wore the highest of heels), and the next moment the door opened, and everything was all right.

'Darling.'

It was the best of welcomes. They embraced, Lucy getting in the way, and as always, hugging Phyllis felt like hugging a bird. A tiny-boned, bright-feathered bird. Today Phyllis was dressed in apricot pink, with cool, glassy beads at her neck and earrings that jangled like Christmas tree decorations. Her child-size hands were laden with rings, her face, as always, perfectly made up. Only her hair looked a little unruly, springing from her brow. It was greying now, but that detracted in no way from the youthful enthusiasm of her face.

'You should have called!'

'I've come on an impulse.'

'Oh, darling, that does sound exciting. Come along!'

Laura followed her indoors, and Phyllis shut the door behind her. But it was not dark, because the narrow hall stretched straight through the house to another door, which led out into the garden, and this stood open. Framed within the aperture, Laura could see the sunny, paved yard, hung about with glossy greenery, and at the far end the white trellis summerhouse.

She stooped and set Lucy down on the ruby-red carpet. Lucy

panted, and Laura dropped her handbag at the foot of the stair and went through to the kitchen to fill Lucy a bowl of water. Phyllis watched from the doorway.

'I was sitting in the garden,' she said, 'but it's almost too hot. Let's go into the sitting room. It's cool there and the French windows are open. Darling, you look terribly thin. Have you been losing weight?'

'I don't know. I suppose I might. I haven't been trying to.'

'Would you like a drink? I've just made some proper lemonade. It's in the fridge.'

'I'd love some.'

Phyllis went to collect glasses. 'You go and make yourself comfortable. Put your feet up, and we'll have a gorgeous chat. It's years since I saw you. How's that handsome Alec?'

'He's all right.'

'You'll have to tell me everything.'

It was heaven to be told to make yourself comfortable and put up your feet. Just like old times. Laura did as she was told, lying back in the corner of Phyllis' great downy sofa. Beyond the open glass doors, the garden stirred in the breeze with a faint rustling sound. There was the smell of wallflowers. It was very serene. Which was funny, really, because Phyllis wasn't a serene person. More like a little gnat, always on the go, her spindly legs carrying her up and down the stairs a hundred times a day.

She was her aunt, the younger sister of Laura's father. Their father was an impoverished Anglican clergyman, and many small economies and penny-pinching had been necessary to raise sufficient cash to send Laura's father to university to study medicine.

There was nothing left over for Phyllis.

Although the era, happily, was past when rectors' daughters were expected to stay meekly at home, helping Mother do the church flowers and run the Sunday School, the brightest prospect for Phyllis might well have been marriage to some solid and suitable man. But Phyllis, from an early age, had ideas of her own. Somehow, she got herself through a secretarial course and set off for London – not without a certain amount of parental opposition – where she found herself, in record time, not only a place to live, but also a job. Junior typist with Hay Macdonalds, an old-established firm of publishers. Before long

6

her enthusiasm and enterprise had been noted. She became secretary to the fiction editor, and then, at the age of twenty-four, was made personal assistant to the chairman, Maurice Hay.

He was a bachelor of fifty-three, and everybody thought that he would remain in this happy state for the rest of his life. But he didn't, because he fell head over heels in love with Phyllis, married her, and bore her off – not exactly on a white charger, but at least in a very large and impressive Bentley – to live in state in his little jewel of a house in Hampstead. She made him very happy, never wasting a day of their time together, which was just as well, because three years later he had a heart attack and died.

To Phyllis he left his house, his furniture, and all his money. He was not a mean nor a jealous man, and there were no nasty codicils attached to his will ruling that she should have to relinquish the lot should she remarry. But even so, Phyllis never did again. The fact that she didn't was a conundrum to all who knew her. It was not that there was a shortage of gentlemen admirers; in fact, the very opposite. A constant stream was almost at once in attendance, telephoning, sending flowers, taking her out for dinner, abroad for holidays, to the theatre in the winter, and to Ascot in the summer.

'But darlings,' she protested when taxed with her independent life-style, 'I don't want to marry again. I'd never find anyone as sweet as Maurice. Anyway, it's much more fun being single. Specially if you're single and rich.'

When Laura was small, Phyllis had been something of a legend, and no wonder. Sometimes, at Christmas, Laura's parents brought her up to London, to see the decorations in Regent Street, and the shops, and to go perhaps to the Palladium or the ballet. Then, they had always stayed with Phyllis, and to Laura, brought up in the busy, humdrum establishment of a country doctor, it was like being suddenly magicked into a dream. Everything was so pretty, so bright, so scented. And Phyllis . . .

'She's just a fly-by-night,' Laura's mother said goodnaturedly on the way home to Dorset, while Laura sat pole-axed in the back seat of the car, stunned by the memories of so much glamour. 'One can't imagine her ever getting to grips with life, doing anything practical . . . and indeed, why should she?'

7

But there Laura's mother was wrong. Because, when Laura was twelve, her parents were both killed, driving home from a harmless dinner party, down a road they had both known all their lives. The pile-up was the direct result of a number of unimagined circumstances: a T-junction, a long-distance lorry, a speeding car with inefficient brakes, all met together in a disaster of hideous finality. Almost, it seemed, before the dust of this horror had settled. Phyllis was there.

She didn't *tell* Laura anything. She didn't tell her to be brave, she didn't tell her not to cry, she didn't say anything about it being God's will. She simply hugged her and asked her very humbly if, just for a little, Laura would be absolutely sweet and come to Hampstead and live with her, just to keep her company.

Laura went, and stayed. Phyllis looked after everything: the funeral, the lawyers, the disposal of the practice, the selling of the furniture. One or two precious and personal things she kept for Laura, and these were installed in the bedroom that was to become Laura's own. A desk of her father's, her dollhouse, her books, and her mother's silver-backed dressing table set.

'Who do you live with, then?' girls at her new London school would ask when their blunt questions evinced the sad truth that Laura was an orphan.

'My aunt Phyllis.'

'Gosh, I wouldn't like to live with an aunt. Has she got a husband?'

'No, she's a widow.'

'Sounds fairly dreary.'

But Laura said nothing, because she knew that if she couldn't be living in Dorset with her own darling mother and father, she would want above everything else in the world to be with Phyllis.

Theirs was, by any standards, an extraordinary relationship. The quiet and studious young girl and her extroverted, gregarious aunt became the closest of friends, never quarrelling or getting on the other's nerves. It was not until Laura was finished with college and qualified to go out and earn her own living that she and Phyllis had their very first difference of opinion. Phyllis wanted Laura to go into Hay Macdonalds; to her it seemed the obvious and natural thing to do.

Laura jibbed at this scheme. She believed that if she did so, it

8

would be a form of nepotism, as well as undermining her determination to be independent.

Phyllis said that she would be independent. She'd be earning her living.

Laura pointed out that she already owed Phyllis enough. She wanted to start her career – whatever it was going to be – under an obligation to nobody.

But nobody was *talking* about obligations. Why turn down a wonderful opening, simply because she was Phyllis' niece?

Laura said that she wanted to stand on her own feet.

Phyllis sighed and explained patiently that she *would* be standing on her own feet. There was no question of nepotism. If she wasn't any good at her job and couldn't do the work, there would be no delicate compunctions about sacking her.

This was scarcely comforting. Laura muttered something about needing a challenge.

But Hay Macdonalds *was* a challenge. Laura might just as well take up this challenge as any other.

The argument continued, spasmodically, for three days, and Laura finally gave in. But at the same time, she broke the news to Phyllis that she had found herself a small, two-room flat in Fulham and that she was leaving Hampstead and going there to live. This decision had been made long ago; it had nothing to do with the argument about the job. It did not mean that she no longer *wanted* to live with Phyllis. She could have stayed forever in that warm and luxurious little house high on the hill above London, but she knew that it could not work. Their circumstances, subtly, had altered. They were no longer aunt and niece, but two adult women, and the unique relationship that they had achieved was too delicate and precious to risk putting into jeopardy.

Phyllis had a life of her own to lead – still full and exciting, despite the fact that she was now well into her fifties. And at nineteen, Laura had a life to *make*, and this could never be achieved unless she had the willpower to fly Phyllis' cosy nest.

After her initial dismay, Phyllis understood this. But, 'It won't be for long,' she prophesied. 'You'll get married.'

'Why should I get married?'

'Because you're the marrying kind. You're the sort of girl who needs a husband.'

'That's what people said to you after Maurice died.'

'You're not me, darling. I'll give you three years as a career girl. Not a moment longer.'

But Phyllis, for once, was wrong. Because it was nine years before Laura set eyes on Alec Haverstock, and another six – by which time Laura was thirty-five – before she married him.

'Here we are. . . .' The tinkle of ice against glass, the tap of high heels. Laura opened her eyes, saw Phyllis beside her, setting down the tray on a low coffee table. 'Were you asleep?'

'No. Just thinking. Remembering, I suppose.'

Phyllis lowered herself onto the other sofa. She did not lean back because to relax in any way was totally foreign to her character. She perched, looking as though at any moment she might spring to her feet and dart away on some vital errand.

'Tell me all. What have you been doing? Shopping, I hope.'

She poured a tall tumbler of lemonade and handed it to Laura. The glass was frosty with cold and agony to hold. Laura took a sip and then put the glass on the floor beside her.

'No, not shopping. I've been to see Doctor Hickley.' Phyllis cocked her head, her face at once assuming an expression of alert interest, her eyebrows raised, her eyes wide. 'No.' said Laura, 'I'm not having a baby.'

'Why did you go and see her, then?'

'Same old trouble.'

'Oh, *darling*.' There wasn't any need to say more. They gazed at each other dolefully. From the garden where she had been having a little necessary visit, Lucy appeared, through the open windows. Her claws made a scratching sound on the parquet as she crossed the floor and leaped lightly up into Laura's lap, where she curled herself into a comfortable ball and proceeded to go to sleep.

'When did this happen?'

'Oh, it's been going on for a bit, but I've been putting off going to see Doctor Hickley because I didn't want to think about it. You know, if you don't take any notice and don't look, perhaps it will go away.'

'That was very silly of you.'

'That's what she said. It didn't make any difference. I've got to go into the hospital again.'

'When?'

'As soon as possible. Maybe a couple of days.'

'But darling, you're going to Scotland.'

'Doctor Hickley says I can't go.'

'I can't *bear* it for you.' Phyllis' voice sank to match the total despair of the situation. 'You've been looking forward to it so much, your first holiday in Scotland with Alec . . . and what's he going to do? He isn't going to want to go without you.'

'That's really why I came to see you. To ask you a favour. Would you mind?'

'I don't know yet what the favour is.'

'Well, can I come and stay with you when I come out of hospital? If Alec knows I'm here with you, he'll go to Glenshandra with the others. It means so much to him. And everything's been planned for months. He's booked the hotel rooms and rented a stretch of the river for fishing. To say nothing of the Boulderstones and the Ansteys.'

'When would that be?'

'Next week. I'll only be in the hospital for a couple of days and I don't need nursing or anything. . . .'

'Darling, it's too *awful*, but I'm going away.'

'You're . . .' It was unthinkable. Laura stared at Phyllis and hoped that she was not going to burst into tears. 'You're . . . not going to be here?'

'I'm going to Florence for a month. With Laurence Haddon and the Birleys. We only arranged it last week. Oh, if you're desperate. I *could* put it off.'

'Of course you mustn't put it off.'

'What about Alec's brother and his wife? The brother who lives in Devon. Couldn't they take care of you?'

'Go to Chagwell, you mean?'

'You don't sound very enthusiastic. I thought you liked them when you stayed with them at Easter.'

'I did like them. They're perfectly sweet. But they've got five children, and it's holiday time, and Janey will have quite enough to do without me arriving, all pale and wan, and expecting breakfast in bed. Besides, I know how one feels after these operations. Absolutely drained. I think it's something to do with the anaesthetic. And the noise at Chagwell is never below about a million decibels. I suppose it's inevitable with five children around the place.'

Phyllis saw her point, abandoned the idea of Chagwell, and sought for other solutions.

11

'There's always Mrs Abney.'

'Alec would never leave me with Mrs Abney. She's getting on now, and she can't cope with the stairs.'

'Would Doctor Hickley consider postponing the operation?'

'No. I asked her, and she said no.' Laura sighed. 'It's on these occasions, Phyllis, that I long to be part of some enormous family. To have brothers and sisters and cousins and grandparents and a mother and a father . . .'

Phyllis said, 'Oh, *darling*,' and Laura was instantly repentant.

'That was a silly thing to say. I'm sorry.'

'Perhaps,' said Phyllis, 'if you got a nurse to look after you, then she and Mrs Abney could cope between them. . . .'

'Or I could just stay in hospital?'

'That's a ridiculous suggestion. In fact this whole conversation is ridiculous. I don't think Alec will want to go to Scotland and leave you behind. After all, you're practically still on your honeymoon!'

'We've been married for nine months.'

'Why doesn't he call the whole thing off and take you to Madeira when you're better?'

'He can't. He can't just take holidays when he wants. He's too horribly important. And Glenshandra is . . . a sort of tradition. He's been going there forever, every July, with the Ansteys and the Boulderstones. He looks forward to it for the whole year. Nothing ever changes. He's told me that, and that's what he loves about it. The same hotel, the river, the same ghillie, the same friends. It's Alec's safety valve, his breath of fresh air, the one thing that keeps him going, slaving away in the City for the rest of the year.'

'You know he loves what you call slaving away. He loves being busy and successful, and chairman of this and that.'

'And he can't let the others down at the last moment. If he doesn't go, they'll think it's all my fault, and my stock will go down to subzero, if I spoil it for them.'

'I don't think,' said Phyllis, 'that your stock with the Ansteys and the Boulderstones matters all that much. You only have to think about Alec.'

'That's just it. I feel I'm letting him down.'

'Oh, don't be ridiculous. You can't help it if your wretched insides suddenly go mad. And you were looking forward to going to Scotland just as much as he was. Or weren't you?'

'Oh, Phyllis, I don't know. If it was just Alec I was going with, it would be so different. When we're together, just the two of us, I can cope. We can be happy. I can make him laugh. It's like being with the other half of myself. But when the others are there too, I feel as though I'd strayed by mistake into some club or other and I know that however hard I try, I can never be a member.'

'Do you want to?'

'I don't know. It's just that they all know one another so well . . . for years and years, and for most of the time Alec was married to Erica. Daphne was Erica's best friend, she's Gabriel's godmother. Erica and Alec had this house called Deepbrook down in the New Forest, and they all used to go their for weekends. Everything they've ever done, everything they remember together, goes back fifteen years or more.'

Phyllis sighed. 'It is fairly daunting. Other people's memories are hard to take, I know. But you must have realized all this when you married Alec.'

'I didn't think about anything like that. I only knew that I wanted to marry him. I didn't want to think about Erica and I didn't want to think about Gabriel. I simply pretended that they didn't exist, which was quite easy, considering that they were both safely miles away, living in America.'

'You wouldn't want Alec to drop all his old friends. Old friends are part of a man. Part of the person that he is. It can't always be easy for them either. You have to see it their way.'

'No, I don't suppose it is.'

'Do they mention Erica and Gabriel?'

'Sometimes. But then there's an ugly silence, and somebody quickly starts another conversation.'

'Perhaps you should bring up the subject yourself.'

'Phyllis, how can I bring the subject up? How can I chat away about the glamorous Erica, who left Alec for another man? How can I talk about Gabriel, when Alec hasn't set eyes on her since the split-up?'

'Does she write to him?'

'No, but he writes to her. From the office. Once, his secretary forgot to put the letter in the post, and he brought it home with him. I saw the address, typewritten. I guessed then that he writes to her every week. But he doesn't ever seem to get one back. There are no photographs of Erica in the house, but there's one of Gabriel on his dressing table and a drawing she did for him when she was about five. It's in a silver frame, from Asprey's. I think if the house caught fire and he had to salvage one precious possession from the flames, that picture would be it.'

'What he needs is another child,' said Phyllis firmly.

'I know. But I may never have one.'

'Of course you will.'

'No.' Laura turned her head on the blue silk cushion and looked at Phyllis. 'I may not. After all, I'm nearly thirty-seven.'

'That's nothing.'

'And if this business with my insides blows up again, then Doctor Hickley says I'll have to have a hysterectomy.'

'Laura, don't think about it.'

'I do want a baby. I really do want one.'

'It will be all right. This time, everything will be all right. Don't be depressed. Think positively. And as for the Ansteys and the Boulderstones, they'll understand. They're perfectly nice, ordinary people. I thought they were all charming when I met them at that lovely dinner party you gave for me.'

Laura's smile was wry. 'Daphne, too?'

'Of course, Daphne too,' said Phyllis stoutly. 'I know she spent the evening flirting with Alec, but some women can't help behaving that way. Even if they are old enough to know better. You *surely* don't think there was ever anything between them?'

'Sometimes, when I'm feeling blue, I wonder. . . . After Erica left him, Alec was on his own for five years.'

'You must be mad. Can you see a man of Alec's integrity having an affair with his best friend's wife? I can't. You're underestimating yourself, Laura. And, which is infinitely more dangerous, you're underestimating Alec.'

Laura put her head back on the sofa cushion and closed her eyes. It was cooler now, but Lucy's weight lay like a hot-water bottle upon her lap. She said, 'What shall I do?'

'Go home,' said Phyllis. 'Have a shower and put on the prettiest garment you own, and when Alec comes home, give him an iced martini and talk to him. And if he wants to give up his holiday and stay with you, then let him.'

'But I want him to go. I really want him to go.'

'Then tell him so. And tell him that if the worst comes to the worst, I'll cancel Florence, and you can come and stay with me.'

'Oh, Phyllis . . .'

'But I'm certain he'll come up with some brilliant brainwave, and all this heart-searching will have been for nothing, so don't let's waste time talking any more about it.' She glanced at her watch. 'And now it's nearly four. What would you say to a delicious cup of China tea?'

2

DEEPBROOK

Alec Haverstock, ex-Winchester and Cambridge, investment analyst, manager of the Forbright Northern Investment Trust, and a director of the Merchant Bank, Sandberg Harpers, hailed – and some people found this surprising – from the heart of the West Country.

He was born at Chagwell, the second son of a family that for three generations had farmed a thousand acres or so of land that lay on the western slopes of Dartmoor. The farmhouse was built of stone, long and low, with large rooms made to accommodate large families. Solid and comforting, it faced southwest, over sloping green pastures where the dairy herds of Guernsey grazed, and down to lush, arable fields and the reedy margins of the little river Chag. Farther still lay the horizon of the English Channel, often veiled in a curtain of mist and rain, but on clear days blue as silk in the sunshine.

The Haverstocks were a prolific family, sprouting various branches all over Devon and Cornwall. Some of these offshoots veered towards the professions and produced a string of lawyers, doctors, and accountants, but on the whole the male members of the clan stayed stubbornly close to the land: building up pedigree herds, raising sheep and ponies on the moor, fishing in the summer, and hunting during the winter months with the local foxhounds. There was usually a youthful Haverstock riding in the yearly Hunt Steeplechase, and broken collarbones were treated as lightly as the common cold.

With the inheritance of land passing from the father to the eldest boy, younger sons were forced to look elsewhere for their livelihood and, following the tradition of Devon men, usually went to sea. Just as there had always been Haverstocks in the farming community of the country, the Navy Lists, for a hundred years or more, were never without their quota of Haverstocks, ranging from junior midshipmen to full captains, and sometimes even an admiral or two.

16

Alec's uncle Gerald had followed this tradition and joined the Royal Navy. With Chagwell entailed to his older brother Brian, Alec was expected to follow the same course. But he was born beneath a different star than his bluff, seagoing forebears, and it led him in a totally different direction. It became very clear after his first term at the local preparation school, that although tough and resourceful, he was also very bright. With the encouragement of the headmaster of this small school, Alec sat for and won a scholarship to Winchester. From Winchester he went to Cambridge, where he rowed, played rugger, and read economics, to emerge at the end of his last year with an honours degree. Before he had even left Cambridge, he had been spotted by a talent scout from Sandberg Harpers and was offered a job with them, in the City of London.

Alec was twenty-two. He bought himself two dark City suits, a furled umbrella, and a briefcase and flung himself into this exciting new world with the reckless enthusiasm of some previous Haverstock riding his hunter straight for a five-barred gate. He was installed in the department of the bank that specialized in investment analysis, and it was at this time that he first met Tom Boulderstone. Tom had already been with Sandberg Harpers for six months, but the two young men had much in common, and when Tom asked Alec to move into his flat with him, Alec accepted with alacrity.

It was a good time. Although they were both kept with their noses firmly pressed to the Harper Sandberg grindstone, there was still plenty of opportunity for the sort of irresponsible enjoyment that only occurs once in most people's lifetime. The little flat bulged with a constant stream of bright young things. Impromptu parties grew out of nothing, with spaghetti boiling up in a saucepan and crates of lager piled on the draining board. Alec bought his first car, and on weekends he and Tom would rustle up a couple of girls and go down to the country to other people's houses, or summer cricket matches, or winter shoots.

It was Alec who introduced Daphne to Tom. Alec had been at Cambridge with Daphne's brother and was asked to be a good fellow and keep his eye on this innocent creature who had just come to work in London. Without much enthusiasm Alec did as he had been asked and was delighted to discover that she

17

was as pretty as paint and marvellously entertaining. He took her out once or twice on his own and then, one Sunday evening, took her back to the flat, where she made him and Tom the worst scrambled eggs he had ever tasted.

Despite this disaster, and somewhat to Alec's surprise, Tom instantly fell in love with Daphne. For a long time she resisted his blandishments and continued to play her own extensive field, but Tom was a dogged fellow and regularly begged her to marry him, only to be fobbed off yet again with endless excuses and procrastinations. His moods, consequently, varied from euphoric elation to the deepest gloom, but, just as he finally decided that he hadn't a hope in hell and was steeling himself to put Daphne out of his life forever, she, perhaps sensing this, suddenly did a *volte-face*, threw over all the other young men, and told Tom that she would marry him after all. Alec was their best man, and Daphne duly moved into Tom's flat, as a very young and very inexperienced Mrs Boulderstone.

It was necessary for Alec to move out, and it was at this early stage in his career that he bought the house in Islington. Nobody else that he knew lived in Islington, but when he first saw it, it seemed to him larger and more attractive than any of the poky mews and cottages that belonged to his friends. It had the added inducement of costing a great deal less than property in other parts of London. And it was only minutes from the City.

The bank helped him with his mortgage and he moved in. The house was tall and thin, but it had a good basement, which he did not really need, so he put an advertisement in the local paper, which was answered by Mrs Abney. She was a widowed lady in early middle age. Her husband had been a builder; she had no children. Only Dicky, her canary. She would have to bring Dicky with her. Alec said that he had no objection to canaries, and it was agreed that Mrs Abney should move in. It was an arrangement to their mutual satisfaction, for now Mrs Abney had a home and Alec a live-in caretaker and someone to iron his shirts.

When Alec had been with Sandberg Harpers for five years, he was transferred to Hong Kong.

Tom was staying in London, and Daphne was wildly jealous. 'I can't think why you're going and Tom isn't.'

18

'He's brighter than I,' said the good-natured Tom.

'He's nothing of the sort. He's just bigger and better looking.'

'Now, that's enough of that.'

Daphne giggled. She loved it when Tom became masterful. 'Anyway, Alec darling, you'll have the most wonderful time and I'm going to give you the address of my best girlfriend, because she's out there just now, staying with her brother.'

'Does he work in Hong Kong?'

'Probably Chinese,' said Tom.

'Oh, don't be silly.'

'Mr Hoo Flung Dung.'

'You know perfectly well that Erica's brother isn't Chinese; he's a captain in the Queen's Loyals.'

'Erica,' said Alec.

'Yes. Erica Douglas. She's frightfully glamorous and good at games and everything.'

'Hearty,' murmured Tom, who was in a maddening mood.

'Oh, all right, *hearty*, if you want to spoil everything.' She turned back to Alec. 'She isn't hearty; she's just the most marvellous person, frightfully attractive.'

Alec said that he was sure that she was. A week later he flew to Hong Kong, and once he had settled himself in, he went in search of Erica. He found her, living with friends, in a beautiful house up on the Peak. A Chinese houseboy answered the door and led him through the house and out onto the shady terrace Below was a sunbaked garden and a blue, kidney-shaped swimming pool. Missy Ellica was swimming, the houseboy told him with a gentle gesture of his hand, and Alec thanked him and set off down the steps. There were six or seven people around the pool. As he approached, an older man observed him and got out of his long chair to come and meet him. Alec introduced himself and explained the reason for his call, and the man smiled and turned towards the pool.

A girl, alone, was swimming there, moving up and down its length with a smooth, expert crawl.

'Erica!' She rolled onto her back, sleek as a seal, her black hair clinging to her head. 'Someone to see you!' She swam to the side of the pool, pulled herself effortlessly out of the water, and came to meet him. She was very beautiful. Tall, long-legged, copper brown, her face and body running with droplets of water.

'Hello.' She smiled and her smile was wide and open, her teeth even and shining white. 'You're Alec Haverstock. Daphne wrote and told me. I got a letter yesterday. Come and have a drink.'

He could scarcely believe his good fortune. He asked her out for dinner that very evening, and after that they were seldom apart. After murky London, Hong Kong was a positive fairground of pleasures to be enjoyed: a crowded, teeming fairground, to be sure, where poverty and riches rubbed shoulders on every corner; a world of contrasts that both shocked and delighted; a world of heat and sunshine and blue skies.

There was, all at once, so much to do. Together they swam and played tennis, went riding in the early mornings, sailed her brother's litttle dinghy on the breezy blue waters of Repulse Bay. At night they were inundated with all the glitter and glamour of Hong Kong's considerable social life. There were dinner parties in establishments more luxurius than he had ever dreamed existed in this day and age. Cocktail parties on board visiting cruisers; regimental occasions – the Queen's Birthday and Beating Retreat; naval occasions. Life for two young people on the brink of falling in love seemed to have no limit to the good things it had to offer, and it finally sank through to Alec that the best thing of all was Erica herself. One evening, as he drove her home after a party, he asked her to marry him, and she gave a typical shout of pure pleasure and flung her arms around his neck, very nearly causing him to run the car off the road.

The next day they went shopping and bought her the biggest star sapphire engagement ring that he could afford. Her brother gave a party for them in the Mess, and there was more champagne drunk that evening than Alec had ever seen consumed in such a relatively short time.

They were married in the cathedral in Hong Kong by the bishop. Erica's parents flew out from England for the ceremony, and Erica wore a dress of fine white cotton lawn, encrusted with white embroidery. They spent their honeymoon in Singapore and then returned to Hong Kong.

And so the first year of their married life was passed in the Far East, but the idyll finally had to end. Alec's term of duty was over, and he was recalled to London. They returned in

November, a gloomy enough month at the best of times, and when they came to the house in Islington, he picked her up and carried her over the doorstep, which meant, at least, that she didn't get her feet wet, because it was pouring with rain at the time.

Erica didn't think much of the house. Seen through her eyes, Alec had to admit that the décor was fairly uninspired, and he told her to do what she wanted to do with it, and he would foot the bill. This delightful ploy kept her happy and busy for some months, and by the time the house had been reconstructed, redecorated, and refurnished to Erica's exacting standards, Gabriel was born.

Holding his daughter for the first time was one of the most astonishing experiences in Alec's life. Nothing had prepared him for the humbleness, the tenderness, the pride he experienced as he pushed aside the baby's shawl and looked for the first time into her small, downy face. He saw the brilliant blue of her open eyes, the high forehead, the crest of spiky, silky, black hair.

'She's yellow,' said Erica. 'She looks like a Chinese.'

'She isn't really yellow.'

Some months after Gabriel's birth he was sent east again, this time to Japan. But now everything was different, and he was almost ashamed of his reluctance to leave his little daughter, even for three months. He admitted this to nobody, not even Erica.

Least of all Erica. Because Erica was not a natural mother. She had always been more interested in horses than children and had shown a sad lack of enthusiasm when she had realized that she was pregnant. The physical manifestations of childbearing revolted her . . . she hated her swollen breasts, her ballooning abdomen. The long wait bored her, and even the interest of doing up the house could not make up for morning sickness, lassitude, and occasional fatigue.

And now, she hated Alec going back to the Far East without her. She resented his going on his own, while she stayed behind, mouldering in London, just because of Gabriel.

'You can't blame Gabriel. Even if we didn't have Gabriel, you couldn't come with me because it's not that sort of a trip.'

'And what am I supposed to do with myself? While you're gallivanting around with the geisha girls?'

'You could go and stay with your mother.'

21

'I don't want to go and stay with my mother. She fusses over Gabriel until I could scream.'

'Well, I tell you what . . .' She was lying on their bed during this particular exchange, and now he sat beside her and laid his hand on the sulky curve of her hip. 'Tom Boulderstone's been on to me about an idea he's had. He and Daphne want to go to Scotland in July . . . for the fishing. The Ansteys are going as well, and they thought that we might go too and make up a party.'

After a bit, 'Whereabouts in Scotland?' Erica asked. She still sounded sulky, but he knew that he had caught her attention.

'Sutherland. It's called Glenshandra. There's a very special hotel, with marvellous food, and you wouldn't have to do anything but enjoy yourself.'

'I know. Daphne told me about it. She and Tom went last year.'

'You'd like fishing.'

'What about Gabriel?'

'Perhaps your mother could have her? What do you think?'

Erica turned over onto her back and pushed her hair out of her eyes and gazed at her husband. She began to smile. She said, 'I'd rather go to Japan.'

He leaned over and kissed her open, smiling mouth. 'Next best thing.'

'All right. Next best thing.'

And so the pattern of their lives evolved, and as the years slipped by, Alec's career broadened and became more involved and more responsible as he climbed his own particular ladder of success. Gabriel was four. Then she was five and starting school. When Alec had time to stop and stand and look at his family life, he supposed that they were as happy as any of his friends. There were ups and downs, of course, but these were only to be expected, and always – like a glittering prize waiting to be grasped at the end of a long run – there was the holiday in Scotland, which had now become an annual event. Even Erica loved this and looked forward to it as much as Alec. A natural athlete, with an athlete's sense of timing and quick observant eye, she had taken to fly-fishing like a duck to water. Her first salmon had reduced her to a mixture of laughter and tears, and her childlike delight and excitement had almost caused Alec to fall in love with her all over again.

22

They were happy in Scotland, the carefree days as refreshing as a gust of clean wind blown through a stuffy house, dispersing resentments, clearing the air.

When Gabriel was old enough, they started taking her with them.

'She'll be a nuisance,' said Erica, but she wasn't a nuisance, because she wasn't that sort of a child. She was charming, and it was at Glenshandra that Alec really got to know his little daughter – to talk to her, to listen to her, or simply to enjoy her companionable silence as she sat on the bank of the river and watched him casting over the brown, peaty water.

But even Glenshandra was not enough, and Erica was restless. She still resented Alec's overseas commitments, his constantly leaving her for glamorous foreign parts. Every time he went, there was a row, and he would fly off, miserable, with the sound of her angry, unforgiving words ringing in his ears. Now, she decided that she hated their house. Initially she had enthused over it, but now it was too small. She was bored with it. Bored with London. He wondered if she was going to tell him that she was bored with him, too.

He could be stubborn. At the end of a long, tiring day, faced with a moody wife, he could be more stubborn than usual. He told her that he had no intention of relinquishing his convenient house for something larger out at the smart end of London, which would cost an arm and a leg and involve even more travelling.

Erica lost her temper. 'You never think about anybody but yourself. You don't have to spend your days in this beastly house, cooped up, surrounded by Islington pavements. What about Tom and Daphne? They've bought a house on Campden Hill.'

It was at this point, listening to her, that Alec first came to realize that there was a chance, a possibility, that one day his marriage to Erica would end up on the rocks. She accused him of thinking about nobody but himself, and although this was not strictly true, what *was* true was that most of his waking hours were spent totally absorbed in his work, with no thought for anything else. But for Erica it was different. Domesticity and motherhood were not enough for her, and although their evenings were packed with social engagements – it seemed to Alec that they were scarcely ever in for dinner – it was natural that Erica's boundless energy yearned for more.

When she had run out of things to complain about and had fallen silent, he asked her what she really wanted.

She told him. 'I want space. A bigger garden, space for Gabriel. That's what I want. Space and freedom. Trees. Somewhere to ride. Do you know, I haven't ridden since we were in Hong Kong. And before that I rode every single day of my life. I want somewhere to be when you're abroad all the time. I want to be able to have people to stay. I want . . .'

What she wanted, of course, was a house in the country.

Alec bought her one. In the New Forest. Erica found it, after three months of frantic searching, and Alec took a deep breath and wrote the enormous cheque demanded of him.

It was a compromise, of course, but he had recognized the danger signals of her desperation and was now in a financial position where he was able to shoulder the added expense of such a luxury. But was it such a luxury? It would mean country weekends and holidays for Gabriel, and property, with looming inflation, was always a good investment.

The house was called Deepbrook. Early Victorian, soundly built, with many rooms, a conservatory, an acre of garden, stabling for four horses, and three acres of paddock. The face of the house was smothered in an enormous, mauve-blossomed wisteria, and there was a big lawn with a cedar tree in the middle and various rather charming, old-fashioned, overgrown rosebushes.

Erica was happy at last. She furnished the house, found a gardener, and acquired for herself a couple of horses and a little pony for Gabriel. Gabriel was now seven and she did not much like the pony, preferring to play for hours on the monkey swing Alec had fixed up in the cedar tree.

Although they seemed to get on well enough, Gabriel and her mother never had very much in common. When she was eight, Erica began to make noises about sending Gabriel to boarding school. Alec was appalled. He did not approve of sending small boys to boarding school at such a tender age, let alone little girls. This argument continued for some time, without coming to any conclusion, but was ended abruptly by Alec having to go to New York for three months.

This time there were no recriminations, no complaints. Erica was schooling a young horse for showing, and she saw him off with scarcely a backward glance, having no thoughts in her head for anything but the job in hand. At least Alec assumed that she had no other thoughts, but when he returned from New York, he was told that she had found the perfect little boarding school for Gabriel, had put her name down, and the child would start there the following term.

It was a Sunday. He had flown into Heathrow that morning and driven straight down to Deepbrook. Erica presented him with her *fait accompli* in the drawing room, while he was pouring her a drink, and it was there, facing each other like antagonists across the hearthrug, that they had their most resounding row.

'You had no business . . .'

'I told you I was going to do it.'

'I told you that you weren't to. I won't have Gabriel being packed off to some boarding school. . . .'

'I'm not packing her off. I'm sending her. For her own good . . .'

'Who are you to decide what's good for her?'

'I know what isn't good for her, and that is staying at that crummy little day school in London. She's an intelligent child –'

'She's only ten.'

'And she's an only child. She needs companionship.'

'You could give her that if you weren't too busy with your bloody horses. . . .'

'That's a lie . . . and why shouldn't I have my horses? God knows I've given up enough of my time taking care of Gabriel. . . . It's not as though I've ever had any help from you . . . you're away half the time.' She began to pace up and down the room. 'And I've tried to interest her in the things I do . . . heaven knows I've tried. I bought her that little pony, but she's more interested in watching television or reading books. How is she ever going to make friends with anybody if she never does anything but that?'

'I don't want her to go to boarding school. . . .'

'Oh, for heaven's sake stop being so selfish. . . .'

'I'm thinking about her. Don't you understand that? I'm thinking about *Gabriel*. . . .'

He was cold with rage, he could feel his anger like a physical thing, knotted hard against his chest. Erica said nothing. Turning at the far end of the room, she stopped, suddenly still, staring not at Alec but beyond him. Her expression did not change; pale and cold she stood there, her hands clenched, taut and bloodless around the scarlet wool of her sweater.

In the silence that followed, Alec laid down his glass and slowly turned. Behind him, in the open doorway, stood Gabriel. She wore old jeans and a sweat shirt with Snoopy on the front. Her feet were bare, her long dark hair like a curtain of silk falling down over her shoulders.

For a long moment he looked into her eyes, and then her gaze fell and she stood there, fiddling with the door handle, waiting to be told something. Waiting to be told anything.

He took a deep breath. He said, 'What's wrong?'

'Nothing.' She shrugged, her thin shoulders hunched. 'I just heard you.'

'I'm sorry.'

Erica said, 'I've just told Daddy about the school, Gabriel. He doesn't want you to go, because he thinks you're too young.'

'How do you feel about it?' Alec asked gently.

Gabriel went on fiddling with the doorknob.

'I don't mind,' she said at last.

He knew that she would say anything to stop them quarrelling; and it occurred to him then, as anger died and sadness took its place, that he had two alternatives. Either he had to make an issue of the situation, which would inevitably involve Gabriel in the subsequent recriminations, or else he had to let the whole thing ride and go quietly along with it. Whatever he decided he knew that Gabriel was going to be the loser.

Later, after he had had a bath and changed, he went along to Gabriel's room to say good-night to her. She was in her night-dress and bedroom slippers, kneeling in the twilight gloom and watching television. He sat on the bed and watched her face, her profile lifted to the screen, her features illuminated by its light. At ten she was neither as pretty as she had been or as beautiful as she would become, but to Alec she seemed so precious, so vulnerable, that his heart turned over at the thought of what might lie ahead for her.

After the programme ended, she got up and switched off the television, then turned on her bedside light and went to draw the curtains. She was an extremely orderly child. When she had done this, he reached out and took her by the arm and drew her gently towards him, holding her between his knees. He kissed her. He said, 'The quarrel's over. I'm sorry. We had no right to make so much noise. I hope you aren't upset.'

She laid her head against his shoulder. He took his hand and touched her hair.

She said, 'Most people go to boarding school sooner or later.'

'Will you mind?'

'Will you come and see me?'

'Of course. Whenever I'm allowed. And there'll be half-terms and things. And holidays.'

'Mummy took me to see the school.'

'What did you think of it?'

'It smelled of polish. But the headmistress had a kind face. And she's quite young. And she doesn't mind if you take teddies and things.'

'Look – if you really *don't* want to go . . .'

She drew away from him and shrugged. 'I don't mind,' she said again.

It was all he could do. He kissed her and left her and went downstairs.

So once again Erica had won, and three weeks later, Gabriel, wearing a grey school uniform and clutching her teddy, entered her new school. Leaving her was like leaving part of himself, and it took some time to get used to returning home to an empty house.

For now the pattern of life was totally changed. Freed from the responsibility of Gabriel, Erica found endless excuses not to come to London, but to stay on her own in the country. There was a new horse to be schooled, some coming event to train for, a Pony Club gymkhana to organize. After a little, it seemed to Alec that they were never together. Sometimes, if there was a party on in London, or she needed to go to the hairdresser or buy some new clothes, she would drive up to town in the middle of the week, and he would get back to the house in Islington to find it full of the fresh flowers she had brought with her from Deepbrook, and smelling of her scent. He would see her fur coat tossed over the banister, hear her voice talking to some girlfriend – probably Daphne – over the telephone.

'Just up for a day or two. Are you going to the Ramseys' this evening? Well, let's lunch tomorrow. The Caprice? All right. About one o'clock. I'll book a table.'

When she was not there, Mrs Abney agreed to keep an eye on Alec. Heavy-footed she would tread up from the basement and produce a shepherd's pie or a stew from the oven. And in the evenings he often sat alone, with a whisky and soda at hand, watching television or reading the paper.

If only for Gabriel's sake, however, it was important to keep up the façade of a sound and lasting marriage. Perhaps the charade convinced no person but himself, but if Alec was in London – for his overseas commitments now were more pressing than ever – he would dutifully drive himself down to Deepbrook on Friday evenings.

But here again things were no longer the same, for lately Erica had taken to filling the house with weekend guests. It was as though she were setting up some sort of a defence against Alec, as though she were reluctant even to spend a few hours alone with him. No sooner had he climbed tiredly out of his car than, it seemed, he was welcoming new arrivals, carrying suitcases, pouring drinks, opening wine. In the old days he had enjoyed the therapy of a little amateur gardening: trimming a hedge or mowing the lawn. There had been time to potter, plant bulbs or prune the roses, saw up a few logs, mend a sagging gate.

But now there were so many people to be taken care of that he never had a moment to himself, and he was too conscientious and courteous a host ever to lose his patience with these demanding hordes and tell them to drive themselves to the Point-to-Point; to find their own way to the National Trust Garden; to fetch their own garden chairs and pour their own bloody drinks.

One Friday evening at the beginning of September, in that blistering summer of 1976, Alec climbed into his car, slammed the door, and set off for Deepbrook. He loved London, it was his home, and like Samuel Pepys, he never tired of it. But for once he felt nothing but relief at the prospect of getting away from the city. The relentless heat, the drought, the dust, and the dirt had become enemies. The parks, usually so green, wilted, dry as deserts. Trodden grass lay dead and brown, and here and there sprouted sinister, unknown weeds, never seen before. The very air was stale and used, doors stood open to the breezeless evening, and the sinking sun, orange in the hazy sky, promised nothing but another scorcher the next day.

Driving, he deliberately put the problems of the week away into the back of his mind. His responsibilities were now so great that he had a long time ago schooled himself to do this, and had discovered that the discipline was a worthwhile one, for when he returned to the office on Monday morning his brain was clear and refreshed, and very often his subconscious mind was ready and waiting to present him with a solution or an idea that previously had eluded him.

Instead, heading south through the sweltering suburbs, he thought about the two days that lay ahead. He did not dread this particular weekend. On the contrary, he was actually looking forward to it. For once, there would not be a houseful of strangers. They had returned, only a month previously, from Glenshandra, and Erica had planned the weekend then, inviting the Ansteys and the Boulderstones to stay.

'We'll have a lovely time,' she told them, 'talking about Glenshandra and exchanging fishing stories.'

As well, Gabriel was home. She was thirteen now. This summer, Alec had bought her a little trout rod of her own, and she had had a happy time with Jamie Rudd, the ghillie, learning to use this new toy. The school about which Alec had had such heart-searching reservations had proved, maddeningly enough, to be a success. Erica was not a fool and had gone to some trouble to find an establishment that would match up to Gabriel's needs, and after a term or so of home-sickness, Gabriel seemed to have shaken down quite happily and made friends for herself. Having the Boulderstones and the Ansteys was like having family to stay – they had been so often, they knew how to take care of themselves. Alec would maybe take Gabriel off by himself one afternoon. Perhaps they would go swimming. The very idea filled him with pleasure. The traffic was thinning. He had reached the motorway and was able to pick up speed, to change up into overdrive. The powerful car surged forward.

In the New Forest it was just as hot, but now it was country heat. Deepbrook drowsed. The shadow of the cedar tree lay black across the lawn, and full-blown roses scented the cooling evening air. The awning was up over the terrace, shading a group of garden chairs, and indoors Erica, for coolness, had drawn all the curtains. This gave the house a blank look, as though the windows were the eyes of a sightless man.

He parked the car beneath the dappled shade of a young silver birch and got out, glad to stretch his legs and get the sweaty cramp out of his shoulders. As he stood there, he heard Gabriel calling him, 'Daddy!' and saw her coming up the lawn towards him. She wore only the skimpiest of bikinis and an old pair of rubber sandals, and she had tied her hair up in a bundle on the top of her head. For some reason this made her look very grown up. In her hand she carried a bunch of yellow flowers.

'Look,' she said, holding them out to show him. 'Kingcups.'

'Where did you find those?'

'Down by the brook. Mummy said she wanted some flowers for her dinner table and everything in the garden's wilting away, because we're not allowed to water *anything*. Every now and then of course we cheat, and do, but there's not much to pick. How are you?' She reached up, and he stooped down and they kissed. 'Isn't it boiling? Isn't it absolutely boiling?'

He agreed that it was boiling. He opened the car door and pulled his suitcase off the back seat, and together they walked slowly across the gravel and into the house.

'Where's Mummy?' he asked, following her into the kitchen.

'She's up at the stables, I think.' She filled a mug with water and put the kingcups into it. Alec opened the fridge and poured himself a glass of fresh orange juice. 'She asked me to lay the table for her because she said she wouldn't have time. The others haven't come yet. I mean the Boulderstones and the Ansteys. Come and see the dinner table and tell me if you think it's all right. Mummy's so fussy, she's bound to say I've forgotten something.'

The dining room, with the curtains drawn, was dim and shadowed, smelling vaguely of other dinner parties, cigars, wine. Gabriel went to draw back the curtains. 'It's cooler now, Mummy won't mind.' Yellow sunlight poured through the windows in dust-moted shafts, glancing off polished silver, crystal, and glass. He looked at the table and said he thought it looked perfect, which it did. Gabriel had used white linen mats and pale yellow napkins. The candles, in their ornate silver candlesticks, were yellow as well. 'That's why I thought of the kingcups, to go with everything else. . . . I thought if I put them in a silver bowl they'd look all right. . . . Mummy's so *good* at doing flowers. . . .' She looked at him. 'What's wrong?'

Alec frowned. 'You've laid for eight. I thought there were only six of us.'

'Seven with me. I'm coming down for dinner. And a man called Strickland Whiteside.'

'Strickland Whiteside?' He almost laughed at the absurdity of the name. 'Who on earth is . . . Strickland Whiteside?' But even as he repeated himself, a chord of familiarity rang like an echo in the back of his mind somewhere. He had heard that man's name before.

'Oh, Daddy, he's Mummy's new chum, and he's terribly famous. He's a frightfully rich American from Virginia and he rides.'

Memory struck. Alec clicked his fingers. 'That's it. I knew I'd heard of him. There was an article in *The Field* about him and his horses. There's one horse in particular. A great beast the height of an elephant.'

'That's right. He's called White Samba.'

'What does he do when he isn't riding?'

'He doesn't do anything else. He doesn't go to an office or anything boring like that. He just rides. He's got an enormous house on the James River and acres of land – he showed me some photographs – and he wins show jumping events all over America, and now he's come over here to train for some of ours.'

'He sounds fairly formidable.'

Gabriel giggled. 'You know Mummy's horsey friends. But actually he's quite nice . . . in a rather overwhelming sort of way.'

'Is he staying?'

'Oh, no, he doesn't have to stay, because he's taken a house over at Tickleigh.'

Alec was intrigued. 'Where did Mummy meet him?'

'At the Alverton Horse Show, I think. I'm not quite sure. Look, have I got the right wineglasses? I always get in a muddle with sherry and port?'

'No. Yes, it's fine. You've got it quite right.' He began to smile. 'Do we have to call him Strickland? If I have to call him

31

Strickland, I don't think I'm going to be able to keep a straight face.'

'Everybody calls him Strick.'

'That's even worse.'

'Oh, he's not so bad. And just think what fun Daphne Boulderstone will have making eyes at him. There's nothing she likes more than a new man. It'll make a lovely change from boring old George Anstey.'

'How about boring old me?'

Gabriel put her arms around his waist and pressed her cheek against his chest.

'*Never* boring old you. Just super, gorgeous, kind you.' She pulled away, responsible and busy. 'Now I must go and do something about the kingcups.'

He was in a cold bath when he heard Erica come upstairs and into their bedroom. He called her name, and she appeared in the open doorway, her arms crossed, a shoulder propped against the wall. She was looking very tanned, very hot, and rather tired. She had tied back her dark hair with a cotton handkerchief and wore old, dirty jeans, riding boots, and a shirt that had once belonged to him. He thought of these as her horse-fangling clothes.

He said, 'Hi.'

'Hello there. You're early. I wasn't expecting you so soon.'

'I wanted to freshen up before the others get here.'

'How was London?'

'Like an oven.'

'It's been hot here too. We're short of water.'

'I hear we have a new acquaintance coming for dinner tonight.'

She met his gaze and smiled. 'Gabriel tell you?'

'He sounds interesting.'

'I don't know if you'll find him particularly interesting, but I thought it would be friendly to ask him along this evening to meet you all.'

'I'm glad you did. Perhaps I shall find that we have American friends in common, and we'll be able to gas about them. What are we eating?'

'Smoked salmon and then grouse.'

'Very smart. White wine or red?'

32

'I think some bottles of both, don't you? Don't be too long, will you, Alec? I'd like to have a bath myself and it's too hot to hurry.' And she turned and went back into the bedroom. He heard her opening the sliding mirrored doors of her wardrobe. Imagined her standing there, trying to decide what she would put on. Thoughtfully, he squeezed dry the sponge and reached for his towel.

Alec, with his guests and his wife already seated, moved around the table pouring the wine. The windows of the dining room were wide open. Outside, it was still light, and very warm. There was not the faintest breeze and the garden drowsed in the scented evening air. On the table the candle flames glowed palely, striking soft reflections on crystal and silver. The kingcups, brilliant butter yellow, seemed to shine with a light all their own.

He put the bottle of wine back on the sideboard and went to take his place at the head of the table.

'. . . of course, you would probably think it was terribly boring after fishing in those wilderness rivers in the United States, but there is something very special about Glenshandra. We all adore it . . . we're like children there.'

That was Daphne, in full cry, monopolizing all conversation.

Strickland, Strick – Alec couldn't decide which was worse – assumed a modest expression. 'I'm not actually much of a fisherman myself.'

'No, of course you aren't, how silly of me, you wouldn't have time.'

'Why wouldn't he have time?' asked Tom.

'Well, darling, of course he wouldn't have time if he's in training for some world-shaking equestrian event.'

'Equestrian.' That was George. 'Daphne, I never realized you knew such long words.'

She pouted at him, and Alec was reminded of the young girl she no longer was.

'But it is the right word, isn't it?'

'Sure,' said Strickland. 'It's the right word.'

'Oh, thank you. You are sweet to be on my side.' She picked up her fork and speared a delicate sliver of rosy-pink smoked salmon.

Erica had placed her guests as she normally did when there

were eight people present. Alec was in his normal chair, at the head of the table, but Erica had moved around to the side and relinquished her place to Strickland Whiteside, in his capacity as guest of honour, so that he and Alec faced each other down the length of the table. In fact, although they sat thus they didn't have a particularly good view of each other because the tall silver candelabra got in the way. When Erica was sitting there, Alec sometimes found this irritating, because if he wanted to say something to her, or to catch her eye, it involved some manoeuvring, but this evening he decided that it was probably a good thing.

He wanted to enjoy his dinner without being conscious the whole time of Strickland Whiteside's disconcertingly pale blue eyes.

Daphne and Erica sat on either side of Strickland and Marjorie Anstey and Gabriel on either side of Alec. Tom and George faced each other across the middle of the table.

Strickland Whiteside also took up his fork. 'Do you ride?' he asked Marjorie.

'Oh, heavens no. I never rode, even at school. I was always far too terrified.'

'She doesn't know a horse's arse from its elbow,' said George, and his wife said '*George*' in tones of extreme disapproval, and glanced towards Gabriel.

'Sorry, Gabriel, forgot you were there.'

Gabriel looked embarrassed, but Erica put back her head and laughed, as much at George's discomfort as at his joke.

Watching her, Alec decided that the time spent pondering over her wardrobe had not been wasted. She wore a caftan of the palest blue Thai silk, with the earrings he had once given her for some long-forgotten birthday and gold bracelets on her slender brown wrists. She looked amazingly young this evening. Her face still beautiful, her jawline firm, her hair without a thread of grey. Of all of them, he decided, she had aged and changed the least. Because, although not old, not even middle-aged, they, who had all been young together, no longer were.

He wondered what Strickland thought of them all. What was his impression of them, as they sat there, dressed up and festive, around the formal dinner table? They were Alec's oldest friends; he had known them for so long that their individual appearances he took totally for granted. But now he let his eyes move around the table deliberately observing each of his guests with the eyes of the stranger who sat in Erica's chair. Daphne, tiny and slender as ever, but with her blond hair now silvery white. George Anstey ponderous and red-faced, his shirt buttons straining over his considerable waistline. Marjorie, who of all of them seemed happy to mature into full solid middle age, without any tiresome backward glances over her ample shoulder.

And Tom. Tom Boulderstone. Affection filled Alec's heart for the man who had been his closest friend for so many years. But this was an objective appraisal, not a sentimental one. So what did Alec see? A man of forty-three, balding, bespectacled, pale, clever. A man who looked more like a priest than a banker. A man whose sombre expression could gleam with hidden laughter. A man who, when called upon, could make an after-dinner speech so witty that it would be quoted in the City for months to come.

Daphne ran out of words at last, and George Anstey took advantage of the subsequent lull to lean forward and ask Strickland what had decided him to come to this country.

'Well' – the American glanced around the table and grinned depreciatingly – 'I seem to have done most everything I could in the States, and I felt there was real new challenge over here.'

'It must have meant the most awful lot of organization,' Marjorie remarked. She was interested in organization. She organized her local Meals on Wheels. 'I mean, renting a house for yourself and getting your horses over . . . what do you do for grooms?'

'I flew them over as well, and a couple of stable lads.'

'Are they black or white?' Daphne wanted to know.

Strickland grinned. 'Both.'

'And what about a housekeeper?' Marjorie persisted. 'Don't say you flew a housekeeper over as well?'

'Yes, I did. There wasn't any point taking Tickleigh Manor if I didn't have some person to look after me.'

Marjorie sat back with a sigh. 'Well, I don't know, but it all sounds like pure heaven to me. I've only got a daily two mornings a week, and she's never even been in an aeroplane.'

'For that you should be thankful,' said Tom dryly. 'Ours flew to Majorca for a holiday and married a waiter and never came back.'

Everybody laughed, but Tom did not even smile. Alec wondered what Tom was making of Strickland Whiteside, but that pale and clever face gave nothing away.

The American had arrived after they were all gathered with their drinks, bathed and shaved and changed and scented and expectant. When they heard the sound of his car drawing up outside the house, Erica went to greet him, and bring him indoors. They returned together, and there was no reason to imagine that they had embraced, but Erica brought with her, out of the fragrant evening, a nervous glitter, like a nimbus of light. Formally she introduced Strickland Whiteside to her husband and her friends. He did not seem in the least put out by being suddenly faced with a roomful of people he had never met before, and all of whom, obviously, knew one another very well. On the contrary, his manner was almost benign, satisfied, as though he knew that the boot was on the other foot, and it was he who must put them at their ease.

He had, Alec guessed, taken some trouble with his dress. He wore a maroon gabardine jacket, brass buttoned, smoothly tailored; a pale blue polo-necked sweater; and a pair of maroon and pale blue plaid slacks. His shoes were white. There was a thick gold watch on one sinewy wrist and a heavy gold signet ring on his left hand. He was a tall man, lean and muscled and obviously immensely strong, but it was hard to guess his age, for while his features were formidable, hawk-nosed, big-jawed, intensely brown, with eyes as pale as sixpences, his hair was corn coloured, thick as the hair of a boy, growing springily from his forehead in a deep wave.

'Glad to meet you,' he said when Alec welcomed him and gripped his hand. It was like shaking hands with a steel spring. 'Erica's spoken so much about you, and it's a real privilege to make your acquaintance at last.'

He continued to be charming. He kissed Gabriel – 'My little girlfriend,' allowed himself to be given a martini, sat in the middle of the sofa with one long ankle hitched up onto a hard-muscled plaid knee. He began at once to ask about Glenshandra, as though knowing that this topic would naturally bring everybody into the conversation and so break the ice. Marjorie was disarmed by this, and Daphne could scarcely keep her eyes off him and for the first five minutes was rendered speechless. After that she scarcely drew breath.

'What's Tickleigh Manor House like? Didn't the Gerrards used to live there?'

'They still do,' Erica said. They were eating grouse now, and Alec poured the red wine.

'Well, they can't live there if Strick's living there.'

'No, they've gone up to London for a couple of months.'

'Were they going anyway, or did Strickland chase them out?'

'I chased them out,' said Strickland.

'He offered them money,' Erica explained to Daphne. 'You know that old-fashioned stuff you keep in your wallet.'

'You mean he *bribed* them . . .!'

'Oh, *Daphne* . . .'

Erica was laughing at Daphne, but there was exasperation in her amusement. Alec sometimes wondered how the friendship of two such totally different women had lasted for so long. They had known each other since school days, and it was doubtful that there was a single secret they did not share, and yet, on analysis, they had nothing in common. It could be that this was the glue that cemented their friendship. Their interests had never overlapped, and so the relationship was not in danger from the destructive touch of jealousy.

Daphne was interested only in men. That was the way she had been made, that was the way she would be even if she lived to be ninety. She came to life only if there was a man in the room, and if she did not have some current admirer tucked up her sleeve, to take her out for little luncheons or to telephone her in the mornings after Tom had gone to work, then life had lost all meaning and she became snappish and despondent.

Tom knew about this and accepted it. Once, very late at night, he had talked to Alec. 'I know she's a fool,' he had said, 'but she's a very sweet fool, and I wouldn't want to lose her.'

Whereas Erica . . . Erica was not really interested in men. Alec knew this. For the last few years he and Erica had lived more or less apart, but agonized conjectures as to how she spent her time had been the least of his worries; in fact, had scarcely entered his mind.

She had always been if not exactly frigid then sexually very cool. The emotions that other women needed – passion and excitement and challenge and affection – were apparently fulfilled by her obsession with her horses. Sometimes Alec was reminded of the small girls who haunted the Pony Club circuit.

Pigtailed, single-minded, cleaning tack, mucking out their ponies. 'It's a sex substitute,' some person had once assured him, when he remarked upon this phenomenon. 'Let them reach fourteen or fifteen, and it'll not be horses they'll be interested in, but men. It's a well-known fact. A natural development.'

Erica must once have been just such a child. *I rode every day of my life until I went to Hong Kong.* But Erica, for some reason, had never grown up. For a little, perhaps, she had loved Alec, but she had never wanted a child, had never experienced the accepted maternal instincts of other young mothers. As soon as humanly possible, she had returned to her original love. That was why she had made him buy Deepbrook. That was, basically, why Gabriel had been sent away to school.

Now, her life revolved around horses. They were the centre of her life, all she truly cared about. And the people who became her new friends were the people who rode them.

Two months after this weekend, on a dark, wet evening in November, Alec drove back to Islington from the city at the end of the day, expecting as usual to find his house empty. He had made no plans for the night and was glad of this, because his briefcase bulged with reading matter that he had had no time to deal with during the day, and there was a directors' meeting planned for the next day, during which he would be expected to make some well-studied pronouncement. He would have his meal early, then light the fire, put on his spectacles, and settle down to work.

He turned at last out of the City Road and into his own street, Abigail Crescent. His house stood at the far end, and he saw the light shining from its windows. Erica, for some reason, had come up to London.

He was puzzled by this. The weather was bad and he knew that her social diary was empty for most of the week. A dentist's appointment perhaps, or a yearly check-up with her doctor in Harley Street?

He parked the car and sat, staring at the lighted house. He had grown accustomed to being alone, but he had never truly come to terms with it. He remembered when they had first come to live here, fresh from Hong Kong, before Gabriel was born. He remembered Erica arranging furniture and hanging curtains and struggling with huge books of carpet samples, but always finding time to come and greet him as he let himself in through the door. That was how it had been. For only a little time, maybe, but that was how it had been. For a moment he let himself imagine that the years between had never happened, that everything was unchanged. Perhaps this time she would come to greet him, kiss him, go into the kitchen to fix him a drink. They would sit with their drinks and exchange the small gossip and doings of their day, and then he would ring some restaurant and take her out for dinner. . . .

The shining windows stared back at him. He was suddenly tired. He closed his eyes, covered them with his hand, as though to wipe fatigue away. After a little he collected his briefcase off the back seat and got out of the car, locked it, and walked across the rain-soaked pavement, with his bulky briefcase bumping against his knee. He got out his key and opened the door.

He saw her coat, slung across the hall chair, a silk Hermes scarf. He smelled her perfume. He closed the door and put down his briefcase.

'Erica.'

He went into the sitting room, and she was there, sitting in an armchair, facing him. She had been reading a paper, but now she folded this and dropped it on the floor beside her. She was wearing a yellow sweater, a grey wool skirt, and long brown leather boots. Her hair, illuminated by the reading lamp that she had lighted, shone like a polished chestnut. She said, 'Hi.'

'This is a surprise. I didn't know you were coming up.'

'I thought about telephoning your office, but there didn't seem much point. I knew you'd be here.'

'For a moment I thought I'd forgotten about some dinner party or other. I haven't, have I?'

'No. There's nothing on. I just wanted to talk to you.'

This was unusual. 'Would you like a drink?' he asked her.

'Yes. If you're having one.'

'What would you like?'

'A whisky would be fine.'

He left her and went into the kitchen and poured the drinks and manhandled ice cubes out of the tray, then carried the two glasses back to where she waited.

He handed her the glass. 'There's not much food in the fridge, I'm afraid, but if you like we could go out for dinner. . . .'

'I shan't be staying for dinner.' He raised his eyebrows, and she went on smoothly, 'I shan't even be staying the night, so you don't need to worry about entertaining me.'

He reached for a chair and pulled it forward and sat facing her across the hearthrug.

'Then why have you come?'

Erica took a mouthful of the whisky, and then laid the glass delicately down on the small marble-topped table that stood by her chair.

'I've come to tell you that I'm leaving you, Alec.'

He did not at once say anything to this. Across the space that divided them, her gaze met his, her eyes unblinking, sombre, quite cold.

After a bit, he said mildly, 'Why?'

'I don't want to live with you anymore.'

'We scarcely live together anyway.'

'Strickland Whiteside has asked me to go to America with him.'

Strickland Whiteside. He said, 'You're going to go and live with *him*?' and he could not keep the appalled incredulity out of his voice.

'You find it astonishing?'

He remembered how they had come indoors together that warm, scented September evening. He remembered the way she had looked, not simply beautiful, but radiant in a way that he had never seen before.

'Are you in love with him?'

She said, 'I don't think I've ever exactly known what being in love means. But I feel about Strick as I've never felt about anyone else. It's not just infatuation. It's doing things together, sharing interests. It's been like that from the moment we met. I can't live away from him.'

'You can't live away from Strickland Whiteside?' The name still sounded absurd. The whole sentence sounded absurd, like a line from some ludicrous farce, and Erica exploded into irritation.

'Oh, stop repeating everything I say. I can't make it any plainer, I can't make it any simpler. Repeating everything I say isn't going to change what I'm trying to tell you.'

He said ridiculously, 'He's younger than you are.'

For a moment she looked a little put out. 'Yes, he is, but what difference does that make?'

'Is he married?'

'No. He's never been married.'

'Does he want to marry you?'

'Yes.'

'So you want a divorce?'

'Yes. Whether or not you agree to a divorce, I'm leaving you. I'm going out to Virginia to be with him. I shall simply live with him. I'm long past the age of minding about what people say. Conventions really don't matter anymore.'

'When are you going?'

'I'm booked on a flight to New York next week.'

'Is Strickland flying with you?'

'No.' For the first time, her gaze faltered. She looked down, her hand reached for her drink. 'He's already gone back to the States. He's in Virginia, waiting for me.'

'What about all these big events he was booked in for?'

'He's given them up . . . cancelled everything.'

'I wonder why he did that.'

Erica raised her eyes. 'He thought it would be better.'

'You mean, he's chickened out. He hadn't the guts to face me and tell me himself.'

'That's not true.'

'He left it for you to do.'

'It's better for me to do it. I wouldn't let him stay. I made him go. I didn't want there to be rows, unpleasantness, things said that are better left unsaid.'

'You could hardly expect me to be delighted.'

'I'm going, Alec. And I'm not coming back.'

'You'd leave Deepbrook?'

'Yes.'

This astonished him almost more than the fact that she was leaving him.

'I always thought that house meant more to you than anything.'

'Not now it doesn't. Anyway, it's your house.'

'And your horses?'

'I'm taking my horses with me. Strickland's arranged for them to be flown to Virginia.'

41

She was, as usual, presenting him with a totally conceived plan, her usual method when she was utterly determined to have her own way. Strickland, Deepbrook, her horses, all had been neatly dealt with, but to Alec none of these things mattered a damn. There was only one real issue at stake. Erica had never been a moral coward. He waited in silence for her to continue, but she simply sat there, watching him with grey eyes unblinking and defiant, and he realized that she was waiting for him to fire the opening shot of the battle for the only thing that really mattered.

'Gabriel?'

Erica said, 'I'm taking Gabriel with me.'

The fight was on. 'Oh no you're not!'

'Now we're not going to start shouting about this. You're going to have to listen to me. I'm her mother, and I've as much right as you – and more – to make plans for our daughter. I'm going to America. I'm going there to live, and nothing is going to change that. If I take Gabriel with me, then she can live with us. Strickland has a beautiful home, with space and land all around it. There are tennis courts, a swimming pool. It's a wonderful opportunity for a girl of Gabriel's age – young people have such a good time in America – life is geared to them. Let her have this chance. Let her take it.'

He said quietly, 'What about her school?'

'I'll take her out of school. She can go to school out there. There's a particularly good one in Maryland. . . .'

'I won't let her go. I won't lose her.'

'Oh, Alec, you won't lose her. We'll share her. You can have access to her whenever you want. She can fly back to this country and stay with you. You can take her to Glenshandra with the others. Nothing's going to change that much.'

'I won't let her go to America.'

'Don't you see, you have no alternative. Even if we drag this thing through the divorce courts and you fight me every inch of the way, ten to one the custody of Gabriel will be given to *me*, because they only separate a child from its mother under the most extreme of circumstances. I'd need to be a drug addict or proved in some way to be totally unfit to bring my daughter up, before they even considered giving her to you. And think what that sort of hideous, public tug-of-war would do to Gabriel. She's sensitive enough as it is, without you and me inflicting that sort of horror on her.'

'Is it any worse than the horror of having her parents divorcing? Is it any worse than the horror of having to go and live in a strange country, in a strange house, under the roof of a man she scarcely knows?'

'And what is the alternative? We have to make a decision now, Alec. There can be no question of putting if off. That's why I came to see you this evening. She has to know what is going to happen to her.'

'I won't let her go.'

'All right, so what do you want? To keep her for yourself. You couldn't look after her, Alec. You haven't the time to give her. Even if she stayed at boarding school in this country, there are still the holidays. What would happen then, when you're working all day? And don't tell me you could leave her with Mrs Abney. Gabriel's an intelligent child, and nobody could say that Mrs Abney's the most stimulating company. She's only got two topics of conversation: one is last week's installment of "Crossroads" and the other is that damned canary of hers. And what would you do with Gabriel when you have to leave on business for Tokyo or Hong Kong? You can hardly take her with you.'

He said, 'I can't just give her to you, Erica. Like some material possession I no longer have any use for.'

'But don't you see, if we do it my way, you *aren't* giving her to me. All right, so we're splitting up and it's a terrible thing to do to a child, but it's happened before and it will happen again, and we have somehow to decide on a course of action that will hurt her the least. I think that my plan is that one. She comes with me next week. That way the cut will be quick, the break clean, and before she's had time to turn round, she'll be caught up in a whole new life, going to a new school, making new friends.' She smiled, and for the first time he saw a glimpse of the old Erica at her most charming, sympathetic, and persuasive. 'Don't let's fight over her, Alec. I know how you feel about Gabriel, but she's my child too, and it's I who brought her up. I don't think I've done such a bad job, and I do think I deserve a little credit for that. Just because you're not going to be there doesn't mean I won't go on bringing her up. And Strick is devoted to her. With us, she'll have the best of everything. A good life.'

He said, 'I thought that was what I was giving her.'

'Oh, Alec, you are. You have. And you can go on doing it. Whenever you want, she can come and see you. We've agreed on that. You can have her all to yourself. You'll love that. Agree to it. For all our sakes. Let her come with me. It's the very best you can do for her. I know it is. Make the sacrifice . . . for Gabriel's sake.'

He said, 'I know your mother's told you what's happened, what's going to happen. But I wanted to talk to you myself, so that if there was anything you were worried about . . .'

Even as he said this, he knew that it was ridiculous. Gabriel's world was falling apart, and he was speaking as though it were some small domestic difficulty that, in a matter of seconds, he could put straight for her.

'I mean . . . it has happened fairly suddenly. There hasn't been time to talk anything over, and you'll be leaving in a week. I didn't want you to go without thinking that I hadn't . . . made some effort to see you. I would like to have had more time to talk things over . . . with *you*. Were you hurt that we didn't discuss it with you?'

Gabriel shrugged. 'It wouldn't have made much difference.'

'Were you surprised when your mother told you about herself and Strickland?'

'I knew she liked him. But she's liked lots of horsey people. I never thought she's want to go and live with him in America.'

'She's going to marry him.'

'I know.'

They walked, together but apart, slowly around a deserted games field. It was a horrible day, English winter weather at its worst. Cold, still, raw, misty. No breeze stirred the empty trees, and only the cawing of the rooks broke the foggy silence. In the distance stood the school buildings. Once they had been an elegant country house, with wings and stables, but these had been converted into gymnasiums and classrooms. Indoors, lessons were in progress, but Gabriel had been allowed to miss a biology lesson in order to speak to her father. Later, no doubt a bell would ring, and the place would erupt with girls dressed for hockey or netball, bundled into sweaters and striped scarves, running and calling to one another and complaining of the cold. Now, except for a few lighted windows that shone through the murk, the place looked deserted, stripped of life.

44

'It could be an adventure, going to America.'

'That's what Mummy says.'

'At least you won't have to play games in weather like this. It makes a difference if you can play games in the sunshine. You might even become a tennis champion.'

Gabriel, with her head drooping and her hands deep in the pocket of her coat, kicked at a stick. So much for tennis. Alec was chilled, disorientated by her lack of response, because it was so out of character. He liked to think that he had always been able to talk to her. But now he was not so sure.

He said, 'I wouldn't have had this happen for anything in the world. You must realize that. But there's nothing I can do to keep your mother with me. You know what she's like once she's made up her mind about something. Wild horses couldn't make her change tracks.'

She said, 'I never never even thought about you and Mummy divorcing.'

'I'm afraid it happens to a lot of children. You must have a lot of friends with divorced parents.'

'But this is *me*.'

Once more, he was lost for words. In silence they paced on, around the corner of the field, passing a pole with a sodden red flag.

He said, 'Whatever happens, you know, you're still my daughter. I shall pay your school fees and give you an allowance. You won't have to ask Strickland for anything. You won't ever have to be beholden to him. You . . . like him, don't you? You don't dislike him?'

'He's all right.'

'Your mother says he's very fond of you.'

'He's so young. He's much younger than Mummy.'

Alec took a deep breath. 'I suppose,' he said carefully, 'if you fall in love with a person, their age doesn't matter.'

Abruptly, Gabriel stopped walking. Alec stopped too, and they stood facing each other, two solitary figures in the middle of nowhere. Not once during this afternoon's encounter had her eyes met his, and now she looked angrily straight ahead, at his coat buttons.

She said, 'Couldn't I have stayed with you?'

He was invaded by an impulse to embrace her, pull his child into his arms, break down her reserve with a demonstration of

45

love that would somehow convince her that this ghastly separation that they spoke of was as abhorrent to him as it was to her. But he had promised himself on the way down to the school to see her that he would not do this. *You mustn't upset her,* Erica had begged him. *Go and see her and talk things over, but don't upset her. She's accepted the situation. If you start getting emotional, then we're all back where we started and your going to break Gabriel into little pieces.*

He tried to smile. He said evenly, 'There's nothing I wanted more. But it wouldn't work. I couldn't look after you. I have too many commitments, I'd be away so much. You need your mother. For the time being, you should be with her. It's better that way.'

She set her mouth as though, faced with the inevitable, she were gathering courage to accept it. She turned from him, and once more they walked.

'You'll come back to see me,' Alec told her. 'We'll go to Glenshandra again next summer. You could maybe try your luck with the salmon this year.'

'What's going to happen to Deepbrook?'

'I suppose I shall sell it. There's not much point hanging on to it if your mother isn't there.'

'And you?'

'I shall stay in Islington.'

She said painfully, 'My bedroom in London . . .'

'It's still your room. It always will be. . . .'

'It isn't that. It's just some books I'd like to take with me. I've . . . I've written down the names.' She took her hand from her pocket and brought out a piece of lined paper torn from an exercise book. He took it from her and unfolded it. He read,

> *The Secret Garden*
> *Adventure of the World*
> *Gone with the Wind*

There were other titles, but for some reason he couldn't go on reading them.

'Of course.' He spoke gruffly, pushing the piece of paper deep into the pocket of his own overcoat. 'Is . . . is there anything else?'

'No. Just the books.'

'I don't know if your mother told you, but I'm going to drive you both to the airport to catch your plane. I'll bring the books with me then. So if you do think of any more things, let me know.'

She shook her head. 'There's nothing else.'

Now, the mist had turned to rain. It beaded her hair and the rough surface of her navy-blue coat. They had rounded the field and were headed back towards the school buildings. They left the grass and walked on gravel, their footsteps crunching. There did not seem to be anything else to talk about. At the foot of the steps that led up to the imposing front door, she stopped and turned once more to face him.

She said, 'I have to go and get ready for games. You'd better not come in.'

He said, 'I'll say goodbye now. I won't say goodbye at the airport.'

'Goodbye, then.'

Her hands remained firmly deep in her coat pockets. He put his hand under her chin and lifted up her face.

'Gabriel.'

'Goodbye.'

He stooped and kissed her cheek. For the first time that afternoon she looked straight at him. For an instant their eyes met, and hers were filled with neither tears nor reproach. Then she was gone, walking away from him up the steps, beneath the pretentious colonnade, through the door.

They left for America the following Thursday, his wife and his child, on the evening flight to New York. As he had promised, Alec drove them to the airport, and after their flight had been called, and he had said goodbye, he made his way up to the observation lounge. It was a wet, dark evening, with much low cloud, and he stood, staring through the streaming glass, waiting for their plane to take off. On time the great jet thundered down the runway, lights flashing through the gloom. He watched it lift off, but seconds later it was lost to sight, swallowed into the clouds. He stayed until the sound of the engines died into the darkness. Only then did he turn away, making the long walk across the polished floor towards the head of the escalator. There were people everywhere, but he did not see them, and no head turned to watch him go. For the first time in his life he knew how it felt to be a nonentity, a failure.

He drove himself back to his empty house. Bad news travels with the speed of light and by now it was common knowledge that his marriage was finished, that Erica had left him for a rich American and had taken Gabriel with her. This, in some measure, was a relief, because it meant that Alec didn't have to tell people, but he shied from social contact and sympathy, and although Tom Boulderstone had asked him around to Campden Hill for supper this evening, he had refused the invitation, and Tom had understood.

He was used to being alone, but now his solitude had a new dimension. He went upstairs, and the bedroom, stripped of Erica's possessions, seemed empty, unfamiliar. He had a shower and changed, and then went downstairs again, poured himself a drink, and took it into the sitting room. Without Erica's pretty ornaments, without any flowers, it looked desolate, and he drew the curtains and told himself that tomorrow he would stop off at the florist and buy himself a potted plant.

It was nearly half past eight, but he was not hungry. He was too exhausted, too drained, for hunger. Later, he would go and investigate, and see what Mrs Abney had concocted and left in the oven for his supper. Later. Now, he switched on the television and collapsed in front of it, his drink in his hand, his chin sunk on his chest.

He stared at the flickering screen. After a moment or two he realized that he was watching a documentary, a programme dealing with the problems of marginal farming. To illustrate the problem, the presenters had chosen a farm in Devon. There was a shot of sheep grazing the rocky slopes of Dartmoor . . . the camera panned down the hill to the farmhouse . . . the lush green slopes of the lower land . . .

It was not Chagwell, but it was a place very similar. The film had been shot in summertime. He saw the blue skies, the high white clouds, their shadows racing down the hillside, to where sunlight sparkled on the waters of a bubbling trout river.

Chagwell.

The past is another country. A long time ago Alec had been conceived, born, brought up in that country; his roots lay deep in that rich red Devon soil. But over the years, diverted by his own success, his own ambitions, and the demands of family life, he had almost totally lost touch.

Chagwell. His father had died, and Brian and his wife, Jenny, now ran the farm between them. In the space of seven years Jenny had borne Brian five blond, freckle-faced children, and the old house bulged with their pets and prams and bicycles and toys.

Erica had no time for Brian and Jenny. They were not her sort of people. Only twice during the whole of their married life had Alec taken her to Chagwell, but the two occasions had been so uncomfortable and so little fun for everybody concerned that, as if by mutual consent, they had never been repeated. Communication dwindled to an exchange of cards at Christmas and the odd letter, but Alec had not seen Brian for five years or more.

Five years. It was too long. Bad news travels with the speed of light, but it would not yet have reached Chagwell. Brian would have to be told about the pending divorce. Alec would write tomorrow, losing no time, for it was unthinkable that Brian should hear about the break-up of his brother's marriage from some other person.

Or he could telephone . . .

The telephone, at his side, began to ring. Alec reached out and picked up the receiver.

'Yes?'

'Alec.'

'Yes.'

'Brian here.'

Brian. He was visited by a sense of blinding unreality, as though his imagination had reached out beyond the limits of his own despair. For a moment he wondered if he was going out of his mind. Automatically, he leaned forward and switched off the television.

'Brian.'

'Who else?' He sounded his usual cheerful, breezy self, his voice as clear as a bell. For whatever reason he was calling, it was plainly not to impart bad news.

'Where are you ringing from?'

'Chagwell, of course, where else?'

Alec saw him sitting at the battered, roll-top desk in the old study at Chagwell, that dusty, book-lined room that had always been used as the farm office. He saw the piles of government forms and dog-eared files, the proud photographs of prizewinning pedigree Guernsey cows.

'You sound astonished,' said Brian.

'It's been five years.'

'I know. Far too long. But I thought you'd like to hear a fairly surprising piece of family news. Uncle Gerald's getting married.'

Gerald. Gerald Haverstock of Tremenheere. Adm. G. J. Haverstock, C.B.E., D.S.O., D.S.C., R.N., once known as the most eligible bachelor in the Royal Navy.

'When did you hear this?'

'This morning. He rang up to tell us. Sounds over the moon. Wants us all to go the wedding.'

'When's that?'

'Weekend after next. In Hampshire.'

Gerald, finally, getting married. 'He must be sixty now.'

'Well, you know what they say, the best wine comes from old bottles.'

'Who's the bride?'

'She's called Eve Ashby. The widow of an old shipmate. It's all very suitable.'

Still, Alec found it hard to believe, for it was indeed an astounding piece of news. Gerald, of all people, the career sailor, the perpetual bachelor, yearned after by countless lovelorn ladies. Gerald, with whom Brian and Alec had spent one blissful summer holiday, the only youngsters in a wholly adult house party. Running wild on the Cornish beaches and playing cricket on the lawn in front of the house, they had yet been treated – for the first time in their lives – as grown-ups. Allowed to stay up for dinner, drink wine, take the sailing dinghy out on their own. Gerald became their hero, and they followed his meteoric career with proprietary pride.

Gerald had been best man at so many weddings that it took some imagination to see him as the bridegroom.

'Are you going to the wedding?' Alec asked.

'Yes, we all are. Kids and all. Gerald wants the lot of us. And you as well. It's not that far from Deepbrook. You could drive over in the afternoon. I don't suppose Erica would particulary want to come, but perhaps you and Gabriel . . .?'

He paused, waiting for a reaction to this suggestion. Alec's mouth was suddenly dry. He saw again the transatlantic jet, taking off, lifting, disappearing into the darkness of night and cloud. She's gone. Gabriel's gone.

After a bit, in a totally different voice, Brian said, 'Is every-thing all right, old boy?'

'Why do you ask?'

'Well, to tell you the truth, the last few days, I've been thinking about you . . . had the feeling you were a bit under the weather. In fact, I've been meaning to ring you. Had this urge to have a word. Telling you about Gerald's wedding was just a good excuse to pick up the telephone.'

Had this urge to have a word.

They had, as boys, been very close. The barriers of distance, the passing years, the two incompatible wives, the lack of communication had not destroyed their closeness. They had always been in touch, linked by a strong, invisible cord of blood and birth. Perhaps this unexpected telephone call, for whatever reason it had been made, was a sort of lifeline.

He clutched at it. He said, 'Yes, everything's wrong,' and told Brian. It did not take very long.

When he was finished, Brian only said, 'I see.'

'I was going to write tomorrow and tell you. Or telephone . . . I'm sorry I didn't get around to telling you before.'

'That's all right, old boy. Look. I'm coming up to London next week for the fatstock show at Smithfield. Would you like to meet?'

No comments, no postmortems, no unnecessary sympathy. 'More than anything,' Alec told his brother. 'Come to my club and I'll give you lunch.'

They fixed on a day and time.

'And what shall I tell Gerald?' Brian asked.

'Tell him I'll be at his wedding. I wouldn't miss it for all the tea in China.'

Brian rang off. Slowly Alec replaced his own receiver. The past is another country.

Images filled his mind, not only of Chagwell, but now, thinking of Gerald, of Tremenheere as well. The old stone house at the very end of Cornwall, where palm trees grew, and camellias and verbena, and scented white jasmine covered the sides of the glass houses in the walled garden.

Chagwell and Tremenheere. They were his roots and his identity. He was Alec Haverstock and he would cope. The world had not come to an end. Gabriel had gone; parting from her had been the worst, but now the worst was over. He had touched bottom and he could only start coming up again.

He stood up and, carrying his empty glass, went through to the kitchen to look for something to eat.

3

ISLINGTON

It was five o'clock before Laura finally reached home. The breeze had dropped and Abigail Crescent drowsed sleepily in the golden sunshine of late afternoon. For once, the street was almost deserted. In all likelihood, her neighbours were sitting in their tiny gardens or had taken their children off to neighbourhood parks for the solace of grass underfoot and shady trees overhead. Only an old lady, with a shopping trolley and an ancient mongrel on a leash, was making her way down the pavement. As Laura drew up in front of her house, even they disappeared, like rabbits down a burrow, descending steps into some basement flat.

She gathered up the day's shopping, her handbag, and her dog and got out of the car, crossed the pavement, and went up the stairs to her front door. She always had to remind herself that it was her own front door every time she found her latchkey and turned the lock. Because the house, which she had lived in for nine months, was still not totally familiar. She was not yet in tune with its moods nor its reactions. It was Alec's home, and it had been Erica's home, and Laura always entered it tentatively, unable to suppress the sensation that she was trespassing upon another person's property.

Now, the warm silence pressed in, thick as a fog. From below, from Mrs Abney's domain, came no sound. Perhaps she had taken herself out or was still asleep. Gradually the humming of the refrigerator in the kitchen made itself heard. Then a clock ticking. Yesterday Laura had bought roses, filled a jug with them. Today their scent, from the sitting room, lay heavy and sweet.

I have come home. This is my home.

It was not a large house. Mrs Abney's basement and, above it, three stories – two rooms at each level and none of them particularly spacious. Here, the cramped hall and stairway; on one side the sitting room, on the other the kitchen, which also served as dining space. Above, the main bedroom and bath-room and Alec's dressing room, doubling as a study. Above again – with dormer windows and sloping ceilings – the attics. A nominal guest room, usually stacked with suitcases and an overflow of furniture, and the nursery, which had once been Gabriel's. That was all.

She set Lucy down and then went into the kitchen to unload the groceries and the chops she had bought for supper. Here were pine fitments, blue-and-white china, a scrubbed table, wheel-back chairs. French windows opened onto a teak deck, and from this a flight of wooden steps led down into a small paved garden, where grew a flowering cherry and a few tubs of geraniums. Laura unbolted these windows and threw them open. Air stirred through the house. Outside on the deck were a couple of garden chairs and a small, wrought-iron table. Later, when Alec came home, and while the chops grilled, they would have their drinks out here, in the dusky twilight, watching the sun drop out of the sky, savouring the coolness of evening.

Perhaps that would be the right time to tell him about not going to Scotland. Her heart sank at the thought, not because she was afraid of him, but because she dreaded spoiling things for him. The kitchen clock stood at ten minutes past five. He would not be home for more than an hour. She went upstairs and took off her clothes, pulled on an airy wrapper, and lay down on her own side of the enormous double bed. Half an hour, she promised herself, and then she would have a shower and change. Half an hour. But almost instantly, like a person dropping down a well, she was asleep.

There was a hospital: long corridors, white-tiled, the hum of half-consciousness loud in her ears, white-masked faces. Nothing to worry about, she was being told. Nothing to worry about. A bell started to jangle. Perhaps there was a fire. Someone had tied her down. Nothing to worry about. The bell went on ringing.

She opened her eyes and lay staring at the ceiling. Her heart was still hammering with the fright of the dream. Automatically she lifted her wrist and looked at her watch. Half past five. The bell rang again.

For airiness, she had left the door open, and now she heard Mrs Abney coming up from the basement, making heavy weather of the climb, a step at a time. Laura lay motionless, listening. She heard the click of the latch, the front door opening.

'Oh, Mrs Boulderstone, it's you!'

Daphne. *Daphne*? What was Daphne doing here at half past five in the afternoon? What on earth could she be wanting? Perhaps, hopefully, Mrs Abney would think Laura was out, and send her away.

'I've been ringing for *hours*.' Daphne's high-pitched voice was clearly audible. 'I was sure somebody had to be in, because Mrs Haverstock's car's there.'

'I know. I had a look for myself when I heard the doorbell ringing. Perhaps she's up in her room.' Hope died. 'Come along in, and I'll pop up and see.'

'I hope you weren't asleep, Mrs Abney.'

'No. Just frying a fishcake for my tea.'

Now, Mrs Abney was climbing the stairs again. Laura sat up with a jerk, pushed aside the light cover, swung her legs over the side of the bed. Sitting there, dizzy and disorientated, she saw Mrs Abney appear at the open door, stopping only to give it a token rap on the panel with her knuckled fist.

'You're not asleep, then.' Mrs Abney, with her frizzy grey hair and her bedroom slippers and her heavy support hose, which did nothing to conceal the ropelike knots of her trouble-some varicose veins. 'Didn't you hear the bell?'

'I *was* asleep. I'm sorry you had to answer the door.'

'Ringing and ringing it was. Thought you must be out.'

'I'm sorry,' Laura said again.

'It's Mrs Boulderstone.'

From downstairs, Daphne was listening in to this exchange. 'Laura, it's me! Don't get out of bed, I'll come up –'

'No . . .' She didn't want Daphne in her bedroom. 'I won't be a moment.'

But her protests did no good, because the next moment Daphne was there. 'Goodness, I'm sorry. I never imagined you'd be in bed at this hour. Poor Mrs Abney. Thank you so much for coming to my rescue. Now you can get back to your fishcakes. We were quite worried about you, Laura. Thought you'd disappeared for good.'

'She never heard the bell,' Mrs Abney explained unnecess-arily. 'Well, if you're all right, then.' And she left them, her bedroom slippers treading heavily away down the creaking stair.

Daphne pulled a comic face at her departing back view. 'I did try to telephone, but there wasn't any reply. Were you out?'

'I went to have tea with Phyllis in Hampstead.'

Daphne tossed her bag and her sunglasses down onto the end of Laura's bed and moved to the dressing table to check her appearance in Laura's mirror. 'I've been having my hair done. It was boiling under the dryer.'

'It looks very nice.' You could tell, not just by her perfectly coifed cap of silvery hair, but by the rich lacquered smell of her, that Daphne had come straight from the beauty salon. She looked, Laura decided in a hopeless sort of way, quite amazingly chic, in thin cotton trousers and pale pink silk shirt. Her figure remained slender as a child's, and as always she was deeply tanned, impeccably made up, scented and elegant. 'Who does it for you?'

'A boy called Antony. He's queer as a coot, but he cuts well.' Apparently satisfied with the way she looked, Daphne turned from the mirror and sank into a small pink velvet armchair that stood by the window. 'I'm exhausted,' she announced.

'What have you been doing all day?'

'Well. I had some shopping to do. . . . I got a divine pair of knickerbockers in Harrods, I thought they'd do for Glenshandra. I've left them in the car, otherwise I'd show them to you. And then I had a gorgeous lunch in the Meridiana, and then I had to come all the way to Euston to pick up a package for Tom. It's a new salmon rod, made for him in Inverness, and they sent it down on the train. *So* . . . as I was coming this way, I though I'd come and see you and we could finalize all our plans for going north. Doesn't that sound businesslike?'

She lay back in the chair, stretching out her legs. Her eyes, large and of an amazing blue, moved around the room. 'You've changed things in here, haven't you? Isn't that a new bed?'

Her lack of perception, of tact, was something that Laura, painfully diffident herself, had never got used to.

'Yes It is new. Alec bought it when we got married.'

'And new curtains as well. That's a very pretty chintz.'

It occurred to Laura that Daphne must have been in this room a thousand times before, gossiping with Erica, just as she now sat and chatted to Laura. She imagined them trying on new clothes, sharing confidences, discussing some party, making plans. Her thin wrapper felt crumpled and sweaty. More than anything, she wanted a shower. She wanted Daphne to go away and leave her alone.

As sometimes occurs on truly desperate occasions, she was visited by a brainwave.

'Would you like a drink?'

'Adore one,' said Daphne promptly.

'You know where Alec keeps the drinks . . . in that cupboard in the kitchen. There's gin there, and tonic. And a lemon in the fridge . . . and some ice. Why don't you go down and help yourself and I'll be with you in a moment. I have to get some clothes on. I can't stay here for the rest of the day, and Alec will be home soon.'

At this Daphne perked up visibly and needed no further persuasion to fall in with Laura's impromptu plan. She pulled herself out of the chair, collected handbag and sunglasses, and went downstairs. Laura waited until she heard cupboard doors opening and the clink of glass. Only then, when she was certain that Daphne would not suddenly appear again, like a Jack-in-the-box, did she get to her feet.

Fifteen minutes later, showered and dressed, she went down and found Daphne relaxed on the sofa, with a cigarette lighted and her drink on the table at her elbow. The sitting room was full of evening sunlight and the scent of roses, and Daphne had found a new *Harpers and Queen*, and was flipping through its glossy pages, but when Laura appeared, she tossed the magazine down and said, 'You haven't changed this room at all, have you? I mean, apart from a few bits and pieces?'

'There wasn't much point. It's pretty enough as it is.'

'Do you like living here? I always think Islington's a bit back of beyondish. It takes such hours to get anywhere.'

'It's handy for the City.'

'That's what Alec always said – stubborn old devil. Which was the reason that Erica made him buy Deepbrook.'

Laura, taken aback, could think of no rejoinder to this. Never before had Daphne come up with such a direct, almost provocative, reference to the past. Why now? Perhaps because there was no Tom here to put a brake on her outspokenness. She and Laura were alone, and she obviously felt that there could be no need for delicate references, tactful evasions. Laura's heart sank and she felt trapped.

Daphne smiled. 'We never talk about Erica, do we? We all tiptoe around the subject as though it were forbidden. But after all, it happened; it's past history now. Water under the bridge.'

'Yes, I suppose it is.'

Daphne's eyes narrowed. She lit another cigarette and then said, 'It must be strange being a second wife. I've often thought it must be strange for you. A whole new experience, and yet it's all happened before, to another woman. It's a classic situation, of course.'

'How do you mean?'

'Well, think of Jane Eyre, or the second Mrs de Winter in *Rebecca*.'

'Except that Alec is neither a bigamist nor a murderer.'

Daphne looked blank. Perhaps she was not as well-read as she made out. Laura thought about explaining, and then decided against it. She saw that Daphne's glass was empty.

'Have another gin and tonic.'

'Adore it.' This seemed to be her stock reply when offered a drink. She held out the glass. 'Or would you like me to get it for myself?'

'No. I'll do it.'

In the kitchen, she poured the drink, filled the glass with ice. Daphne had been out for lunch – doubtless with one of her mysterious admirers. Doubtless, too, she had been plied with martinis and wine. Laura wondered if, possibly, she was slightly drunk. What else could explain her extraordinary burst of frankness? She looked at the clock and longed for Alec to come home and rescue her from this situation. She carried the glass back into the sitting room.

'Oh, gorgeous.' Daphne took it from her. 'Aren't you having anything?'

'No. I'm . . . not really thirsty.'

'Well, cheers!' She drank, and then set the glass down again. 'I was just thinking . . . you know, it's nearly six years since Erica went to America. It doesn't seem possible that it was so long ago. I suppose, as we all get older, time flies by more quickly . . . or something. But it doesn't seem so long.' She settled herself more comfortably in her corner of the sofa, tucking her feet up beneath her, the very picture of a woman getting down to an intimate chat. 'She was my best friend. Did you know that?'

'Yes, I think I did.'

'We were at school together. We were always friends. It was I who introduced her to Alec. At least, I didn't introduce them, because she was in Hong Kong, but I brought them together. When they got married, I was terribly thrilled, but I was also just the teensiest weensiest bit jealous. You see, Alec was one of my first boyfriends. I knew him before I met Tom. Silly to feel that way about a man, but let's face it, there's no love like a first love.'

'Unless it's the last love.'

Daphne's expression was at once surprised and hurt, as though she had just been bitten by a worm. 'I wasn't being bitchy, I promise you. Just making a tiny confession. After all, he is a very attractive man.'

'I expect,' said Laura, in some desperation, 'you missed Erica very much.'

'Oh, dreadfully. At first I couldn't believe that she wasn't coming back, and then the divorce came through and Alec sold Deepbrook, and after that I knew we'd never go back. It was like the end of an era. Weekends without Deepbrook to escape to seemed very strange. We worried about Alec, too, being on his own so much, but he took up with his brother again and used to disappear off to Devon on Friday evenings. I expect he's taken you there?'

'To Chagwell, you mean? Yes, we've been, we went for Easter. But mostly we just stay here.' (Those weekends were the best of all. Just the two of them and Lucy, the door closed and the windows open and the little house to themselves.)

'Do you like them? Brian Haverstock and his wife, I mean. Erica couldn't stand going there. She said the furniture was covered in dog's hairs and the children never stopped screaming.'

'With such a big family, it's bound to be fairly disorganized and rowdy . . . but it's fun, too.'

'Erica couldn't stand undisciplined children. Gabriel was charming.' She stubbed out her cigarette. 'Does Alec ever hear from Gabriel?'

This was getting worse and worse. Uncontrollable. Laura lied. 'Oh, yes,' and was astonished at her own coolness.

'She's probably a real little American by now. Young people out there have such a marvellous time. I suppose that was why she never came back to this country to see Alec. He always imagined that she would. Each year he'd start making noises about her joining us at Glenshandra, and he'd book a room for her in the hotel and get himself all organized. But she never came. Talking of which,' she went on, with no change of expression in her voice, 'that's really why I came to see you, not to talk about my past life. Glenshandra. Are you all prepared to face the frozen north? I hope you've got heaps of warm clothes, because it can be bitterly cold on the river, even in July. One year it rained nonstop and we nearly froze. And you'll need something formal for the evenings, just in case we get asked out for dinner. That's the sort of thing husbands never remember to tell you, and there isn't a shop for a hundred miles, so you can't go out and buy anything.'

She stopped and waited for Laura to make some response to this. Laura could think of nothing to say. Daphne rattled on.

'Alec told us that you'd never actually fished, but you are going to try it, aren't you? It'll be boring otherwise, left at the hotel all on your own. You don't look very excited at the prospect. Aren't you looking forward to it?'

'Well . . . yes . . . but . . .'

'There's nothing wrong, is there?'

She would have to know sooner or later. Everybody would have to know. 'I – I don't think I'm going to be able to come.'

'Not *come*?'

'I've got to go into hospital. It's just a small thing . . . a small operation, but the doctor says I've got to rest up afterwards. She says I can't go to Scotland.'

'But *when*? When do you have to go into hospital?'

'In a day or two.'

'But does that mean *Alec* can't come?' Daphne sounded appalled at this prospect, as though without Alec the entire holiday were doomed to disaster.

'Yes, of course he can. There's no reason for him to stay.'

'But . . . won't you *mind*?'

'I want him to go. I want him to come with you all.'

'But *you*. Poor you. What a wretched thing to happen. And who's going to look after you? Mrs Abney?'

'I'll maybe go and stay with Phyllis.'

'You mean, your aunt, who lives in Hampstead?'

A car was drawing up in the street outside. The engine stopped; a door slammed. Laura prayed for it to be Alec. 'That's why I went to see her this afternoon.' Footsteps; his key in the lock. 'That's Alec now.'

They met as he opened the front door, and she had never been so glad to see him.

'Laura . . .'

Before he had time to kiss her, she said in clear tones, 'Hello, isn't it lovely, Daphne's here.'

He froze, one arm around his wife, the other hand still holding his briefcase. 'Daphne?' He looked amazed.

'Yes, it's me!' Daphne called from the sitting room. Alec put down his briefcase and shut the door behind him. 'Isn't that a nice surprise for you?'

He went through the open door, with Laura behind him, and stood there, with his hands in his pockets, smiling down at Daphne.

'What are you doing here?'

She smiled back at him, tilting her head, so that her earrings bobbed to one side.

'Just having a little girlish gossip. I had to pick up a parcel at Euston and it seemed a good opportunity. It's not often I'm in this neck of the woods.'

He stooped to kiss her upturned face. 'Lovely to see you.'

'I really came to talk to Laura about Glenshandra. . . .'

Behind Alec's back Laura made an agonized face, but Daphne either did not notice this frantic telegram or else was too engrossed in Alec to pay attention, '. . . but she's just told me that she isn't going to be able to come.'

In that instant, Laura could have strangled Daphne. Or strangled herself for having been such a fool as to confide in her.

Alec turned and looked at her, frowning and completely at a loss. 'Not able to come . . .?'

'Oh, Daphne, Alec doesn't *know* about it yet. At least he didn't until you told him.'

'And you wanted to tell him yourself! How ghastly, and now I've let the cat out of the bag. Tom's always telling me I talk too much. I had no idea. . . .'

'I *told* you. I only saw the doctor this afternoon!'

'I didn't know you were going to see the doctor,' said Alec.

'I didn't want to tell you. Until I'd been. Until I knew. I didn't want you to be worrying. . . .' To her horror she heard the break in her own voice. But Alec heard it too and came to her rescue, stemming her distress and confusion.

'We don't need to talk about it now, you can tell me later. When Daphne's gone.'

'Oh, darling, is that a hint? Does that mean I've got to take myself off?'

'No, of course not. I'm going to have a drink. Let me give you another.'

'Well' – she cradled her glass in her hand – 'perhaps a tiny one. Not too strong, though, because I've got to drive myself home, and Tom will kill me if I bash up the car.'

She went at last. They watched the weaving back view of her car disappear around the curve of the crescent.

'Hope she doesn't kill herself,' said Alec. They went indoors and he shut the door. Laura instantly burst into tears.

Almost as instantly he had his arms around her.

'Now come along. Calm down. What's all this about?'

'I didn't want *her* to be the one to tell you. I wanted to tell you myself, when we were having a drink. . . . I didn't mean to tell her, but she went on and on about Glenshandra and in the end I couldn't do anything else. . . .'

'That doesn't matter. All that matters is you. . . . Come along.' With his arm around her he led her into the sitting room, pushed her gently down where Daphne had sat, and lifted her feet up on to the sofa. The cushion under Laura's head smelled of Daphne. She couldn't stop crying.

'I . . . kept putting off going to see Doctor Hickley because I didn't want to be told I'd have to have another operation, and because I thought perhaps everything would sort itself out. But it hasn't. It's just got worse.'

Tears were streaming down her face. He sat on the edge of the sofa and gave her the clean linen handkerchief out of his top pocket. She blew her nose, but it didn't seem to do much good.

'When have you got to go into hospital?'

'In a day or two. Doctor Hickley's going to ring me. . . .'

'I'm sorry. But after all, it's not the end of the world.'

'It will be if it doesn't work this time, because if it happens again . . . she says I'll have to have a hysterectomy, and I don't want that to happen. I'm frightened of that happening . . . I don't think I could bear it . . . I want to have a baby . . . I want to have your baby. . . .'

She looked up at him, but she could not see his face because it was drowned in her own tears. And then she couldn't see it, because he had gathered her up into his arms, and her own face was buried against the warm comfort of his shoulder.

He said, 'It won't happen again.'

'That's what Phyllis said, but we don't know.' She wept into his navy-blue, chalk-striped suit. 'I want to *know*.'

'We can't know everything.'

'I want a child. . . .' *I want to give you a child to make up for Gabriel.*

Why couldn't she say it? What was wrong with their marriage that she couldn't bring herself to say Gabriel's name? What was wrong with their marriage that Alec never mentioned his daughter, wrote letters to her from the privacy of his office, and, if she ever replied to these letters, kept these a secret from Laura? There shouldn't be secrets. They should be able to talk about anything, tell each other everything.

It wasn't even as though she had gone without trace. Upstairs in the attics was her room, filled with her furniture, her toys, her pictures, her desk. On the chest of drawers in Alec's dressing room stood Gabriel's photograph, the drawing that she had done for him, proud in its silver frame. Why couldn't he realize that this refusal to admit even her existence was creating a void between them that Laura was incapable of crossing?

She sighed deeply and pulled away from him, and lay back on the pillow, hating herself for crying so much, for looking hideous, for being so unhappy. His handkerchief was already sodden with her grief. She tugged viciously at its hemstitched corner. She said, 'If I can't give you a child, I can't give you *anything*.'

Being Alec, he came out with no comforting cliché. But after a little he said, in a marvellously normal way, 'Have you had a drink?'

Laura shook her head.

'I'll get you a brandy.' He stood up and went out of the room. She heard him moving around the kitchen. Lucy, disturbed by his presence, got out of her basket. Laura heard the scratch of her claws on the linoleum. Then she came into the room and ran to jump up into Laura's lap. She licked Laura's face and, tasting salt tears, licked it again. She curled up and went back to sleep. Laura blew her nose again and pushed a straggling lock of dark hair away from her face. Alec returned, with whisky for himself and a little glass of brandy for Laura. He gave it to her and pulled up a low stool and sat facing her. He smiled and she smiled back, feebly.

'Better?'

She nodded.

'The brandy's medicinal,' he told her. She took a mouthful and felt it slip, burning, down her throat and into her stomach. Its strength was comforting.

'Now,' he said, 'we'll talk about Glenshandra. Doctor Hickley says you're not to come?'

'She says I can't.'

'And there's no question of the operation being postponed?'

Laura shook her head.

'In that case we'll have to call Glenshandra off.'

She took a deep breath. 'That's what I *really* don't want. I really don't want you not to go.'

'But I can't leave you here alone.'

'I – I thought we could get a nurse in or something. I know Mrs Abney couldn't manage by herself, but we could perhaps get somebody to help her.'

'Laura, I couldn't leave you here.'

'I *knew* you'd say that. I just *knew* you'd say that.'

'Well, what did you expect me to say? Laura, Glenshandra doesn't matter.'

'It does matter. You know it matters.' She began to cry again, and there was no way she could stop the flood of tears. 'You look forward to it all year, it's your holiday, you have to go. And the others . . .'

'They'll understand.'

She thought of Daphne's face of horror, Daphne saying, *Does that mean Alec can't come*?

'They won't understand. They'll just think I'm being as useless and boring about this as they do about everything else.'

'That's unfair.'

'I want you to go. I want you to. Don't you realize that's why

64

I'm so miserably upset, because I know I'm ruining everything for you?'

'You can't go into hospital and have an operation if you're in this state.'

'Then think of something. Phyllis said you'd be able to think of something.'

'Phyllis?'

'I went to see her this afternoon. After Doctor Hickley. I thought I'd ask her if I could go and stay with her when I come out of hospital, because I thought if you knew I was with her, then you'd go to Glenshandra, but she can't have me because she's going to Florence. She says she'll put it off, but I can't let her do that. . . .'

'No, of course we can't let her do that.'

'I told her it's the first time in my life I wished I had a family of my own. A real family, with masses of close relations. I've never wished that before. I wish I still had a cosy mother, and I could go and stay with her and she'd put hot-water bottles in my bed.'

She looked at him to see if he was smiling at this useless fancy, but he was not smiling. He said gently, 'You haven't got a family, but I have.'

Laura thought about this, and then said, with a notable lack of enthusiasm, 'You mean Chagwell?'

He laughed. 'No. Not Chagwell. I love my brother and his wife and their brood of children very much, but Chagwell is a house where you can stay only if you are in the rudest of health.'

Laura felt relieved. 'I'm glad you said that, and not me.'

He said, 'You could go to Tremenheere.'

'Where's Tremenheere?'

'Cornwall. The very end of Cornwall. Heaven on earth. An old Elizabethan manor and a view of the bay.'

'You sound like a travel agent. Who lives there?'

'Gerald and Eve Haverstock. He's my uncle, and she's a darling.'

Laura remembered. 'They sent us crystal wineglasses for a wedding present.'

'That's right.'

'And a sweet letter.'

'Right again.'

'And he's a retired admiral?'

'Who didn't get married until he was sixty.'

'What a complicated family you have.'

'But all charming. Like me.'

'When were you at this place . . . Tremenheere?' The word was difficult to say, especially after a neat brandy.

'When I was a boy. Brian and I spent a summer holiday there.'

'But I've never met them. Gerald and Eve, I mean.'

'That doesn't matter.'

'We don't even know if they can have me to stay.'

'I'll ring them later on and fix it.'

'What if they say no?'

'They won't say no, but if they do, we'll think of something else.'

'I'll be a nuisance.'

'I don't think so.'

'How would I get there?'

'I'll drive you down once you're out of hospital.'

'You'll be at Glenshandra.'

'I shan't go to Glenshandra until you're safely delivered. Like a parcel.'

'You'll miss some of your holiday. Some of the fishing.'

'That won't kill me.'

She had finally run out of objections. Tremenheere was a compromise, but it was at least a plan. It would mean meeting new people, living in a stranger's house, but as well it meant that Phyllis would go to Florence and Alec would go to Scotland.

She turned her head on the cushion and looked at him, sitting there, with his drink cradled between his knees. She saw his thick hair, black, streaked with white, like silver fox fur. His face, not conventionally handsome, but arresting and distinguished, the sort of face that seen once could never be forgotten. She saw his tallness, easily disposed upon the low stool, his long legs spread, his hands clasped loosely around his glass. She looked into his eyes, which were dark as her own, and he smiled, and her heart turned over.

He is, after all, a very attractive man.

Phyllis had said, *Can you see a man of Alec's integrity having an affair with his best friend's wife?* But how Daphne would love having him at Glenshandra on his own.

The thought filled Laura with a pain that was ludicrous,

66

because she had spent the last half hour persuading him to go. Ashamed of herself, filled with love for Alec, she put out her hand, and he took it in his own.

'If Gerald and Eve say they can have me, and if I say that I'll go, you promise you'll go to Scotland.'

'If that's what you want.'

'That is what I want, Alec.'

He bent his head and kissed the palm of her hand and closed her fingers around the kiss as though it were some precious gift.

She said, 'I probably wouldn't be much good at fishing anyway . . . and you won't have to spend all your time trying to teach me.'

'There'll be another year.'

Another year. Perhaps in another year, everything would be better.

'Tell me about Tremenheere.'

4

TREMENHEERE

The day had been perfect. Long, hot, sun-soaked. The tide was out, and the beach, viewed from the sea, where Eve, after an energetic swim, drifted blissfully on the rise and fall of gathering waves, revealed itself as a curve of cliff, a sickle of rocks, and then the wide, clean sweep of the sand.

It was, for this particular beach, crowded. Now, at the end of July, the holiday season was at its peak and the scene was littered with bright spots of colour: bathing towels and striped windbreaks; children in scarlet and canary-yellow bathing suits; sun umbrellas and huge, inflatable rubber balls. Overhead, gulls swooped and screamed, perched on the clifftops, dived to devour the flotsam of a hundred picnics, dropped in the sand. Their screams were matched by human cries, which, across the distance, pierced the air. Boys playing football, mothers shrieking at wayward toddlers, the happy screams of a girl being mobbed by a couple of youths who appeared to be trying to drown her.

The sea at first had seemed icy, but the swim had got her circulation going and now she was aware only of a marvellous, invigorating, salty coolness. She lay on her back and watched the cloudless sky, her mind empty of anything save the physical perfection of now.

I am fifty-eight, she reminded herself, but had long since decided that one of the good things about being fifty-eight was the fact that one took time to appreciate the really marvellous moments that still came one's way. They weren't happiness, exactly. Years ago, happiness had ceased to pounce, unawares, with the reasonless ecstacy of youth. They were something better. Eve had never much liked being pounced on, by happiness or anything else. It had always frightened and disconcerted her to be taken unawares.

Lulled, as though in a cradle, by the movement of the sea, she let herself be gently washed ashore by the incoming tide.

Now, the waves gathered their puny momentum, curved into shallow breakers. Her hands touched sand. Another wave, and she lay, beached, letting the incoming tide flow over her body, and after the depths in which she had been swimming, the water now felt actually warm.

That was it. It was over. There was no time for more. She got to her feet and walked up onto the blistering sand towards the outcrop of rock where she had left her thick white towel robe. She picked up the robe and pulled it on, felt it warm against the cold wetness of her shoulders and arms. She tied the sash, pushed her feet into thong sandals, started the long walk up towards the narrow footpath that led to the clifftop and the car park.

It was nearly six o'clock. The first of the holiday people were starting to pack up, the children, reluctant, protesting, howling with exhaustion and too much sun. Some people were already well tanned, but others, who had perhaps arrived only yesterday or the day before, were boiled pink as lobsters and were in for a couple of days of agony and peeling shoulders before they could safely venture out again. They never learned. It happened every hot summer, and the doctors' surgeries were filled with them, sitting in rows with flaming faces and blistered backs.

The cliff path was steep. At the top, Eve paused for breath, turning back to look at the sea, framed between two bastions of rock. Inshore, over the sand it was green as jade, but farther out lay a ribbon of the most intense indigo blue. The horizon was hazed in lavender, the sky azure.

A young family caught up with her, the father carrying the toddler, the mother dragging the older child by the hand. He was in tears. 'I don't want to go 'ome termorrer. I want to stay 'ere for another week. I want to stay 'ere forever.'

Eve caught the young mother's eye. She was close to exasperation. Eve could identify with her. She remembered being that age, with Ivan, a stocky little blond boy, clinging to her hand. She could feel his hand, small and dry and rough, in her own. Don't be angry with him, she wanted to say. Don't spoil it. Before you know where you are, he'll be grown up and you'll have lost him forever. Savour every fleeting moment of your child's life, even if he does, from time to time, drive you out of your mind.

69

'I don't want to go 'ome.' The drone continued. The mother made a resigned face in Eve's direction and Eve smiled back wryly, but her tender heart bled for the lot of them, who tomorrow would have to leave Cornwall and make the long, tedious journey back to London; to crowds, and streets and offices and jobs and buses and the smell of petrol fumes. It seemed grossly unfair that they should have to go and she should stay. She could stay here forever, because this was where she lived.

Walking towards her car, she prayed for the heat wave to continue. Alec and Laura were arriving this evening in time for dinner, which was the reason Eve could not linger on the beach. They were driving down from London, and tomorrow morning, at some ungodly hour, Alec was leaving again, to make the unimaginably long drive to Scotland and his salmon fishing. Laura would stay at Tremenheere for the next ten days or so, and then Alec would return to take her back to London.

Alec, Eve knew. Pale and stony-faced, still pole-axed by his newly broken marriage, he had come to their wedding, and she had always loved him for this. Since then, slightly less shattered, he had come, once or twice, to stay with Gerald and Eve. But Laura was a stranger. Laura had been ill, in hospital. Laura was coming to Tremenheere to recover.

Which made it even more necessary for the weather to go on being conveniently perfect. Laura would have breakfast in bed and lie, peacefully, in the garden with no person to bother her. She would rest and recover. When she was stronger, perhaps, she, Eve, would bring her here, and they would bask on the beach and swim together.

It made everything so much easier if the weather was good. Living here, in the farthest corner of Cornwall, Eve and Gerald were inundated each summer with visitors: relations, friends from London, young families unable to afford the hideous cost of hotels. They always had a good time because Eve made sure that they did, but sometimes even she became disheartened by constant rain and unseasonable winds, and although she knew perfectly well that it wasn't, she could never quite get rid of the idea that it was all her fault.

These reflections got her into her car, which was boiling hot, despite the fact that she had parked it in the meagre shade of a hawthorn bush. Still bundled in her towel robe, and with the air from the open window cold on her damp hair, she started for home. Up the hill from the cove and onto the main road. Through a village and along by the edge of the sea. The road crossed the railway by means of a bridge and then ran, parallel to the railway lines, towards the town.

In the old days, Gerald had once told her, before the war, here had been only agricultural land, small farms and hidden villages with tiny square-towered churches. The churches still stood, but the fields where the broccoli and the early potatoes had grown were now lost to development and progress. Holiday homes and blocks of flats, petrol stations and super-markets, lined the road.

There was the heliport that served the Scilly Islands and then the big gates of a mansion house that was now a hotel. Once there had been trees beyond the gates, but these had been cut down and space made for a glittering blue swimming pool.

Between this hotel and the start of the town, a road turned up to the right, signposted to Penvarloe. Into this road Eve turned, away from the stream of traffic. The road narrowed to a lane, high hedged, winding up onto the hill. At once she was back in rural, unspoiled countryside. Small fields, stone-walled, where herds of Guernseys grazed. Deep valleys, dark with thickets of wood. After a mile or so, the road curved steeply and the village of Penvarloe lay ahead, low cottages clinging to the edge of the street. She passed the pub – where tables stood out on the cobbled forecourt – and the tenth-century church, embedded, like some prehistoric rock, surrounded by yews and ancient, leaning gravestones.

The village post office was also the general store and sold vegetables, fizzy drinks, and deep-frozen goodies for the holiday trade. Its open door (for it did not close until seven o'clock in the evening) was flanked with crates of fruit, and as Eve approached, a slender woman, with a mop of curling grey hair, emerged through this door. She wore sunglasses and a pale blue, sleeveless dress and carried a wicker basket of shopping. Eve tooted her horn, and the woman saw her and waved, and Eve slowed the car and drew up at the side of the road.

'Silvia.'

Silvia Marten crossed the pavement and came over to talk, stooping, supported by a hand on the roof of the car. From a distance, despite the grey hair, her appearance was incredibly youthful, so that close up, the lined weather-beaten skin, the sharp angle of her jawbone, the sagging flesh beneath her chin, were somehow shocking. She set down her basket and pushed her sunglasses to the top of her head, and Eve stared up into those amazing eyes, neither yellow no green, very wide, very open, and fringed with thickly mascaraed lashes. Her eye shadow was a pale translucent green and her eyebrows immaculately shaped and plucked.

'Hello, Eve.' Her voice was deep and husky. 'Have you been swimming?'

'Yes, I went to Gwenvoe. I've been busy all day and I simply had to have a cool-off.'

'How energetic you are. Didn't Gerald want to come with you?'

'He's been cutting the grass, I think.'

'Are you going to be in this evening? I've got some chrysanthemum cuttings I promised him, and I've run out of space in my greenhouse. Thought I might bring them up, take a drink off you.'

'Oh, how sweet of you. Of course.' Then she hesitated. 'The only thing is, Alec and Laura are arriving sometime. . . .'

'Alec? Alec Haverstock . . .?' she smiled suddenly, and her smile was disarming as a small boy's grin, transforming her expression, dissolving the tautness of her features. 'Is he coming to stay?'

'Not to stay. Just for a night. Laura's staying on for a bit, though. She's been in hospital; come for a rest cure. Of course' – she slapped the flat of her hand against the driving wheel – 'I always forget you've known Alec for so long.'

'We used to play on the beach centuries ago. Well . . . I . . . won't come this evening. Another time.

'No.' Eve could not bear to disappoint Silvia, to imagine her returning to her empty house, to spend the rest of this lovely day on her own. 'Come. Come anyway. Gerald would love to see you. If I ask him he'll make us some Pimms.'

'Well, if you're *sure*.'

Eve nodded.

'Heaven, then; love to come.' She picked up her basket again. 'I'll just take this home and collect the cuttings. Be about half an hour.'

They parted, Silvia walking up the street in the direction of her little house, Eve to pass her and drive on, through the length of the village and a hundred yards or so beyond the last cottage. Now, she was running alongside the garden of Tremenheere. There was a stone wall, and thick clumps of rhododendrons beyond. The gates stood open, and the drive curved around a stand of azaleas and stopped in a sweep of gravel below the front door. This was framed in honeysuckle, and as Eve got out of the car, she could smell its heavy fragrance, drowsy and sweet in the warmth of the breezeless evening.

She went, not indoors, but in search of Gerald, through the escallonia archway that led into the garden. She saw the sweep of the lawn, newly cut, neatly striped in two shades of green. She saw her husband on the flagged terrace, supine in a long chair, with his old sailing hat on his head, a gin and tonic conveniently to hand, and the *Times* on his lap.

The sight of him was, as always, eminently satisfying. One of the best things about Gerald was that he never pottered. Some husbands Eve knew pottered the day away, always apparently on the go, but never actually achieving anything. Gerald was always either intensely busy or intensely idle. He had spent the day cutting the grass; now he was going to be lazy for an hour or two.

Her white coat caught his eye. He looked up and saw her, laid down the newspaper, took off his spectacles.

'Hello, my darling.' She reached his side, put her hands on the arms of his chair, leaned down to kiss him. 'Did you have a lovely swim?'

'Quite delicious.'

'Sit down and tell me about it.'

'I can't. I've got to go and pick raspberries.'

'Stay for a second.'

She sat at his feet, cross-legged. Scented thyme grew between the cracks in the flagstones, and she pulled up a tiny sprig and crushed it between her fingers, releasing the herby, aromatic smell.

She said, 'I've just seen Silvia. She's coming round for a drink. She's got some chrysanthemum cuttings for you. I said you'd maybe make us some Pimms.'

'Can't she come another evening? Alec and Laura will probably arrive while she's here.'

'I think she'd like to see Alec. They said they wouldn't be here until dinnertime. Perhaps –' She had been going to suggest that they should invite Silvia to stay on for dinner, but Gerald interrupted her.

'You're not to ask her to stay for dinner.'

'Why not?'

'Because Laura won't feel like meeting new people, not just yet. Not after two days in hospital and a long drive on a hot day.'

'But it's so embarrassing when people come for a drink and then one has to bundle them off home because it's time to start eating the soup. It seems so inhospitable.'

'You wouldn't know how to be inhospitable. And with a bit of luck, Silvia will have gone before they arrive.'

'You're heartless, Gerald. Silvia's lonely. She's all alone. After all, it's not very long since Tom died.'

'He's been dead for a year.' Gerald never minced words nor talked in platitudes. 'And I'm not heartless. I'm very fond of Silvia and I find her extremely decorative and amusing. But we all have our own lives to live. And I won't have you exhausting yourself, looking after all your lame ducks at the same time. They must wait in a tidy queue and take their turn. And this evening it's Laura's turn.'

'Gerald, I do hope she's nice.'

'I'm sure she's charming.'

'How can you be so sure? You couldn't stand Erica. You said that she drove a wedge between Alec and his family.'

'Never said that. Never met the woman. It was Brian who couldn't stand her.'

'But men who remarry nearly always follow a pattern. I mean, the second time around they often marry somebody the spitting image of the first wife.'

'I don't think that's happened with Alec. Brian approves of this one.'

'She's terribly young. Only a bit older than Ivan.'

'In that case, you will be able to look on her as a daughter.'

'Yes.' Eve thought about this, holding the sprig of thyme to her nose and looking at the garden.

From the terrace and the house the newly cut lawn sloped away, flanked by glossy-leaved camellias, which in May were a riot of pink and white flowers. The prospect, carefully land-

74

scaped by some long-dead gardener, enclosed the distant view much as a frame surrounds a painting. She saw the bay, the wedge of blue sea, dotted with the white sails of small boats.

Still worrying about Silvia she said, 'If we asked Ivan as well he could make up an even number for dinner, and we would tell Silvia – '

'No,' said Gerald. He fixed Eve with a stern blue eye. 'Absolutely no.'

Eve capitulated. 'All right.' They smiled, understanding, in total accord.

She was his first wife, and he was her second husband, but she loved him – although in a totally different sort of way – as much as she had loved Philip Ashby, Ivan's father. Gerald now was sixty-six – balding, bespectacled, white-haired, but still as distinguished and attractive as he had been when Eve first met him, as her husband's commanding officer, and quite the most eligible bachelor in the service. Active and energetic, he had retained his long-legged (all the Haverstocks had long legs), flat-stomached physique, and at parties was constantly surrounded by quite young ladies or cornered in sofas by elderly ones who remembered Gerald as a young man and had never ceased to be charmed by him. Eve didn't mind all this in the slightest. On the contrary, it made her feel quite smug and proud, because at the end of the day, she was the female he searched for and claimed, and took home to Tremenheere.

Gerald had put on his glasses and was once more immersed in the cricket scores. Eve got to her feet and left him there, going indoors.

The British Empire was built by naval officers with private fortunes. Although Gerald Haverstock was born a hundred years or so too late to take part in this enterprise, the principle of the old saying still applied. His success in the service was due, in the larger part, to his own courage, ability, and resource, but as well, he had the courage to take risks and to gamble on his career. He could do this because he could afford to. He loved the navy and was keenly ambitious, but promotion, although desirable, was never financially essential. As a commanding officer, faced with nerve-racking dilemmas involving the future safety of men, expensive equipment, and even international relations, he had never taken the easy, the timid, nor the obvious way out. This dashing behaviour paid off and earned for Gerald a reputation for coolheaded nerve, which had stood him in good stead and finally earned his right to a flag officer's ensign on the front of his large, black, official car.

He had, of course, been lucky as well, and Tremenheere was part of his luck. It was bequeathed to him by an elderly godmother when he was only twenty-six. With the estate went a sizeable fortune, originally amassed by astute dealings with the Great Western Railway, and Gerald's financial future was assured for the rest of his charmed life. It was thought then that he might leave the navy, settle in Cornwall, and take up the existence of a country squire, but he loved his job too much for this, and Tremenheere was left, until the day he retired, to run, more or less, on its own momentum.

A local land agent took over the administration, a tenant was found for the home farm. At times, for long periods, the house was let. Between lets, a caretaker kept an eye on the place, and a full-time gardener tended the lawns and the flowerbeds and kept the two walled gardens neatly dug and filled with rows of vegetables.

Sometimes, home from abroad and with a long leave under his belt, Gerald stayed there himself, filling Tremenheere with family, nephews and nieces, and his own naval friends. Then the old house came to life again, ringing with voices and laughter. Cars stood parked by the front door, children played French cricket on the lawn, doors and windows stood open, enormous meals were partaken around the scrubbed kitchen table or, more formally, in the panelled, candlelit dining room.

The house took all this unorthodox treatment in its stride. It remained, like an elderly sweet-tempered relation, undisturbed, unchanged: still filled with the old godmother's furniture, the curtains she had chosen, the faded prints on the chairs, the Victorian furniture, the silver-framed photographs, the pictures, the china.

Eve, brought here as Gerald's bride six years ago, had made only a few changes. 'It's dreadfully shabby,' Gerald had told her, 'but you can do what you want with it. Do the whole place over if you want to.' But she hadn't wanted to, because Tremenheere, to her, seemed perfect. There was a peace about it, a tranquillity. She loved the ornate Victoriana, the low-lapped chairs, the brass bedsteads, the faded floral carpets. She was reluctant to replace even the curtains, and when one by one they finally shredded to pieces and fell apart, she spent days searching through pattern books from Liberty trying to find designs that would match, as closely as possible, the original chintzes.

Now, she entered the house through the French windows that led from the terrace into the drawing room. After the brightness of the day outside, the interior seemed very cool and dim, and smelled of the sweet peas that, this morning, Eve had arranged in a great bowl and placed on the round marquetry table that stood in the middle of the room. Beyond the drawing room, a wide, oak floored passage led to the hall, and from this spacious entrance, a square wooden staircase with carved newels rose past a soaring window to the upper floor. Here were old portraits, a carved armoire that had once contained linen. The door to their bedroom stood open, and inside the room felt airy, the rose-trellised curtains stirring in the first breeze of the evening. Eve pulled off her towel robe and her bathing suit and went into the bathroom and took a shower, washing the salt out of her dried hair. Then she found clean clothes, a pair of pale pink jeans, a cream silk shirt. She combed her hair, which had once been blonde and was now nearly white, put on some lipstick, and sprayed herself with cologne.

She was now ready to pick raspberries. She left her room and went down the passage to the door that stood at the top of the back stairs leading to the kitchens. But, holding the door handle, she hesitated, changed her mind, and instead went on down the passage to where once had been the nursery wing, and where now May lived.

She tapped on the door. 'May?'

No reply.

'May?' She opened the door and went inside. The room, which was at the back of the house, smelled stuffy and airless. The window had a charming view of the courtyard and the fields beyond, but was firmly shut. In old age May felt the cold and saw no point in suffering what she called howling draughts. As well as being stuffy, the room was crowded, not only with the original Tremenheere nursery furniture, but as well with May's bits and pieces, which she had brought with her from

Hampshire: her own chair, her varnished tea-trolley, a fireside rug, hectic with cabbage roses, which May's sister had once hooked for her. The mantelpiece was crowded with china mementoes from forgotten seaside resorts, jostling for place with a plethora of framed snapshots, all of which depicted either Eve or her son Ivan as small children, because once, in the long distant past, May had been Eve's nursery maid and had remained, willy-nilly, to become – in the not so distant past – Ivan's nanny.

A table stood in the middle of the room, where May sat to do the mending or eat her supper. Eve saw the scrapbook, scissors, the pot of paste. The scrapbook was a new ploy for May. She had bought it in Woolworth's on one of her weekly outings to Truro, where she would lunch with an old friend and potter around the shops. It was a child's scrapbook, with Mickey Mouse on the cover, and already beginning to bulge with cuttings. Eve hesitated and then turned the pages. Pictures of the Princess of Wales, a sailing boat, a view of Brighton, an unknown baby in a pram – all clipped from newspapers or magazines, neatly arranged, but without any apparent reason or cohesions.

Oh, May.

She closed the book. 'May?' Still no reply. A sort of panic filled Eve's heart. Nowadays, she was always anxious for her, fearing the worst. A heart attack, maybe, or a stroke. She crossed to the bedroom door and looked inside, steeling herself to discover May prostrate on the carpet or dead on the bed. But this room too was empty, neat, and stuffy. A small ticking clock stood on the bedside table, and the bed lay smooth beneath May's own crocheted counterpane.

She went downstairs and found May where she had feared to find her, in the kitchen, pottering about, putting things away in the wrong cupboards, boiling up a kettle. . . .

May wasn't meant to work in the kitchen, but she was always sneaking down there when Eve wasn't looking, in the hope of finding some dishes to wash or potatoes to peel. This was because she wanted to be useful, and Eve understood this and tried to make a point of giving May small harmless chores like shelling peas or ironing napkins, while Eve cooked the dinner.

But May stumbling around the kitchen on her own was a perpetual anxiety. Her legs had become unsteady, and she was

78

always losing her balance and having to grab onto something to stop herself from falling. As well, her sight was bad and her coordination beginning to fail, so that the most mundane of tasks, like chopping vegetables, making tea, or going up and down stairs, became occupations fraught with danger. This was Eve's nightmare. That May would cut herself, or scald herself, or break a hip, and the doctor would have to be called, and an ambulance would arrive to wheel May off to hospital. Because in hospital, without doubt, May would be a terror. They would examine her and probably be insulted by her. She would do something mad and irrational, like stealing another patient's grapes or throwing her dinner out of the window. The authorities would become suspicious and officious and start asking questions. They would put May into a home.

This was the nub of the nightmare, because Eve knew that May was becoming senile. The Mickey Mouse scrapbook was only one of her disconcerting purchases. About a month ago she had returned from Truro with a child's woollen hat, which she now wore like a tea cosy, pulled down over her ears, whenever she went out of doors. A letter that Eve had given May to post, she had found three days later in the door of the refrigerator. A freshly made casserole May dumped into the pig bucket.

Eve unloaded her anxieties on to Gerald, and he told her firmly that she was not to start worrying until there was something to worry about. He didn't care, he assured her, if May was nutty as a fruitcake, she was doing no person any harm, and provided she didn't set fire to the curtains or scream blue murder in the middle of the night, like poor Mrs Rochester, she could stay at Tremenheere until she turned up her toes and died.

'But what if she has an accident?'

'We'll cross that bridge when we get to it.'

So far there had been no accident. But, 'Oh, May darling, what are you up to?'

'Didn't like the smell of that milk jug. Just going to give it a scald.'

'It's absolutely clean; it doesn't need scalding.'

'You don't scald jugs in this weather, and we'll all be coming down with diarrhea.'

She had once been quite round and plump, but now, at

79

nearly eighty years old, had become painfully thin, the joints of her fingers gnarled and twisted as old tree roots, her stockings wrinkled on her legs, her eyes pale and myopic.

She had been a perfect nanny, loving, patient, and very sensible. But even as a young woman, she had held strong views, attended church each Sunday, and was a passionate believer in strict temperance. Old age had rendered her intolerant to the point of bigotry. When she first came with Eve to live at Tremenheere, she refused to go to the village church, but joined some obscure chapel in the town, a grim edifice in a back street, where the minister preached sermons on the horrors of drink and May, with the rest of the congregation, renewed her pledges and raised her cracked voice in joyless praise.

The kettle boiled. Eve said, 'I'll pour the water into the jug,' and did so. May's expression was sour. To placate her, Eve had to think of something for May to do. 'Oh, May, I wonder if you'd be an angel and fill up the salt cellars for me, and put them on the dining room table. I've laid it and done the flowers, but I forgot about the salt.' She was searching in cupboards. 'Where's the big bowl with the blue stripe? I want it for picking raspberries.'

May, with a certain grim satisfaction produced it from the shelf where the saucepans lived.

'What time are Mr and Mrs Alec coming?' she asked, although Eve had already told her twenty times.

'They said they'd be here in time for dinner. But Mrs Marten's bringing some cuttings for us . . . she should be here any moment, and she's going to stay for a drink. If you hear her, tell her the Admiral's on the terrace. He'll look after her till I get back.'

May's mouth pursed over her dentures, her eyes narrowing. This was her disapproving face, which Eve had expected, because May approved neither of drink nor of Silvia Marten. Although it was never mentioned, everybody – including May – knew that Tom Marten had died of an excess of alcohol. This was part of Silvia's tragedy and had left her not only widowed but with very little money. It was one of the reasons Eve was so painfully sorry for her and tried so hard to help her and be kind.

As well, May thought Silvia a flighty piece. 'Always kissing the Admiral,' she would mumble complainingly, and it wasn't any good pointing out that she had known the Admiral for most of her life. May could never be convinced that Silvia did not have ulterior motives.

'It's nice for her to come here. She must be dreadfully lonely.'

'Hm.' May remained unconvinced. 'Lonely. I could tell you some things you wouldn't like to hear.'

Eve lost her patience. 'Well, I don't want to hear them,' she said, and put an end to the conversation by turning her back on May and going out through the door. This led directly into the spacious courtyard, sheltered from the winds, and now somnolent with evening sunshine. The four sides of this quadrangle were formed by garages, the old coach house, and a cottage where undergardeners had once lived. Beyond a high wall lay one of the vegetable gardens, and in the centre of the courtyard was a pigeon cote, where a flock of white doves roosted, cooing gently and fluttering about in brief bursts of flight. Strung between the pigeon cote and the garage wall were lines of washing, shining white pillowcases and tea towels, and not-so-shining white nappies, all crisp and dry. All about stood a variety of tubs, planted with geraniums or herbs. There was the spicy scent of rosemary.

When Gerald retired and returned to Tremenheere to live for good, the coach house and the cottage had long stood empty. Derelict, unused, they had become repositories for broken garden machinery, rotting harnesses, and rusting tools, all of which offended his navy-engrained sense of order. Accordingly he had gone to some trouble and expense to reconstruct and convert them. Furnished and equipped, they were rented out, in short lets, as holiday homes.

Now, both the houses were occupied, but not by holiday people. Ivan, Eve's son, had been living in the coach house for nearly a year, paying Gerald a generous rent for this privilege. The undergardener's cottage was inhabited by the mysterious Drusilla and her fat brown baby Joshua. They were Joshua's nappies that hung upon the washing line. So far, Drusilla had paid no rent at all.

Ivan was not at home. His car was gone and his front door, flanked by wooden tubs of pink pelargoniums, closed. This was because early this morning, he and his partner Mathie Thomas had loaded Mathie's truck with samples of furniture from their little factory at Carnellow and had driven to Bristol, in the hopes of getting regular orders from some of the big stores there. Eve had no idea when they would be back.

Drusilla's door, however, stood open. There was no sign of Drusilla or her baby, but as Eve stood there, from inside the little house a sweet piping started up, and the warm, scented evening was filled with the floating strains of music. Eve, listening, charmed, recognized Villa-Lobos.

Drusilla was practising her flute. Heaven knew what Joshua was doing.

She sighed.

I won't have you exhausting yourself, looking after all your lame ducks.

So many lame ducks. Silvia and Laura and May and Drusilla and Joshua and . . .

Eve pulled her thoughts to a stop. No. Not Ivan. Ivan was not a lame duck. Ivan was a man of thirty-three, a qualified architect, and totally independent. Exasperating, perhaps, and far too attractive for his own good, but still perfectly capable of taking care of himself.

She would go and pick raspberries. She would not start worrying about Ivan.

By the time she had finished this, Silvia had arrived. Eve came through the French windows on to the terrace to find her and Gerald sitting there, looking relaxed and civilized and chatting lazily. While Eve picked raspberries, Gerald had stirred himself and arranged a tray of drinks, glasses and bottles, sliced lime, and a bucket of ice, and this stood between them on a low table.

Silvia looked up, saw Eve, and raised her glass. 'Here I am, being perfectly looked after!'

Eve drew up another chair and sat beside her husband.

'What do you want my darling?'

'A Pimms would be delicious.'

'With lime, too, what a treat. . . .' Sylvia said. 'Where do you get limes? I haven't seen one for years.'

'I found them in the supermarket in the town.'

'I shall have to go and buy some before they all go.'

'I'm sorry I wasn't here when you came. Did you find Gerald all right?'

'Well, not exactly' – Silvia smiled her small boy's grin – 'I went into the house and was calling, rather pathetically, because there didn't seem to be anybody about, and May finally came to my aid and told me Gerald was here. I must say' – Silvia crinkled her nose – 'she didn't look exactly delighted to see me. But then, come to think of it, she never does.'

'You mustn't take any notice of May.'

'She is a funny old thing, isn't she? Do you know I met her in the village the other day, and it was swelteringly hot and she was wearing the most extraordinary woollen hat. I couldn't believe it. She must have been boiling.'

Eve leaned back in her chair and shook her head, smiling, torn between anxiety and amusement.

'Oh, dear, I know. Isn't it awful? She bought it in Truro a couple of weeks ago and she's been wearing it ever since.' Automatically, she lowered her voice, although it was unlikely that May – wherever she was – would overhear. 'She bought herself a scrapbook, too, with a Mickey Mouse on the cover, and she's started cutting things out of the paper and sticking them in.'

'There's nothing very heinous about that,' Gerald pointed out.

'No. It's just . . . unpredictable. Odd. I've got to the point when I never quite know what she's going to do next. I –' She stopped, realizing that she had already said too much.

'You don't think she's going off her head?' Silvia sounded horrified, and Eve said stoutly, 'No, of course I don't.' She had her own private fears, but no one else was allowed to. 'She's just getting old.'

'Well, I don't know, but I think you and Gerald are a pair of saints, looking after the old girl.'

'I'm not a saint. May and I have been together for most of my life. For years she looked after me, and then Ivan. She was always there when things went wrong, like a rock in times of crisis. When Philip was so ill . . . well, I couldn't have lasted the course without May. No, I'm not a saint. If anybody's a saint, Gerald is, taking her on when he married me, and giving her a home.'

'I didn't have much option,' Gerald pointed out. 'I asked Eve to marry me, and she said that if she did, I'd have to marry May as well.' Having poured his wife's drink, he now handed it to her. 'A fairly shaking thing to be told.'

'Didn't May mind leaving Hampshire and coming to live down here?'

'Oh, no, she took it all in her stride.'

'She was at our wedding,' Gerald enlarged on this, 'wearing the most fantastic hat, like a cake tin covered in roses. She looked like a very old, very cross bridesmaid.'

Silvia laughed, 'Did she come on your honeymoon as well?'

'No, I put my foot down there. But by the time we got back to Tremenheere she was already installed, with a nice little list compiled of things to complain about.'

'Oh, Gerald, that isn't fair. . . .'

'I know. I'm only teasing. Besides, with May here, I get my shirts ironed and my socks darned, despite the fact that they take about an hour to find, because she's always put them away in the wrong drawer.'

'She does all Ivan's laundry as well,' said Eve, 'and I'm sure she's longing to get her hands on Joshua's pale grey nappies and give them a good boil. Actually, I suspect she's longing to get her hands on Joshua as well, but so far she's made no move. I expect she's torn between her nanny instincts and the fact that she hasn't quite made up her mind yet about Drusilla.'

'Drusilla.' Silvia repeated the improbable name. 'When you come to think of it, she couldn't be called anything but Drusilla, could she? Totally outlandish. How long is she staying here?'

'No idea,' said Gerald peaceably.

'Isn't she a bit of a nuisance?'

'No nuisance at all,' Eve assured her. 'We see very little of her. She's really Ivan's friend. In the evenings they sometimes sit outside her house on kitchen chairs and have a glass of wine. What with the washing line and the doves cooing, and the geraniums, and both of them looking faintly bohemian, Tremenheere suddenly feels like Naples, or one of those little courtyards you unexpectedly come upon in Spain. It's nice. And then at other times, you can hear her practising her flute. She was playing this evening. It's rather romantic.'

'Is that what she and Ivan are doing now? Drinking wine beneath the shade of the washing line?'

'No, Ivan and Mathie have been in Bristol all day, trying to drum up some business.'

'How's the factory going?'

84

Gerald answered, 'All right as far as we know. They don't seem to be going bankrupt. Silvia, your glass is empty . . . have another.'

'Well' – she made a show of glancing at her watch – 'won't Alec and his wife be here in a moment . . .?'

'They aren't here yet.'

'I'd love one, then . . . but after that I must take myself off.'

'I feel awful,' said Eve, 'not asking you to stay for dinner, but I think Laura will be feeling exhausted, and we'll probably have an early meal, so that she can get to bed.'

'I can't wait to meet her.'

'You must come for dinner another evening, when I know how much social life she can cope with.'

'. . . and I'd love to see Alec.'

'You can see him when he comes back to fetch her, and take her back to London.'

'The last time he was here Tom was still alive. . . . Oh, thank you, Gerald. Do you remember? We all went out for dinner at the Lobster Pot.'

Yes, thought Eve, *and Tom got paralytically drunk.* She wondered if Silvia remembered this too, and then decided that she didn't, otherwise she would never have mentioned that occasion in the first place. Perhaps the passing months since Tom's death were being kind to Silvia, clouding memory over, so that the bad moments were fading and only the happy ones remained. This happened to other people, she knew, but it had never happened to Eve. When Philip died, there had been no bad memories, only the recollection of twenty-five years of good companionship and laughter and love. She had been blessed with so much good fortune; Silvia, it seemed, had had so little. Life, when it came to handing out the goodies, was really dreadfully unfair.

The sun was now low in the sky. It was cooler, but the midges were beginning to bite. Silvia slapped one away and leaned back in her chair, gazing out over the newly cut lawn.

She said, 'Tremenheere always looks so fantastically neat. Not a weed in sight. Not even on the paths. How do you keep them down, Gerald?'

'I'm afraid I spray them with weed killer,' Gerald admitted.

'Tom used to do that, too, but I just use the hoe. Somehow I think it makes a better job, and at least they don't all come up again. Talking of which, I got buttonholed by the vicar, and he told me you were running the garden stall for the fête next month. Do you need any plants?'

'I certainly do.'

'I'm sure I can find something in my greenhouse for you.' Silvia had finished her second drink. Now, she laid down the empty glass and reached for her bag, preparing to depart. 'I took some cuttings of those little geraniums with the delicious lemon-scented leaves. . . .'

Eve stopped listening to them. Out of the silence of the evening, she had heard the soft purr of a car coming up the road from the village. It changed down, came through the gate; there was the scrunch of tyres on gravel. She sprang to her feet. 'They're here.'

The others got up and they all made their way across the lawn and through the escallonia arch to greet the new arrivals. In front of the house, alongside Silvia's shabby little car, stood parked a beautiful dark red BMW coupé. Alec had already got out of the car and was holding the door open for his wife, a hand under her elbow to help her out.

Eve's first impression was of a girl much younger than she had expected. A slender girl, with dark eyes and thick dark hair, loose upon her shoulders. She wore, like a teenager, faded Levis and a loose blue cotton shirt. Her feet were bare in open sandals, and she carried in her arms a small long-haired dachshund (which looked, thought Eve, like a cross between a fox and a squirrel), and the first thing she ever said to Eve was, 'I am so sorry, I hope you don't mind having Lucy to stay as well as me.'

Silvia trundled home in her little car. There was a new and unexplained rattle from the engine and the choke didn't seem to be working properly. Her gate, with the name *Roskenwyn* painted upon it, stood open. A pretentious name, she always thought, for such a small and ordinary house, but that was what it had been called when she and Tom bought it, and they had never got around to thinking up anything better.

She parked outside her door, collected her handbag off the seat, and went indoors. The cramped hallway seemed deathly quiet. She looked for letters, forgetting that the postman had already passed, leaving none for her. She dropped her handbag at the foot of the stairs. The silence pressed upon her, a physical thing. Silence, stirred only by the slow ticking of the clock on the upstairs landing.

She went across the hall and into her sitting room, an apartment so small that there was room only for a sofa and a couple of armchairs and desk, with bookshelves over it. In the grate lay the dusty ashes of a fire, although she had not lit one for days.

She found a cigarette and lit it and stooped to switch on the television; she punched the buttons to change channels, was bored by everything, and switched it off. After the moment's burst of meaningless voices, silence pressed in upon her again. It was only eight o'clock. She could not, reasonably, go to bed for at least two hours. She thought of pouring herself a drink, but already had had two with Eve and Gerald, and it was best to be careful with alcohol. Supper, then? But she felt no healthy pang of hunger, no inclination to eat.

A glass door stood open, leading out into her garden. She threw the half-smoked cigarette into the empty fireplace and went out of doors, stooping to pick up a pair of scissors from a wooden basket. Now, with the sun nearly gone, the lawn lay dark with long shadows. She crossed the grass towards her rosebed, began aimlessly to snip off a few dead heads.

A wayward briar became entangled in the hem of her dress, snagging the material. Impatient, angry, she jerked it free, but in her clumsiness caught her thumb on a jagged thorn.

She gave a little cry of pain, holding up her hand to inspect the damage. From the tiny agonizing wound blood swelled. A dot of blood, a bead, a trickle. She watched its progress, a miniature scarlet river, flowing down into the palm of her hand.

As though in sympathy, tears welled in her eyes, brimmed, overflowed. She stood there in the gloomy twilight, numbed by the misery of loneliness, bleeding, and weeping for herself.

The room that they had been given seemed, after Abigail Crescent, enormous. It had a pinkish, flower-patterned carpet, a fireplace, and two long windows, curtained in faded chintz, with tasselled ropes to hold them back. The brass bedstead was of a size to match, and the linen sheets and the pillowcases on the great, downy pillows were elaborately hemstitched and embroidered. There was a mahogany dressing table for Laura and a tall chest of drawers for Alec, and beyond an open door was their own bathroom. The bathroom had once been a dressing room, but conversation from one to another seemed to have been achieved simply by replacing the bed by a bath, so that it too was carpeted and had a fireplace and even one or two rather comfortable-looking chairs.

Laura lay in bed and waited for Alec. She had retired straight after dinner, suddenly overcome with physical exhaustion, but Alec had remained downstairs, in the dining room, drinking a glass of port with Gerald and putting the world to rights, with their chairs pushed back from the table and the air redolent with the scent of cigar smoke.

Laura found the house comfortingly reassuring. Wobbly after the operation, easily prone to tears and apprehensions, she had felt naturally nervous about coming on this long visit, being left by herself, abandoned to strangers. She had kept these fears to herself, in case Alec at the last moment changed his mind and decided to give up all thoughts of Glenshandra and the salmon that were waiting to be hooked out of the river, but as the long car journey progressed and they drew closer by the minute to their destination she had fallen silent.

She had been afraid that Tremenheere would be overwhelmingly grand; that the glittering Gerald would be frighteningly sophisticated; that she would find nothing to say to Eve; and that both Eve and Gerald would think her a dreary ninny and would curse the day they had let Alec talk them into this undertaking.

But it was going to be all right. Their genuinely delighted faces, their obvious fondness for Alec, the warmth of their welcome had dispelled Laura's doubts and melted her shyness. Even the appearance of Lucy they had taken in their stride. And the house, far from being grand, was in fact rather shabby in the very nicest and most comfortable sort of way. Laura had been allowed, at once, to have a bath, which was what she needed more than anything in the world, and after that they had a glass of sherry in the drawing room and then moved into the dining room, which was panelled and candlelit, and hung with Victorian seascapes of great detail and charm, and dinner was grilled trout and a salad, and raspberries smothered in Cornish cream.

'They're our own raspberries,' Eve had told her. 'Tomorrow we'll pick some more. Even if we don't eat them all, we can put them in the freezer.'

Tomorrow. Tomorrow Alec would be gone.

She closed her eyes and moved her feet, which were beginning to get cramped because Lucy, under the quilt, was lying upon them. Her body, beneath the cool, smooth linen sheet, felt flat and insubstantial . . . denuded in some extraordinary way. The operation had left her in no sort of pain, but drained of energy and heavy with lassitude, and it was bliss to be, at last, in bed.

She was still awake when Alec came. He closed the door and came over to the bed to kiss her forehead. Then he turned back the quilt and lifted Lucy from her hiding place and put her in her basket by the fireplace. Lucy's expression at this treatment was one of cold reproach, but she settled in her basket and stayed there. She knew when she was beaten.

He stood with his back to Laura and emptied his pockets, placing his keys, watch, small change, and wallet in a neat row on the top of the chest of drawers. He loosened his tie and pulled it off.

Watching him, Laura decided that security was lying in bed and watching your husband get ready to join you. She remembered, years ago, after some minor childhood illness, being allowed to sleep with her mother. Lying in her mother's bed as she lay now and seeing, through eyes heavy with drowsiness, her mother brush her hair, cream her face, slip on her filmy nightgown.

Alec turned off the lights and got into bed beside her. Laura raised her head from the pillow, so that he could slip an arm beneath it. Now they were really together. He turned towards her, laying his other hand against her rib cage. His fingers moved slowly, caressing, comforting. Through the open windows the warm night air flowed in upon them, laden with mysterious scents and small unexplained country sounds.

He said, 'You're going to be all right.'

It was a statement of fact and not a question.

She said, 'Yes.'

'They love you. They think you're charming.' She could hear the smile in his voice.

'It's a lovely place. They're lovely people.'

'I'm beginning to wish I weren't going to Scotland.'

'Alec!'

'Tremenheere always has this effect on me.'

To this remark, thought Laura, other women, other wives, more sure of themselves, would say teasingly, *Tremenheere! I hoped it was me that you didn't want to leave.* But she had neither the heart nor the courage to risk such coyness.

She said, 'The moment you go through that gate, you'll start looking forward to Glenshandra.' The others would be there already, waiting for him. His old friends. He would be absorbed into his old, pre-Laura life, about which she knew too little and yet too much. Her eyes filled with tears. But this is what I *want* him to do. She said, doing her best to sound down-to-earth, 'In magazines, they're always telling you that being apart every now and then adds spice to a marriage.'

'Sounds like a cookery recipe.'

The tears fell. 'And ten days isn't *really* very long.'

She wiped the tears away. Alec kissed her. 'When I come back for you,' he told her, 'I shall expect to find you fat and sunburned and well again. Now, go to sleep.'

He had set an alarm, which rang at five thirty the following morning, shrilling them both awake. He got out of bed, and Laura lay, sleepily, while he bathed and shaved, and then she watched him dress and put his few things into an overnight bag. When he was ready, she too got out of bed and pulled on her dressing gown. She lifted Lucy out of her basket, and they went out of the room and down the stairs. The old house and its occupants slept on. Alec unlocked the front door and they went out into the chill, misty dawn. Laura set Lucy down and stood, shivering, watching while he stowed his bag in the car, found a duster, and wiped the morning dew from his windscreen. He tossed the duster back into the car and turned to her.

'Laura.'

She went to his side, was enfolded in his arms. Through his sweater, his shirt, she could hear the beating of his heart. She thought of him throughout the coming day, bombing his way north on the great motorways that led to Scotland.

She said, 'Don't have a crash.'

'I'll try not to.'

'Stop for the night if you get too tired.'

'I will.'

'You're too precious to lose.'

He smiled and kissed her, then let her go. He got into the car, fixed his seat belt, and slammed the door. He started the powerful engine. The next moment, he had gone, around the azaleas, through the gate, down the road through the village. She stood there, listening until there was nothing more to hear. Then she called to Lucy and went back indoors and up to their room. She was very cold, but when she got back into bed, it was lovely and warm because before they went downstairs Alec had switched on the electric blanket.

She slept until midday and awoke to find the room filled with bright noon sunshine. Out of bed, she went to the window and leaned out, her bare arms on the warm sill. The garden simmered in the heat of yet another good day. A man in overalls was working in one of the flowerbeds; the distant sea was a cup of blue.

She dressed and went downstairs, and made her way to the kitchen, whence came sounds and voices. There she found Eve, in an apron, stirring something on the Aga stove and a very old lady sitting at the kitchen table, podding peas. They both looked up as she appeared.

'I'm sorry I'm so late.'

'It doesn't matter a bit, you were meant to sleep. Did Alec get off all right?'

'Yes, at about quarter to six.'

'Oh, Laura, this is May . . . you didn't meet her last night. May lives here with us.'

Laura and May shook hands. May's hand felt cold from the peas and was knotted with arthritis.

'How do you do?'

'Pleased to meet you,' said May and went on with her podding.

'Can I do something to help?'

'You don't have to. You're meant to be having a rest.'

'I shall feel quite purposeless if I'm not allowed to do something.'

'In that case' – Eve left her saucepan and stooped to a cupboard to find a bowl – 'we'll need more raspberries for this evening.'

'Where do I pick them?'

'I'll show you.'

She led the way out into the courtyard and pointed out the door that gave on to the vegetable garden. 'The canes are up at the far end, under a cage, because otherwise the birds eat all the fruit. And if you see somebody picking peas, it'll be Drusilla. I said she could take some for herself.'

'Who's Drusilla?'

'She lives there, in that cottage. She plays the flute. She's got a baby called Joshua. I expect he's up there with her. She looks a bit odd, but she's quite harmless.'

The vegetable garden was very old, the various beds neatly squared off from one another by hedges of box. Inside the sheltering walls it was very hot; no breath of breeze stirred. The air smelled of box and mint and thyme and newly turned earth. Laura walked up the path. At the end of this stood an enormous old-fashioned pram, containing a large baby. He wore no sun hat and no clothes at all and was as brown as a berry. Nearby, veiled in the green of pea vines, his mother was hard at work.

Laura stopped to admire the baby. Drusilla, disturbed, looked up, and their eyes met over the top of the peas.

'Hello,' said Laura.

'Hello.' Drusilla laid down her basket and came to chat, folding her arms and propping a shoulder against a post.

'What a nice baby.'

'He's called Joshua.'

'I know. Eve told me. I'm Laura Haverstock.'

'I'm Drusilla.'

Her accent was sensible North Country, which was somehow surprising, because her appearance was quite outlandish. She was a very small and thin girl – it was hard to believe that the lusty Joshua had sprung from such meagre roots – with pale eyes and a great deal of bushy tow-coloured hair, which did not look as though it had ever seen a pair of scissors. In an attempt to keep it under some sort of control, Drusilla had bound her head with a length of braid. Above this, her hair bulged like a bathing cap; below it stuck out sideways, thick and dry and frizzy.

Her clothes were no more conventional than her hairstyle. She wore a low-necked black vest, beneath which her breasts were flat as a child's. Over this, despite the heat, a velvet jacket, touched here and there with scraps of moth-eaten fur.

92

Her skirt of heavy cotton was long and full, reaching nearly to her ankles. Her feet were bare and dirty.

To complete the bizarre assemblage of garments, Drusilla had added further adornment: a single dangling earring, set with blue stones; a string of beads around her neck and a silver chain or two. Bangles rattled on her thin wrists and there were many rings on her small and surprisingly elegant hands. You could see them playing a flute.

'Eve told me I'd find you here. I've got to pick some raspberries for her.'

'They're over there . You came last night, didn't you?'

'That's right.'

'How long are you staying?'

'About ten days, I think.'

'Eve said you'd not been well.'

'I was in hospital for a couple of days. Nothing very serious.'

'You'll get better here. It's peaceful. It's got good vibes. Don't you think? Don't you think it's got good vibes?'

Laura said, yes, she did. She thought it had lovely vibes.

'She's a really nice person, Eve. She's good. She lent me that pram, because I didn't have one for Josh. Used to lug him around in an old grocery carton, and he weighs a bloody ton. Makes life a bit easier having a pram.'

'Yes, it must.'

'Well' – Drusilla heaved her shoulder from the support of the post – 'I must get on with my picking. We're having peas for lunch today, aren't we, my duck? Peas and macaroni. That's what Josh loves. See you around.'

'I hope so.'

Drusilla disappeared once more into the thicket of leaves, and Laura, carrying her bowl, went in search of raspberries.

That afternoon, they lay on deckchairs in the garden, which Eve arranged beneath the dappled shade of a mulberry tree, because it was too hot to sit out in the full sunshine. Gerald had gone to Falmouth for some meeting to do with a sailing club, and May, after the dishes were done, had taken herself off upstairs to her own rooms.

'We could go to the beach,' Eve had said, but after some discussion they had both agreed that it was too hot to get into the car and drive there, even with the lure of a swim at the end of the drive, and had settled for the garden. It was very pleasant, the air scented with roses and filled with birdsong.

Eve had brought her tapestry with her and was stitching industriously, but Laura was happy to be totally idle, simply watching Lucy, who, a small russet shape with pluming tail, was happily nosing through the borders and shrubberies after rabbit smells. Finally this delightful occupation palled, she came across the lawn and leaped lightly into Laura's lap. Her fur, beneath Laura's hands, felt velvety and warm.

'She is a charming little animal,' said Eve. 'So well behaved. Have you had her long?'

'About three years. She lived with me in my flat in Fulham and she used to come to the office with me and sleep under my desk. She's used to being well behaved.'

'I don't even know what you did before you married Alec.'

'I worked for a publisher. I was with them for fifteen years. It sounds rather unenterprising, staying in one place for so long, but I was happy there, and I ended up as an editor.'

'Why unenterprising?'

'Oh, I don't know. Other girls seemed to do such adventurous things . . . like being cooks on yachts or hitchhiking to Australia. But I wasn't ever a very adventurous person.'

They fell silent. It was very warm, even under the shade of the tree. Laura closed her eyes. Eve said, 'I've started working seats for all the dining room chairs. I've only done two, and there are still eight to go. At the rate I'm going, I'll be dead before I finish them.'

'It's such a lovely house. You've made it so pretty.'

'I didn't make it pretty. I just found it pretty.'

'It must be big to run, though. Don't you have any help?'

'Oh, yes. We have a gardener who lives in the village, and his wife comes in most mornings and gives me a hand. And then there's always May, although she's getting a bit past it now. . . . She's nearly eighty, you know. It's extraordinary to think of a person actually remembering life before the First World War, at the turn of the century. But May has total recall about her childhood, remembers every detail. What she *can't* remember is where she's hidden Gerald's socks or who it was who telephoned and left a message for me to ring them back. She lives with us because she was my nanny, and then she looked after Ivan.'

Ivan. Alec had told Laura a little about Ivan. Eve's son, whom he had met at Eve and Gerald's wedding, to which – by some slipup in his social planning – he had brought, not one girl, but two, neither of whom could stand the sight of the other. Ivan, who had trained as an architect, joined a firm in Cheltenham and seemed set for a good solid career, only to blot his copybook by getting engaged to some girl and then deciding to disengage himself. This would not have been so bad, Alec pointed out, if he had not waited until all the wedding invitations had been sent out, all the wedding presents had come in, and an enormous marquee was about to be erected for the reception. Before the repercussions of this outrageous behaviour had even settled, Ivan had thrown up his job and come to live in Cornwall. Which did not make him sound a very reliable proposition.

'Ivan's your son, isn't he?'

'Yes. My son, not Gerald's. Of course, I keep forgetting, you haven't met him yet. He lives in the coach house at the back of the courtyard. He's been in Bristol, on business. I thought he'd be back by now. Perhaps that's a good sign. Perhaps he's sold lots of furniture.'

'I thought he was an architect.'

'No, he's started up a little factory in a disused chapel up at Carnellow . . . that's about six miles from here, up on the moor. He's got a partner, Mathie Thomas. He met him in a pub. Such a nice man.'

'It must be lovely for you, having him so close.'

'We don't see that much of him.'

'Do he and Gerald get on?'

'Oh, yes. They're very fond of each other. But then, you see, Gerald was very fond of Ivan's father. He's known Ivan since he was quite a little boy.'

'I think Gerald's a darling,' said Laura and was astonished that she had, without thinking, come out with this totally spontaneous remark. But Eve was not disconcerted, simply delighted.

'Oh, isn't he? I am glad you think so.'

'He's so good-looking.'

'You should have seen him when he was a young man.'

'Did you know him then?'

'Oh, yes, but not very well – for one thing, I was married to Philip, and for another, Gerald was Philip's commanding officer, and I felt very junior and respectful. Then, when they both retired, Gerald to Cornwall and Philip and I to Hampshire, we didn't see each other for a bit. But then Philip . . . became ill. And Gerald used to come and see him, on his way to London, or if he happened to be staying nearby. When Philip died, Gerald came to his funeral. And then he stayed with me for a day or two, to help untangle all the legal and financial problems and show me how to cope with things like insurance and income tax. I remember he mended a toaster that hadn't worked properly for months and gave me the most frightful row because I hadn't had the car serviced.'

'Was your husband ill for long?'

'About six months. Long enough to forget about servicing the car.'

'And then you married Gerald.'

'Yes. I married him. Sometimes I look back at my life and I simply can't believe my good fortune.'

'I feel that way too,' said Laura.

'I'm glad you do. If Gerald is a darling, then Alec is too. You must be very happy with him.'

'Yes,' said Laura.

There was a small pause. She still lay with her eyes closed, but she imagined Eve beside her, with needle poised, looking up over the rims of her pale blue spectacles. Eve said, 'He had a rough deal. We never met Erica or Gabriel. Gerald always says that Erica came between Alec and his family . . . the Haverstocks, I mean. But after the divorce, when he came to stay with us, he never talked about her, so we never really knew what happened.'

'She ran away to America with another man.'

'I think we knew that much . . . but little more. Not that we wanted to. Does he ever hear from her?'

'No.'

'Does he ever hear from Gabriel?'

'I don't think so.'

'So sad. How unhappy people can make each other. I always feel guilty, all the time, about Silvia Marten.'

'She was here last night when we arrived?'

'I wanted to ask her to stay and have dinner with us all, but Gerald wouldn't let me.'

'Who is she?'

'Oh, she's lived here always. She used to be Silvia Trescarne. When Alec and his brother were young, they came to Tremenheere for a summer holiday, and they used to play cricket with Silvia on the beach. She married a man called Tom Marten, and for a bit they were very happy, and very social, darting hither and thither from one party to another. But then Tom started drinking, and it seemed that he simply couldn't stop. It was terrible to witness . . . a sort of physical disintegration. He had once been quite attractive, but by the end he was repulsive, with a plum-coloured face, hands he couldn't keep still, and eyes that could never quite meet yours. He died last year.'

'How dreadful.'

'Yes. Dreadful. And particularly dreadful for Silvia because she's the sort of woman who really needs a man in her life. There were always men around Silvia, like bees round a honeypot. They were usually Tom's friends, but he didn't seem to mind. Some women need that little extra bit of attention and admiration. I don't suppose it does any harm.'

Laura was reminded, instantly, of Daphne Boulderstone. She said, 'I know somebody just like that. She's the wife of Alec's friend. She's forever having intimate lunches with mysterious gentlemen. I don't know how she finds the time or the energy.'

Eve smiled. 'I know. One's imagination reels.'

'She's so attractive. Silvia, I mean. She'll probably get married again.'

'I wish she would. But the sad truth is that after Tom died, Silvia's admirers rather fell by the wayside. I suppose it became a different kettle of fish, once she was on her own and free to remarry. Nobody wanted a serious involvement.'

'Does she?'

'Of *course*!'

'It doesn't always follow. I've got an Aunt Phyllis. She's the prettiest thing you've ever seen and she's been widowed for years. She simply doesn't want to get married again.'

'Was she, as they say, richly left?'

'Yes. She was,' Laura admitted.

'I'm afraid that makes a terrible difference. Drinking yourself to death is an expensive way of committing suicide, and Tom left Silvia with very little money. That's one of the reasons

I worry so much about her. I felt so mean letting her go home alone yesterday evening, when all of us had one another and were so happy together.'

'Couldn't she come another evening?'

'Yes, of course,' Eve cheered up. 'We'll ask her for supper in a day or two, and when Alec comes back to collect you, we'll all go out for dinner together. Somewhere terribly smart. That's what Silvia really enjoys. An expensive dinner in a smart restaurant. It would be such a treat for her. And now, would you believe it, it's nearly half past four? What would you say to having tea out here in the garden?'

5

LANDROCK

Everything baked. Up in the vegetable garden, beyond the pea vines, the gardener toiled, stripped to the waist, planting young lettuces. On a browning patch of lawn, Gerald set up the sprinkler. The sun, shining through the spinning sprays of water, made rainbows. In the house, Eve drew down the drawing room blinds, and outside her cottage Drusilla sat on her doorstep while Joshua squatted beside her, digging up the corner of Eve's herb bed with an old tin spoon.

Wednesday. May's day off. She had to be driven to the station to catch the train to Truro and Laura volunteered for this job. She went to fetch Eve's car from the garage, backed it cautiously out, and waited for May by the back door. When May emerged, she leaned across to open the door for her and the old lady got in beside her. May was dressed up for her outing in a seemly brown dress patterned with squiggles and her child's woollen hat with the bobble on top. She carried her ponderous handbag and a plastic carrier patterned with a Union Jack, which made her look as though she were about to go and cheer royalty.

As instructed, Laura helped May buy her return ticket and saw her on to the train.

'Have a good day, May.'

'Thanks very much, dear.'

She drove back to Tremenheere, parked the car once more in the shade of the garage. Drusilla and her child had disappeared, retreating to the cool of the cottage, and going into the kitchen, Laura saw that Gerald, too, had been defeated by the heat and was sitting at the kitchen table, drinking cold beer and reading the *Times*. Around him, Eve was trying to lay the table for lunch.

'Oh, Laura, you angel.' She looked up as Laura came through the open door. 'Did you get her off all right?'

'Yes.' Laura pulled out a chair and sat facing Gerald's open newspaper. 'But won't she expire in that hat?'

'Imagine. Trailing round Truro in this heat, wearing a tea cosy on your head. It's market day, too. Don't let's think about it. I've given up.'

Gerald shut the *Times* and set it aside. 'Let me get you both a drink.' He pulled himself to his feet and went over to the fridge. 'There's lager here, or orange juice. . . .'

They both opted for orange juice. Eve pulled off her apron, ran a hand through her short, silvery hair, and collapsed into a chair at the top of the long, scrubbed table.

'What time does she get back? May, I mean.'

'About seven. Somebody has to go and fetch her from the train. We'll think about that later. What are we going to do with ourselves today? It's almost too hot to decide. . . . Oh, thank you, darling, how delicious.'

Ice bobbed against the tall glasses. 'Don't worry about me,' said Laura. 'I'm perfectly happy doing nothing in the garden.'

'I suppose we could go to the beach.' She touched Gerald's hand as he sat beside her. 'What are you going to do, my darling?'

'I shall take a siesta. Get my head down for a couple of hours. Then when it's cooler, I shall maybe contemplate a little gentle hoeing. The border's like a jungle.'

'You wouldn't like to come to the beach with us?'

'You know I never go to the beach in July or August. I object to being showered with sand, deafened by transistors, and anaesthetized by the smell of suntan oil.'

'Well, perhaps –'

But he interrupted her. 'Eve, it's too hot to be organized. Let's have something to eat and then decide what we're going to do.'

Lunch was cold ham and crusty bread and butter and a dish of tomatoes. As they ate this delicious food, the simmering quiet of the day beyond the open door was broken by the sound of a car coming up from the gate and through the archway into the courtyard. There it stopped. A door slammed with a heavy thud. Eve laid down her fork and listened, turning her head towards the door. Footsteps came across the gravel and down the flagged walkway. A shadow fell across the patch of sunlight on the kitchen floor.

'Hello, there.'

Eve smiled. 'Darling, you're back.' She turned up her face to be kissed. 'Have you been in Bristol all this time?'

'Got back this morning. Hello, Gerald.'

'Hello, old boy.'

'And this' – he was looking down at Laura – 'this has to be Alec's Laura.'

His saying that – *Alec's Laura* – melted any shyness or restraint. He held out his hand, and Laura put her own into it and smiled up into his face.

She saw a young man of good height, but not as tall as Gerald or Alec. Broad-shouldered and very tanned, with blunt, boyish features, his mother's bright speedwell blue eyes, and thick fair hair. He wore a pair of washed-out cotton trousers patched over the knees and a blue-and-white checked shirt. A thick serviceable watch encircled one wrist, and around his neck, revealed by the low-buttoned shirt, hung a gold medallion on a thin silver chain.

'How do you do,' they both said, formally and at the same time. This sounded ridiculous, and Ivan laughed. His smile was wide and ingenuous, disarming as his mother's, and Laura recognized the famous charm that had landed him in so much trouble over the years.

'Had any lunch?' Gerald asked him, and he let go of Laura's hand and turned to his stepfather.

'No, I haven't, actually. Is there any to spare?'

'Heaps,' said his mother. She got to her feet and went to collect another plate, a glass, knives and forks.

'Where's May? Oh, of course, it's Wednesday, isn't it? Truro day. I should think she might die in this heat.'

'How did you get on in Bristol?' Gerald asked.

'Very successful.' He went to the fridge for a can of lager and came back to the table, drawing up a chair alongside Laura and letting Eve lay a place in front of him. He opened the can and reached for a glass and poured the lager neatly, with no head to it. 'We got two orders from one store and a tentative order from another. The head buyer was away on holiday and the other chap didn't want to commit himself. That's why we were so long.'

'Oh, darling, that is good. . . . Mathie must be thrilled.'

'Yes, it's encouraging.' Ivan leaned forward to cut himself a thick slice of bread. His hands, doing this, were neat and strong and competent, their backs, and his bare forearms, downed in sun-bleached hair.

101

'Where did you stay in Bristol?' Eve asked.

'Oh, some pub Mathie knew.'

'Lots of traffic on the motorway?'

'Not too bad . . . middle-of-the-week stuff.' He took a tomato and began to slice it. He said to Laura, 'You've brought the good weather with you. I heard the forecast on the radio. It seems to be set fair for a few more days. How's Alec?'

'He's very well, thank you.'

'I was sorry to miss him. But he's coming back for you, isn't he? That's fine, I'll see him then.'

'You can come out to dinner with us,' said Eve. 'Laura and I have decided that one night, we're all going to go somewhere terribly expensive and grand for dinner, and we're going to ask Silvia to come with us.'

'She'll love that,' said Ivan. 'Head waiters to hand and a quick fox-trot between courses.'

'Who's going to pay the bill?' asked Gerald.

'You are, of course, my darling.'

He was not in the least put out by this, as Eve knew he would not be. 'Very well. But remember to ring and book a table in good time. And don't let it be that place where they gave us rotten scampi. Took me days to get over it.'

Ivan made the coffee. 'What are you all doing this afternoon?'

'Good question,' said Gerald.

'Gerald's going to have a little nap. He says he won't come to the beach with us.'

'Are you going to the beach?'

'We haven't decided.' Eve took a sip of her coffee. 'What are *you* going to do? Go up to the factory, I suppose?'

'No, I have to drive to Landrock. Old Mr Coleshill's got some old pine pieces in . . . there's been a sale at some big house. He's given us first refusal, and if I don't go today, the dealers are going to find out about them.'

Eve took another sip of coffee. 'Why don't you take Laura with you?' she suggested. 'It's a pretty drive, and she'd probably enjoy nosing round Mr Coleshill's antiques.'

'Of course,' said Ivan at once. He turned to Laura. 'Would you like to come with me?'

This unexpected suggestion took Laura unawares. 'Well . . . yes. But, please, don't worry about me.'

Eve and Ivan laughed. 'We're not worrying,' Eve told her, 'and you don't have to go if you'd rather rest. But you might enjoy it. And the shop's filled with pretty china as well as a mass of dusty junk. It's fun nosing around.'

Laura loved antique shops almost as much as she loved bookshops. 'I think I'd like to come. . . . Would you mind if I brought my dog as well?'

'Not at all, provided it's not a Great Dane prone to car sickness.'

Eve said, 'She's a dear little dachshund, but I think she'd be happier left with me. She can play in the garden.'

'That's settled, then.' Ivan pushed back his chair. 'We're off to Landrock. And on the way back, we'll maybe stop at Gwenvoe and have a bathe.'

'I was there two days ago,' his mother told him. 'The tide's out just now and the swimming's perfect.'

'Would you like that, Laura?'

'I'd love it.'

'We'll leave in about fifteen minutes. I've got a couple of phone calls to make . . . and don't forget your swimming things.'

His car was just what she had expected, an open coupé, which meant that the wind blew her hair from the back, all over her face. She tried to hold it back, but it was an impossible task, so Ivan produced an old silk scarf and she tied her head up in that, wondering how many of his girlfriends had already done just this thing.

They followed the main road for a mile or so, moving at great speed, and then turned off into a maze of winding high-hedged lanes. These, with their narrowness and blind corners, Ivan treated with respect and took at a leisurely pace. They trundled peacefully along, every now and then passing small villages or isolated farms, where the air was heavy with the smell of manure and farmhouse gardens bright with flowers. Fuchsias grew in the hedges, purple and deep pink, and ditches were filled with buttercups and tall, creamy stalks of cow parsley.

'It's so peaceful,' said Laura.

'We could have taken the main road, but I always come to Landrock this way.'

'If you build new furniture, why do you have to go and buy old furniture?'

'We do both. When I first met Mathie, he was in the pine-stripping business. Had quite a good little concern going and no shortage of material. But then stripped pine became suddenly very fashionable and all the London dealers were down, buying anything they could get their hands on. The supply started petering out.'

'What did he do?'

'He couldn't do anything much. He couldn't afford to top their prices, and after a bit he couldn't supply his own customers. That's when I came in, a year ago. I met him in a pub, and he poured out his troubles to me over a glass of beer. He's such a good chap, I went the next day to look at his workshop, and I saw some chairs he'd made himself, and a table. I asked him why he didn't start up manufacturing the stuff himself, and he said he couldn't, because he hadn't the capital to buy machinery and generally shoulder all the over-heads involved. So we went into partnership. I put up the money, and Mathie put up the expertise. We've had a few thin months, but I'm more hopeful now. I think it's beginning to pay off.'

'I thought you were an architect.'

'Yes, I am. I was a practising architect for a number of years, in Cheltenham of all places. But when I came down here to live I realized that there simply wasn't enough work. There was no call for a man with my qualifications. Anyway, designing furniture isn't that different from designing houses, and I've always liked working with my hands.'

'Are you going to stay here always?'

'If I can. Provided I don't blot my copybook with Gerald and get flung out of Tremenheere. It's your first visit, isn't it? How do you like it?'

'It's heaven.'

'Mind you, you're seeing it under ideal conditions. Just wait till the winds blow and the rain starts pouring down. You'd think it would never stop.'

'I was a bit apprehensive about coming,' she admitted, and somehow it was possible to do this, because he was an easy person to talk to. 'You know, to stay, by myself, with people I'd never met. Even though they are Alec's relations. But the doctor said I wasn't to go to Scotland, and I didn't actually have anywhere else to go.'

'What . . .?' he sounded astonished. 'No relations of your own?'

'No. Not one.'

'I don't know whether to envy you or be sorry for you. Well, don't worry about it anyway. My mother's most favourite thing is looking after people. Every now and then Gerald has to put his foot down, but she persists. He grumbles that she's turned his house into a bloody commune, but he only becomes annoyed with all us hangers-on when he thinks that Eve's looking tired. Have you met Drusilla?'

'Yes.'

'And the dreaded Joshua? I'm afraid Drusilla's coming to Tremenheere was my responsiblity.'

'Who is she?'

'I've really no idea. She turned up at Lanyon about a year ago, with the infant Joshua and a man called Kev. I suppose he was Joshua's father. He called himself an artist, but his pictures were so appalling that no person in his wildest moment would dream of paying good money for them. They lived in a little house on the moor, and then one evening when they'd been there about nine months, Drusilla turned up at the pub with her backpack and her flute case and her baby in a grocery carton and the news that Kev had decamped on her and gone back to London and another woman.'

'What a brute.'

'Oh, she was quite philosophical about it all. Not particularly resentful. Just homeless and broke. Mathie was in the pub that evening, and at closing time he took pity on her and took her home to his wife, and they looked after her for a couple of days, but it was obvious that she couldn't stay there, so I had a word with Gerald and she moved into the cottage at Tremenheere. She seems to have settled down very nicely.'

'But where does she come from?'

'Huddersfield, I think. I don't know her background. I don't know anything about her. Except that she is a trained musician. I think she once played in an orchestra. You'll hear her practising her flute. She's very good.'

'How old is she?'

'No idea. I suppose about twenty-five.'

'But what does she live on?'

'Social Security, I imagine.'

'But what will *happen* to her?' Laura persisted. She found this all fascinating, a glimpse into a life that she had never had to imagine.

'Again, no idea. Down here, we don't ask those sort of questions. But have no fears for Drusilla. She and Joshua are born survivors.'

As they talked, the road had climbed, the terrain altered. Bosky lanes had given way to open countryside, reclaimed moorland, with distant views of rounded hills topped here and there with the engine houses of disused tin mines, piercing the skyline like jagged teeth.

They came to a sign, Landrock, and a moment later entered the village, not as picturesque as the others they had come through, but a collection of bleak stone terraces, built around a crossroads. On the four corners of this stood a pub, a newsagent, a post office, and a long rambling building that had once, perhaps, been a barn. It had small, dusty windows crammed with seductive junk, and over the door hung a sign.

WM. COLESHILL
SECONDHAND FURNITURE
BRIC-À-BRAC
ANTIQUES

Ivan slowed down and drew up at the pavement's edge. They got out of the car. Up here, on the hill, it was cooler, the air fresh. There did not seem to be anybody about. They went through the open door of the shop, down a step. Inside the temperature dropped by ten degrees or more, and there was the smell of damp and decay and musty old furniture and wax polish. It took some time to grow accustomed to the dark after the bright sunshine out of doors, and as they stood there, a stirring came from the back of the shop. A chair was pushed back. Out of the gloom, edging his way between cliffs of stacked furniture, emerged an old man in a sagging cardigan. He took off his glasses, the better to see.

'Ah . . . Ivan!'

'Hello, Mr Coleshill.'

Laura was introduced. Remarks were made about the weather. Mr Coleshill asked after Eve; then he and Ivan disappeared into some dim recess to look at the pine furniture the old man had acquired. Left alone, and very happy, Laura pottered around, squeezing herself into inaccessible corners, tripping over coal scuttles, milking stools, broken umbrella stands, piles of china.

But she was not simply pottering, because she was looking for a present for Eve. There had not been time before she left London to buy a gift for her hostess, and she had felt badly arriving as she did, empty-handed. When at last she came upon the pair of china figures, the shepherd and the shepherdess, she knew at once that they were exactly what she had been searching for. She inspected them for cracks or chips or mends, but they appeared to be in perfect condition, if a little dusty. She blew at the dust and wiped the shepherd on the skirt of her dress. His face was white and pink, his hat blue, encircled by tiny flowers. She wanted them for herself, which is perhaps the best criterion of all when giving presents. Holding her find, she made her way back into the main part of the shop, where Ivan and Mr Coleshill, having apparently transacted their business successfully, were waiting for her.

'I'm sorry. I didn't realize how long I'd been. I found these. . . . How much are they?'

Mr Coleshill told her and she reeled. 'They're genuine Dresden,' he assured her and turned them up in his dirty long-nailed hands to show her the mark on the bottom. 'Dresden and in perfect condition.'

'I'll have them.'

While she wrote the cheque, Mr Coleshill went away and returned with her purchase, bulkily wrapped in dirty newspaper. She gave him the cheque and took the precious parcel from him. He went to the door to open it for them and let them out. They said goodbye and got into the car. After the chill of the shop, it was good to be warm again.

Ivan said, 'I think you probably paid too much for them.'

'I don't care.'

'They're charming.'

'They're for your mother. Do you think she'll like them?'

'For Eve? What a darling girl you are!'

'I'll have to wash them before I give them to her. They can't have had a bath in years. And perhaps, on the way home, we could stop off somewhere to get some pretty tissue paper. I can't give them to her wrapped in dirty newspaper.'

She looked a him. He was smiling. 'You're obviously a person who loves to give presents.'

'Yes, I do. I always have. But . . .,' she added, in a burst of confidence, 'before I married Alec I could never afford to give people the sort of presents I really wanted to buy. But now I can.' She hoped that she did not sound mercenary. 'It's a lovely feeling,' she said apologetically.

'There's a gift shop in the town. We'll get some paper there when we've had our swim.'

Laura stowed the parcel at her feet, where it could not fall and break. She said, 'And you? Are you pleased with what you've bought?'

'Yes. Quite satisfied. Although like you I've probably been rooked. But so what? He has to make a living. Now' – he started up the engine – 'let's forget about shopping and go to Gwenvoe and jump into the sea.'

Silvia lay in the deck chair, where yesterday Laura had lain. After his stint of hoeing, Gerald had taken himself off to the town to deal with a few small masculine errands, and Eve had grasped the opportunity to calm her troubled conscience, and telephoned Silvia to ask her for tea. Silvia has accepted the modest invitation with alarming alacrity and come at once, walking the short distance up the road from her little house.

It was now five thirty, and they had had their tea. The remains of this stood on a low table between them, the empty teapot, the thin Rockingham cups and saucers, a few biscuits that had not been eaten. Lucy, who had decided that if she couldn't be with Laura, she might as well be with Eve, was curled up in the shade beneath Eve's chair. Eve was stitching at her tapestry.

She glanced at her watch. 'I'd have thought they'd be home by now. I hope Ivan hasn't made Laura do too much. . . . At Gwenvoe he usually walks up the cliff path for a bit and swims from the rocks, but that really would be too much of a climb for her. I should have said something.'

'I should think Laura's perfectly capable of looking after herself,' said Silvia.

'Yes, I suppose so. . . .' Eve raised her head, needle poised. A car roared up through the village. 'Talk of the devil, there they are now. I wonder if I should go and make a fresh pot of tea.'

'Wait and see if they want one,' said Silvia sensibly.

They listened. Car doors slammed. Voices could be heard. Laughter. Next moment Ivan and Laura appeared through the escallonia arch and began to walk across the sunlit grass towards the two watching, waiting women. Ivan and . . . yes, it was Laura. But so subtly changed from the pale girl who had arrived at Tremenheere two days ago that Eve, for an astonished second, scarcely recognized her. But of course it was Laura. Laura with her dark hair wet and sleek from swimming, wearing a loose sleeveless sundress that exposed long bare arms and legs already tanned to a warm honey brown. As they watched, one of her sandals came loose. She stood on one leg to deal with this, and Ivan put his hand on her arm to support her. He said something and she laughed.

Lucy heard her laughter. She sat up, pricked her ears, saw Laura, and ran to greet her, tail and ears flying. Laura, with her sandal fixed, stooped and gathered Lucy up into her arms and got her face licked for her pains. They came on, across the grass, the fair young man, the dark pretty girl, the little dog.

'Hello!' called Eve when they were within earshot. 'We wondered what had happened to you. Did you have a lovely time?'

'Yes. Gorgeous. We're cool at last. Hello, Silvia, I didn't know you were here.' Ivan stooped and kissed Silvia's cheek beneath the enormous black sunglasses, and then took the lid off the teapot.

'Anything left? I've got a hell of a thirst.'

Eve laid down her tapestry. 'I'll make some more,' but Ivan stopped her, with a hand on her shoulder.

'Don't stir yourself, we'll get some for ourselves.' He collapsed on the grass, leaning back on his elbows. Laura knelt at Silvia's feet and set Lucy down beside her. She smiled at Silvia. 'Hello!'

'Where did you take her?' Silvia asked Ivan.

'To Gwenvoe. It was packed with screaming people, but you were right. The swimming was perfect.'

'I hope you're not too tired,' Eve said to Laura.

'No. I feel marvellous. All refreshed.' She knelt there on the grass, glowing from her bathe, looking, thought Eve, about fifteen.

'Have you never been down to Cornwall before?' Silvia asked her.

'No. This is my first visit. When I was a child I lived in Dorset and we used to go to Lyme Regis in the summertime.'

Alec and I used to play on the beach here together when we were both very young. . . . I'm sorry I didn't have the chance to chat with him when he was here, but Eve's promised that we shall have a good gossip when he comes back to fetch you. He's gone to Scotland?'

'Yes. Salmon fishing.'

'And you still live in London?'

'Yes. The house Alec's always had, in Islington.'

'I used to go to London quite often, in the old days, when my husband was alive. It was always rather a treat. But I haven't been for ages. Hotels are so dreadfully expensive now, and everything costs so much . . . even taking a taxi practically bankrupts me.'

'We've got a spare bedroom. It's not very smart, but you'd be more than welcome if ever you wanted to make use of it.'

'How very kind.'

'You just have to ask. Alec would love to have you, I'm certain. It's Abigail Crescent. Number thirty-three. Or you could telephone. Eve's got the number.'

'Oh, I do think that's thoughtful. I'll maybe take you up on it one day.'

'I really mean it. I wish you would.'

Eve was talking to Ivan. 'How did you get on with Mr Coleshill?'

Silvia heard the name and joined in with their conversation. 'Did you find any pretty things, Ivan?'

'Yes, it was a worthwhile trip. I got a beautiful dresser and some very nice wheel-back chairs. So good-looking, I think they might be worth copying. Mathie will be thrilled.'

'Oh, darling, what a lovely, successful few days you've had,' said Eve.

'I know. Laura and I have decided that we should celebrate. So there's going to be a cocktail hour in the coach house this evening. Or it might even be a champagne cocktail hour if I can find the right sort of bottles. Silvia, you're invited too. About seven o'clock.'

Silvia turned her blind, black gaze in his direction. 'Oh . . . I don't think –' she began, but Eve interrupted her.

'Now, don't start making excuses, Silvia. Of course you must come. It wouldn't be a proper party without you. And if you can't find any champagne, Ivan, I'm sure Gerald's –'

But no, said Ivan. 'I'll go out and buy some and put it on ice. This is my party.'

And hour later Laura was in her bath when Eve came to call her. 'Laura, you're wanted on the telephone. Long-distance from Scotland. It must be Alec.'

'Oh, heavens.' She got out of the warm, scented water, wrapped herself in a large white towel, and went downstairs – her bare feet leaving damp marks on the polished treads – to where the telephone stood on a chest by the front door. She picked up the receiver.

'Hello.'

'Laura.'

He sounded very far away, as indeed he was.

'Oh, Alec.'

'How are you?'

'I'm all right. Did you have a good drive?'

'Yes. Did it in one go. Got here about nine o'clock in the evening.'

'You must have been exhausted.'

'Not really.'

Laura hated the telephone. She always found it hard to speak naturally over the horrid instrument, or even to think of anything to say.

'What's the weather like?' she asked now.

'Pouring with rain and pretty cold, but the river's full and there are plenty of fish. Daphne caught her first salmon today.'

Pouring with rain and pretty cold. Laura looked up and saw through the long windows the cloudless sky and sunbaked garden of Tremenheere. She might have been abroad, oceans away from her husband. She tried to imagine Glenshandra drenched and chill, but it was unimaginable, and this was not just because she had never been there. She thought of Daphne, booted and mackintoshed, wielding her hefty salmon rod . . . the talk in the evening over large whiskys, sitting in some little lounge by a necessarily blazing fire. She was grateful not to be there, and this shameful gratitude immediately filled her with guilt.

'Oh, how lovely.' She made herself sound pleased and enthusiastic, smiling into the telephone receiver as though Alec could see her. 'Send her my love.' And then, 'Send them all my love.'

'What have you been doing?' he asked. 'Resting, I hope.'

'Well, I rested yesterday, but today I met Ivan and we went to a lovely beach and swam.'

'Ivan's back, then?'

'Yes. Yes, he got back this morning.'

'How did Bristol go?'

'I think successfully. He's celebrating tonight. Has asked us all for drinks in his house.' She added, 'Champagne cocktails if we're lucky.'

'Well, it sounds as though you're enjoying yourself.'

'Oh, Alec, I am. I really am.'

'Don't do too much.'

'I won't.'

'I'll ring you again.'

'Yes, do.'

'Goodbye, then.'

'Goodbye . . .' She hesitated. 'Goodbye, darling.'

But she had hesitated too long, and he had already put down the receiver.

Eve, showered and changed into a thin dress, came out of her bedroom and made her way, by the back stairs, down to the kitchen. Here, after Ivan's party, they were all going to partake of an informal supper. She had already laid the table and it looked rustic and pretty, with checked napkins and white candles and a pottery jug filled with marguerite daisies.

Gerald, already changed, had gone to fetch May from the station. May always had her evening meal upstairs in her room, but Eve had set places for both Ivan and Silvia and now stood wondering whether she should set one for Drusilla as well. She didn't know if Ivan had invited Drusilla to what he insisted on calling his cocktail hour, but that didn't mean that she wouldn't come. With Drusilla, one never quite knew. In the end, she decided against it. If necessary an extra place could be added at the last moment.

Having made up her mind, she left the kitchen and went out into the warmth and herb-scented air of the courtyard. From their rooftop the doves cooed and murmured, indulged in sudden bursts of flight, their wings spread white against the deep blue sky. Ivan had no garden to his house, but she saw that he had arranged chairs and small tables in a companionable group outside his open front door. Silvia had already arrived and was sitting with a cigarette lighted and a wineglass in her hand. Ivan, talking to her, leaned against a table, but as his mother approached, he straightened.

'Come along. You're just in time for the first brew-up.'

Silvia held up her glass. 'Champagne, Eve. Such a treat.'

She wore a dress of palest yellow, a dress that Eve had seen her wear often before, but which she thought particularly becoming. Her thick grey hair curled about her lively face like the petals of a chrysanthemum, and she had taken much time and trouble over her makeup. Gold studs shone in her earlobes, and around one wrist she had fastened her gold chain bracelet, jangling with old seals and charms.

Eve sat beside her. 'Silvia, you *are* looking glamorous.'

'Well, I felt I had to dress up for such an occasion. Where's Gerald?'

'He's gone to fetch May. He'll be here in a moment.'

'And Laura?' said Ivan.

'She's on her way. Alec phoned from Scotland, so that probably delayed her a little.' She lowered her voice. The door of Drusilla's cottage stood open. 'Did you ask Drusilla?'

'No,' said Ivan. He poured a glass of champagne for his mother and handed it to her. 'But she'll probably appear,' he finished comfortably.

At that moment they were joined by Laura, coming, as Eve had come, through the kitchen door and walking across the gravel towards them. She looked, thought Eve, deliciously pretty, in an airy dress of peacock blue lawn, delicately stiched and smocked. Her aquamarine earrings, set in diamonds, echoed this rich colour, and she had darkened, with mascara, her long, bristly lashes, which had the effect of making her eyes appear luminous and very large.

'I hope I'm not late.'

'Yes, you are,' Ivan told her. 'Dreadfully late. At least two minutes. I refuse to be kept waiting like this.'

She made a comic face and turned to Eve. 'This is for you,' she said.

She had been carrying what Eve thought to be a small

handbag, but which now she saw was a parcel, wrapped in pink tissue paper and tied with pale blue ribbon.

'For me?' She set her glass on the table and took the package from Laura's hand. 'Oh, but how exciting. You shouldn't have bought me a present.'

'It's really a hostess present,' Laura explained, sitting down, 'but I didn't have a chance to get one in London, so I bought it today.'

With all of them watching, Eve undid the ribbons and the paper. First pink tissue and then white. The two little china figures were revealed. She had never seen anything so pretty and was wordless with delight.

'Oh . . . oh, *thank you*.' She leaned forward and kissed Laura. 'Oh, how can I thank you? They're enchanting.'

'Let me see,' said Silvia and took one from her. She turned it up, as Mr Coleshill had done, to inspect the mark. 'Dresden.' She looked at Laura, and Laura met her topaz-coloured gaze and silently begged her not to refer to their astronomical price. After a second, Silvia got the message and smiled. She turned the shepherd the right way up and set him down on the table. 'They are very lovely. How clever of you to find them, Laura.'

'I shall keep them in my bedroom,' Eve announced. 'All my most precious things I keep in my bedroom, because I can enjoy them first thing in the morning and last thing at night. Did you get them at Mr Coleshill's?'

'Yes.'

'He's a dreadful old rogue,' said Silvia, 'but he does have some good stuff mixed up with all that dusty tat. Even if you do have to pay through the nose for it.'

'Well,' said Ivan, 'like I said, he has to make a living. And Dresden's rare these days.'

'I shall wrap them up again, before they get broken.' Eve began to do this. 'You really are a darling, Laura. Now tell me about Alec. How is he?'

Laura began to tell her, but before she had time to say more than the fact that Alec had arrived at Glenshandra safely, Gerald's car came through the gate, drove past them all through the courtyard, and disappeared into the garage. In a moment he reappeared, with May at his side.

May was still wearing her woollen hat, but definitely gone in the legs. Eve, with a sinking heart, saw this immediately. She must have had a tiring day and walked too far, and seemed glad of Gerald's support, his hand beneath her elbow. In her other hand she carried her bag and the Union Jack carrier, bulging mysteriously. Eve's heart sank even further at the thought of what it might contain.

They halted.

'Did you have a good day, May?' Eve asked.

'Oh, it was all right,' said May. But she did not smile. Her old eyes looked at them all, moving from one face to another. They took in the champagne bottles and the glasses. Her mouth folded over her dentures.

'You must be tired. Would you like me to come and get you a little supper?'

'No, no, I'll manage.' Firmly, she detached her arm from Gerald's. 'Thanks for coming to get me,' she said to him, and then she turned her back on them all. They watched her make her slow way towards the house. She went through the door into the kitchen.

'Cross old thing,' said Silvia.

The door closed, with some firmness, behind May.

'Silvia, you mustn't say things like that. She'd be terribly hurt if she heard.'

'Oh, Eve, come off it, she *is* a cross old thing. I've never been given such a look in my life. We might have been having an orgy.'

Eve sighed. It was no good trying to explain to anybody. As Gerald came to join them, she looked up and caught Ivan's eye. Ivan knew what she was thinking, and he smiled reassuringly, before turning away and drawing up a chair for his stepfather.

His smile made Eve feel better, but not much. The occasion was so pleasant, the company so delightful, the champagne so delicious, the evening so beautiful, however, that it would have been morally wrong to waste it all in fretting over May. The present was now, and every precious moment of it to be appreciated.

The sun was sinking, the shadows lengthening. At this hour Tremenheere became a magic place. The blue hour. *L'heure bleu*. Eve recalled other, long-ago evenings spent with good friends and a bottle of wine on cool terraces after days of Mediterranean sunshine. Terraces wreathed in pink and purple bougainvillaea, the air resinous with pine. A full moon rising over a dark and silent sea. The sound of cicadas. Malta, when she had been married to Philip. The south of France on her honeymoon with Gerald.

She looked up and saw that Gerald was watching her. She smiled, and across the little space that divided them, he threw her a secret kiss.

Drusilla did not appear, but inside her cottage, as dusk gathered, she began to play her flute. By now, Ivan's cocktail hour was in full swing. They all seemed to have drunk a great deal of his champagne, and Silvia had started to tell Gerald an old anecdote that she knew always made him laugh, but as the first sweet notes floated out into the evening air, the laughter and the voices died away, and even Silvia fell silent.

Mozart. The Eine Kleine Nachtmusik. Magical. Extraordinary to think that the outlandish Drusilla should have, locked within her, this amazing talent. Listening, lost in pleasure, Eve remembered Glyndebourne and the first time Gerald had taken her. She decided that this occasion was not all that different, and the heady enchantment of Drusilla's music just as sweet.

When the little concert was over, they sat spellbound for an instant, and then spontaneously began to applaud. Gerald got to his feet. 'Drusilla!' A standing ovation. 'Drusilla! Bravo! Come and join us. You've earned a reward for giving us so much pleasure.'

After a moment, she appeared in her open doorway and stood there, arms crossed and one shoulder propped against the lintel, a marvellously strange and picturesque figure, with her untamed mass of pale hair and her archaic clothes.

She said, 'Did you enjoy it?'

'"Enjoy" isn't a strong enough word. You play like an angel. Come and drink champagne with us.'

Drusilla turned her head and, as May had done, looked them all over. Her face was never, at the best of times, expressive, but now it was impossible to guess what she was thinking.

After a bit, 'No, I won't,' she said. 'Thanks all the same.'

And she went into her cottage and shut the door. She did not play her flute again.

6

PENJIZAL

The weather was changing, the barometer dropping. A wind had arisen, flowing in from the southwest, warm and blustery. On the horizon, clouds banked, in dark billows, but the sky remained blue, crossed by chasing banks of white cumulus. The sea, observed from the gardens of Tremenheere, no longer lay blue and flat as silk, but was whipped into flecks of surf. Doors slammed and windows rattled, and sheets and pillowcases and Joshua's nappies flapped and bellied on the washing line, making a noise like badly set sails.

It was Saturday, and Eve for once had her kitchen blissfully to herself. May had taken a pile of mending up to her room and, hopefully, would not appear again until lunchtime. Drusilla had gone down to the village to do her shopping, pushing Joshua in the old pram. In deference to the wind, she had wound a woollen shawl about her shoulders and as well, Eve was glad to notice, had put clothes on to Joshua: a nappy and a felted sweater that his mother had bought at a jumble sale.

Because it was a Saturday and the factory was closed, Ivan had placed his free day at the disposal of Laura and taken her off in his car to show her the north coast in general and Penjizal Cove in particular. Eve had packed a picnic for them and warned Ivan about letting Laura do too much or walk too far.

'She's been ill; you mustn't forget that. That's why she's here.'

'You are a fussy old hen,' he told her. 'What do you think I'm going to do? Take her on a ten-mile hike?'

'I know what you're like, and I have a responsibility to Alec.'

'What am I like?'

'Energetic,' she told him, thinking that she could have said a great many other things.

'We'll have a picnic and we'll maybe have a swim.'

'Won't it be terribly cold?'

'If the wind stays in this quarter, it'll be sheltered at Penjizal. And don't worry. I'll take care of her.'

So, she was alone and it was eleven o'clock and she was making coffee for herself and Gerald. She put two cups on a tray with the milk and sugar and a ginger biscuit for Gerald and went out of the kitchen and down the passage to where he had his study. She found him sitting behind his desk, dealing with the paper work that nowadays seemed inevitable if one were to run any sort of an establishment. As she appeared, he laid down his pen, leaned back in his chair, and took off his spectacles.

He said, 'The house seems quite extraordinarily quiet.'

'Of course it does. There's nobody in it except you and me and May, and she's upstairs darning your socks.' She put the tray in front of him.

'Two cups,' he observed.

'One is for me. I shall sit and drink it with you and we shall have a companionable five minutes together with no interruptions.'

'That'll make a nice change.'

She picked up her cup and carried it over to the big chair by the window, where Gerald sometimes took an afternoon snooze or read the papers in the evening. It was a very comfortable and masculine chair, in which her small form was lost, but then this was a comfortable and masculine room, with panelled walls and photographs of ships and various other mementoes of Gerald's naval career.

'What's Laura doing?' he asked.

'Ivan's taken her off for the day in his car. I've given them a picnic. I think they're going to Penjizal to look for seals.'

'I hope he behaves himself.'

'I've told him not to let her get tired.'

'I didn't mean that,' said Gerald. He was fond of Ivan but had no illusions about him.

'Oh, Gerald, you must give him some credit. He's just being kind. Besides, Laura's Alec's wife, and she's older than Ivan.'

'That's what I call an alternative defence. She's very pretty.'

'Yes, she is, isn't she? I didn't think she'd be pretty. I thought she'd be rather a mouse. I think she *was* probably rather a mouse when Alec found her, but it's marvellous what a bit of loving care and some expensive clothes will do to even the plainest of women.'

118

'Why do you think she was a mouse?'

'Oh, just things she's told me over the course of the last few days. An only child, parents killed in a car crash, brought up by an aunt.'

'What, a spinster aunt?'

'No, rather a jolly-sounding aunt. A widow. They lived in Hampstead. But then when she grew up, she got herself a job and a little place of her own, and as far as I can gather, that was her life for the next fifteen years. She worked for a publisher's. She ended up as an editor.'

'Which proves that she's not unintelligent, but doesn't prove that she was a mouse.'

'No, but it does sound a little unadventurous. And Laura is the first to admit it.'

Gerald stirred his coffee. 'You like her, don't you?'

'Immensely.'

'Do you think she's happy with Alec?'

'Yes. I think so.'

'You sound doubtful.'

'She's reserved. She doesn't speak all that much about him.'

'Perhaps she's just being private.'

'She wants to have a child.'

'What's stopping her?'

'Oh, mysterious female complications. You wouldn't understand.'

Gerald, that man of the world, accepted this sweeping statement with good grace. He said, 'Would it matter very much if they didn't have a child?'

'I think it would matter to her.'

'And Alec? Alec must be fifty now. Would Alec want a squalling brat about the place?'

'I wouldn't know.' She smiled sweetly. 'I haven't asked him.'

'Perhaps if . . .'

The telephone on his desk suddenly rang. He said, 'Oh, damn.'

'Don't let's answer it. Let's pretend we're out. . . .'

But Gerald had already picked it up.

'Tremenheere.'

'Gerald.'

'Yes.'

'It's Silvia . . . I . . . oh, Gerald . . .'

Eve could hear her voice quite clearly and was appalled to realize, instantly, that Silvia was in floods of tears.

Gerald frowned. 'What's wrong?'

'Something horible . . . ghastly . . . vile . . .'

'Silvia, what is it?'

'I can't . . . I can't tell you over the telephone. Oh, will you come? You and Eve? Nobody else. Just you and Eve . . .'

'What, come *now*?'

'Yes . . . right away. Please. I'm sorry, but there's nobody . . .'

Gerald looked at Eve. Frantically, she nodded.

'We'll come,' he said. His voice was even, reassuring. 'You just wait for us and try to calm down. We'll be there in five minutes or so.'

Firmly, he replaced the receiver. Across the desk, before she could say more, he met his wife's agonized, questioning gaze.

'Silvia,' he said unnecessarily. 'So much for our companionable time together.'

'Whatever was all that about?'

'God knows. Damned woman. She's hysterical about something.' He stood up, pushing back his chair. Eve, too, got to her feet, still carrying the coffee cup. Her hand was shaking and the cup rattled in the saucer with a tiny tinkling sound. Gerald came and took it from her and set it down on the tray.

'Come along.' He put his arm around her, supporting her, urging her gently forward. 'We'd better take the car.'

The road to the village was strewn with green leaves, blown from the trees. They turned into the gates of Silvia's house, and Eve saw that the front door stood open. Feeling physically sick with apprehension, she was out of the car before Gerald had even switched off the engine.

'Silvia.'

As she ran into the house, Silvia emerged from the sitting room, her face distorted with distress, and the two women came together in the cramped hallway.

'Oh . . . Eve, I'm so glad to see you.'

She fell into Eve's arms, weeping and incoherent. Eve held her close, patted her shoulder, murmured words of comfort that didn't really mean anything at all.

'There . . . there, it's all right. We're here.'

Gerald, on the heels of his wife, firmly shut the door behind them all. He waited for a decent moment or two, and then said, 'Now, come along Silvia. Calm down.'

'I'm sorry . . . you are angels. . . .' With an effort Silvia pulled herself together, drew away from Eve, felt up the sleeve of her sweater for a handkerchief, mopped pathetically at her streaming face. Eve was deeply shocked by her appearance. She had scarcely ever seen Silvia without makeup, and now she looked exposed, defenceless, much older. Her hair was awry, her hands, sunburned and rough from gardening, shook uncontrollably.

'Let us all go,' said Gerald, 'and sit down quietly. Then you can tell us all about it.'

'Yes . . . yes, of course. . . .'

She turned and they followed her into her little sitting room. Eve, whose legs were beginning to feel like rubber, sat in a corner of the sofa. Gerald took hold of the chair by the desk, turned it, and settled himself there, upright and unflappable. He had obviously determined to bring some sense of order to the occasion.

'Now. What's this all about?'

Silvia told them, her voice unsteady, every now and then gasping with intermittent sobs. She had been into the town to do some shopping. When she returned, the morning post lay upon her doormat. A couple of bills and . . . this . . .

It lay on her open desk. She picked it up and gave it to Gerald. A small, plain, brown business envelope.

'Do you want me to open it?' he asked her.

'Yes.'

He put on his spectacles and took out the letter. A sheet of pale pink writing paper. He unfolded it and read its contents. It did not take a moment. After a bit, he said, 'I see.'

'What is it?' Eve asked.

He stood up and silently handed it across to her. Gingerly, as though it were contaminated, Eve took it from him. He sat down again and began, minutely, to examine the envelope.

She saw the child's lined writing paper, the sickly picture of a fairy at the top. The message was composed by letters cut from newspaper headlines and neatly stuck to form words.

YoU WEnT WItH OTheR MEn
anD DrOVE YoUR hUSbanD
to dRiNK
YOu ShoULd bE asHaMed OF
YoURseLF

She felt that for the first time in her life she was truly seeing evil, but on the heels of this repulsion came the most terrible fear.

'Oh, Silvia.'

'Wh – what am I to do?'

Eve swallowed. It was very important to be objective. 'How does the address on the envelope look?'

Gerald handed it over, and she saw that this had been printed, not very evenly, in separate letters, and by means of a rubber stamp. A child's printing set perhaps. A second-class stamp. Their local postmark and yesterday's date. That was all.

She gave the letter and the envelope back to Gerald.

'Silvia, have you the slightest idea who could have sent you such a horrible thing?'

Silvia, who had been standing by the window staring out at her garden, turned her head and looked at Eve. The amazing eyes, her best feature, were swollen with weeping. For a long moment Eve met her gaze. Silvia said nothing. Eve turned to Gerald, longing for reassurance, but he only watched her over the rim of his spectacles, and his expression was both grave and unhappy. All of them knew what the other was thinking. None of them could bring themselves to actually say the name.

Eve took a deep breath and let it out again in a long, trembling sigh.

'You think it's May, don't you?'

Neither Gerald nor Silvia spoke.

'You think it's May. I know you think it's May. . . .' Her voice, rising, began to shake. She clenched her jaw against incipient tears.

'Do *you* think it's May?' Gerald asked quietly.

She shook her head. 'I don't know what to think.'

He looked at Silvia. 'Why should May write you a letter like this? What possible motive could she have?'

'I don't know.' The worst of her weeping seemed to be over, and she was calmer now, more like her usual self. With her hands deep in the pockets of her trousers, she came away from the window and began to pace the floor of the tiny sitting room. 'Except that she doesn't like me.'

'Oh, Silvia . . .'

'It's true, Eve. It's never mattered particularly. It's just that for some reason May could never stand the sight of me.'

Eve, knowing that it *was* true, sat in miserable silence.

Gerald said, 'Even so, it's not sufficient motive.'

'All right. So Tom drank himself to death.'

Eve was shocked at her coolness and at the same time filled with admiration. To speak thus of her own personal tragedy seemed to Eve both sensible and very brave.

Gerald said, 'I know May's strong views on drink and temperance sometimes become a little tedious, but why should she take them out on you?'

'"Went with other men," then. Is that what you're driving at, Gerald?'

'I'm not driving at anything. I'm trying to be objective. And I can't see that your friends, or your private life, are any concern of May's.'

'They might be, if the friend was Ivan.'

'Ivan.' Eve's voice, even to herself, sounded shrill with incredulous disbelief. 'You can't be serious.'

'Why not? Oh, Eve, darling, don't look like . . . what I meant was, that sometimes, when you and Gerald are away from home, Ivan asks me up to the coach house for a drink. . . . He's just being kind. Another time, he gave me a lift to a party over at Falmouth that we'd both been asked to. Nothing. *Nothing*. But I've seen old May spying away out of her upstairs window. Nothing goes on beyond that window that she doesn't know about. Perhaps she thought I was undermining his morals or something. Old nannies are always possessive, and after all, he was her baby.'

Eve's hands clenched tightly together in her lap. She heard May's voice. *Hmmm. Lonely. I could tell you some things you wouldn't like to hear*.

She saw the scrapbook. The unexplained scrapbook, the newspapers, the scissors, and the paste.

She thought of May's Union Jack carrier bag, bulging mysteriously with things that she had bought on her day out. Had they included the fairy writing paper, the child's printing set?

123

Oh, May, my darling May, what have you done?

She said, 'You mustn't tell anybody.'

Silvia frowned. 'What do you mean?'

'We mustn't tell anybody about this terrible thing.'

'But it's criminal.'

'May's a very old lady. . . .'

'She would have to be mad to send a thing like that.'

'Perhaps . . . perhaps she is . . . a little . . .' She could not say the word *mad*. She finished, feebly, 'confused.'

Gerald was studying the envelope again. 'It was posted yesterday. Did May go to the village yesterday?'

'Oh, Gerald, I don't know. She's always pottering up and down to the post office. It's her little bit of exercise. She gets her pension there and buys peppermints and darning wool.'

'Would the girl in the post office remember seeing her?'

'She wouldn't have had to go into the post office. She always keeps a book of stamps in her bag. I'm constantly borrowing stamps from May. She could simply have posted the letter and come home again.'

Gerald nodded, accepting this. They fell silent, Eve haunted by visions of May in her woollen hat making her slow way out of the gates at Tremenheere, down the road to the village, dropping the venomous envelope into the mouth of the scarlet letter box.

Silvia went to the fireplace, took a cigarette from a packet on the mantelpiece, and lit it. She stood looking down into the empty, uncleared grate. She said again, 'She could never stand me. I've always known that. I don't think I've ever had a civil word from the old cow.'

'You *mustn't* call her that! You mustn't call May a cow. She isn't. She may have done this appalling thing, but that's because she's muddled and old. And if anyone gets to hear of it . . . if we tell the police or anyone we ought to tell, then there'll be questions, and . . . nobody will understand . . . and May really will go out of her mind . . . and they'll take her . . . and . . .'

She had tried so hard not to cry, but now she couldn't stop. In a single movement, Gerald had left his chair and come to her side on the sofa. His arms were around her, her face pressed to the familiar warmth of his chest. Shoulders heaving, she wept into the lapel of his naval blazer.

'There,' said Gerald, comforting her in much the same way that Eve had comforted Silvia, with pats and gentle words. 'That's all right. That's all right.'

She finally pulled herself together and apologized to Silvia. 'I'm sorry. It's we who came to help you, and now I go all to pieces.'

Silvia actually laughed. Without much humour, perhaps, but she did at least laugh. 'Poor Gerald, what a pair of females we are. I really feel badly about landing you with this, but I knew that you had to know. I mean, after the ghastly shock of opening the letter and reading those horrible words, I couldn't think of anybody but May.' She had stopped her pacing and halted behind the sofa. Now she leaned down and kissed Eve's cheek. 'Don't be upset. I'm not going to be upset about it anymore. And I know how fond you are of her. . . .'

Eve blew her nose. Gerald glanced at his wristwatch. 'I think,' he said, 'that we should have a drink. I suppose, Silvia, you wouldn't have any brandy in the house?'

She had. They each had a snifter and talked things over. In the end they decided to do nothing, to tell nobody. If it was May who had sent the letter, Gerald pointed out, hopefully, she would have shot her bolt. Probably, by now, she would have forgotten all about it, so unreliable was her memory. But if anything remotely similar should happen again, then Silvia must let Gerald know at once.

She agreed to this. As for the letter, she intended burning it.

'I'm afraid you mustn't do that,' Gerald told her gravely. 'We never know. If things turn out badly, it might be needed as some sort of evidence. If you like, I'll keep it for you.'

'I couldn't let you. I couldn't bear the thought of it con- taminating Tremenheere. No, I'll shut it away in a drawer in my desk and forget all about it.'

'You promise not to burn it.'

'I promise, Gerald.' She smiled. The familiar endearing grin. 'What a fool I was to be so upset.'

'Not a fool at all. A poison-pen letter is a frightening thing.'

'I am so sorry,' said Eve. 'I'm so dreadfully sorry. In a way I feel personally responsible. But if you try to forgive poor May and understand the position I'm in . . .'

'Of course I understand.'

In silence, they drove the short distance home to Tremenheere. Gerald parked the car in the courtyard, and they went into the house through the back door. Eve crossed the kitchen and started up the back stairs.

'Where are you going?' Gerald asked.

She stopped, a hand on the banister, and turned to look down at him. She said, 'I'm going up to see May.'

'Why?'

'I shan't say anything. I just want to make sure that she's all right.'

By the time lunch was finished, Eve had been overcome by a blinding, throbbing headache. Gerald observed that under the circumstances, this was hardly surprising. She swallowed two asprin and took to her bed, a thing she very seldom did. The asprin did their work, and she slept through the afternoon. She was awakened by the telephone ringing. Looking at her watch, she saw that it was past six o'clock. She reached out a hand and picked up the receiver.

'Tremenheere.'

'Eve.'

It was Alec, calling from Scotland, wanting to speak to Laura.

'She's not here, Alec. She went to Penjizal with Ivan, and I don't think they're back yet. Shall I tell her to ring you back?'

'No, I'll ring her later. About nine.'

They exchanged a few more remarks and then rang off.

Eve lay for a little while and watched the clouds race across the sky beyond her open window. Her headache had, mercifully, gone, but for some reason she still felt very tired. Dinner must be prepared, however. After a bit, she got out of bed and went to the bathroom to take a shower.

The lane that led to the clifftop was rutted and winding and so narrow that the gorse bushes on either side scratched and scraped against the wings of Ivan's car. They were covered with yellow flowers and smelled of almonds, and beyond them lay fields where dairy cows grazed. These fields were small and irregular in shape, stitched into a patchwork by meandering stone walls. It was rocky terrain, and here and there outcrops of granite broke the surface of the rich green pasture.

The lane ended finally in a farmyard. A man on a tractor was loading dung on a forklift. Ivan got out of the car and went to speak to him, raising his voice to be heard over the sound of the tractor engine.

'Hullo, Harry.'

''Ullo there, Ivan.'

'All right if we leave the car here? We're going down to the cove.'

'That's all right. It's in nobody's way there.'

Ivan returned to the car, and the farmer continued his work.

'Come on,' Ivan said to Laura and Lucy, 'out you get!' He shouldered the haversack and, carrying the picnic basket, led the way towards the sea. The path narrowed to a stony track, plunging down into a tiny valley, where fuchsia grew in profusion and a small stream, concealed by hazel thickets, kept them company. As they neared the cliffs, this valley opened out into a deep cleft, thick with bracken and brambles, and the sea lay ahead.

Now the little stream revealed itself, bubbling down the hill through carpets of kingcups. They crossed a rough wooden bridge and paused at the rim of the cliff before descending farther.

Underfoot, sea pinks and heather grew in the tussock-grass, and the wind pounced upon them, salty and fresh, and blew Laura's hair all over her face. The tide was out. Here, there was no beach, only rocks, stretching to the rim of the sea. Wet with emerald seaweed, cruel and jagged, these rocks glittered and dazzled in the sunshine. From the ocean – the Atlantic now, she told herself – enormous waves, stirred up by the freshening wind, gathered themselves up – quite far out – to pour in upon the shore, breaking on the coastline in a fury of pounding white surf. The sound of this was ceaseless.

Beyond the breakers the sea stretched to the horizon and seemed to Laura's enchanted eyes to contain within its depths every shade of blue: turquoise, aquamarine, indigo, violet, purple. She had never seen such colour.

She said, unbelieving, 'Does it always look like this?'

'Heavens, no. It can look green. Or navy blue. Or, on a dark, cold winter evening, a particularly sinister shade of grey.' He pointed – 'That's where we're headed for.'

She followed the line of his arm and finger, and saw, caught within a bastion of rocks, a large natural pool, shining in the sunlight like an enormous jewel.

'How do we get there?'

'Down this little path and over the rocks. I'll lead the way. Watch your feet, because it's treacherous. And perhaps you'd better carry Lucy. We don't want her going over the edge.'

It was a long, tough scramble before they finally reached their destination, and took the best part of half an hour. But they were there at last. Laura edged her way around the final overhanging hazard and joined Ivan on a great flat rock, which sloped to the edge of the pool.

He wedged the picnic basket into a crevice, dropped the haversack, which contained their swimming things. He smiled at her. 'Well done. We've made it.'

Laura set Lucy down on her feet. Lucy went at once to explore, but there were no rabbit smells here. Only seaweed and limpets. After a bit she got bored and hot, found herself a shady corner, and curled up to sleep.

They changed at once and then swam, diving into cold, salty water, twenty feet deep or more, clear and blue as Bristol glass. The bottom of this was strewn with round, pale stones, and Ivan, diving deeply, brought one of these to the surface and placed it at Laura's feet.

'It isn't a pearl, but it will have to do.'

After a little, they stopped swimming and came out and lay in the sunshine, sheltered from the wind by the surrounding rocks. Laura unpacked the picnic, and they ate cold chicken, Tremenheere tomatoes, crusty bread, and peaches with the bloom still upon them, unbruised and dripping with juice. They drank wine, which Ivan had cooled by the simple expedient of placing the bottle in a handy rock pool. There were shrimps in the pool, who scurried away when this strange object invaded their private world.

'They probably think it's a Martian,' said Ivan. 'A creature from outer space.'

The sun beat down, the rocks were warm.

'There were clouds at Tremenheere,' Laura observed, lying on her back and gazing at the sky.

'All blown away along the other coast.'

'Why is it so different here?'

'A different coast, a different ocean. At Tremenheere we

grow palm trees and camellias. Here, they can scarcely grow a tree, and escallonia's about the only shrub that can stand the wind.'

She said, 'It's like another country. Like going abroad.'

'How many times have you been abroad?'

'Not very often. I went once to Switzerland in a party to ski. And Alec took me to Paris for our honeymoon.'

'That sounds very romantic.'

'It was, but it was only for a weekend, because he was in the middle of some enormous deal, and he had to get back to London.'

'When were you married?'

'In November, last year.'

'Where?'

'In London. In a registry office . . . It rained all day.'

'Who came to your wedding?'

Laura opened her eyes. He lay beside her, propped on one elbow, looking down into her face.

She smiled. 'Why do you want to know?'

'I want to be able to picture it.'

'Well . . . nobody came, really. At least, Phyllis came, and Alec's driver, because we had to have two witnesses.' She had already told him about Phyllis. 'And then Alec took Phyllis and me out for Lunch at the Ritz, and then we caught the plane to Paris.'

'What did you wear?'

She began to laugh. 'I can't even remember. Oh, yes, I can. A dress I'd had for ages. And Alec bought me some flowers to hold. They were carnations and freesias. The carnations smelled of bread sauce, but the freesias smelled divine.'

'How long had you known Alec?'

'A month, maybe.'

'Were you living together?'

'No.'

'When did you first meet?'

'Oh' – she sat up, resting her elbows on her knees – 'at a dinner party. Very banal.' She watched the surf pouring over the rocks. 'Ivan, the tide's coming in.'

'I know. It does. It's the natural course of events. Something to do with the moon. But we don't have to move just yet.'

'Does it cover the pool?'

'Yes, which is why the water is so clean and clear. It gets laundered twice a day. And the sea covers where we're sitting and a great deal more besides. But not for another hour or so. If we're lucky and keep our eyes open, we'll see the seals. They always appear on a rising tide.'

She raised her face to the breeze, letting it blow her wet hair back over her shoulders.

He said, 'Go on about Alec.'

'There's nothing more to go on about. We got married. We had a honeymoon. We went back to London.'

'Are you happy with him?'

'Of course.'

'He's so much older than you.'

'Only fifteen years.'

'Only.' He laughed. 'If I married a girl fifteen years younger than I am she'd be . . . *eighteen.*'

'That's old enough.'

'I suppose so. But the very idea seems ludicrous.'

'Do you think me being married to Alec is ludicrous?'

'No. I think it's fantastic. I think he's a very lucky man.'

She said, 'I'm lucky.'

'Do you love him?'

'Of course.'

'Did you fall in love with him? It's different from just loving, isn't it?'

'Yes. Yes, it's different.' She bent her head and picked with her fingers at a crack in the rock, dislodging a tiny pebble. She lifted her arm and threw this, and it bounced on the rock and landed in the pool with a miniature splash. It sank, disappearing forever.

'So. You met Alec at a dinner party. "This is Alec Haverstock," your hostess said, and your eyes met over the cocktail tray, and . . .'

'No,' said Laura.

'No?'

'No. It wasn't like that.'

'How was it?'

She said, 'It was the first time we'd met, but it wasn't the first time I saw Alec.'

'Tell me.'

'You won't laugh?'

130

'I never laugh at important things.'

'Well . . . I actually first saw Alec six years before I met him. It was lunchtime, and I'd gone to see a girlfriend who worked in an art gallery in Bond Street. We were meant to be having lunch together, but she couldn't get away. That's why I went to see her. And it was quiet, and there weren't many people about, so we just sat and talked. And Alec walked in and spoke to my friend and bought a catalogue, and then went to look at the paintings. And I watched him go and I thought, "That's the man I'm going to marry." And I asked my friend who he was. And she said Alec Haverstock. She said he often came in at lunchtimes, just to look around and sometimes buy pictures. And I said, "What does he do?" And she told me . . . Sandberg Harpers, Northern Investment Trust . . . very successful, married to a beautiful wife, father of a beautiful daughter. And I thought, "Funny. Because he's going to marry me."'

She fell silent. Found another scrap of rock, threw it into the pool with some force.

'Is that all?' asked Ivan.

'Yes.'

'I think that's amazing.'

She turned to look at him. 'It's true.'

'But what did you do with your life during those six years? Sit and twiddle your thumbs?'

'No. Worked. Lived. Existed.'

'When you met him at the dinner party, did you know then that his marriage had broken and he was divorced?'

'Yes.'

'Did you leap at him, crying "At last," and fling your arms around his neck?'

'No.'

'But you still knew?'

'Yes, I knew.'

'And he, presumably, knew too?'

'Presumably.'

'How fortunate you are, Laura.'

'What, to be married to Alec?'

'Yes. But mostly, to have been so sure.'

'Have you never been sure?'

He shook his head. 'Not really. That's why I'm still a single, available, desirable, eligible bachelor. Or so I like to think.'

'I think you're desirable,' Laura told him. 'I can't imagine why you're not married.'

'That's a long story.'

'You were engaged. I know that because Alec told me.'

'If I start on that we'll be here till nightfall.'

'Do you hate talking about it?'

'No, not particularly. It was just a mistake. But the gruesome thing was that I didn't realize it was a mistake until it was almost too late to do anything about it.'

'What was she called?'

'Is that important?'

'I answered all your questions. Now it's your turn to answer mine.'

'Oh, all right. She was called June. And she lived in the heart of the Cotswolds, in a beautiful stone house with mullioned windows. And in the stables were beautiful horses on which she used to ride to hounds. And in the garden was a blue, kidney-shaped swimming pool, and a hard tennis court, and a lot of statues and unnatural-looking shrubs. And we got engaged, and there were tremendous celebrations, and her mother spent the next seven months planning the largest, most expensive wedding the neighbours had witnessed in years.'

'Oh, dear,' said Laura.

'It's all water under the bridge. I turned tail at the last moment and fled, like the coward I am. I just knew that the magic wasn't there, that I wasn't sure, and I liked the poor girl too much to condemn her to a loveless alliance.'

'I think you were very brave.'

'Nobody else did. Even Eve was angry, not so much because I'd broken off the engagement, but because she'd bought a new hat, and she never wears hats.'

'But why did you throw up your job? Surely you didn't have to throw up your job as well as your engagement.'

'I had to, really. You see, the senior partner of my firm happened to be June's father. Tricky?'

Laura found this unanswerable.

It was seven o'clock before they got back to Tremenheere. Driving over the moor and down into the long, wooded valley that led to the village, they saw that the clouds to the south had thickened and moved inshore. After the brilliance of the north

132

coast, this mist came as something of a surprise. The town was cloaked in it, invisible. It swallowed the low evening sun and was blown, in drifts, up from the sea towards them.

'I'm glad we didn't spend the day here,' said Ivan. 'WE'D HAve been sitting in a fog with sweaters on, instead of sunbathing on the rocks.'

'Is that the end of the good weather, or will the sun come back?'

'Oh, the sun'll come back. It always comes back. We could have another scorcher tomorrow. It's just a sea fog.'

The sun always comes back. The confident way Ivan said this filled Laura with comfort. Optimism is a lovely thing, and one of Ivan's most endearing qualities was that he seemed to radiate optimism. She could not imagine him being downhearted, and if he ever was, then it would not last for long. Even the saga of his disastrous engagement and the loss of his job, which could in a less resilient man have been the source of much retrospective gloom, he had recounted with good humour, turning the whole episode into a joke against himself.

This optimism was catching. Sitting beside him in the open car, tired, sunburned, and salty, Laura felt carefree as a child and more hopeful about the future than she had for a long time. She was, after all, only thirty-seven. That was young. With a bit of luck, fingers crossed, she would be able to start a baby. Perhaps then Alec would sell the house in Islington and buy another, bigger, with a garden. And the house would be Laura's, not Erica's. And the nursery upstairs would be their baby's nursery, not Gabriel's. And when Daphne Boulderstone came to call, she would not be able to sit in Laura's bedroom and make remarks about the furniture and the curtains, because there would be no memories of Erica to justify them.

Now they were turning into the gates of Tremenheere, driving under the arch, stopping by Ivan's front door.

'Ivan, thank you very much. It's been the most perfect day.'

'Thank you for coming.' Lucy, curled up in Laura's lap, sat up and yawned and looked about her. Ivan caressed her head, pulled her long, silky ears. Then he picked up Laura's hand and kissed the back of it in the most natural and unconsidered way. 'I hope I haven't exhausted the pair of you.'

'I don't know about Lucy, but I haven't felt so well in years.' She added, 'Or so happy.'

They parted. Ivan had a phone call to make; he would take a shower and change. Perhaps, later, they would all meet for a drink. It depended on what arrangements Eve and Gerald had made. He emptied the haversack and took the damp swimming things and slung them over the washing line, where they hung, sandy and unpegged, in the gathering mist. Laura carried the picnic basket into the kitchen. There was nobody about. She gave Lucy a drink of water and then unpacked the basket, throwing away the rubbish and washing up the plastic plates and glasses. She went out of the door and down the passage in search of Eve.

She found her, for once sitting down, in the drawing room. Because of the mist and the gloom of the prospect from the window, she had kindled a little fire, and this burned cheerfully in the grate.

She had already changed for the evening and was doing her tapestry, but as Laura came through the door, she set this down and took off her spectacles.

'Did you have a lovely day?'

'Oh, heavenly . . .' Laura flopped down into a chair and told Eve about it. 'We went to Penjizal and it was gorgeous weather there, not a cloud in the sky. And then we swam and had lunch – thank you for the lunch – and sat and watched the tide come in. And we saw heaps of seals, all bobbing about with darling doggy faces. And then the tide *did* come in, so we went back onto the cliffs and spent the rest of the afternoon there, and then Ivan took me to Lanyon, and we had a beer in the pub, and then we came home. I'm sorry we're so late. I haven't done anything to help you with dinner or anything . . .'

'Oh, don't worry, that's all been seen to.'

'You've lit a fire.'

'Yes, I felt rather shivery.'

Laura looked at her more closely. She said, 'You're pale. Are you feeling all right?'

'Yes, of course. I – I had a bit of a headache at lunchtime, but I've had a sleep and I'm fine now. Laura, Alec called. Just after six. But he's ringing back at nine.'

'Alec . . . What was he ringing about?'

'I've no idea. Probably just wanted a chat with you. Anyway, like I said, he's ringing back.' She smiled. 'You're looking wonderfully well, Laura. Quite a different person. Alec's not going to recognize you when he sees you again.'

134

'I feel well,' Laura told her. She pulled herself out of the chair and went to the door, headed for her bedroom and a bath. 'I feel quite a different person.' She went, closing the door behind her. Eve sat looking at the closed door, frowning a little. Then she sighed, put on her spectacles again, and went back to her tapestry.

Gerald stood at his dressing table, chin raised, squinting into the mirror, pulling up the knot of his tie. A dark blue silk tie, patterned with red naval crowns. It settled neatly between the two crisp points of his collar. That done, he took up his ivory-backed brushes and attended to what remained of his hair, which was not very much.

Meticulously, he replaced the brushes, neatly lined up with his clothes brush, his stud box, his nail scissors, and the silver-framed photograph of Eve, taken on their wedding day.

His dressing room – as his sea cabin had been – was always a model of order. Clothes were folded, shoes placed in pairs, nothing ever left lying about. It even looked like a sea cabin. The single bed, where he sometimes slept if he had a cold, or Eve a headache, was narrow and functional, and neatly squared off under a navy-blue blanket. The dressing table was an old sea chest, with recessed brass handles at either side. The walls were lined with group photographs: his term at Dartmouth, and the ship's company of H.M.S. *Excellent*, the year that Gerald had been gunnery commander.

Order was engrained in him   order and a set of ethics by which he had lived his life, and he had decided long ago that the old, rigid maxims of the Royal Navy could be profitably applied to ordinary, day-to-day existence.

A ship is known by her boats.

That meant that if the front entrance of a house looked clean and scrubbed, with brasses polished and floor shining, then visitors assumed that the rest of the house was just as spotless. It didn't necessarily have to be, and in the case of Tremenheere, frequently wasn't. It was just the first impression that mattered so much.

A dirty submarine is a lost submarine.

In Gerald's opinion this was particularly appropriate to the endless headaches of modern industry. Any establishment, mismanaged and inefficiently run, was doomed as well. He was, in the main part, a calm and easygoing man, but sometimes, reading accounts in the *Times* of strife, strikes, and picket lines, misunderstanding and noncommunication, he came near to grinding his teeth in rage, longing to be, not retired, but in action again, convinced that with a bit of sensible, seamanlike cooperation, all could be resolved.

And then the last, the final conceit. *The difficult we can do at once, the impossible may take a little longer.*

The difficult we can do at once. He put on his blazer, took a clean handkerchief from his drawer, and tucked it into his top pocket. He let himself out of the room, crossed the landing, to where a window looked out over the courtyard. Ivan's car was parked outside his door. Eve, Gerald knew, was having a sit-down in the drawing room. Quietly he went down the back stairs and through the deserted kitchen.

Outside, the mist had thickened and it was damp and cold. From far out to sea he could hear the faint, regular moaning of the coast-guard foghorn. He crossed the courtyard and opened the door of Ivan's house.

The impossible may take a little longer.

'Ivan.'

From above he heard the sound of running water, as bath water gurgled down a drain. As well, Ivan had his radio on, a blast of cheerful dance music.

The door led straight into the spacious kitchen living room, which comprised the entire ground floor of the house. A table stood in the middle of this, and comfortable chairs were drawn up before a log-burning stove. Most of the furniture in the room belonged to Gerald, but Ivan had added things of his own: the blue-and-white china on the dresser, some pictures, a pink-and-red Japanese paper bird, suspended from the ceiling. An open flight of wooden steps, like a ship's ladder, gave access to the upper floor, where the old hay loft now contained two small bedrooms and a bathroom. He went to the foot of these and called again, 'Ivan.'

Abruptly, the radio was silenced. The water gurgled away. The next moment Ivan appeared at the head of the stairs, dressed in a small towel and with his wet fair hair standing on end.

'Gerald. Sorry I didn't hear you.'

'I'm not surprised. I want a word.'

'Of course, make yourself at home. I won't be a moment. It felt so damp and miserable, I lit the fire. I hope it hasn't gone out. Anyway, pour yourself a drink. You know where it is.'

He disappeared, could be heard thumping about overhead. Gerald checked on the stove, which had not gone out. A faint warmth already emanated from its black iron walls. He found a bottle of Haig in the cupboard over the sink, poured a tot into a tumbler, and filled it with water from the tap. Holding this, he began to walk up and down the length of the room. Pacing the quarterdeck, Eve always called it. But at least it was better than sitting down, doing nothing.

Eve. *We won't tell anyone,* they had all agreed. *Oh, Gerald,* she had said, *we mustn't ever tell anyone.*

And now he was going to break his word, because he knew that he had to tell Ivan.

His stepson came down the steep stairs full tilt, like an experienced sailor, damp hair slicked down, and wearing blue jeans and a dark blue polo sweater.

'Sorry about that. You've got a drink? Is the fire all right?'

'Yes, it's going.'

'Extraordinary how quickly it gets cold.' He went to get himself a drink. 'Up on the other coast it was really warm, not a cloud in the sky.'

'You had a good day, then?'

'Perfect. How about you? What have you and Eve been up to?'

'We,' said Gerald, 'have not had a good day. That is why I'm here.'

Ivan turned at once, the tumbler in his hand, half-filled with neat whisky.

'I suggest you put some water in that, and then we'll sit down and I'll tell you.'

Their eyes met. Gerald did not smile. Ivan turned on the tap and filled up the glass. He brought it over to the fireside and they sat facing each other across the white sheepskin hearthrug.

'Fire away.'

Quietly, Gerald recounted to him the happenings of the morning. The hysterical telephone call from Silvia. Their instant response to her appeal. The letter.

'What sort of a letter?'

137

'A poison-pen letter.'

'A . . .' Ivan's jaw dropped. 'A poison-pen letter? You have to be joking.'

'It is, unfortunately, true.'

'Bu– but who's it from? Who the hell would write Silvia a poison-pen letter?'

'We don't know.'

'Where is it?'

'She has it still. I told her to keep it.'

'What did it say?'

'It said . . .' As soon as he had got home, and before he forgot the exact words, Gerald had written them down, in his neat script, at the back of his diary. Now he took his diary out of his breast pocket, put on his spectacles, opened the diary, and read aloud. '"You went with other men and drove your husband to drink. You killed him. You should be ashamed of yourself."'

He sounded like a barrister, reading aloud in court the intimate details of some sleazy divorce. His cultured voice reduced to cool impersonality the ill-framed, evil-intentioned words. But the venom, still, was there.

'How revolting.'

'Yes.'

'Was it handwritten?'

'No, the classic method was used: letters cut from newspaper headlines and stuck on to writing paper. Child's writing paper. The envelope printed with a rubber stamp . . . you know the sort of thing. Local postmark, yesterday's date.'

'Has she any idea who could have sent it?'

'Have you?'

Ivan actually laughed. 'Gerald, I hope you don't think it was me!'

But Gerald did not laugh. 'No. We think it was May.'

'*May?*'

'Yes, May. May, according to Silvia, has never been able to stand the sight of her. May has this fetish about drink. You know that as well as we do. . . .'

'But not May.' Ivan got to his feet, started pacing the floor, much as Gerald had paced it a few moments earlier.

'May is an old lady, Ivan. Over the last few months, her behaviour has become odder by the day. Eve suspects she's going senile and I'm inclined to agree with her.'

'But it's so out of character. I know May. She may not like Silvia, but deep down she's bound to be sorry for her. May can be maddening, I know, but she was never one to bear a grudge or be resentful. She was never wicked. You'd have to be totally wicked to think up a thing like that.'

'Yes, but on the other hand, she's always held very strong views. Not just about drink, but moral behaviour in general.'

'What's that meant to mean?'

'"You went with other men." Perhaps she thinks Silvia's promiscuous.'

'Well, she probably is. Was. Never did May any harm.'

'Perhaps May thought she was being promiscuous with you.'

Ivan swung around, as though Gerald had landed a blow at him. He stared, incredulous, at his stepfather, his blue eyes unblinking and blazing with indignation.

'With me? Who thought that one up?'

'Nobody thought it up. But Silvia's an attractive woman. She comes and goes at Tremenheere all the time. She told us that you'd driven her to some party . . .'

'So I did. Why waste petrol taking two cars? Is that being promiscuous?'

'. . . and that sometimes, when we're away, you have her up here for a drink or a meal.'

'Gerald, she's Eve's friend. Eve keeps an eye on Silvia. If Eve's away, I ask her here. . . .'

'Silvia thinks that May has watched from her window and disapproved.'

'Oh, for God's sake, what's Silvia trying to get me into?'

Gerald spread his hands. 'Nothing.'

'Well, it sounds like something to me. Next thing, I'll be accused of seducing the bloody woman.'

'Did you?'

'Did I? She's old enough to be my bloody *mother*!'

'Did you sleep with her?'

'*No, I bloody never did!*'

The shouted words left a sort of vacuum behind them. In the silence that followed, Ivan tipped back his head and poured the last of his drink down his throat. He went to pour himself another. The bottle clinked against the side of the glass.

Gerald said, 'I believe you.'

139

Ivan filled the glass with water. With his back still turned to Gerald, he said, 'I'm sorry. I had no right to shout.'

'I'm sorry too. And you mustn't hold this against Silvia. She made not the smallest insinuation against you. It was just that I had to be sure.'

Ivan turned, leaning with grace against the edge of the draining board. His quick anger had died, and he grinned ruefully. 'Yes, I can see that. After all, my track record hasn't always been perfect.'

'There's nothing wrong with your track record.' Gerald put the diary back in his pocket, took off his spectacles.

'What are you going to do about the letter?'

'Nothing.'

'What if there's another one?'

'We'll cross that bridge when we get to it.'

'Is Silvia prepared to take no action?'

'Yes, Only she and I and Eve know about it. And now you. And you will of course say nothing. Not even to Eve, because she doesn't know that I've told you.'

'Is she very upset?'

'Very. I think more deeply upset than poor Silvia. She's frightened of what May might do next. She has nightmares about having to watch while poor May is wheeled off to some geriatric mental home. She protects May. Just as I protect Eve.'

Ivan said, 'Well, May protected us. She looked after me, and she stood by my mother all the time my father was ill and dying. She was like a rock then. Never faltering. And now this. Dear old May, I can't bear to think about it. We owe her so much.' He thought about this. 'I suppose we all owe debts to each other.'

'Yes,' said Gerald. 'It's a sad business.'

They smiled at each other. 'Let me give you the other half,' said Ivan.

Eve and Laura sat in the firelit drawing room, listening to a concert on BBC 2. The Brahms Piano Concerto. It was past nine o'clock, and Gerald, not wishing to spoil their pleasure, had taken himself off to his study to watch the news in there.

Laura lay curled up in one of the big armchairs, Lucy in her lap. Ivan had not reappeared. While she changed, Laura had

140

heard his car go through the gate and take off up the hill in the direction of Lanyon. She guessed that he was off to the pub, perhaps to have a beer with Mathie Thomas.

Across the room, Eve stitched at her tapestry. She looked, thought Laura, tired this evening and very fragile, her fine skin taut over her cheekbones and dark bruises of fatigue beneath her eyes. She had spoken little, and it had been Gerald who made conversation over the grilled chops and fruit salad, while Eve picked at the delicious food and drank water instead of wine. Laura, watching her through sleepy, half-closed eyes, felt concern. Eve did so much, was always on the go, cooking and organizing and generally looking after them all. When the concert was finished, Laura would suggest bed. Perhaps Eve would let her make a hot drink for her, fill a hot-water bottle . . .

The telephone began to ring. Eve looked up from her work. 'That'll be Alec, Laura.'

Laura pulled herself out of the chair and went out of the room, with Lucy at her heels, down the passage to the hall. She sat on the carved chest and picked up the receiver.

'Tremenheere.'

'Laura.' The line was better this time, his voice as clear as if he spoke from the next room.

'Alec. I'm sorry I wasn't here when you called before. We didn't get back till seven.'

'Did you have a good day?'

'Yes, it was lovely. . . . How is everything with you?'

'Fine, but that's not why I'm calling. Look, something's come up. I'm not going to be able to come back to Tremenheere to fetch you. As soon as we get back to London, Tom and I have got to go to New York. We only heard this morning. I got a phone call from the chairman.'

'But how long have you got to be away?'

'Only a week. The thing is, we can take our wives with us. There's a fair amount of socializing to be done. Daphne's coming with Tom, and I wondered if you'd like to come too. It'll be pretty hectic, but you've never been to New York and I want to show it to you. But it would mean getting back to London under your own steam and meeting me there. How do you feel about it?'

How Laura felt was appalled.

This instinctive reaction to a suggestion made by Alec, whom she loved, and intended for Laura's pleasure, filled her heart with a sort of horrified guilt. What was wrong? What was happening to her? Alec was asking her to go to New York with him, and she didn't want to go. She didn't want to make the journey. She didn't want to be in New York in August, especially with Daphne Boulderstone. She did not want to sit in some air-conditioned hotel with Daphne while the men attended to their business, nor pound the sizzling pavements of Fifth Avenue, window-shopping.

But worse was the realization that she did not want to get the train back to London. Nor be torn by the roots from this lovely, carefree existence. Nor leave Tremenheere.

All this took only a second to flash, with hideous clarity, through her mind.

'When are you going?' she asked, stalling for time.

'Wednesday evening. We're flying Concorde.'

'Have you booked a seat for me?'

'Provisionally.'

'How – how long would we be in New York?'

'Laura, I told you. A week.' And then he said, 'You don't sound very enthusiastic. Don't you want to come?'

'Oh, Alec I do. . . . It's sweet of you to ask me . . . but . . .'

'But?'

'It's just that it's all a bit sudden. I haven't had time to take it in.'

'You don't need much time. It's not a very complicated plan.' She bit her lip. 'Perhaps you don't feel up to it yet.'

She grasped at this excuse, the proverbial drowning man with his wretched bit of straw. 'Well, actually, I don't know if I do. I mean, I'm fine . . . but I don't know if flying's an awfully good idea. And New York will be so dreadfully hot. . . . It would be so awful if anything happened, and I spoiled it all for you . . . by being ill. . . .' She sounded, even to herself, hopelessly irresolute.

'Well, don't worry. We can cancel the fourth seat.'

'Oh, I am sorry. I feel so feeble. . . . Perhaps, another time.'

'Yes, another time.' He dismissed the idea. 'It doesn't matter.'

'When will you be back again?'

'The following Tuesday, I suppose.'

142

'And what shall I do? Stay here?'

'If Eve doesn't mind. You'll have to ask her.'

'And will you be able to come and fetch me then?' This sounded even more selfish than saying she would not go to New York with him. 'You don't have to. I – I can easily catch the train.'

'No. I think I'll be able to drive down. I'll see how things go. I'll need to contact you later about that.'

He might have been planning some office meeting. The hated telephone separated them, rather than brought them together. She longed to be with him, to see his face, watch his reactions. To touch him, make him understand that she loved him more than anyone in the world, but she didn't want to go to New York with Daphne Boulderstone.

Not for the first time, she was aware of the gap that yawned between them. Trying to bridge this she said, 'I miss you so much.'

'I miss you too.'

It hadn't worked. 'How's the fishing?' she asked him.

'We're having a great time. Everyone sends their love.'

'Ring me before you leave for New York.'

'I'll do that.'

'And I'm sorry, Alec.'

'Think no more about it. Just a suggestion. Good night. Sleep well.'

'Good night, Alec.'

7

SAINT THOMAS

At five thirty in the morning, Gabriel Haverstock, who had lain awake since three, pushed aside the rumpled sheet and climbed silently out of her bunk. Across the cabin, a man still slept, his hair and stubbled chin dark against the pale pillow. His arm lay across his chest, his head was turned away from her. She pulled on an old tee shirt that had once belonged to him and made her way, barefoot, aft to the day cabin. She found a match and lit a ring on the small, gimballed gas cooker, filled a kettle and put it on to boil, and then went up the steps and out into the cockpit. There had been a dew, and the deck was damp, beaded with moisture.

In the dawn light, the waters of the harbour lay like a sheet of glass. All about, at their moorings, other boats slumbered, moving so slightly that it was as though they breathed in their sleep. Ashore, the dockside was beginning to stir. A car started up, and from the jetty a black man climbed down into a wooden dinghy, cast off, and began to row. Across the water, each dip of his oars was clearly audible. The boat moved out into the harbour, its wake causing only an arrow-shaped ripple.

Saint Thomas, United States Virgin Islands. During the night, two cruise liners had moved in under cover of darkness and tied up. It was like being unexpectedly invaded by skyscrapers. Gabriel looked up and saw, high on the superstructure, sailors working, winching cables, sluicing decks. Below them, the tall cliff of the ship's side was studded with rows and layers of portholes, behind which, in their cabins, the tourists slept. Later in the morning, they would emerge, wearing their Bermuda shorts and their hectically patterned fun shirts, to lean over the rail and gaze down at the yachts, just as Gabriel was gazing up at them now. Later, they would go ashore, slung with cameras and mad to spend their dollars on straw baskets and sandals and carved wooden statuettes of black ladies with fruit on their heads.

144

Behind her, in the cabin, the kettle began to boil.

She went below and made a pot of tea. They had run out of milk, so she cut a slice of lemon, put it in a mug, and poured tea over it. Carrying the mug, she went to wake him.

'Umm?' He turned when she shook his naked shoulder, buried his face in the pillow, scratched his head, yawned. He opened his eyes and looked up, saw her standing over him.

He said, 'What time is it?'

'About a quarter to six.'

'Oh, God.' He yawned again, heaved himself up into a sitting position, pulling the pillow from beneath him and stuffing it behind his head.

She said, 'I made you some tea.' He took the mug and tried a scalding sip. 'It's got lemon in, because there's no milk.'

'So I see.'

She left him, poured another mug for herself, took it out into the cockpit, and drank it there. It was getting lighter by the minute, the sky turning blue. As the sun came up, it would burn all moisture away, in a drift of vapour. And then another day, another hot, cloudless, West Indian day.

After a bit, he joined her. He had dressed, was wearing his old dirty white shorts and a grey sweat shirt. His feet were bare. He stepped up onto the deck and went aft, busying himself with the painter of the dinghy, which had got fouled up with the stern anchor chain.

Gabriel finished her tea and went below again. She cleaned her teeth and washed in the tiny basin, put on jeans and a pair of canvas sneakers and a blue-and-white-striped tee shirt. Her red nylon kit bag, which she had packed last night, stood at the foot of her bunk. She had left it open and now stowed in it the last of her stuff – her sponge bag, her hairbrush, a thick sweater for the journey. There wasn't anything else. Six months of living on a boat had done nothing for her wardrobe. She pulled the ties at the top of the kit bag and tied them with a seaman-like knot.

Carrying this, and her shoulder bag, she went back on deck. He was already in the dinghy, waiting for her. She handed him the kit bag and then climbed down the ladder, stepped into the fragile craft, and sat on the forward thwart, holding the kitbag between her knees.

He started the outboard. It hiccupped and then fired, making a noise like a motor bicycle. As they moved out over the water, and the distance widened, she looked back at the yacht – the beautiful, fifty-foot, single-masted sloop white-painted and graceful with her name, *Enterprise of Tortola* emblazoned in gold upon her transom. Over his shoulder, she watched it go for the last time.

At the jetty, he tied up, tossed her luggage onto the dock, and heaved himself up after it. He gave her a hand and helped her up beside him. Once, there had been a set of wooden steps for this purpose, but they had been blown away in some hurricane and never replaced. They walked down the dock and up the steps, into the complex of the hotel. They went through the gardens, past the deserted swimming pool. Beyond the reception bulding, beneath the palm trees, was a forecourt, where a couple of taxis stood, the sleepy drivers dozing. He woke one, who stretched and yawned, disposed of the kit bag, started the engine, and generally prepared himself for a trip to the airport.

He turned to Gabriel. 'I suppose, then, this is goodbye.'

'Yes. It's goodbye.'

'Will I ever see you again?'

'I don't suppose so.'

'It's been good.'

'Yes. It's been good. Thank you for it.'

'Thank you.'

He put an arm around her shoulder and kissed her. He had not shaved and the stubble on his chin scratched her cheek. She looked into his face for the last time, and then turned and got into the taxi and slammed the door. The old car trundled forward, but she never looked back, so that she never knew if he waited until they were out of his sight.

From Saint Thomas she flew to Saint Croix. From Saint Croix to San Juan. San Juan to Miami. Miami to New York. At Kennedy, they lost her kit bag and she had to wait for an hour by the empty, turning carousel until it finally appeared.

She went out of the building into the warm, humid, New York dusk, the air foggy and smelling of fuel oil, and waited by the sign until an airport bus came her way. It was full, and she had to stand, strap-hanging, with her kit bag between her knees. At the British Airways terminal, she bought a ticket for London, and then went upstairs to sit for three hours, waiting for the flight to be called.

The plane was full, and she realized that she had been lucky to get a seat on it. She sat next to an elderly blue-haired lady who was making her first trip to Britain. She had been saving up, she told Gabriel, for two years. She was on a tour – most of the passengers were on the same tour – and they were going to see the Tower of London and Westminster Abbey and Buckingham Palace, and make trips farther afield as well. Edinburgh, for a day or two of the festival, Stratford-on-Avon.

'I just can't wait to see Stratford, and Anne Hathaway's cottage.'

The excursion, to Gabriel, sounded mind-boggling, but she smiled and said, 'How lovely.'

'And you, dear, where are you going?'

'I'm going home,' said Gabriel.

She did not sleep on the plane. There was not enough night to go to sleep. No sooner had they finished dinner than, it seemed, they were being handed hot towels to wash their faces and given glasses of orange juice. At Heathrow, it was raining. Soft, sweet English rain, like mist on her face. Everything looked very gentle and green, and even the airport smelled different.

Before she left Saint Thomas, he had given her some English money – a few ill-assorted notes from the back of his wallet – but there was not enough to pay for a taxi, so she caught the tube from Heathrow to King's Cross. At King's Cross she changed to another train that took her to the Angel.

From the Angel, she walked, her kit bag under her arm. It was not very far. She saw that changes were taking place in the once-familiar streets. A block of old houses had been bulldozed away and a new and enormous structure was going up in their place. A wall of wooden hoardings protected this building operation from the pavement, and these were spray-painted with graffiti. Skids Rule, she read, and Jobs not Bombs.

She went down the old Islington High Street and through the Campden Passage, between the shuttered jewellers and anti-que dealers, past the toy shop where once she had bought, in a dusty box labelled three shillings and sixpence, a doll's china tea set. She turned down a narrow, paved lane, and emerged into Abigail Crescent.

Abigail Crescent had not changed. A few more houses had

had their faces cleaned, a neighbour had added a dormer window to his roof. That was all. The house where she had spent her childhood looked exactly as it always had, which was comforting, but her father's private parking space stood empty, which was not so comforting. Perhaps, although it was only half past eight in the morning, he had already gone to work.

She went up the steps and rang the bell. Inside the house, she heard it ringing, but no one came to the door. After a little she put her hand to her neck and drew from beneath her sweater a long silver chain, from which hung a latchkey. Long ago, when she was still at day school in London, her father had given her the key . . . in case of emergencies, he had said, but she had never had to use it, because there was always somebody there when she got home.

She used it now, turning the lock. The door opened, and as it did, Gariel saw a figure making its slow way up the basement stairs towards her.

'Who's that?' The voice was shrill and sharp, even a little agitated.

'It's all right, Mrs Abney,' said Gabriel. 'It's only me.'

Mrs Abney did all the things people are meant to do if they have turns or heart attacks. She stopped dead, gasped as if for air, placed her hand on her chest, clutched the banister.

'Gabriel!'

'I'm sorry, did I frighten you?'

'You certainly did!'

'I didn't think anyone was in. . . .'

'I was in all right and heard the bell, but I can't get up the stairs like a dose of salts, can I?'

Gabriel lugged the kit bag into the hall and closed the door behind her.

'Where have you sprung from?' asked Mrs Abney.

'From the West Indies. I've been flying since . . .' It was too long ago to remember and, with time changes and jet lag, too complicated to try to explain. '. . . . oh, forever. Where's my father?'

'He's away. He didn't say anything about you coming.'

'He didn't know I was coming. I suppose he's in Scotland.'

'Oh, no. He's *been* to Scotland. Got back Wednesday . . . yesterday, that is. And flew off again yesterday evening.'

'Flew off?' Gabriel's heart sank. 'Where to?'

'New York. A business trip. With Mr and Mrs Boulderstone.'

'Oh . . .' Gabriel's legs felt suddenly weak. She sat at the bottom of the stairs and bowed her head, pushing her fingers through her hair. He'd gone to New York. She'd missed him by only a few hours. Their planes must have crossed in the night, both of them travelling in the wrong direction.

Mrs Abney, seeing her wilt with tiredness and disappointment, became motherly.

'There's nothing in the kitchen, because the house is empty. But why don't you come downstairs with me and I'll make you a cup of tea. . . . It'll seem like old times, having you there. Remember how I used to give you your tea after school when your mum was out? Just like old times.'

Mrs Abney's basement was another of the things that hadn't changed, dim and cosy as a badger's holt, with lace curtains shutting off what light seeped in from the area, and her little range, even in August, hot as a ship's boiler.

While Mrs Abney put on a kettle and collected cups and saucers, Gabriel pulled out a chair and sat at the table. She looked around her, seeing familiar photographs, the framed calender of bluebells in a wood, the china dogs at either end of the mantelshelf.

She said. 'Where's Dicky?'

'Oh, my little Dicky, he died. About a year ago. My nephew wanted to give me a budgie, but I hadn't the heart.' She made the tea. 'Do you want anything to eat?'

'No, just tea would be fine.'

'You sure? When did you last have a meal?'

Gabriel couldn't remember. 'Oh, sometime.'

'I could do a bit of bread and butter.'

'No, really.'

Mrs Abney sat facing her and poured the tea. She said, 'I shall want to hear all your news. And about your mother. Mother's all right, is she? That's good. My goodness, it seems a long time since you went . . . must be nearly six years now. How old are you now? Nineteen? Yes, I thought you must be just about nineteen. You haven't changed that much. Recognized you at once. Except your hair's short. And you've dyed it blond.'

'No, I didn't dye it. It just bleached itself with West Indian sunshine and chlorinated swimming pools.'

'You look like a boy. That's what I thought when I saw you

149

standing there. That's why I got such a scare. Some nasty boys around the place these days . . . I have to take good care of the house when your father's away.'

Gabriel took a mouthful of the tea, which was dark and sweet and strong, the way Mrs Abney had always liked it.

'And his new wife . . . has she gone to New York too?'

'No. I told you, just the Boulderstones. No, the new Mrs Haverstock's gone to Cornwall. She's been there for a bit.' Mrs Abney dropped her voice to a confidential whisper. 'Had to have this little operation. You know, dear. Insides.'

'Oh, dear.'

'Anyway,' Mrs Abney continued in her normal tones, 'the doctor wouldn't let her go to Scotland, so she went to Cornwall instead.' She took another sip of tea and laid the cup down in the saucer. 'To get better.'

'Do you know where she is?'

'No, I don't know where. Mr Haverstock didn't give me her address. Just to some relation of his, in Cornwall.'

'There are dozens of Haverstocks in Devon and Cornwall. She could be anywhere.'

'Well, I'm sorry, but I don't know where she is . . . except . . . a letter came yesterday evening. I think it came from Cornwall. Just wait and I'll get it.' She got to her feet and went over to her sideboard and opened a drawer. 'Your father's secretary drops by each morning and picks up all the mail, and deals with it in the office. But she hasn't come yet, and this is all I've got to give her.'

She handed the envelope to Gabriel. A plain brown envelope with her father's name and the address apparently printed on, as though it had been done with a rubber stamp. The postmark was Truro, Cornwall, and in the opposite corner someone had written, in felt pen, Urgent, and underlined it.

'What an extraordinary-looking letter.'

'It *might* be from Mrs Haverstock. The new Mrs Haverstock, that is,' she added tactfully.

'I can't *open* it.' She looked at Mrs Abney. 'Can I?'

'Well, I don't know, dear. It's up to you. If you want to get hold of Mrs Haverstock and the address is in the letter, then I don't see why you shouldn't have a peep. Though I must say, it's a funny way to write the address. Must have taken hours.'

Gabriel laid down the envelope and then picked it up again.

She said, 'I really *have* to know where she is, Mrs Abney. If I can't see my father, I have to see her.'

'Then open it,' said Mrs Abney. 'After all, "Urgent" doesn't mean private.'

Gabriel put her thumb beneath the flap and slit the envelope. She drew out a sheet of pale pink writing paper and unfolded it. Lined paper, headed by a stamp-size picture of a fairy. The lines of black, uneven print shouted at her like a bad-news headline.

> YOur WiFe aT TreMEnhEeRe iS
> HaViNG AN AFfaIR wITh IvAN
> AShbY. ThOUgHt yOu shOUld KnoW
> A WEll-wisHEr.

Her heart was hammering. She felt the blood drain from her face.

'Any use?' asked Mrs Abney, craning her neck to peer.

Gabriel quickly folded the letter and stuffed it back into the envelope before Mrs Abney should see.

'No. Yes. It's . . . not from her. Just a note from somebody else. But she's at a place called Tremenheere.'

'There you are! Now you know.' Her eyes narrowed. 'Are you all right? You've gone deathly pale.'

'Yes, I am all right, but I'm tired.' She pushed the horrible envelope into the pocket of her jeans. 'I haven't slept for hours. I think, if you don't mind, I'll go and lie down.'

'You do that. Your bed's not made up, but it's been aired. You can get in under the blankets. Have a bit of shut-eye.'

'Yes. You are kind, Mrs Abney. I'm sorry I suddenly burst in on you, surprised you.'

'It's nice to have you here again. Nice to have a bit of company with everyone away. Your dad'll be pleased when he knows you're back.'

Gabriel went upstairs and into the sitting room. Picked up the telephone and dialled a number. A man answered, 'Directory enquiries.'

'I want a number in Cornwall, please. The name is Haverstock. I'm afraid I don't know the initial. And the address is Tremenheere.'

'Hold on a mo.'

151

She held on. He was a cheerful man, singing at his work. 'Oh, when e'er the darkest cloud is in the sky, You mustn't sigh. And you mustn't cry. . . .'

The sitting room was much as she remembered it. The same curtains, the same covers on the chairs. The cushions that her mother had chosen. Some new ornaments, another picture or two . . .

'Tremenheere. Here we are. Penvarloe two three eight.'

Gabriel, ready with a pencil, wrote it down.

'And it's Mister . . .?'

'No, not Mister. Admiral. Admiral G. J. Haverstock.'

She said, 'Penvarloe,' and then, sounding helpless, 'Oh, dear.'

'What's wrong now?'

'I've got to get there by train. I wonder which would be the nearest railway station.'

'I can tell you that.' And he did so.

'How do you know?'

'The wife and I were down there for our summer holidays last year.'

'How amazing.'

'Amazing all right,' said the cheerful voice. 'Rained the whole bloody time.'

She went out of the room, picked up her things, and trailed upstairs. On the first landing, she dropped the kit bag and went into her father's dressing room. It smelled, as it had always smelled, of Bay Rum. She opened the wardrobe and touched his clothes, lifting the sleeve of a tweed jacket and holding it against her cheek. She saw his salmon rod, in its canvas case, neatly stowed in a corner; his open desk, stuffed with his ordered confusion of papers and cheque stubs and some accounts, waiting to be paid. On the chest of drawers stood a photograph of herself, taken years ago, and a terrible drawing she had once done for him. As well there was a photograph of . . . Laura? Not a studio portrait but an enlarged snap, informal and laughing. She had a lot of dark hair and dark eyes and a lovely smile. She looked so happy.

Your wife at Tremenheere is having an affair with Ivan Ashby.

Gabriel went out through the door and closed it behind her. Dragging the kit bag again, she started up the last flight. *Your*

152

room will always be there, he had promised her. *Waiting for you*. She opened the door and went in. Her bed, her books, her bears, her dollhouse. The Beatrix Potter frieze around the walls, the blue-and-white-striped curtains.

The kit bag fell upon the floor with a soft thud. She kicked off her shoes and pulled back the covers and got into the bed. The blankets felt soft and warm, more comforting than any sheet. She stared at the ceiling, too tired to sleep.

Your wife at Tremenheere . . .

Too tired even to cry. She closed her eyes.

Later, she got up and had a hot bath and put on some other clothes. Another pair of jeans, another tee shirt, hauled, un-ironed, from the kit bag, but at least clean. She picked up her shoulder bag and let herself out of the house and walked around the corner to the local bank that her parents had always used. She asked to see the manager, identified herself, and was allowed to cash a cheque. With money to spend, she realized that she was ravenously hungry. She found a delicatessen and bought fresh bread, butter, a carton of milk, some pâté, and half a pound of tomatoes. When she got back to Abigail Crescent, she unloaded all this onto the kitchen table, and there assembled and consumed the impromptu meal. It was now nearly three thirty. She went through to the sitting room and rang Paddington Station and booked herself a sleeper on the night train. After that there wasn't anything to do except wait.

The station was at the end of the line. For the last mile or so of the journey, the railway ran alongside the sea, and when Gabriel opened the door of the train and stepped down onto the platform, it was to be met by the strong, salty smell of seaweed and fish, while overhead a lot of gulls, screaming into the fresh morning breeze, were flying about.

The platform clock stood at half past seven. She walked down the platform and out into the station yard. Beyond this was a harbour, filled with fishing boats and small pleasure craft. There was a taxi rank, with two or three cars lined up, so she went to the first and asked the man to take her to Tremenheere.

'Got any luggage, 'ave you?'

'Only this.'

He opened the door, and she got in and he slung the red kit bag in after her.

'Is it very far?' she asked him, as he started up the road behind the station and then turned back in the direction from which the train had come.

'No, only a mile or two. Going to stay with the Admiral?'

'Do you know him?'

'No, I don't know 'im. Know *of* 'im. Lovely 'ouse 'e's got.'

'I hope it's not too early for them. I'm not expected.'

'Bound to be someone around.'

Already, they had left the town behind them, turned up a winding lane, climbing a hill. There were little fields and farms and a lot of wild rhododendrons. Then a village. 'This 'ere's Penvarloe,' and then gates, and a short driveway, and a big and very beautiful stone Elizabethan house was revealed.

They stopped by the front door, which stood, irrefutably shut, locked against them. At the side of it was a wrought-iron bellpull, but the thought of actually pulling it and waking a houseful of sleeping people was more than Gabriel could face.

'Just drop me here, and I'll wait.'

'Let's go round the back and see if there's anyone there.'

The taxi moved on cautiously, under an archway and into a courtyard at the back of the house. Still, there was no sign of life. Gabriel got out and heaved her kit bag after her.

'Don't worry,' she told the driver. 'I'll be all right now. How much do I owe you?'

He told her, and she paid him and thanked him. He backed cautiously out of the courtyard, through the archway, and she heard him drive away. As she stood there trying to decide what to do next, the quiet was shattered by the sound of a window opening, and a man's voice said, 'Are you looking for somebody?'

Not the big house, but the small house opposite, on the far side of the square. It had pink pelargoniums in tubs on either side of its door, and from the upper window a man leaned, his forearms resting on the stone ledge. He might have been totally naked, but Gabriel could only see his top half, so she couldn't be sure.

She said, 'Yes.'

'Who?'

'Mrs Haverstock.'

154

'You have a choice. We have two Mrs Haverstocks here. Which would you like?'

'Mrs Alec Haverstock.'

'Hold on a moment,' said the naked man, 'and I'll come down and let you in.'

Gabriel carried the kit bag across the courtyard and waited. She did not have to wait for long. A moment later, the door of the little house opened – he obviously never locked it – and he reappeared, barelegged and barefooted, but with the rest of him decently wrapped in a blue towel robe, the sash of which he was in the process of knotting around his waist. He was unshaven and his fair hair stood on end.

He said, 'Hello.'

'I'm afraid I woke you up.'

'Yes, you did, or at least the taxi did. You're looking for Laura. She won't be up yet; none of them ever appear until about nine o'clock.'

Gabriel looked at her watch. 'Oh, dear . . .'

He picked up her kit bag and stood aside, holding the door open. 'Come on in.'

'But, aren't you . . .?'

'Come on, it's all right. I can't go back to bed, even if I wanted to. I've got to get to work. . . .'

Gabriel went through the door, and he closed it behind them. She saw the big room, which appeared to serve all functions; the pleasant clutter of scrubbed pine and blue-and-white china; saucepans neatly ranged over a small electric cooker; a black stove with armchairs drawn up to its comfort. There was a table in the middle of the room, on which stood a brown jug filled with roses. From the ceiling, suspended by a thread, hung a pink-and-red paper bird.

She said, 'What a nice room.'

'I like it.' She turned to face him. 'Does Laura know you're coming?'

'No.'

'Who are you?'

'Gabriel Haverstock.' He stared. 'Alec's my father.'

'But you're in America.'

'No, I'm not. I'm here. It's my father who's in America now. He flew to New York on Wednesday evening. Our planes must have crossed in the middle of the night.'

'He didn't know you were coming, either?'

'No.'

'How did you get here?'

'On the night train from Paddington.'

'Well . . .' He seemed to be lost for words. 'This is a turn-up for the books. Are you going to stay?'

'I don't know. That depends on whether anybody asks me.'

'You don't sound very sure.'

'I'm not.'

'Do you know Gerald?'

'My father used to talk about him, but I've never met him.'

'So you won't have met Eve?'

'No, I haven't met either of them. And I haven't met Laura.'

He laughed, scratching the back of his head, the very picture of a man in perplexity. 'What a jolly time everybody's going to have, meeting each other. Well, we'll just have to wait until they all stir their stumps. Would you like some breakfast?'

'Are you going to have some?'

'Of course I am. You don't imagine I go to work on an empty stomach.'

He went over to the little cooker, switched it on, opened the fridge, took out a packet of bacon. Gabriel pulled a chair away from the table and sat and watched him. He looked, she thought, marvellously dishevelled, like an advertisement for Eau Savage.

She said, 'Where do you work?'

'I have part shares in a small furniture factory, up on the moor at a place called Carnellow.'

'Have you lived here long?'

'Only a year.' He plugged in the electric kettle, put bread in the toaster. 'I rent this place from Gerald. It used to be a coach house, but he converted it.' He found a tin and started spooning coffee into an enamel jug. 'You've been in Virginia, haven't you?'

'Yes. But not for a bit. For the last six months I've been in the Virgin Islands, living on a yacht.'

He turned to grin at her over his shoulder. 'Have you? How fantastic. The lotus eater's dream. Is that where you've come from?'

'Yes. Saint Thomas to Saint Croix, Saint Croix to San Juan, San Juan to Miami, Miami to Kennedy, Kennedy to London . . .'

'London to Tremenheere.'

'Right.'

The crisp smell of bacon filled the room mingled with the aroma of coffee. From a cupboard he took plates, cups, saucers; from a drawer, knives and forks. He dumped all these on the table. 'Be a good girl and lay the table, would you?' He went back to the cooker. 'One egg or two?'

'Two,' said Gabriel, who, once again, was feeling famished. She set out the china and the cutlery.

'What else do we need?' he asked.

She tried to remember traditional British breakfasts. 'Marmalade? Honey? Porridge? Kidneys? Kedgeree?'

'Don't get overexcited.'

'Butter, then.'

He found some in the fridge, a pale yellow chunk on an earthenware dish, dumped it on the table, returned to his cooking.

He said, 'What were the Virgin Islands like?'

'Full of mosquitoes.'

'You have to be joking!'

'But perfect if you were at sea.'

'Where were you based?'

'Saint Thomas.'

'Where did you sail?'

'Everywhere. Saint John. Virgin Gorda . . .' His back view was the most attractive back view she had ever seen, even, dressed as he was, in a bathrobe and with his hair on end. He had the most beautiful, capable hands. . . . 'Norman Island.'

'Norman Island. Sounds like a hairdresser.'

'The original Treasure Island. You know. Robert Louis Stevenson.'

'Did he go there?'

'Must have.'

He piled the bacon and eggs onto two plates, carried them over to the table. 'Is that enough for you?'

'More than enough.'

'I can add tomatoes. If you want mushrooms and kidneys, you'll have to wait while I make a quick dash down to the post office in the village.'

'I don't want them.'

'Coffee, then?'

'Lovely.'

He sat down opposite her. 'Go on about Norman Island.'

'Nothing to go on about.'

'Banyan trees and white strands.'

'You've got it in one.'

'Why did you leave?'

Gabriel picked up her fork in her right hand, saw that he was watching her, transferred the fork to her left hand, and picked up a knife in her right hand.

He said, 'Transatlantic customs.'

'I forget easily. I'm in Britain now.'

'We are divided by a common language.'

'But you make great ham and eggs.'

'Why did you leave?'

She looked down at her plate, shrugged. 'Oh, time to come home, I guess.'

It was a delicious breakfast, but he did not linger. With his second cup of coffee in his hand, he told Gabriel that he had to go and shave. But before he did this, he went to open the door, to check on the morning situation in the big house.

'Not a movement. Nor a stir. It's only half past eight. There won't be a face at the window for another half hour.' He came back into the room, leaving the door open. Sunshine was beginning to seep into the courtyard. A long golden diamond of it lay on the scrubbed wooden floor. 'Can you look after yourself while I go up and dress?'

'Of course.'

'You don't have to do the washing up' – he headed for the open staircase – 'but it would be nice if you did.'

She said, 'I don't know who you are.'

Halfway up, he turned, looking down at her from eyes as brightly blue as hummingbird feathers, or the water at Caneel Bay, or speedwells.

'I'm sorry, didn't I tell you? Eve's my mother.'

'But I still don't know your name.'

'It's Ivan Ashby.'

He disappeared upstairs. His footsteps moved overhead. Presently she heard the radio turned on, cheerful, early-morning music. A tap ran water into a basin.

Ivan Ashby.

Gabriel pushed back her chair, gathered up the breakfast

dishes, and took them to the sink. She washed everything up, stacking it neatly in a rack to dry. With this done, she went out into the courtyard. Overhead a flock of white doves fluttered, settling on the bleached tiles of a pigeon cote. No movement showed in the big house. An upstairs window still had the curtains drawn.

But there was another cottage in the courtyard, and this had already wakened. Smoke blew from the single chimney and the door stood open. As Gabriel watched, a figure appeared in this doorway, a girl, wearing a long dark skirt and a white garment, like a choirboys surplice, touched here and there with bedraggled lace. She paused, savouring the warm freshness of the summer morning, and then, with a sort of timeless grace, settled herself on the doorstep in the sun.

Intriguing. A young woman emerging from her house at eight o'clock in the morning and simply sitting down, doing nothing, was a charming novelty.

> What is this life so full of care,
> We have no time to stop and stare.

Gabriel stared. The girl, becoming aware that she was being watched, looked up and saw her.

She said, 'Hello.'

'Hello,' said Gabriel.

'Lovely morning.'

'Yes.' She began to walk over towards the cottage. 'You've got the right idea.'

The girl was quite young, with a small head made enormous by a frizzy mop of pale hair. Her feet were bare, her hands covered with rings. She said, 'Where have you sprung from?'

She looked like an insubstantial gipsy, but her voice was bright and strong, with the long vowels of the North Country.

'I've just arrived. Got off the train this morning.'

Gabriel had reached her side. The girl shunted herself along the doorstep, making space, and Gabriel sat beside her.

'I'm Drusilla,' said the girl.

'I'm Gabriel.'

'Have you come to stay?'

'I hope so.'

'Join the club, then!'

159

'Do you live here?'

'Yes. I've got a baby inside. He hasn't woken up yet, that's why I'm sitting here. Nice to have a bit of peace.'

'How long have you lived here?'

'Oh, a month or two. Before that I was out at Lanyon. But I've been down in this part of the world for about a year.'

'Do you work here?'

'No, I'm not working. Just looking after Josh. I'm a flautist,' she added.

'Sorry?'

'A flautist. I play the flute.'

'Do you?' More and more intriguing. 'Professionally?'

'That's right. Professionally. Used to play in an orchestra in Huddersfield – that's my hometown – but then the orchestra ran out of funds, and I haven't really worked since. I went to London to try to get a job there, but I didn't have any luck.'

'So what did you do?'

'Well, I met this man. Kev. He was a painter. He had a little place in Earls Court, so I moved in with him for a bit. He didn't have much luck in London, either, so we decided to come down here. Some chums of his were here already, and they helped us find somewhere to live. We got this little house out on the moor at Lanyon, but it wasn't much of a place. Nothing like this. Didn't even have a lavatory.'

'How old is your baby?'

'Ten months.'

'And . . . are you and Kev still together?'

'God, no. He lit out on me. Went back to London. I had to get out of the cottage – the man who owned it wouldn't let me stay there on my own. Anyroad, I couldn't pay the rent.'

'What did you do?'

'Couldn't do much, could I? Got out. Mathie Thomas – do you know Mathie Thomas?'

'I don't know anybody.'

'He took me in for a night or two, and then Ivan found me this place. Ivan's Mathie's partner.'

'He's just given me breakfast.'

'Has he?' Drusilla smiled. 'Isn't he smashing? I think he's a lovely person. Really fancy him. Wouldn't mind taking up with Ivan any day of the week.'

' . . . his mother . . . ?'

'Eve? She's a lovely person too. And the Admiral. Have you met the Admiral?'

'I told you, I don't know anybody.'

'We're a regular commune, I can tell you.' Gabriel had caught Drusilla in one of her expansive moods. 'There's an old nanny as well, older than God she is, and twice as disagreeable.' She thought this over. 'No' – she wrinkled her nose – 'that's not fair. She's not a bad old thing. She goes to Truro every Wednesday, it's her day off, and I asked her to buy a bottle of Ribena for Josh, because I can't get it in the post office, and she brought him back a little rabbit. Not a real one, a toy one, with a ribbon round its neck. He'd never had a toy like that before. I thought it was really kind of her. But her face when she handed it over! Sour as an old prune. Some people are funny, no doubt. There's none so queer as old folks.'

'Who else is there?'

'There's Laura. Some relation of the Admiral's. Here to convalesce. She's had an operation. She doesn't live here, though. Just staying. And then there are various hangers-on. You know, popping in and out. There's the gardener, and his wife – she helps in the house sometimes. And a woman called Mrs Marten who lives in the village, but I can't stand her.'

'Does she help in the house, too?'

'God, no. She's a friend of Eve's. I think she's a toffee-nosed bitch. Never handed me a good word, never so much as looks at Josh. And never a day passes but she isn't here for some reason or another. Taking advantage. You know.'

Gabriel, who did not know but was loath to stem this flood of fascinating information, nodded.

'To tell the truth, I think she resents me being here, wants to be the only pebble on the beach. She was up for a drink the other evening. . . . They were all sitting outside Ivan's house in the sun and drinking champagne, and the Admiral asked me to join them. But when I saw her there as well, I said I wouldn't and came into the house and shut the door. And it was champagne they were drinking, too. I wouldn't have minded. . . .'

She stopped. From behind them, in the house, came the indignant wail of a small child, just woken, and thinking itself abandoned.

'That's Josh,' said Drusilla and got up and went indoors. A

161

moment later she appeared again, bearing the baby in her arms. She sat down and set him on his fat bare feet between her knees. He wore a shrunken nightgown and was immensely fat and brown, with sparse hair and black, boot-button eyes.

'Who's my duck, then?' Drusilla asked him tenderly and pressed a kiss into his fat neck.

He took no notice of her, being absorbed in Gabriel. After a bit he smiled, revealing a small tooth or two. Gabriel put out her hand and he clutched at her finger and tried to put it into his mouth. When she would not let him he roared in rage, and Drusilla bent to kiss him again, hold him close, rock him lazily to and fro.

'Did you . . .?' Gabriel asked. 'When you were having a baby, did you ever think about having an abortion?'

Drusilla looked up, wrinkling her nose in disgust.

'God no. What a gruesome idea. Not have Josh?'

Gabriel said, 'I'm having a baby.'

'Are you?' Drusilla's voice was not only delighted, but interested. 'When?'

'Ages yet. I mean, I've only just realized that I am having a baby. You're the first person I've told.'

'Get away.'

'You won't say anything, will you?'

'I won't say a word. Do you know who the father is?'

'Yes, of course.'

'Does he know?'

'No. And he isn't going to.'

Drusilla smiled approvingly. This sort of independent stand was right up her street.

'Good for you,' she said.

May, lying in bed, with her teeth in a tumbler beside her, awoke to the soft murmur of voices beneath her window. Last night, she had worked for a bit at her scrapbook, stuck in some lovely pictures, and then watched television till there was nothing left to watch. But in old age, sleep did not come easily, and the new day was dawning before she finally dropped off. Now . . .

She put a hand out and found her spectacles, fumbling, got them on. She picked up her watch. A quarter to nine. Changed days. In the old days, she'd been out of bed at six thirty, and sometimes sooner if there was a baby to be fed. The voices murmured on, making, she decided, a pleasant sound. She wondered who was there.

After a bit, she got out of bed, put in her teeth, and pulled on her dressing gown. She went to the window and drew back the curtains. Below, the courtyard lay washed in the first sunshine of another fine day. Outside Drusilla's cottage Drusilla sat with Joshua and a girl beside her. One of her funny friends, no doubt.

She did not lean out of the window, because that was not May's way. She watched them. The new girl wore trousers, had dyed-looking hair. May pursed her lips, settling her dentures. She saw Ivan come out of his house and walk across the courtyard towards the two girls.

'Anybody stirred yet?' he asked them. May opened her window. 'I'm stirring,' she told him. He stopped and looked up. 'Morning, May.'

'What are you all doing down there, chattering?' May wanted to know.

'May, be an angel and go and see if my mother's awake. Now. I've got to go to work and I want to see her before I leave.'

'I'll have to get me clothes on.'

'No time. Go now. You look smashing in your dressing gown.'

May bridled. 'Get away.' But she shut the window and turned back into her room. She found her bedroom slippers and put them on, went out of the door and down the passage. Outside Gerald and Eve's bedroom, she paused, listening. They were talking. She knocked.

Eve sat up in her side of the big, padded bed, with a shawl around her shoulders, drinking her morning cup of tea. Gerald, up and dressed, was sitting at the end of her chaise longue tying his shoelaces. Encouraged by the continuing good weather, she was trying to talk him into the idea of a lunch picnic the following day. ' . . . we could go to Gwenvoe and walk along the cliffs for a bit. I haven't been there for ages, and there wouldn't be any people there to kick sand in your face. Do say you'll come. I think we all need to get away from the house. . . .'

A knock on the door. Eve instantly felt apprehensive. After

163

the letter, she felt apprehensive all the time, and even more so when May's face appeared around the edge of the door.

'May, what is it?'

'Ivan wants you. He's out in the courtyard.'

'Ivan? What's happened? What's the matter?'

'I don't think anything's the matter. Just says he wants a word before he goes to the factory. Drusilla's out there too, and another girl . . . think she must be friend of Drusilla's. Got dyed hair.'

'Heavens,' said Eve.

'Ivan says to come.'

'Thank you, May. I'll be there in a moment.'

The door closed. 'Gerald, why have I got to go and see Ivan and a girl with dyed hair?'

'Don't look so worried. It sounds interesting. I shall come with you.'

'All the time, I think something terrible's going to happen. . . .'

'You mustn't.' She turned back the covers and got out of bed, dropping her shawl. Gerald got to his feet and helped her on with her pale blue quilted robe. He said, 'Do you think the girl with dyed hair belongs to Drusilla or to Ivan?'

Despite herself, Eve had to smile. 'Oh, don't say things like that!'

'You know, Tremenheere was very dull until I married you. I hope she's not another lame duck.'

'A lame duck with dyed hair?'

'The imagination boggles,' said Gerald.

They went together down the back stairs and through the kitchen. The table was laid with three places for breakfast. Laura's tray waited on the dresser. Gerald unbolted the back door and opened it.

'We thought you were never going to appear,' Ivan told them.

'What's so urgent?' Gerald asked. Eve looked over his shoulder. Drusilla's friend. She had been sitting on the doorstep of the cottage, but now she stood up and came towards them. She was tall and slender, long-legged. Her face brown, her hair the colour of straw. She had, Eve had time to notice, remarkably beautiful grey eyes.

From her doorway, Drusilla and the baby watched.

'Do you know who this is?' Ivan asked. It was unlike Ivan to ask idiotic questions. How could she and Gerald know who she was? Eve shook her head.

'Gabriel,' said Ivan.

Lucy was not well. In the middle of the night, she had woken Laura, standing on her back legs by the bed, scratching at the sheet and whining miserably. In the still darkness, Laura had carried her downstairs, unbolted the front door, and taken Lucy out into the garden, where she had promptly been sick. Upstairs again, she had drunk copiously from her water bowl and then gone back to her basket, digging her way in under her blanket, for warmth.

When Laura woke, she was still there, only her face visible, her eyes dark and reproachful, her silky ears drooping.

'How do you feel?' Laura asked her, but Lucy did not stir at the sound of her voice. She sighed and rested her chin on the edge of the basket and looked more miserable than ever.

She must have eaten something. For all her pretty looks, she was a terrible scavenger. Perhaps she had found the compost heap, or dug up a rotten bone. Perhaps she would have to be taken to the vet.

She looked at her watch. It was nearly nine o'clock and another beautiful morning. It seemed sinful still to be lying in bed, but she was not allowed by Eve to appear downstairs until she had eaten her breakfast, which Eve insisted on bringing up to her on a tray. Laura was now so totally recovered that she would have been happy to join the others in the kitchen and save Eve a trek up the stairs, but Eve so enjoyed this little bit of spoiling that it would have been churlish not to accept with good grace.

After a bit, she got up and cleaned her teeth and brushed her hair, and thought about Alec in New York. She immediately felt guilty again. She had written to him, an air letter, apologizing and trying to explain, but the letter somehow did not express what she wanted to say, and posting it had not made her feel any better. When he came back to Tremenheere to fetch her, it would be better. She would stop being so reserved. She would stop being polite about Daphne Boulderstone. Perhaps she would discover that Alec felt exactly the same about Daphne as Laura did, but had never actually put his feelings into words, and then they would laugh together, and everything would be all right.

She crouched by Lucy's basket, touched the little dog's head, put the back of her hand to Lucy's nose, which was warm and feverish. She was there when Eve's footsteps came down the passage from the top of the back stairs, and Eve's light tap sounded on the door.

'Eve, I'm up.'

Eve appeared, carrying the wicker breakfast tray. She was still in her quilted robe and looking more cheerful than she had looked for days.

She put the tray down on the bed and said, 'Are you feeling strong?'

Laura stood up. 'Why?'

'Really strong? Ready for a surprise? A lovely surprise.'

A lovely surprise. She could only think of Alec. But it wasn't Alec who followed Eve through the door and there stopped, not smiling exactly, but looking secret and a little bit wary. She was very young, with short, bleached hair and huge grey eyes that met Laura's, unblinking.

Nobody said anything, and it was Eve who had to break the silence.

'Laura, it's Gabriel. It's Alec's Gabriel.'

'But where have you come from?'

'Saint Thomas. The Virgin Islands.'

Eve had left them, and they sat on the big bed together, Gabriel with her legs curled beneath her and her back supported by the great brass bedstead.

'Did you see your father?'

'No. He'd already left for New York.' She went on, explaining exactly what had happened. Her journey home sounded to Laura like a nightmare, but Gabriel seemed to take it all in stride. She had gone back to Islington and seen Mrs Abney, spent a day in London, and then come to Tremenheere.

She had come to Tremenheere, not to see Alec, but Laura. It was Gabriel, and she was home. She was a person, a girl, a daughter, sitting on the end of Laura's bed. No longer a name that nobody mentioned. No longer a photograph, a drawing, a deserted attic room filled with a child's possessions. She was here. Within touch. Gabriel.

166

'We must let Alec know you've come.'

'No, don't,' said Gabriel. 'He'll only worry, and there's nothing to worry about. Eve said he'd be coming back to fetch you, so let's surprise him then. It's only for a few days. Let's keep it a secret from him.'

'But don't you have to go back to America?'

'No, I don't have to go back.'

'But . . . what will you do?'

'I thought I might stay in England.'

'But that would be *marvellous*. I can't think of anything nicer. And Alec . . . oh, Gabriel, he's missed you so much. I know he missed you so much.'

Gabriel said, 'Yes.' She got off the bed and stood with her back to Laura, looking out of the window. 'What a heavenly place this is. And palm trees too. It's like the West Indies all over again.' She turned her head and saw Lucy in her basket. 'Is this your dog?' She squatted beside Lucy.

'Yes. But she's not well. She was sick in the night. Luckily, she told me, and I got her out into the garden in time. I think she's eaten something. She's called Lucy.'

Watching Gabriel, she realized what had been subconsciously puzzling her. 'Gabriel, how did you find me? How did you know I was here, at Tremenheere?'

'Oh,' Gabriel leaned forward to stroke Lucy. 'Mrs Abney knew. She told me.'

'Alec must have told her before he left for New York.'

'Yes,' said Gabriel. 'I guess so.' She straightened up. She said, 'I'm going downstairs. Eve said she'd give me a cup of coffee. I'll leave you to have your breakfast in peace. Your boiled egg will be hard as a stone if you don't eat it soon.'

'When I come down,' said Laura, 'let's talk. There's so much I want to ask you.'

'Sure. We'll sit in the garden and gas.'

Gabriel closed the door behind her and went to the head of the great staircase. She stopped there, hesitating, then put her hand into the pocket of her jeans and took out the creased brown envelope. *Your wife at Tremenheere is having an affair with Ivan Ashby*.

Tough and young, with the resilience and open-mindedness of her generation, Gabriel had been shocked by the evil intent of the letter, but not shocked by the actual accusation. Now, within a couple of hours of arriving at Tremenheere, she had met both Ivan and Laura. An almost frighteningly attractive man, of whom one could believe almost anything. But a woman who looked and behaved like a total innocent, naïve in her transparent pleasure at Gabriel's appearance. Faced with an unknown step-daughter, she could, under any circumstances, have been wary, suspicious, or even jealous, but no trace of these emotions had shown in her candid delight, and her patent sincerity was clear as glass.

For the first time, Gabriel knew stirrings of suspicion. For the first time it occurred to her that it was possible that the letter was totally untrue. In which case, who hated Laura and Ivan so much that they had fabricated such a dangerous slander?

She went downstairs. As she crossed the polished hall, she saw the kitchen door open, and Gerald emerged, carrying his newspaper. He did not see Gabriel, but walked away from her, headed down the passage.

'Gerald.'

He turned. She went towards him. 'Do you think I could talk to you for a moment?'

He took her into his study, a pleasant room, smelling of cigars and books and wood ash.

'Is this where you come to read the paper?'

'Yes.' He was a very good-looking man. 'Gets me out of the way. Sit down, Gabriel.'

She sat, not in the armchair he indicated, but in an upright one, so that they faced each other across his desk.

She said, 'You've been so kind . . . I'm sorry I didn't let you know I was coming, but there really wasn't time.'

'Delighted. Delighted to see you. Delighted to meet you, for that matter.'

She said, 'I've just told Laura that Mrs Abney – she's the housekeeper at the house in Islington – that she told me where I could find Laura. But that wasn't true.'

'How did you know she was here, then?'

Gabriel said, 'I opened this,' and she laid the envelope on his blotter.

Gerald, leaning back in his chair, did not move. He sat looking at the brown envelope and then raised his eyes and met Gabriel's. His expression was grave. He said, 'I see.'

'What do you see?'

'There has already been a similar letter. Sent to a friend of ours in the village . . . a poison-pen letter.'

'Well, this is another. I opened it because I saw the Truro postmark and I knew Laura was somewhere in Cornwall. Mrs Abney and I thought it would be all right.'

'Did you show it to Mrs Abney?'

'No. I haven't shown it to anybody.'

He sighed deeply and picked it up. 'It was posted in Truro, on Wednesday.'

'Yes, I know.'

He took the letter out and read it. Then he put his elbow on the desk and covered the bottom half of his face with his hand. He said, 'Oh, God.'

'It's horrible, isn't it?'

'You had breakfast with Ivan. Did you say anything to him?'

'No, of course not. Nor to Laura. I told you. You're the first person I've shown it to.'

'What a good girl you are.'

'Who wrote it?'

'We don't know.'

'But what about the other one. Didn't you follow the first letter up?'

'No. For . . . reasons . . . we let it slide. We hoped there wouldn't be a second letter. Now, I'm beginning to think we made a mistake.'

'But it's criminal to write things like that. It's a crime.'

'Gabriel, there's no word of truth in it. You know that, don't you?'

'I wondered. But how do we *know* it isn't true?'

'Because I know Ivan and I know Laura. Believe me, I've lived long enough, and I've seen enough of my fellow men to know very well if something – clandestine, as this infers – was going on under my roof. Ivan's my stepson, not always the most discreet or sensible of men, but he would never be such a fool, or such a knave, as to seduce Alec's wife. As for Laura' – he spread his hands – 'you've met her yourself. Can you see her doing a thing like that?'

'No, I can't,' Gabriel admitted. 'I'd worked that out for myself. But there must be *some* justification. . . .'

'Oh, a couple of outings together. To an antique shop . . .

169

for a picnic. Ivan's a kind fellow. He enjoys the company of any attractive woman, but basically his intentions are triggered off by a sheer goodness of heart. And it's landed him in trouble, I can tell you, over the years.'

Gabriel smiled. It was like having a weight lifted from her heart to hear Ivan described in such glowing terms, even if he was Gerald's stepson, and Gerald was bound to be slightly biased.

'In that case, what are we going to do?'

'Perhaps we should get in touch with your father.'

'No, we mustn't do that.'

'Not even to let him know you're here?'

'Let's keep it a surprise. After all, he hasn't seen me for six years, and he thinks I'm still in Virginia. . . . It's not as though he'll be worrying.'

'I'd be happier telling him.'

'Oh, don't. Please don't. If you don't mind me staying on here until he comes, that's what I'd rather do.'

Gerald gave in. 'All right.'

'But I still don't know what you're going to do about the letter.'

'Will you leave that to me?'

'I think we should tell the police.'

'I will if we have to, but for Eve's sake I'd rather not.'

'What's Eve got to do with it?'

'Everything,' he told her. 'I'll explain another time. The first letter made her ill with worry, but she's looking better now than she has for days, and I'm hoping that your unexpected appearance has put it out of her mind. Meanwhile, I think you should try to do that too. It's not your responsibility any longer. So why don't you just enjoy yourself? Go and sit in the sun in the garden. Go and find Laura and make friends?'

When she left, he read the letter again, then put it back into its envelope and stowed it away in the breast pocket of his old tweed jacket. He got to his feet and went out of the study and back to the kitchen, where he found Eve in her cooking apron, chopping vegetables for soup.

'Darling.'

He kissed her. 'I have to go out for half an hour.'

'Are you going into the town? I need some groceries.'

'Not just at the moment. I'll go later, though, if you want.'

'You are a love. I'll make a shopping list.'

He opened the back door. She said, 'Gerald.' He turned. She smiled her old smile. She said, 'She's sweet, isn't she? Gabriel, I mean.'

'Charming,' said Gerald and went out.

In his car he turned left at the gate and headed up the hill on the road that led over the moor. After a mile or two he came to a fork and a signpost, one arm of which pointed to Lanyon, the other to Carnellow. He took the road to Carnellow.

It had once been an isolated tin-mining village. A couple of rows of blank-faced cottages, a ruined engine house and stack, a bleak chapel. Up here, high on the moor, even on the stillest day, there was always a wind. When he got out of the car, this wind whined in his ears, and all about him, the moor rolled, patched here and there with the emerald green of bog, tall grasses leaning in the breeze.

From the old chapel came the clangor of activity. The whine of a circular saw, the banging of wooden mallets. The original doorway had been opened up into an aperature the size of a double garage, and heavy doors, on runners, were pushed aside to reveal the interior of the workshop. Over this entrance was a new sign, recently erected: Ashby and Thomas.

Outside the factory, timber was stacked, seasoning beneath a makeshift shelter. There were a couple of vans and Ivan's car. Shavings, like ringlets, blew about. He could smell the sweet, new-sawn wood.

A boy appeared, carrying a chair, which he was loading into one of the vans.

'Good morning,' said Gerald.

''Ullo.'

'Is Ivan in there?'

'Yes, 'e's about somewhere.'

'Get him, would you? Say it's Admiral Haverstock.'

The boy, perhaps impressed by Gerald's authoritative manner as much as his title, set down the chair and disappeared, only to return a moment later with Ivan beside him. Ivan in shirt sleeves and a pair of old-fashioned bib-and-brace overalls.

'Gerald.'

'Sorry to disturb you. Won't take a moment. Let's go and sit in the car.'

He told Ivan the sorry tale and showed him the second letter.

171

As Ivan read it, Gerald saw his fist clench on his knee so tightly that the knuckles turned white. As Gerald had said, Ivan said, 'Oh, God.'

'Nasty business,' said Gerald. 'But this time, of course, I know it's not true.'

Ivan said drily, 'Well, that's a good start anyway. What a filthy thing. And you say Gabriel read it in London and brought it with her! She must have thought I was a real four-letter man.'

'She knows there's no word of truth in it. I told her so and I got the impression that she was happy to believe me.'

'You don't still think it's May?'

Gerald shrugged. 'Posted in Truro on Wednesday. Same format.'

'Gerald, I don't believe it's May.'

'Well, who is it, old boy?'

'You don't think . . . ? I wondered about this after the first letter, but I didn't say anything. You don't think it could be Drusilla?'

'*Drusilla*?'

'Yes, Drusilla.'

'Why should it be her? What would she get out of writing scurrilous poison-pen letters?'

'I don't know. Except that' – Ivan began to look faintly embarassed – 'well, after I helped her, you know, fixed for her to come and live in the cottage . . . she did come over one evening and made it quite plain that she was grateful and if she could repay me in any way, she'd be more than pleased. But it wasn't anything to do with . . . loving. Just a business proposition.'

'Did you take her up on it?'

'No, of course I didn't. I thanked her and said she didn't owe me anything and sent her home again. She bore no grudge.' He thought about this, and added, 'Apparently.'

'Would Drusilla be capable of writing a thing like that?'

'She's a funny girl. I don't know. I don't know her. None of us does. We don't know her background, we don't know what makes her tick. She's a mystery.'

'I agree with that. But why should she want to hurt Silvia?'

'No idea. I don't think she's particularly fond of Silvia, but that hardly merits sending the poor woman a poison-pen letter.

And Drusilla certainly doesn't have strong views about drink. She enjoys her jar.'

Gerald thought this over. 'Ivan, that letter was posted in Truro on Wednesday. Drusilla never goes farther than the village. She can't, with the baby in the pram. There's no way she could get to Truro.'

'She could have asked May to post the letter for her. In an odd fashion, they seem to have made friends. May sometimes gets things for her when she's in Truro, stuff for Joshua that Drusilla can't buy in the village. So why shouldn't she have posted a letter for Drusilla?'

It all seemed perfectly reasonable. And so impossibly awful that Gerald wished that, like Eve, he could somehow put the whole sorry business out of his mind.

Ivan said, 'What are we going to do now?'

'I suggested to Gabriel that we should get in touch with Alec, but she wouldn't let me. She doesn't want him worried. Anyway, he'll be here by Tuesday.'

'Gerald, we have to do something before he comes.'

'What?'

'Don't you think we should get the police in?'

'And what if it *is* May?'

After a bit, Ivan said, 'Yes, I see your point.'

'Let's leave it for another day.'

Ivan smiled at his stepfather. 'You're not acting in character, Gerald. Procrastinating. I thought naval time was five minutes beforehand.'

'It is.'

'"The difficult we can do at once, the impossible may take a little longer."'

'Don't you quote myself at me. And perhaps this is an impossible one. Perhaps it will take a little longer. When will you be back, Ivan?'

'I'll maybe take a make and mend, be home for lunch. You look like a man who needs a little moral support.' He got out of the car, slammed the door behind him. 'See you later.'

Gerald, his heart filled with affection and gratitude, watched him go. When Ivan had disappeared back into his workshop, Gerald started up the engine of his car and drove back to Tremenheere.

*   *   *

173

'It wasn't so bad at first. It wasn't as bad as I thought it was going to be. Virginia's beautiful, and Strick had this lovely place, on a bluff above the James River. It was an enormous house, with acres of land all around, green pastures for the horses, and white split-rail fences. And there were dogwoods and wild oaks, and in front of the house a garden with a vast swimming pool and tennis courts. It was so mild and so sunny, even in winter. And I had a huge room all to myself and a bathroom as well, and there were servants. A cook and a housemaid, and a coloured butler called David, who came to work each day in a pink Studebaker. Even the school my mother sent me to was all right. It was a boarding school and, I imagine, wildly expensive, because all the girls' parents seemed to be just as rich as Strickland was, and after a bit, when they'd got used to the idea of me being English and having a British accent, I became a sort of novelty, and it wasn't so difficult to make friends.'

They were in the garden together, under the mulberry tree. They had carried out a rug and some cushions, and lay, side by side, on their stomachs, like a couple of schoolgirls exchanging confidences. Being like that somehow made it easier to talk.

'Were you never lonely?'

'Oh, heavens, yes. All the time, really, but it was a funny sort of loneliness. A little part of me that I carried around all the time, but it was hidden. Very deep. Like a stone at the bottom of a pond. I mean, I never ever felt that I belonged, but it wasn't too difficult to behave as though I did.'

'What about when you weren't at school.'

'Even that wasn't too bad. They knew I didn't want to ride, so they left me alone. I've never, actually, minded being alone, and besides, there were usually people around the place. Friends staying, with children of my age, or people coming for tennis, or to swim.' She smiled, 'I can swim really well, and I can even play tennis too, though I'm not what you call a champion.'

'Gabriel, why did you never come back and see your father?'

Gabriel looked away, pulled at a tuft of grass within reach, shredded it between her fingers.

'I don't know. It just never worked out. At first I thought I'd come back and be with him when he went to Glenshandra. That was where we really were together, just him and me. He used to take me out on the river with him, and we spent hours . . . just the two of us. I wanted to go to Glenshandra, but when I tried to tell my mother, she said she'd fixed for me to go to summer camp, and why not leave it for this year. There'd be other years. When you're only fourteen, it's not easy to argue and get your own way. And my mother is an almost impossible person to argue with. She has answers for absolutely everything, and in the end you're always defeated. So I went to summer camp, and I thought my father would write and be furiously angry with us all. But he didn't. He just said the same thing. Perhaps next year. And that hurt me, because I guessed perhaps he hadn't cared as much as I thought he would.'

'Did he write to you?'

'Yes, he wrote. And I got presents at Christmas and for my birthday.'

'Did you write back?'

'Oh, yes. Thank-you letters.'

'But he must have missed you so much. Those five years when he was all on his own. He must have longed to have you with him. Just sometimes.'

Gabriel said, 'He should never have let me go. I wanted to stay with him. I told my mother that, and she said that it was impossible. Apart from the practical problems, he was too busy, too involved with his work. His job always came before anything else.'

'Did you tell your father?'

'I tried to. He came to see me at the school in England, and we walked around the games field, but somehow by then it was too late to get through to him. All he said to me was, "I have too many commitments. You need your mother."'

'And you've never forgiven him for that?'

'It's not a question of forgiving, Laura. It's a question of adapting. If I hadn't adapted, I'd have become a screwed-up mess, the sort of nutty kid who has to be wheeled off to the local headshrinker. And once I'd adapted, it was too late to go back, even for a little while. Do you see that?'

'Yes,' said Laura slowly. 'I think I do see. I think you did very well. At least you accepted an impossible situation and made some sort of a life for yourself.'

'Oh, I made a life all right.'

'What happened when you left school?'

'Mother wanted me to go to college, but I jibbed at that. We really had a row, but for once, I stuck my toes in and won, and did what I wanted to do, which was to study fine arts at a place in Washington.'

'How fascinating.'

'Yes, it was great. I had a little apartment and a car of my own, and if I wanted to, at weekends, I could go back to Virginia and take my friends. Mother didn't approve of any of the friends, who all voted Democrat and had long hair, but apart from that it was O.K. At least, it was for a bit . . .'

'Why only for a bit . . .?'

Gabriel sighed and pulled up another piece of Gerald's lawn. She said, 'I don't know if you know anything about Strickland Whiteside.'

'No. Nothing. Alec's never spoken of him. I'm afraid he hardly spoke about your mother.'

'After I left school . . . I don't know, nothing happened, but I used to catch Strickland watching me, and I felt sleazy, and I knew things weren't the same any longer. I started taking some trouble to keep out of his way. That's one of the reasons I went to Washington, to get away from Virginia. But of course, finally, when I'd got my little degree, I had to go back, and the first night I was home, my mother went to bed early, and Strickland made the most violent pass at me. He'd had a few drinks and I think he was feeling a bit randy, but it was horrible.'

'Oh, Gabriel.'

'I knew I couldn't stay. The next morning I told my mother I was going to New York, to stay with a girl who'd been a friend of mine at school. She bucked slightly, but she didn't raise any objections. Perhaps she had an idea of what was going on in Strickland's pin-brain, but if she did, she gave no indication. She's always been a very controlled person. I never saw her lose control of any situation. So I called the girlfriend, packed, and got myself to New York. I thought I'd get a job or something, but New York was never my scene, and the first morning I was there, I caught sight of my reflection in one of the Fifth Avenue store windows and I thought, "What the hell are you doing here?" Anyway, after two days I still hadn't found anything to do, but as it turned out that didn't matter. Because that evening we went to a party down in Greenwich Village, and I met this man. He was British and funny and nice; we talked the same language, were on the same wavelength. And oh, the joy of being with someone who laughed at the same idiotic things as I did. Anyway, he took me out for dinner and said that he had this yacht down in the Virgin Islands, and he'd asked some friends down for a cruise, and would I like to go too. So I went. It was great. The most beautiful yacht, and heavenly sailing, and gorgeous romantic little coves with white sand and palm trees. And then the two weeks were over, and all the others went back to New York, but he stayed on. And so did I. I stayed with him for six months. We lived together for six months. I said goodbye to him two days ago. Two days. It feels like two years.'

'But who was he, Gabriel?'

'I suppose you'd call him an upper-class drifter. I told you, he was English. He'd been in the army. I think he had a wife somewhere. A lot of money, because he didn't have a job, and it costs something to keep a fifty-foot sloop in the Virgin Islands.'

'Were you happy with him?'

'Oh, sure. We had a great time.'

'What was his name?'

'I'm not going to tell you. It's of no account.'

'But if you were happy, then why did you come back to England?'

Gabriel said, 'I've started a baby.'

There was a silence, which was not a silence at all, because the garden was filled with birdsong. Then Laura, inadequately, said, 'Oh, Gabriel.'

'I only realized that I had – about a week ago.'

'Have you seen a doctor?'

'No, nothing like that, but I'm perfectly sure. And at the same time, I knew that if I wasn't going to have a child, if I was going to have an abortion, I had to move pretty quickly. But that wasn't the only reason I came straight home. The real reason was that I wanted my father. I just wanted him. I needed him. I needed to tell him, and to talk to him, and to hear his advice and . . . oh, just to be with him, Laura. And then when I got to London and he wasn't there, I thought that the only thing I could do was to find you and talk to you.'

'But you didn't even know me.'

'I had to tell somebody.'

Laura's eyes filled with tears, and swiftly, ashamedly, she brushed them away. She said, 'I've never had very strong views about abortion. I mean, I've never campaigned either way, for or against. But hearing you even say the word fills me with such horror and revulsion. . . . Oh, Gabriel, you mustn't have an abortion!'

Gabriel grinned. 'Don't worry. I've already decided I couldn't go through with it. I decided this morning, when I was talking to Drusilla, before you were all awake. When I saw that great fat baby of hers, I was suddenly, absolutely, sure that I wanted this one.'

'Does the father know about it?'

'No, I didn't say anything.'

'Oh, darling . . .' The tears started again. 'So silly to cry, but I can't help it. Perhaps I shouldn't be, but I'm happy for you.'

'You don't think Alec's going to flip when we tell him?'

'You know him better than that.'

'What I'd really like to do,' said Gabriel, 'is to come back to London with you both . . . maybe stay till the baby's born.'

'Stay as long as you want.'

'We'll be a bit of a tight fit in that little house.'

'We'll get Alec to buy us a bigger one, with a garden.'

They laughed together, two women conspiring gently against the man they both loved. 'It's what I've always wanted. Not a bigger house, but a baby. But I'm thirty-seven now, and every now and then my insides go mad, and so far I haven't been very lucky. That's why I had to have this operation. That's why I'm here and why I didn't go to Glenshandra or New York with him. But if I can't have a child, then you having one . . .'

'Will be the next best thing?'

'No. Never that. Never next best.'

A movement from the house disturbed them. Looking up, they saw Gerald emerge onto the terrace through the French windows from the drawing room. They watched while he collected the folded garden furniture, set it up in the sunshine around the white iron table. When this was done, he picked up some small piece of rubbish – a matchstick perhaps – and stooped to pull a stray weed or two from between the stone flags. Then, apparently satisfied that all was shipshape, he disappeared indoors.

'What a marvellous guy,' Gabriel observed.

'Yes, marvellous. He was always Alec's hero. Poor man. A bachelor for sixty years, and here he is with a houseful of women. So many of us. Women on their own. Women without men. Old May, up in her room, darning socks and with her life behind her. Drusilla, with nobody but her baby. Silvia Marten, Eve's friend, coming and going, hungry for company. She's probably the loneliest of all. And you. And me.'

'You, lonely? But Laura, you have Alec.'

'Yes, I have Alec. And it's been very nearly perfect.'

'What's missing?'

'Nothing's missing. Just another lifetime that I had no part of.'

'You mean my mother. And Deepbrook. And me.'

'You most of all. Alec would never talk to me about you. It was like a barrier between us and I never had the confidence nor the resolution to break it down.'

'Were you jealous of me?'

'No, I don't mean that.' She lay, trying to work it out, to find the right, tremendously important, words. 'I think I was lonely for the same reason as Alec. You weren't a barrier, Gabriel, but a void. You should have been there, with us, but you weren't.'

Gabriel smiled. 'Well, I'm sure here now.'

'How about Erica? Will she be worrying about you?'

'No. She thinks I'm still cruising round the Virgin Islands with a jolly party of socially acceptable New Yorkers. When my father gets back and the future's a little clearer, I'll write to her, tell her what's happening.'

'She'll miss you.'

'I don't think so.'

'Is she ever lonely? Is she one of the lonely ones?'

'Never. You see, she has her horses.'

They stayed there for a little longer, and then Laura looked at her watch, stirred herself, and sat up.

'Where are you going?' Gabriel asked.

'I've been neglecting Eve. I must go and help her. We're such a houseful and she does all the cooking herself.'

'Shall I come too? I'm a dab hand at peeling potatoes.'

'No, you stay. You're allowed to be lazy on your first morning. I'll give you a shout when it's time for lunch.'

She went across the grass, the breeze blowing her pink cotton skirt, her long dark hair. She climbed the steps onto the terrace and disappeared into the house. Gabriel watched her go, and then rolled over onto her back, the cushion beneath her head.

The baby was there. Would be born. She laid a hand on her abdomen, cherishing the future. A tiny seed, already growing. An entity. Last night on the train, she had scarcely slept, and because of this or, perhaps, delayed jet lag, she was all at once overcome with drowsiness. With her face to the sun, she closed her eyes.

Later, she stirred. Consciousness came gently, tranquilly. There was another sensation, one at first unrecognized, and then remembered from long ago, from childhood. Security, like a warm blanket. A presence.

She opened her eyes. Ivan, cross-legged, sat beside her on the rug, watching her, and his being there seemed so natural that she felt none of the normal embarrassment of a person found asleep, vulnerable and defenceless.

After a bit, he said, 'Hello.'

Gabriel said the first thing that came into her head, which was, 'You weren't having an affair with Laura.'

He shook his head. 'No.'

She frowned, trying to think what had made her say this, when they had not before even spoken of the letter. As though he knew what was going on in her head, he said, 'Gerald showed me the letter. He came up to Carnellow to show it to me. I'm so sorry about everything. Sorry it was written, but mostly sorry that it was you who had to read it.'

'I only opened it because I wanted to find Laura. And I think it's a mercy that I did. It could have been so dangerous, Ivan. If Alec had read it before he went to New York, it could really have been very dangerous.'

'It can't have made meeting Laura for the first time very easy.'

'No. But in the last few days I seem to have done a lot of things that weren't easy.'

'I just hate that you had that uncertainty about us. Even if it was only for a single day.'

'It wasn't your fault.'

'There's already been one like it. Gerald told you.'

180

'Yes, he told me. But, like he said, it was a pack of lies. It's no longer my responsibility.' She stretched, yawned, and sat up. The garden was dazzled in sunshine, scented with wallflowers. The sun had moved, and beneath the mulberry tree the grass lay dappled in light and shadow. 'How long have I been asleep?'

'I don't know. It's half past twelve. I was sent out to tell you it will soon be lunchtime.'

He was wearing a pale blue shirt, open-necked, the sleeves rolled up and away from his wrists. Beneath this, against the brown skin of his chest, she saw the glint of a silver chain. His hands, which she had already decided were beautiful, hung loosely between his knees. She saw his wristwatch, the heavy gold signet ring.

'Do you feel like something to eat?' he asked.

She dragged her eyes away from his hands and looked up into his face. 'Do you always come home for lunch?'

'No. But today I'm taking a make and mend.'

'Sorry?'

'Six months in a yacht and you don't speak the language! Naval slang for a half-day.'

'I see. And what are you going to do with it?'

'Nothing, I think. How about you?'

'Sounds a good idea.'

He smiled and got to his feet, and put out a hand to help Gabriel up. 'In that case,' he said, 'let's do nothing together.'

They were all sitting around the kitchen table, having a drink before lunch, and waiting for May. When she appeared cautiously descending the back stairs, it was immediately obvious, from the sour displeasure on her wrinkled features, that something was very amiss.

'May, what is it?' Eve asked.

May folded her hands over her stomach, set her mouth, and told them. The door of Laura's bedroom had been left open. Lucy had got out of her basket, found her way along the passage to May's room, and had there been extremely sick in the middle of May's good rug.

At five o'clock that evening, Laura, carrying a punnet of tomatoes, walked down to the village by herself. She and Eve had picked the tomatoes together. They came from the Tremenheere greenhouse, and with the warm weather, dozens of them had ripened at the same moment. They had spent the afternoon concocting soups and purées, and yet there were pounds left over. Drusilla gladly accepted a bowlful, and a basket was set aside for the vicar's wife, but still there were more.

'Why do the beastly things all have to come at once?' Eve wanted to know, flushed in the face from all this culinary effort. 'I can't bear to waste them.' Then she was visited by a brainwave. 'I know, we'll give them to Silvia.'

'Doesn't she have her own?'

'No, she grows just about everything else, but not tomatoes. I'll give her a ring and see if she'd like some.' She went off to the telephone and returned triumphant. 'She's simply delighted. She says she's been buying them in the post office, and they're overcharging. We'll take them down later.'

'I'll take them down if you like.'

'Oh, would you? You've never seen her garden, anyway, and it's a dream, and she's always glad of someone to chat to. And perhaps she'd like to come to Gwenvoe with us tomorrow.' Over lunch, she had finally persuaded her reluctant husband into agreeing, not only that a Saturday picnic would be a good idea, but that he would take part and accompany them all. 'If she would, tell her we'll bring the food, and one of us will pick her up. We'll have to take two cars anyway.'

As she came around the corner of the house, Laura had glanced into the garden. At the far end of the lawn Ivan and Gabriel sat cross-legged, talking. They had been there all afternoon, apparently engrossed, like a pair of old acquaintances catching up on the news of a lifetime. Laura was glad that he had not taken her off for the day on one of his energetic and exhausting expeditions. She felt protective as a mother about Gabriel.

She had not been to Silvia's house, but it was not difficult to find. The gate stood open, with the name on it, Roskenwyn. Laura went up the short gravelled drive and in through the open front door.

'Silvia.'

There was no reply, but the sitting room door stood open, and on the other side of this, a glass door led out into the garden. Here, she found Silvia, on her knees, working at her border with a small weeding fork.

'Silvia.'

'Hello.' She sat back on her heels, the fork held loosely in her hand. She was in old jeans and a checked shirt, her face as usual almost concealed by her huge dark glasses.

'I've brought you the tomatoes.'

'Oh, you are an angel.' She dropped the fork and stripped off her earth-stained gloves.

'Don't stop if you don't want to.'

'But I do want to. I've been at it all afternoon.' She got to her feet. 'Let's have a drink.'

'It's only five.'

'It doesn't need to be alcohol. I'll make a cup of tea if you like. Or we could have some lemonade.'

'Lemonade would be delicious!'

'Right.' She took the basket from Laura's hand. 'I'll bring it out. You can move around my garden and say ooh and aah, and when I come back you can tell me how good it's looking.'

'I don't know much about gardens.'

'Even better. I like uncritical admiration.'

She disappeared into the house and Laura, obediently, walked around the beautifully staked and tended borders, which were a mass of flowers in every shade of pink and blue and mauve. No red, no orange, no yellow. Delphiniums stood high as a tall man, and smoky lupins smelled of every summer Laura could remember. Silvia's roses were almost indecently flamboyant, thickly planted, and with heads as large as saucers.

Sitting on Silvia's little patio, with the tray of lemonade between them, 'How on earth do you grow roses like that?' she asked.

'I feed them. Horse manure. I get it from the farmer up the road.'

'But don't you have to spray them and all that sort of thing?'

'Oh, yes. Like mad. Otherwise they get bitten to death by greenflies.'

'I don't know much about gardening. In London we've only got a sort of yard with a few tubs.'

'Don't tell me Gerald hasn't got you weeding yet? He's a great one for organizing what he calls work parties.'

'No. Nobody's got me doing anything. Except pick a bit of fruit. I've been treated like the most expensive sort of guest.'

'Well, it's certainly worked.' Silvia turned her blank, black stare onto Laura's face. 'You look marvellous. Better each day. Today you look particularly well. You've lost that rather . . . anxious expression.'

'Perhaps I'm not anxious anymore.'

Silvia had finished her lemonade. Now she reached for the jug and refilled her glass. 'Any particular reason?'

'Yes, a very particular one. Gabriel's with us. Alec's daughter. She arrived this morning, off the night train.'

Silvia put the jug back on the tray. 'Gabriel. But she's in Virginia, isn't she?'

'She was, but she's come home. Nobody was expecting her. It was just the most wonderful surprise.'

'I thought she never visited her father.'

'She didn't. And this isn't a visit. She's staying. She's going to live with us. She's not going back.'

It occurred to Laura then that happiness was a strange thing, at times as uncontrollable as grief. All day, she had felt as though she were walking on air, and now was suddenly visited by the compulsion to share this happiness, to confide. And why not Silvia, who had known Alec since they were children, and had seen him at Tremenheere in his loneliness. 'We'll be a family. And I've only just discovered that that was what I always wanted. That's what has been missing.'

'Missing in your marriage?'

'Yes,' Laura admitted. 'Marrying a man who was married before, for quite a long time, to another woman . . . it's not always very easy. There are great chunks of his life that are shut away from you, like a locked room where you're not allowed inside. But now Gabriel's back, it's going to be different. It's as though she were the key that unlocks the door.' She smiled at her own inadequacy. 'I'm afraid I'm not very good at explaining. It's just that, now, I know everything's going to be marvellous.'

'Well, I hope you're right,' said Silvia. 'But I wouldn't allow yourself to be too euphoric. You've only known the girl for a day. After a month of living with her, you'll probably be glad to see the back of her. She'll go off and find herself a flat of her own. They all do, these young things.'

'No. I don't think she will. Anyway, not for a bit.'

'What makes you so sure?'

Laura took a deep breath and then let it all out again without saying anything. Silvia said, 'You're looking guilty, like a woman with a secret.'

'I am. I haven't even told Eve yet because it isn't my secret to tell.'

'Laura, I'm the soul of discretion.'

'All right. But don't say anything.' She smiled, because just being able to say it, aloud, filled her with joy. 'She's going to have a baby.'

'*Gabriel* is?'

'You mustn't be shocked. You mustn't sound shocked.'

'Is she going to get married?'

'No. That's why she's coming back to London with us.'

'What on earth is Alec going to say?'

'I think he's going to be so thrilled that she came back to him, that the fact that she's pregnant simply won't matter.'

'I don't understand you. You look as though you were telling me you'd started a baby yourself. All radiant.'

'Perhaps,' said Laura, 'that's a bit how I feel. I'm happy for Gabriel and Alec, but mostly I'm happy for myself. That's selfish, isn't it? But you see, Silvia, from now on, we're all going to be *together*.'

With all this excitement, it wasn't until she was leaving that Laura remembered the other message she had to give Silvia.

'I nearly forgot. We're all going for a lunch picnic to Gwenvoe tomorrow, and Eve wondered if you'd like to come with us.'

'Tomorrow. Saturday?' Silvia, as Gerald was constantly doing, stooped and pulled a weed from between the gravel chips of her driveway. 'Oh, what a bore, I can't. I've got an old girlfriend staying at the Castle Hotel in Porthkerris, and I promised I'd go over and see her. I'd much rather come to Gwenvoe, but I can't let her down.'

'What a shame. But I'll explain to Eve.'

'I thought something was missing,' said Silvia suddenly. 'Where's your little dog? She's always with you.'

'She's not well. May's not talking to anybody because Lucy got into her room and was sick on May's rug.'

'What's wrong with her? The dog, I mean.'

'I think she's eaten something. She's a dreadful scavenger.'

'The beaches begin to be filthy at this time of the year.'

'I never thought of that. Perhaps I won't take her to Gwenvoe tomorrow. Anyway, she gets so hot in the sand, and she won't go into the sea, because she doesn't like getting her fur wet.'

'Like a cat.'

Laura smiled. 'Yes, just like a cat. Silvia, I must go.'

'Thanks for bringing the tomatoes.'

'Thank you for the lemonade.'

Laura walked away from her. At the gate, she turned to wave and then disappeared behind the wall. Silvia stood outside her house. She looked down and saw another weed, groundsel this time. She stooped and jerked it out, and it's fragile roots were covered in damp brown earth, dirtying her hands.

Gerald sat on a rock, in the shade of another one, and watched his family swimming. His assorted family, he corrected himself. His wife, his great-niece, her stepmother, and his own stepson. It was five thirty in the evening, and he was ready to go home. They had been here since noon, and although they had the spot to themselves, he was looking forward to a shower, a gin and tonic, the cool drawing room, and the evening paper, but just as he had started to make noises about departing, Eve and the others all decided to swim again.

They were at Gwenvoe, but not on the beach. Instead, on leaving the car park, they had walked half a mile or so along the cliff path, and then dropped down onto the rocks. At first the sea had been far out, but as the afternoon slipped by, the tide came in, filling a deep gully, which split the face of the cliff like a fiord, and forming a natural pool. The water here was the deepest turquoise, clear and sparkling in the evening sunshine. Which was why nobody had been able to resist it.

Except Gerald, who had had enough and chose to observe. Eve, his darling Eve, who was perfectly seaworthy, but the only person he had ever seen who could swim in a totally upright position, and Gerald had never got around to solving the sheer mathematics of this extraordinary feat. Laura was more conventional, with her unambitious breast stroke, but Gabriel swam like a boy, head down, brown arms moving smoothly, slipping through the water in a beautifully professional crawl. At intervals, she and Ivan would clamber up onto a convenient ledge and dive. She was waiting now to do this thing, perched on the rock like a sleek wet mermaid, wearing the smallest bikini Gerald had ever seen, her brown body sparkling with droplets.

Eve and Laura came out at last, sat beside him, rubbing at their hair with towels, dripping all over the sizzling rock.

Gerald asked wistfully, 'Do you think we could go home now?'

'Oh, my darling.' Eve reached up her face and gave him a cool, salty kiss. 'Of course. You've been very good and not complained once. And I think I've had enough for the day, although it's always sad to end a day when it's been so perfect.'

'You should always leave a party when you're still enjoying yourself.'

'Anyway, I must get back and start thinking about dinner. By the time we've got everything packed up and we've walked back to the car . . .'

She slid down the straps of her bathing suit, preparing to get dressed. 'How about you, Laura?'

'I'll come with you.'

'And the others?'

They looked towards Ivan and Gabriel. Gabriel was in the water in the pool, treading water, looking up to where Ivan stood, high above her, poised to dive.

'Ivan,' Gerald called.

He relaxed, turned his face in their direction. 'What is it?'

'We're going now. What do you want to do?'

'We'll stay for a bit, I think. . . .'

'All right, we'll see you later.'

'Leave some of the baskets for me to carry.'

'We'll do that.'

At Tremenheere, he drove the car under the archway and parked in the courtyard. Drusilla and Joshua were there, playing with a rubber ball, Joshua chasing it on his hands and knees, as he had not yet mastered the art of walking. He wore a grubby cotton vest and nothing else, and as they got out of the car, he sat on his fat brown bottom to observe them.

'Have a good day?' Drusilla asked.

'Perfect,' said Eve. 'How about you?'

'We went up to the walled garden, and I turned the hose on Joshua. I hope you don't mind.'

'What a good idea. Did he like it?'

'Thought it was a great joke. Couldn't stop laughing.'

They carried the picnic baskets into the kitchen. After the warmth out of doors, it felt marvellously cool.

'I think,' said Laura, 'I'll just run up and see how Lucy is, give her a little walk in the garden.'

'What a good thing we didn't take her,' said Eve. 'She'd have hated it being so hot.'

Laura ran up the back stairs, and Eve began unpacking the remains of the picnic – always, she thought, a distasteful job, and the sooner accomplished the better. While she was doing this, Gerald joined her, carrying the hamper that had contained the wine bottles and the coffee thermos.

Eve smiled at him. 'Darling, it was lovely that you came with us. It wouldn't have been the same without you there. Just leave that, and go up and have a shower. I know you're longing for one.'

'How did you guess?'

'You've got a sort of hot and sweaty look. I'll clear up, it won't take me a moment. I'll stack it all in the dishwasher, and –'

'Eve.'

Laura, calling from upstairs.

'*Eve!*'

They heard the panic is her voice, shrill as a scream for help, and looked at each other, their eyes meeting in apprehension. Then, with accord, they dropped what they were doing and made for the stairs. Eve was first, down the passage, and in through the open door of Laura's bedroom. They found her standing there, with Lucy in her arms. The little bowl that Laura had left filled with milk was empty, and it seemed that she had struggled from her basket and tried to reach the door, for there were small pools of vomit all across the carpet. The smell was sour and sickening.

'Laura.'

The dog's supple body was strangely rigid, her usually silky fur staring, her back paws dangling pathetically. Her eyes were open, but sightless and glazed, and her lips curled back from her pointed teeth in an agonized snarl.

She was, quite obviously, dead.

'Laura. Oh, Laura.' Eve's instinct was to embrace, to touch, to comfort, but somehow she could do none of these things. She put out her hand and laid it on Lucy's head. 'She must have been much sicker than any of us realized. Poor little thing . . .' She dissolved into tears, hating herself for succumbing, but it was all too tragic, and she was incapable of controlling her distress. 'Oh, Gerald.'

Laura did not cry. Slowly she looked from Eve's face to Gerald's. He saw her dark eyes blank with the misery of loss. After a little, 'I want Alec,' she told him.

He went to her side, gently loosened the frantic grip of her fingers, and took Lucy's body away from her, holding it against his chest. He left the women and went out of the room, and carried Lucy downstairs to the kitchen. He found a cardboard grocery carton and there, decently, laid the little body, covered it with the lid. He carried the box out into the woodshed, set it down on the floor, and came out, closing the door behind him. Later, he would dig a grave and bury Lucy in the garden. But now, there were more urgent things to be done.

It being a Saturday made everything infinitely more complicated. In the end, with the assistance of directory enquiries, he obtained the home telephone number of Alec's chairman at Sandberg Harpers and put a call through to him. By the greatest of good fortune he caught that eminent gentleman at home, explained the bare facts of his dilemma, and was given, in return, a New York number at which Alec might be reached.

It was now six thirty. One thirty in New York. He put the call through, but was told there would be a little delay. If he would care to stay by the telephone, he would be rung back. He set down the receiver and sat back to wait.

It was while he was doing this that Eve came to find him. He looked up as she came into his study.

'Is Laura all right?' he asked.

'No. She's desperately shocked. She didn't cry, she just started shivering. I put her to bed with the electric blanket on. I gave her a sleeping pill. I couldn't think of anything else to do.'

She came to his side, and he put his arms around her and for a little they said nothing, just indulged in wordless, mutual comfort. After a bit, she drew away from him and went to sit in his big armchair. She looked, he thought, desperately tired.

She said, 'What are you doing?'

'Waiting to speak to Alec. I've put a call through to New York.'

She looked at her watch. 'What time is it there?'

'One thirty.'

'Will he be there?'

'I hope so.'

'What are you going to say to him?'

'I'm going to tell him to get the first plane home.'

Eve frowned. 'You're going to tell him to come home? But Alec . . .'

'He has to come. It's all too serious.'

'I don't understand.'

'I didn't want to tell you. But there was another of those dreadful letters. And Lucy didn't die from natural causes, Eve. She was poisoned.'

8

ROSKENWYN

Dawn. Sunday morning. The great jet dropped out of the sky above London, circled once, lined up on the runway at Heathrow, and floated down to a perfect landing.

Home.

Alec Haverstock, with no luggage save a small grip, which he carried, went straight through Immigration and Customs, across the terminal, and out into the cool, grey damp air of an English summer morning.

He looked for the car and found it. His own dark red BMW, with Rogerson, the office driver, standing alongside. Rogerson was a formal fellow, and although it was Sunday, and officially his day off, he had come to the airport in full rig: peaked cap, leather gloves, and all.

'Morning, Mr Haverstock. Have a good flight?'

'Yes, fine, thank you.' Although he had not slept at all. 'Thank you for bringing the car.'

'That's all right, sir.' He took Alec's bag and stowed it in the boot. 'She's all filled up — you shouldn't have to stop for a bit.'

'How are you getting back to town?'

'I'll take the tube, sir.'

'I'm sorry to have to put you to so much trouble on a Sunday. I appreciate it.'

'Anytime, sir.' His gloved hand received Alec's grateful fiver discreetly. 'Thank you very much, sir.'

He drove, and the morning lightened all about him. On either side of the motorway small villages slowly came to life. By the time he was in Devon, church bells had started to ring. By the time he crossed the bridge over the Tamar, the sun was high in the sky and the roads were filling with aimless Sunday traffic.

The miles flashed by. Now it was sixty, now fifty, now forty to Tremenheere. He crested a rise, and the road ran downhill to the northern estuaries, the sand dunes, and the sea. He could see the small hills, crested with monoliths and cairns of granite that had stood there since before the very beginning of time. The road swung south, into the sun. He saw the other sea, shimmering with sun pennies. There were yachts out – some small regatta, perhaps – and the narrow beaches were lined with screaming, happy holiday-makers.

Penvarloe. He turned up the hill and into the familiar, quiet lanes and was through the village and out the other side in the same moment, turning in through the remembered gates.

It was half past twelve.

He saw her at once. She was sitting on the front doorstep of Tremenheere, with her knees drawn up to her chin, waiting for him. He wondered how long she had been there. As he drew up and stopped the engine, she rose slowly to her feet.

He unlatched his safety belt and got out of the car, and stood by the open door looking at her. Across the small distance that separated them he saw the beautiful grey eyes, the best thing that she could have inherited from her mother. She had grown tall and long-legged, but she hadn't changed. Once, her hair had been long and dark, and now it was short and bleached the colour of straw. But she hadn't changed.

She said, 'You took your time,' but the tough words were belied by the shake in her voice. He slammed the car door shut and held out his arms, and his daughter said, 'Oh, Daddy!' and burst into tears, and catapulted herself into his embrace, all at one and the same time.

Later, he went upstairs in search of his wife. He found her in their bedroom, sitting at the dressing table, brushing her hair. The room was neat and airy, the bed made. Lucy's basket was gone. In the mirror, their eyes met.

'Darling.'

She dropped the brush and turned into his arms. He pulled her to her feet, and for a long moment they embraced, her slenderness held so close that he could feel the beating of her heart. He kissed the top of her clean, sweet-smelling head, touched her hair with his hand.

'Darling Laura.'

She said, into his shoulder, the words sounded muffled, 'I didn't come down because I wanted you to see Gabriel first. I wanted her to be the first one to see you.'

'She was waiting.' He said, 'I'm sorry about Lucy.'

He felt her shake her head, wordless, not wanting to talk about the tragedy, not trusting herself to speak.

He did not say, 'I'll buy you another,' because that would be like telling a bereaved mother that you would buy her another child. For Laura, there could never be another. A new puppy, perhaps, in time, but never another Lucy.

After a little, he held her gently away from him and stared down into her face. She looked brown and marvellously better, but dreadfully sad. He put his hands on either side of her head, with his thumbs touching the dark smudges beneath her eyes as though they were marks that he could rub away.

She said, 'Did you speak to Gabriel?'

'Yes.'

'Did she tell you?'

'Yes.'

'About the baby?' He nodded. She said, 'She came home to you, Alec. That's why she came home. To be with you.'

'I know.'

'She can stay with us.'

'Of course.'

'She's had a bad time.'

'She's survived it.'

'She's a lovely person.'

He smiled. 'That's what she said about you.'

'You would never speak about her, Alec. Why would you never speak about Gabriel to me?'

'Did that worry you so much?'

'Yes. It made me feel so dreadfully inadequate, as though you thought I didn't love you enough. As though I hadn't enough love for you to let Gabriel be part of our life together.'

He thought that over. He said, 'It sounds complicated. I think we'd better sit down. . . .' Taking Laura's hand, he led her to the old sofa that stood in front of the window. He sank into the corner of this, drawing her down beside him, still holding her hands within his own.

He said, 'You have to listen. I didn't talk about Gabriel, partly because I didn't think it was fair to you. My life with Erica was over years ago, and Gabriel physically left me then. In truth, by the time I married you, I'd given up all hopes of ever seeing her again. As well, I *couldn't* talk about her. It was

193

as simple as that. Losing her, seeing her go, was the worst thing that ever happened to me. Over the years, I shut the memory away, like something shut in a box, with the lid tightly closed. That was the only way I could live with it.'

'But now you can open the box.'

'Gabriel's opened it herself. Escaped. Free. She's come home.'

'Oh, Alec.'

He kissed her. He said, 'You know, I've missed you so much. Without you with me, Glenshandra lost its magic. I kept wanting the holiday to be over, so that I could get home to you. And in New York, I kept thinking that I saw you, in restaurants and on sidewalks, and I'd look and the girl would turn round, and I'd see that she didn't look in the least like you, and my imagination had been playing me tricks.'

'Did it matter very much, leaving New York in the middle of your business and coming back? When . . . Lucy died, I told Gerald that I wanted you, but I never thought he'd go to all that trouble to get you here.'

'Tom's still there. He's quite capable of handling things on his own.'

'Did you get my letter?'

He shook his head. 'Did you write?'

'Yes, but it wouldn't have got to you. It was only to say how sorry I was about not coming with you.'

'I understood.'

'I hate telephones.'

'So do I. I use them all the time, but they're impossible instruments if you're trying to get close to someone.'

'Alec, it wasn't just that I didn't want to fly, or that I was still feeling ill. It was just that . . . I couldn't . . .' She hesitated, and then it all came out in a rush '. . . I couldn't face a week in New York with Daphne Boulderstone.'

For a second Alec was silenced into blank astonishment. And then he started to laugh. 'I thought you were going to tell me something horrendous.'

'Isn't that horrendous?'

'What, being driven around the twist by Daphne Boulderstone? My darling, we all are, constantly. Even her husband. She's the most maddening woman in the world. . . .'

'Oh, Alec, it isn't just that. It's that . . . she always . . . well, she makes me feel an idiot. As though I don't know anything. That day she came to see me, she went on about Erica, and Erica's curtains and things, and how she'd been Erica's best friend, and nothing was the same after Deepbrook was sold, and how she'd been your friend before she even met Tom, and how important first loves were, and . . .'

Alec laid his hand over her mouth. She looked up and saw his eyes sympathetic, but still, dancing with amusement.

He said, 'That's the most garbled sentence I've ever heard in my life.' He took his hand away. 'But I do understand.' He kissed her mouth. 'And I'm sorry. It was stupid of me to even imagine you'd have wanted to spend a week with Daphne. It was just that I wanted you so much to be with me.'

'They're like a club, the Boulderstones and the Ansteys. One that I can never belong to . . .'

'Yes, I know. I've been very unperceptive. Sometimes I forget how much older we all are than you. I've been involved with them so long that sometimes I lose track of the real essentials.'

'Like what?'

'Oh, I don't know. Like having a beautiful wife. And a beautiful daughter.'

'And a beautiful grandchild.'

He smiled. 'That too.'

'We'll be a bit of a squash in Abigail Crescent.'

'I think I've lived in Abigail Crescent long enough. When we get back to London, we'll look for a bigger house. One with a garden. And there, no doubt, we shall all live happily ever after.'

'When do we have to leave?'

'Tomorrow morning.'

She said, 'I want to go home. Eve and Gerald have been unbelievably kind, but I want to go home.'

'That reminds me.' He looked at his watch. 'I had a word with them before I came to find you. Lunch is at half past one. Are you feeling hungry?'

'I think I'm too happy to be hungry.'

'Impossible,' said Alec. He stood up and pulled her to her feet. 'Look at me. And I can't wait to get my teeth into Eve's cold roast beef and new potatoes.'

*   *   *

. . . so that's the situation. After Silvia received that first letter, we were all, reluctantly, pretty sure that poor old May was responsible. Had composed it in a moment of total lunacy. In her old age, she behaves very oddly every now and again, and it seemed at the time a reasonable explanation. But when Gabriel produced that second letter, the one that was addressed to you, Ivan suggested that it could possible be Drusilla who was writing them, the girl who lives in the cottage. She's apparently quite a nice creature, but as Ivan pointed out, a complete mystery to all of us. She came here to live because she had nowhere else to go. And I think, probably, she rather fancied Ivan.' He shrugged. 'I don't know, Alec. I really don't know.'

'And then Lucy!'

'Yes. And this horror leaves me without explanations at all. Even if she was stark staring bonkers, May could never, would never, do such a thing. And Drusilla's a sort of earth-mother type. I simply can't see her taking life.'

'You're sure the dog was poisoned?'

'Absolutely no doubt. That's why you had to come back from New York. As soon as I saw the dog I was filled with fears for Laura.'

It was now three o'clock in the afternoon, and they had been closeted together in Gerald's study since lunchtime. Finally, they seemed to have come to the end of the road. The letter and its envelope lay on the desk between them, and Alec now took it up and read it yet again. The black, uneven words were burned into his memory, as though his brain had taken a sharp, clear-edged photograph, but still he felt compelled to read them, just once more.

'We haven't got the first letter?'

'No, Silvia has it. She wouldn't let me take it. I told her not to destroy it.'

'Perhaps, before we make any further decisions, I'd better see it. Anyway, if we do have to take . . . further steps . . . we'll need it for evidence. Perhaps I'd better go down and see Silvia. Do you think she'll be there?'

'Give her a ring,' said Gerald. He picked up his telephone, dialled the number, and handed the receiver across to Alec. He heard the ringing tone. After a moment, 'Hello' came Silvia's cheerful, husky voice.

'Silvia, it's Alec.'

'Alec.' She sounded delighted. 'Hello! You're back?'

'I wondered, are you going to be around for the next hour?'

'Heavens, yes. I'm always around.'

'Thought I might walk down. Come and see you.'

'Lovely. I'll be in the garden, but I'll leave the front door open. Just walk through. See you.'

Out of doors, the warmth of the slumberous Sunday afternoon was tempered by a cool breeze, blowing off the sea. It was very quiet, and for once Tremenheere was deserted. Ivan had taken Gabriel off in his car, with a vacuum flask of tea and their swimming things packed into a haversack. Eve and Laura, both looking exhausted, had been persuaded by their husbands to take to their beds and rest.

Even Drusilla and Joshua were gone. During the morning, observed by Ivan, a very small, old, open car had rattled into the courtyard, driven by one of Drusilla's mysterious friends, a large man with a biblical beard. On the back seat of the car was parked, like an upright passenger, an enormous black 'cello case. There had been a discussion with Drusilla, and presently they had all driven off together, Drusilla with Joshua on her knee. As well, she had taken her flute, so presumably some unimaginable musical occasion was planned. Ivan had watched them drive away and reported all this to the others over lunch.

Eve became quite excited. 'Perhaps this is a new romance for Drusilla.'

'I wouldn't count on it,' said Ivan. 'They looked quite bizarre, but very sedate, setting off. I'm sure they're just going to make beautiful music together, but not the kind you envisage.'

'But . . .'

'I shouldn't push it, if I were you. I should think the last thing Gerald needs right now is a bearded cellist moving in to Tremenheere.'

So much for Drusilla. So much for everybody. Alec walked through the gate and down the road towards the village. There was no traffic in the shady lane, but somewhere from across the valley came the barking of a dog. Above him, the topmost branches of the trees shivered in the wind.

He found Silvia, as she had said that he would, in her garden. She was working in her rosebed, and as he walked across the garden towards her, it occurred to him that, with her slender figure, her brown arms, and her curly mop of grey hair, she looked like an advertisement for some life insurance company. Invest with us and your retirement will be carefree. All that was missing was the handsome, white-haired husband, snipping away at the dead heads and smiling because he had no financial worries.

All that was missing. He remembered Tom, but Tom had not been handsome and white-haired. Tom, the last time Alec had seen him, had become shambling and shifty-eyed, with a beetroot-coloured face and hands that shook unless they were firmly clasped around a glass.

'Silvia.'

She turned her face towards him. She was wearing sunglasses, so that he could not see her eyes, but at once she smiled, appearing delighted to see him.

'Alec!' She edged herself out from among her roses and came to meet him. He kissed her.

'This is a lovely surprise. I didn't know you were back from New York. And I hardly had a glimpse of you when you were here before, leaving Laura.'

'I was just thinking about Tom. I don't think I ever wrote to you when he died. And there wasn't time that other evening to say anything. But I was sorry.'

'Oh, never mind. Poor old Tom. It was strange without him at first, but I suppose I'm getting used to it now.'

'Your garden's looking fantastic, as it always does.' There were tools lying on the grass. A rake and a hoe, a pair of scissors, a small fork. A wheelbarrow was filled with weeds and dead rose heads and prunings. 'You must work like a beaver.'

'It keeps me busy. Gives me something to do. But I'm going to stop now and talk to you. I'll just go and wash my hands first. Would you like a cup of tea? Or a drink?'

'No, I'm fine. What about all this stuff? Would you like me to put them away?'

'Oh, you are an angel. They live in the potting shed.' She started towards the house. 'I shan't be a moment.'

He gathered up the things and carried them to the small garden shed that stood in a corner of the garden, discreetly disguised by a trellis, smothered in clematis. Behind the shed was a compost heap and the remains of a bonfire, where Silvia had been burning garden rubbish. Alec went back for the wheelbarrow and dealt with that as well, tipping its contents onto the top of the compost heap and then setting the barrow neatly against the back wall of the shed.

There was earth on his hands. He took out his handkerchief and wiped them. As he did this, he glanced down and saw that on her bonfire, Silvia had disposed of not only rubbish from her garden, but also old newspapers, cardboard packets, letters. Half-burned scraps of paper, inevitably, had survived, littered around the blackened ash. Scraps of paper. His hands were still. After a bit, he put his handkerchief away and stooped to pick up one of these. A corner – a triangle, charred along its longest edge.

He went back into the garden shed. It was neatly kept and very orderly. Long-handled tools leaned against one wall, small tools hung from a pegboard. There were stacks of earthenware flowerpots, a box of white plastic labels. At eye level was a shelf, ranged with packets and bottles. Grass seed, rose food, a bottle of methylated spirits. A can of engine oil, some fly repellent. A packet of Garotta for the compost heap. His eye moved down the shelf. A large green bottle with a white cap. Gordon's gin. Thinking of poor old Tom, he lifted it down and read the label. The bottle was still half full. Thoughtfully, he set it back in its place, stepped out of the shed, and walked slowly back towards the house.

As he went into the living room, Silvia appeared through the other door, rubbing cream into her hands. She had not taken off her dark glasses, but had combed her hair and doused herself in perfume. The room was heavy with its musky fragrance.

She said, 'It's *so* lovely to see you again.'

'It's not actually a social visit, Silvia. It's about that letter you got.'

'That letter?'

'The poison-pen letter. You see, I got one too.'

'You . . .' She looked horrified, as the meaning of this sunk in. '*Alec*!'

'Gerald tells me that you still have the one that was sent to you. I wondered if I might have a look at it.'

'Of course. Gerald said I had to keep it, otherwise I'd have burned the horrible thing.' She went to her desk. 'It's here somewhere.' She opened a drawer, took it out, handed it to him.

He drew, from the brown envelope, the sheet of paper. Brought from his pocket the second one, which had been addressed to him. He held them, fanned like a pair of playing cards.

'But they're exactly the same! A child's writing paper.'

'So is this,' said Alec.

It was the charred scrap that he had found. Pink, and lined, with the sickly little fairy only half burned away.

'What's that?' Her voice was sharp, almost indignant.

'I found it at the edge of your bonfire. I saw it when I emptied your wheelbarrow.'

'I didn't ask you to empty the wheelbarrow.'

'Where did it come from?'

'I've no idea.'

'It's the same paper, Silvia.'

'So what?' All this time, she had been wringing her hands, rubbing in the cream. Now she suddenly stopped doing this and went to the mantelpiece to find a cigarette. She lit it and flung the matchstick into the empty grate. Her hands were shaking. She took a long drag on the cigarette, blew out a plume of smoke. Then she turned to face him, her arms folded across her chest, as though she were trying to hold herself together.

'So what,' she said again. 'I don't know where it came from.'

He said, 'I think you sent that first letter to yourself. So that you could send the second letter to me, and nobody would even think of suspecting you.'

'That's not true.'

'You must have bought a packet of the child's writing paper. You'd only have needed two sheets. So you burned the rest.'

'I don't know what you're talking about.'

'You wanted everybody to think it was May. You posted the first letter locally. But the second time, you drove to Truro and posted that one there. On a Wednesday. That's the day that May always goes to Truro. It arrived in London the following day, but by then I'd already left for New York. So I never saw it. It was Gabriel who found it. Gabriel opened it, because she wanted to find out where Laura was staying, and she thought some clue might be in the letter. As it happens, you told her everything she wanted to know, but it wasn't a very nice way for her to find out.'

'You can't prove anything.'

'I don't think I have to. I just have to try to find out *why*. I thought we were friends. Why send me this sort of malevolent rubbish?'

'Rubbish? How do you know it's rubbish? You haven't been here, watching them, seeing them. Carrying on together.'

She sounded like May at her most disagreeable.

'But why should you want to come between me and my wife? She's done nothing to harm you.'

Silvia had finished her cigarette. She stubbed it out viciously, flung it into the hearth, fumbled for another.

She said, 'She has everything.'

'Laura?'

She lit the cigarette.

'Yes. Laura.' She began to pace up and down the small room, still holding herself as though she were icy cold, up and down, like a tigress in a cage.

'You were part of my life, Alec, part of growing up. Do you remember, when we were all children, you and I and Brian, playing cricket on the beach, and climbing the cliffs and swimming togther? Do you remember, once, you kissed me? It was the first time a man ever kissed me.'

'I wasn't a man. I was a boy.'

'And then I didn't see you for years and years. But then you came back to Tremenheere, and your first marriage was finished and I saw you all over again. Do you remember, we all went out for dinner. You and Eve and Gerald and Tom and I . . . And Tom got drunker than usual, and you came back with me and helped me get him to bed. . . .'

He did remember, and it was not an occasion that he enjoyed remembering. But he had come because it was obvious that Silvia could not cope on her own with a totally inebriated husband, six feet tall, sodden with alcohol and likely at any moment to pass out or be violently sick. Between them, he and Silvia had somehow got him into the house, upstairs, onto his bed. Afterwards, they had sat in this room, and she had given him a drink, and he – feeling pitifully sorry for her – had sat and talked for a little.

'. . . you were so sweet to me that night. And that was the first time I thought about Tom dying. That was the first time I faced the fact that he would never get better, never dry out. He didn't want to. Death was all that was left for him. And I

201

thought then, "If Tom dies – when Tom dies – then Alec will be there, and Alec will take care of me." Just a fantasy, but when you left me that night, you kissed me with such tenderness that all at once it seemed perfectly reasonable and possible.'

He did not remember kissing her, but he supposed that he had.

'But Tom didn't die. Not for a year. By the end it was like living with a shadow, a nonentity. A sort of wraith, whose only aim in life was to get his hand around the neck of a whisky bottle. And by the time he did die, you'd married again. And when I saw Laura I knew why. She has everything,' she repeated, and this time the word came out through clenched teeth with envious rage. 'She's younger and she's beautiful. She has an expensive car, and expensive clothes and jewellery that any woman would give her eyes for. She can afford to buy expensive presents. Presents for Eve, and Eve is *my* friend. I can never give Eve presents like that. Tom left me so broke, I can scarcely make ends meet, let alone buy presents. And everybody went on and on about her, as though she were some sort of saint. Even Ivan. Especially Ivan. Before, Ivan used to come and see me sometimes, ask me up for a drink if I was feeling blue, but once Laura arrived, that was it; he had time for no one but her. They used to go off together, did you know that, Alec? God knows what they were up to, but they'd get back to Tremenheere all secret and laughing, and your wife looking sleek and smug as a cat. It was true, what I told you. It was true . . . they had to be lovers. Fulfilled . . . that's how she looked. I know. I can tell. Fulfilled.'

Alec said nothing. Filled with sadness and pity he listened, watching the tireless figure pacing to and fro, hearing the voice, which was deep and husky no longer, but shrill with desperation.

'. . . do you know what it's like to be alone, Alec? Really alone? You were without Erica for five years, but you can't know what it's like to be truly alone. It's as though your unhappiness is contagious, and people keep away from you. When Tom was alive there were always people coming around, friends of his, even at the end when he was so impossible. They came to see *me*. But after he died, they didn't come anymore. They left me alone. They were afraid of involvements, afraid of a woman on her own. The last few years of his life Tom was no use to me, but I . . . managed. And I wasn't ashamed of it either, because I had to have some sort of love, some sort of physical stimulus to keep me going. But after he died . . . Everyone was so sorry for me. They talked about the empty house the empty chair by the fire, but they were all too delicate to mention the empty bed. That was the worst nightmare of all.'

He began to wonder if, possibly, she were a little mad. He said, 'Why did you kill Laura's dog?'

'She has everything. . . . She has you and now she has Gabriel. When she told me about Gabriel, I knew that I'd lost you forever. You might have chucked *her* over, but you'd never leave your daughter. . . .'

'But why the little dog?'

'The dog was ill. It died.'

'She was poisoned.'

'That's a lie.'

'I found a Gordon's gin bottle in your toolshed.'

She almost laughed. 'That would be one of Tom's. He used to keep them hidden everywhere. After a year I'm still finding bottles stashed away.'

'This one didn't have gin in it. It was labelled. It's Paraquat.'

'What's Paraquat?'

'A weed killer. Just about the most deadly poison there is. You can't buy it in a shop. You have to sign for it.'

'Tom must have got it. I never use weed killer. I don't know anything about it.'

'I think you do.'

'I don't know anything.' She flung her cigarette out through the open garden door. 'I tell you I don't know anything.' She seemed about to turn on him. He caught her by the elbows, but she jerked herself away, and in doing this, her hand caught her sunglasses and knocked them off. Revealed, unprotected, her strange-coloured eyes stared into his. The dark pupils were hugely distended, but there was no life, no expression there. Not even anger. It was disturbing. Like looking into a mirror and finding no reflection.

'You killed the dog. Yesterday, when they were all at Gwenvoe. You walked up the road and into the open house. May was in her bedroom, Drusilla and her baby out at the back. There was nobody there to see you. You simply walked up the stairs and into our bedroom. You put probably just the smallest drop of Paraquat into Lucy's milk. That's all it would have needed. She didn't die at once, but she was dead by the time Laura found her. Did you really think, Silvia, did you honestly imagine that May would be blamed?'

'She hated the dog. It had been sick in her room.'

'Have you any conception of the agony of mind you've put Eve through? No woman could have a better, kinder friend than Eve, but if this had gone the way you meant it to go, there wouldn't have been a thing Eve could do to help May. You were prepared to crucify the pair of them, just to satisfy a fantasy that could never have been more than a shred of your imagination. . . .'

'That's not true. . . . You and I . . .'

'*Never!*'

'But I love you . . . I did it for you, Alec . . . you . . .'

Now she was screaming the words at him, trying to get her thin arms around his neck, turning up her blank-eyed face in a travesty of passion, her mouth open and hungry for some physical assuagement of her pathetic and unbearable need. 'Can't you see, you fool, I did it for you . . .?'

The force of her assault on him was manic, but he was a good deal stronger than she, and the distasteful struggle was over almost as soon as it began. In his arms, he felt her go limp. As he held her, she sagged against him and began, horribly, to cry. He picked her up in his arms and carried her to the sofa, and laid her down, arranging a cushion beneath her head. She went on weeping, a dreadful sound, choking and gasping, her head turned away from him. He drew forward a chair, and sat and watched her, waiting until hysteria was spent. At last, she lay still, exhausted, her breathing heavy and deep, her eyes closed. She looked like a person who had suffered a devastating fit, as though she were slowly coming out of a coma.

He reached out and took her hand. 'Silvia.'

Her hand in his was lifeless. She gave no indication that she had heard him speak.

'Silvia. You must see a doctor. Who is your doctor?'

Presently she sighed deeply and turned her tear-ravaged face towards him, but she did not open her eyes.

'I'll call him. What's his name?'

'Doctor Williams.' It was no more than a whisper.

204

He laid down her hand and left her there, and went out to the hall where the telephone stood. He looked up the number in her own private book, found it written in her neat hand. He dialled, praying that the doctor would be in.

He was, and answered the call himself. Alec, as clearly and simply as he could, explained what had happened. The doctor listened.

When Alec had finished. 'What's she doing now?' he asked.

'She's quiet. She's lying down. But I think she's a very sick woman.'

'Yes,' said the doctor. And then, 'I've been afraid something like this might happen. I've been seeing her, on and off, since her husband died. She's been under great stress. It wouldn't have taken much to trigger this off.'

'Will you come?'

'Yes. I'll come. I'll come now. Will you stay there with her until I arrive? I'll be as quick as I can.'

'Of course.'

He went back to Silvia. She seemed to be sleeping. Grateful for this, he took a rug from the back of a chair and covered her, tucking the soft wool around her shoulders and over her feet. Looking down into her lined, unconscious face, racked with tension and spent despair, she seemed to him as old as May. Older, for May had never lost her innocence.

When at last he heard the doctor's car, he left Silvia and went out to meet him. He saw that the doctor had brought a nurse with him, a bustling woman in a white apron.

'I'm sorry about this,' said Alec.

'I'm sorry too. Good of you to call. Good of you to stay with her. If I want to get hold of you, where will you be?'

'I'm staying at Tremenheere. But I have to go back to London tomorrow morning.'

'If I need to, I can always get in touch with the Admiral. I don't think you can do any more. We'll take over now.'

'Will she be all right?'

'There's an ambulance on the way. Like I said, it's out of your hands now.'

Walking slowly back up the road to Tremenheere, Alec found himself recalling, not the shattering confrontation that had just taken place, but that long-ago time when he and Brian had been boys, staying with their dashing young uncle Gerald, and tasting the first heady sip of adulthood. Perhaps this was what happened to very old people. This was why May could remember in minute detail the Sunday School picnics and snowy Christmases of her childhood, and yet had no recollection of what she had done the day before. Hardening of the arteries, the medical profession called it, but perhaps the causes lay deeper than the physical disintegration of the extremely elderly. Perhaps it was simply a withdrawal, a rejection of the reality of failing sight, failing hearing, unsteady legs, and hands that fumbled, crippled with arthritis.

So now, Silvia was, in his memory, fourteen again. A child, but, for the first time, patently aware of the potential heady excitement of the opposite sex. Her legs and arms were long and skinny and brown, but her tiny breasts belied this childishness, and her red-gold mop of hair framed a face filled with a promise of great beauty. The three of them had played cricket and climbed cliffs, with the innocence of all youngsters of their age, but swimming together, as though the cold salt sea washed away the timid inhibitions of puberty, was a different matter altogether. Tumbling in the surf, their bodies touched. Diving, they came together underwater, hand met hand, cheek brushed against cheek. When, finally, Alec plucked up the courage to kiss her, a boy's first fumbling kiss, she had moved her face so that her open mouth touched his lips, and after that, the kiss wasn't such a fumbling affair after all. So much she had taught him. She had so much to give.

In all his life he could not remember feeling so tired. Never a man to yearn for the comfort of alcohol, he found himself, now, deeply in need of an enormous drink. But that would have to wait. Reaching Tremenheere, he went indoors through the open front door and stood for a moment in the empty hall, listening. There were no voices, no sound. He climbed the great, polished oak staircase, went along the passage to their bedroom, gently opened the door. The curtains were still drawn against the sunlight, and in the great double bed, Laura slept. For a moment he watched her, her dark hair spread on the white pillow, and was overwhelmed by tenderness and love. His marriage to her was the most important thing in his life, and the thought of losing her, for any reason, filled him with anguish. Perhaps they had both made mistakes, been too reserved, too respectful of the other's privacy, but he promised himself that from now on they would share everything fate flung their way, good or bad.

Her face, in sleep, was untroubled and innocent, so that she looked much younger than her years. And it occurred to him then, with a sort of amazed gratitude, that she *was* innocent.

She, of all of them, knew nothing of the malevolent letters. She did not know that Lucy had died because she had been poisoned. It was important that she should never know, but this was the last secret that Alec would keep from her. She stirred, but did not wake. Quietly, he went from the room, closing the door behind him.

Eve and Gerald were nowhere in the house. Searching for them, Alec made his way through the deserted kitchen and out into the courtyard. Here, he saw that Drusilla and her friend had returned from their outing. His car, resembling nothing so much as a very old sewing machine on wheels, stood parked, apparently held together with knots of string and bits of wire. He and Drusilla and Joshua were outside her cottage. A rocking chair had been carried out, and in this the friend sat, looking like some ancient prophet, with Joshua squatting at his feet. Drusilla sat on the doorstep and was playing her flute.

Alec, diverted from his intent by the charming scene they presented, stopped to look and listen. Drusilla's music pierced the air with all the clarity and precision of water dropping into a fountain. He recognized 'The Lark in the Clear Air,' an old North Country song, which she probably carried with her from her childhood. It was the perfect accompaniment for a summer evening. Her friend, rocking gently in his chair, sat and watched her. Joshua, bored with playing on the ground, all at once struggled to his feet, hauling himself upright against the man's knees. He leaned forward and lifted the child into his lap, bare bottom and all, and held him, cradled in the curve of his massive arm.

So maybe Ivan had been wrong. Maybe Drusilla and her friend were going to make more than beautiful music together. He looked a nice sort of fellow, and Alec, silently, wished them well.

The last note died away. Drusilla lowered her flute and looked up and saw him standing there.

He said, 'Well done. That was beautiful.'

'Are you looking for Eve?'

'Yes.'

'They're up in the garden picking raspberries.'

He found himself comforted by this little encounter. Tremenheere had not lost its magic, its gift of soothing the spirit. But even so, as he went through the door in the wall and up the path between the box hedges, his heart was heavy as that of a man about to break the news of a tragic family bereavement. As he approached, they stopped their picking, their faces turned towards him. It seemed an eternity since Alec had last seen them, and yet it took only moments to relate the sombre details of the afternoon. They stood there, in the sunshine, in the scented, tranquil walled garden, and it was all told in a few bare, painful sentences. It was finished. Over. They were still together. Relationships had survived, undamaged. It seemed to Alec nothing short of a miracle.

But Eve, being Eve, had thoughts only for Silvia.

'. . . an ambulance? A nurse? Oh, dear heaven, Alec, what are they going to do to her?'

'I think they'll take her to hospital. She needs caring for, Eve.'

'But I must go and see her . . . I must.'

'My darling,' Gerald laid a hand on her arm. 'Let it be. For the moment, let it be. There's nothing you can do.'

'But we can't abandon her. Whatever she's done, she had nobody but us to turn to. We can't abandon her.'

'We won't abandon her.'

She turned to Alec, appealing to him. He said, 'She's sick, Eve.' Still she did not understand. 'She's had a nervous breakdown.'

'But . . .'

Gerald abandoned euphemisms. 'My darling, she has gone off her head.'

'But that's ghastly . . . tragic . . .'

'You must accept it. It's better for you to accept it. If you don't, then you have only one alternative, and that is infinitely worse. We suspected both Drusilla and May; two totally innocent women might have been blamed for something they knew nothing about. And that is what Silvia wanted. To destroy not only Alec and Laura's marriage but May as well. . . .'

'Oh, Gerald – ' Her hand went over her mouth, shutting off the rest of the sentence. Her blue eyes filled with tears. 'May . . . my darling May . . .'

She dropped her basket of fruit and turned away from them, running down the path in the direction of the house. Her going was so sudden that Alec, instinctively, started after her, but Gerald put out a hand to stop him.

'Leave her. She'll be all right.'

May was sitting at her table, pasting pictures into her scrapbook. Lovely, it had been, hearing Drusilla play that nice tune. Funny girl she was. Got a new admirer by the looks of things, though May had never been much of a one for beards. She'd found some nice photos in the Sunday papers. One of the Queen Mother in a blue chiffon hat. She'd always had a pretty smile. And a comic one of a kitten in a jug with a bow round its neck. Pity about Mrs Alec's little dog. Nice little creature, even if it had been sick on her rug.

Because she was so deaf, she did not hear Eve coming down the passage, and the first thing she knew was her door bursting open and Eve there in the room. Such a start it gave her that she was quite annoyed and looked up crossly over her spectacles, but before she had time to say a word, Eve was across the room and on her knees at May's side.

'Oh, May . . .'

She was in floods of tears. Her arms were around May's waist, her face buried in May's meagre bosom.

'Oh, darling May . . .'

'Well, whatever's all this about?' asked May in the rallying tones she had used when Eve was a very small child and had cut her knee or broken her doll. 'My word, what's upset you? All those tears. And all about nothing, I shouldn't wonder. There now.' Her gnarled arthritic hand stroked the back of Eve's head. Such a pretty blond she'd been, and now she was quite white. 'There now.' Oh well, thought May, we're none of us getting any younger. 'There. Nothing to cry about. May's here.'

She had no idea what all the fuss was about. She was never to know. She never asked, and she was never told.

9

HOMES

Laura was alone in her bedroom, doing the last of the packing: emptying drawers, checking on the contents of the wardrobe, trying to remember where she had put a red leather belt or whether it was already in her suitcase. She had left Alec and Gabriel at the breakfast table, eating the last of the toast and drinking a second cup of coffee. As soon as they had finished, and Alec had assembled their various bits of luggage, they would be leaving. The car waited at the front door. Tremenheere was almost over.

She was in the bathroom, collecting her sponge and toothbrush and Alec's shaving things, when there came a knock on the bedroom door.

'Hello?'

She heard the door open. 'Laura.' It was Gabriel. Carrying all the various bits and pieces, Laura emerged from the bathroom.

'Oh, darling, I won't be a moment. Is Alec making impatient noises? I've just got to get these things sorted, and then I'll be ready. Is your suitcase in the car? And I've got a bottle of Elizabeth Arden somewhere . . . or have I put it in?'

'Laura.'

Laura looked at her.

Gabriel smiled. 'Listen to me.'

'Darling, I'm listening.' She put the things down on the bed. 'What is it?'

'It's just that . . . would you mind most frightfully if I didn't come back with you? If I stayed here . . .?'

Laura was taken aback, but did her best not to show it. 'But of course. I mean, there's no rush. If you want to stay on for a bit, why shouldn't you? It's a good idea. I should have thought of it myself. You can join us later.'

'It's not like that, Laura. What I'm trying to say is that . . . I don't think I'll be coming to London at all. After all,' she added unnecessarily.

'You won't . . .?' Thoughts flew, undisciplined, in all directions. '. . . but what about the baby?'

'I'll probably have the baby here.'

'You mean, you're going to stay here with Eve?'

'No.' Gabriel laughed ruefully. 'Laura, you're being dreadfully thick. You're not making it the least bit easy for me. I'm going to stay with Ivan.'

'With I–' Laura felt, quite suddenly, all weak at the knees and found it necessary to sit down on the edge of the bed. She saw to her surprise that Gabriel, rather endearingly, was blushing.

'Gabriel!'

'Does that horrify you?'

'No, of course it doesn't horrify me. But it is a little surprising. . . . You've only just met him. You scarcely know him.'

'That's why I'm going to stay with him. So that we really can get to know each other.'

'Are you sure this is what you want to do?'

'Yes, I'm sure. And he's sure too.' When Laura did not reply, Gabriel came to curl up on the bed beside her. 'We've fallen in love, Laura. At least, I think that's what happened to us. I don't know for certain, because it's never happened to me before. I never really believed in it. And as for falling in love at first sight, I always told myself that was just a lot of sentimental twaddle.'

'It isn't,' Laura told her. 'I know, because I fell in love with your father at first sight. Before I even knew who he was.'

'Then you understand. You don't think I'm behaving like an idiot. You don't think it's all a wild figment of my imagination, or something to do with hormones or being pregnant.'

'No. I don't think that.'

'I'm so happy, Laura.'

'Do you think you'll marry him?'

'I expect so. One day. We'll probably walk down to the church in the village, just the two of us, and come back man and wife. You wouldn't mind if we did that, would you? You wouldn't mind losing out on all the hassle of a family wedding?'

'I don't think you should ask me that. I think you should ask Alec.'

'Ivan's downstairs now, telling him what I'm telling you. We thought it would be easier that way. For everybody.'

'Does he know about the baby?'

'Of course.'

'And he doesn't mind?'

'No. He says, in a funny way, it just makes him more certain that this is what he wants.'

'Oh, Gabriel.' She put her arms around her stepdaughter, and for the first time they embraced, hugging enormously, kissing with a true and tender affection. 'He's such a special person. Almost as special as you are. You both deserve all the happiness in the world.'

Gabriel drew away. 'When the baby comes, will you come back to Tremenheere? I'd like you to be around when it's born.'

'Wild horses wouldn't keep me away.'

'And you're not upset about me not coming back to London with you after all?'

'It's your life. You must live it your way. Just know that your father's always there if you need him. You didn't realize it before, but that's the way it's always been.'

Gabriel grinned. 'I guess so,' she said.

She was still there, still endeavouring, in a bemused fashion, to finish the packing, when Alec came to find her. As he opened the door, she straightened from her suitcase, a hairbrush in one hand and the elusive bottle of Elizabeth Arden in the other. For a long moment they looked at each other across the room, in silence, not because they had nothing to say, but because words were unnecessary. He shut the door, with some force, behind him. His expression was serious, his features set grimly, the corners of his mouth turned down, but his eyes, bright with amusement, gave him away. And Laura knew that he was laughing, not at Ivan and Gabriel, but at themselves.

It was he who broke the silence. 'We look,' he told Laura, 'the very picture of two long-suffering parents, trying to come to terms with the dotty inconsistencies of the younger generation.'

She dissolved into laughter. 'Darling, however hard you try, you'll never sound like a Victorian father.'

'I wanted you to believe I was enraged.'

'You haven't succeeded. You don't mind?'

'Mind? That's the understatement of the year. I'm punch-drunk with body blows, most of them beneath the belt. Ivan and Gabriel.' He cocked an eyebrow. 'What do you think about it?'

'I think,' said Laura, stowing the bottle and the hairbrush, and shutting the suitcase, 'I think they need each other.' She fastened the locks. 'I think they're in love, but I think they like each other too.'

'They don't know each other.'

'Oh, yes, they do. They made friends right away, and they've been together constantly over the last two days. He's a very kind man, and Gabriel, for all that veneer of toughness, needs kindness. Especially now, with the baby on the way.'

'That's the other extraordinary thing. He doesn't give a damn about a baby being on the way. Just makes him more sure than ever that he wants to spend the rest of his life with her.'

'Alec, he loves her.'

At that, he had to smile, shaking his head. 'Laura, my darling, you're a romantic.'

'I think Gabriel's probably a romantic too, although she doesn't want to admit it.'

He thought this over. 'There's one good thing about all this. If she stays here, I won't need to go hunting for a bigger house.'

'Don't count on it.'

'What does that mean?'

'I'm coming back to Tremenheere when Gabriel has the baby. That's in eight months' time. I may be pregnant myself by then. You never know.'

Alec smiled again, his eyes filled with love. 'That's right,' he said, 'you never know.' He kissed her. 'Now, are you ready? Because they're all hanging around downstairs in the hall, waiting to see us off. My father always used to say, if you're going, go. Let's not keep them waiting.'

She shut the last of the cases, and he picked them up and made for the door, but Laura lingered for a last look around. Lucy's basket was gone, for Gerald had burned it. And Lucy was buried here, at Tremenheere, in the garden. Gerald had offered to have a little headstone carved, but somehow that did not seem quite right, so instead Eve had promised to plant a rose over the spot where Lucy lay. An old-fashioned rose. *Perpétué et Félicité,* perhaps. Darling little pale pink flowers. Just right for Lucy.

Perpétué et Félicité. She thought of Lucy, running across the grass towards her, eyes shining, ears streaming, tail whisking with delight. It was a good way to remember her, and *Félicité*

213

meant happiness. Her eyes had misted with tears – it was still impossible to think of Lucy without tears – but she brushed them swiftly away and turned and followed her husband through the door.

Behind them, the deserted room lay empty and still, but for a curtain stirring, caught by the summer morning breeze.